THE
SAMARITAN'S
PISTOL

Visit us at www.jollyfishpress.com.

For information, write to Jolly Fish Press, PO Box 1773, Provo, UT 84603-1773.

THIS TITLE IS ALSO AVAILABLE AS AN EBOOK.

Library of Congress Cataloging-in-Publication Data

Bishop, Eric, 1967-
 The samaritan's pistol : a novel / by Eric Bishop.
  pages cm
  ISBN 978-1-939967-12-1 (hardcover : alk. paper)—ISBN 978-1-939967-13-8 (pbk. : alk. paper)
 1. Ranchers—Fiction. 2. Gangsters—Fiction   I. Title.
 PS3602.I7564S26 2013
 813'.6--dc23

2013030338

Printed in the United States of America

10   9   8   7   6   5   4   3   2

For my Grandfather Bishop, my first saddle partner.

THE
SAMARITAN'S
PISTOL

a Rocky Mountain Thriller

ERIC **BISHOP**

JOLLY
FISH
PRESS

PROVO, UTAH

1

The dog nosed his fingers, and Jim shivered to life on a lumpy bed of horse blankets.

"Mornin', Duke." Jim yawned and then rubbed the dog's head as clouds spit lightning over craggy peaks. The attendant thunder boomed through everything. Rain started, and Jim pulled an old tarp over himself and the dog. The pitter-patter might have lulled him back to sleep, but Duke nosed his hand again.

"Who needs an alarm clock?" Jim petted the dog's head before rolling to his elbow. His thirty-eight-year-old body ached, so he pinched an Ibuprofen from his shirt pocket and twisted open a canteen.

Oil for a rusty hinge, he thought as cold, black coffee chased the tablet.

Dry beneath the tarp, he rubbed both eyes then lifted the edge, revealing long shadows and a gray sky. To the east, the sun was burning through the clouds, coloring the continental divide's ridges a postcard-worthy mix of violet and orange.

In addition to the view, the cash in the safe back at the ranch made the cold morning worth the effort. Four grand doubled the most he'd ever charged for packing clients into the mountains.

Jim burrowed into the saddle blankets again, waiting for the caffeine to jump-start his morning and wondering about the man who hired him.

Chris Cobb was as anxious to fly fish Wyoming's high country as a newborn foal was to stand, but only half as steady. Calling at late notice, he'd begged Jim to pack him and six friends—plus gear—deep into the Wyoming Rockies for a fly-fishing trip.

Chris didn't matter now. The raindrops ceased, typical of a fast-moving, high country storm. Jim tugged on his boots and rolled to his knees, pulled the tarp away and stood. His breath hung in the frosty air, but he ignored the chill. With fingers for a comb, he swept back a thick but graying mane, smashing it into place with a battered old cowboy hat. He stretched for a moment but quit, knowing the best way to alleviate the aches was to get moving.

Looking toward the meadow and his horses, Duke pushed against his leg.

"Would you like some help?" a voice asked.

Jim turned and found Chris emerging from a tent.

"You're up early for someone on vacation," Jim said, turning again toward the horses.

"Packing all our gear in here on late notice, it's the least I owe you."

"You paid me plenty." Jim took a bridle from where it hung on a tree branch. "Everyone else still asleep?"

"The hike in wore them out." Chris eyed Jim's makeshift bed. "How come you don't sleep in a tent?"

"Can't see the stars."

"How can I help?" Chris asked.

"Unsnap the picket ropes at the halters," Jim instructed as they headed to the horses. "I'll ride the buckskin. The rest'll follow like true believers."

"You don't want me to lead them?"

"Nah." Jim shook his head. "They know the drill."

The tall meadow grass soaked Jim's pants to the knee. He pulled the buckskin's stake, coiled the wet picket rope into a bundle, and slipped it over his shoulder. Then he slipped the bit into the horse's mouth, while gently pulling its ears under the bridle. He led the buckskin closer to a pair of horses, and after unsnapping their ropes, jumped aboard the buckskin's bareback and headed toward camp.

Chris did as instructed and watched as the horses trotted toward Jim like football players toward a water break. As they reached the fire ring, Jim tied each horse to a tree and started brushing the buckskin with long, fluid strokes.

"Show me what to do," Chris offered.

"You brush, and I'll saddle." Jim demonstrated how to groom his horses, insisting Chris focus on any spots of dirt that would wear a sore beneath the cinches. Then he went to the pile where he'd slept for an armful of saddle blankets and packsaddles. Forty-five minutes later, all of the horses were tied head-to-tail and ready to go.

"Appreciate the help," Jim said, extending his hand to Chris.

"That's quite a grip."

Jim didn't reply, thinking it was the typical city-dude comment.

"I get up early back in Vegas, so I don't mind," Chris continued.

"Vegas?" Jim rolled his eyes and made his tone as sympathetic as possible. "What do you do there?"

"I'm a CPA."

"A money man." Jim brightened, then thinking about the four grand added. "You must be good."

Chris smiled. "I am."

"Well, this week you're a fisherman." Jim swung into the saddle. "I'll be back Friday."

"You don't want to stay for breakfast?" Chris offered.

"There's a leftover sandwich in my saddle bags." The horse shifted. "Steady Sam." Jim reined the buckskin still. "I'll make the trailhead by noon if I get moving."

Chris nodded.

"Got your pepper spray?" Jim asked.

"Right here." Chris patted his vest pocket.

"A clean camp'll keep the bears away more than anything," Jim said over his shoulder as he led the seven packhorses down the trail.

THE ZIP-TIES DUG INTO LARRY'S wrists, stinging flesh worn away from traveling sixteen hours in the back of the Escalade. The vehicle veered right, rolling his six-seven frame against the side of the car, along with the golf clubs the three kidnappers had piled over him. The irons and woods jangled against each other as the road became rougher. Larry suspected one of his captors had partially opened a window; dust from the gravel road seeped in, mixing with cigarette smoke and dried turf from golf spikes.

"Are we there yet?" a voice Larry only knew as Johnny asked. "C'mon uncles, are we there yet?"

The vehicle bounced through a pothole.

"Are we there yet?" Johnny continued, the cadence and tone changing each time.

"Where'd that come from?" a threadbare smoker's voice asked. If Larry remembered right, the smoker was Johnny's uncle, Simon.

"Answer me!" Johnny said, his voice a mixture of playful and impatient. "Are we there yet?"

"It's Donkey from Shrek," a third voice, belonging to Johnny's uncle Marcus, answered through a yawn. "My kids watch it every day."

"I like that boulder," Johnny paused. "That is a nice boulder!"

Simon cleared his throat. "Guess I'll have to see the movie."

Larry's head thudded against the rear seat as the Escalade stopped. In addition to reigniting the stinging in his wrists, the sudden stop compressed his full bladder and cramped legs.

"Earth to Johnny—this is Uncle Simon."

"We're there?"

"We're there," Simon chuckled into a dry cough. "Go wiz while we call your dad."

"Right on." The door opened with the attendant chime, and then the door slammed.

"Maybe we should gag the nephew on the way home," Marcus said.

"There's an idea."

"Put the call on speakerphone," Marcus suggested.

The phone rang twice before a splatter of static over someone's voice filled the vehicle.

"You there? Michael?" Marcus asked. "We're in the woods."

"Did you find him?" The question rattled the speakerphone.

"Now I hear you Mike. We're still looking and we're outta road."

"Whaddaya mean outta road?"

"We're at a trail head. We think the accountant went camping. We're gonna go dump the cargo in the woods while we look."

Larry's stomach sank, knowing he was the cargo.

"How's Johnny been?" Michael's voice asked through the phone.

"Johnny's Johnny," Marcus answered. "You love him or hate him."

"Appreciate you taking him."

"What's to thank? We're family," Simon responded.

"Shit!" Michael said in a tone indicating he'd just realized something important. "Make sure to call our old man out in Florida. Today's his eighty-fourth."

"Did anyone remember?" Simon turned to Marcus. "You get him anything?"

Marcus shrugged.

"I got it." Michael's voice filled the vehicle. "You two can't get anything done out there. I'll have a limo take him to dinner from all of us."

"Thanks, Mike."

"Yeah, thanks," Marcus agreed. "What about Johnny?"

"Have him call. His grandpa loves that kid. Talk to me when you know something," Michael ordered, and then the phone clicked off.

The front doors opened and shut with the crisp air-tight sound of a new vehicle. Even though Larry expected it, the rear hatch lifting startled him. The clubs were taken away, and then a clawing hand grasped his belt, squeezing his bladder as they dragged him from the Escalade.

The parking lot was a football field compared to the cargo space. Larry stretched his legs and squinted at sagebrush and a few aspen trees at the gravel's edge. A rusty old gooseneck livestock trailer attached to a dented Dodge pick-up was parked next to the Escalade. At the far end of the parking lot was a wooden corral, where a watering trough overflowed into a muddy spot a few yards from the parking lot's gravel edge. To the right, shaded by a giant pine tree was an outhouse, complete with a half-moon cut into the door.

"Hey, Sambo, wasn't you a former athlete?" Simon lit a cigarette then rolled it between pudgy be-ringed fingers.

"Cut me loose, and I'll show you." Larry shifted to where Simon's muffin-top belly eclipsed the rising sun.

"And have you gone Mike Tyson on me?" Simon inhaled, turning the ash bright red before exhaling dragon-like from both nostrils.

"I'm gonna play golf." Johnny grabbed a driver and unzipped the bag's side compartment, spilling several balls onto the gravel. "Where's the tees?"

"Put it away," Marcus ordered. "You need to call your grandpa to wish him happy birthday."

Johnny dropped the driver and a second later was thumbing his phone. "Dear Gramps," Johnny narrated the text. "Happy birthday. You're the best."

The three men had kidnapped Larry from behind, throwing him directly into the Escalade. Viewing his captors for the first time, Larry wondered if Marcus and Simon were twins. Designer golf shirts clung to protruding bellies, while watches and bracelets hung loose around their wrists. Displayed against tan skin were gold necklaces nestled in thick chest hair. Simon stood an inch taller than Marcus. They both had fringes of gray around their ears.

Johnny was measuring his swing. Nickel-sized gauges stretched each earlobe. Skater shorts hung beyond his knees. The t-shirt sleeves reached his elbows, and his forearms were inked to his wrists.

"Could I take a leak?" Larry asked.

The golf ball sliced at a ninety-degree angle and shattered the Escalade's side mirror.

"Fuck." Simon flicked the ash from his smoke. "Put the clubs away."

"Glad you drove." Marcus smiled at his brother.

"I'm about to piss myself here." Larry doubted they'd let him, but it was worth asking.

"What?" Simon turned from the mirror.

"I need to pee."

"Go ahead." Simon flicked the cigarette's ash. "You've used your hands for the last time."

"Don't be such a hard-ass." Johnny stepped back and took a practice swing at another ball. "Let the man pee."

Simon dangled the cigarette from his lips and pulled a pistol from behind his back. He nodded to Marcus, who took a knife from his pocket and sliced the ties.

Larry's numb fingers responded like prosthetic appendages as he struggled with the zipper before relieving his bladder. Tingling ignited in his palms as he finished.

They'll shoot if I run, Larry thought. *I'm dead anyway.* He bolted, but only made three steps before the bullet's impact sprayed gravel against his calves. Larry stopped knowing the next slug would hit flesh.

"Tie him up." Simon held the pistol on Larry as Marcus went to the vehicle and returned with two new ties.

Larry rubbed the already rising welts where the gravel had peppered his bare skin, before placing his hands behind his back.

Marcus cinched Larry's hands then pulled backward, toppling him to the ground. Larry tried to stand, but Marcus grabbed his neck with both hands and squeezed hard enough to stifle the scream as Simon sizzled the cigarette into Larry's shoulder.

"Who needs an ashtray?" Marcus asked as his brother crumpled the butt.

The radiating agony from his shoulder and the scent of his own charred flesh mixed with tobacco smoke and the pressure on his throat made Larry gag.

Simon flicked the butt into the gravel behind the livestock trailer. He knelt close to Larry and exhaled in his face. "Think about it as we hike—quick and painless, or a human ashtray?"

Larry turned away from Simon's gaze and putrid breath to see Johnny, club in hand, eyes big, and mouth open. Johnny's mouth shut. Then he swallowed; the snake tattoo on his throat looked like the snake had actually swallowed a mouse.

"Sorry," Johnny mouthed.

"Me, too." Larry waited until Johnny's eyes dropped and turned away.

Larry stood, and Marcus tied a rope to his wrists. A yank reignited the sting even though his hands had already passed from tingling to numb.

"Put the clubs back." Simon strode past Johnny to the front passenger door, where he rummaged through the glove compartment. He came back with a revolver that he handed to his nephew.

"Let's move," Marcus said from behind.

A rocky trail wound upward, with chest-high sagebrush on both sides. A few hundred yards from the parking lot, they reached the forest's edge. Despite shade from the pines and the cool morning, sweat still dripped from Larry's brow.

2

Two hours after leaving Chris and the others, Jim studied the tree canopy with a smile of contentment, moving between patches of light and shadow as the horse carried him down the trail.

"Hardly sucks at all, Sam," he said to the horse. "This is the place to spend Sunday."

He checked on the pack string over his shoulder. They resembled a kindergarten class, holding hands as they crossed the road. Each horse followed the one in front, pulling and giving slack as Jim and Sam led them through the woods.

The short rainstorm amplified the smell of the pines, and Jim expanded his lungs, knowing that within a few hours he'd be branding and inoculating steers at his ranch in the hot, dusty valley.

The caravan approached a spot where the trail descended through a twisting granite chute. Car-sized boulders made an obstacle course the horses would have to skirt—a slip or stumble would send them over the cliff's edge. In the middle of it all stood an old growth pine, nearly three feet in diameter, rubbed free of bark on one side from passing pack animals.

Jim twisted in the saddle to check on the horses. Instead of moving smoothly, the third horse's head bobbed up and down, indicating a limp.

Jim leapt from Sam, who stopped immediately.

"Easy boy," he said as he approached the horse and lifted the hoof. A small, sharp rock was wedged in the crevice by the frog of the hoof. After using his multi-tool to dislodge the stone, he tossed it into the woods. Then, he watched as the horse put all his weight on the limb.

"Easier without the shrapnel?" Jim asked, petting the animal's neck.

He climbed back on Sam, watching as the string followed in single-file.

With the rough section behind them, Jim relaxed, taking in the sights, sounds, and smells.

Rustling in a thicket of wild raspberries startled the horses as they approached a meadow. Black bears loved raspberries, and whatever was shaking the bushes was running toward them. Sam snorted, turned to look, his ears pointed toward the potential threat.

Snaking his hand beneath his shirt, Jim gripped his subcompact .45 caliber Kimber 1911 pistol, but didn't draw. "Let me know if that's you, Duke!"

A friendly bark and Jim unclenched the gun as Duke burst from the thicket. Sam and Duke exchanged sniffs, and Sam resumed walking with no urging from Jim.

"Thanks for the chaos." Jim shook his head and smiled at the dog that was now trotting at the horse's side.

As the caravan rattled down the trail, Jim ate the sandwich from his saddlebags in a half-dozen bites, but his stomach still rumbled. The trailhead was over an hour away, so he reached in his shirt pocket and took out a butterscotch candy. Partially unwrapped, specks of lint clung to the sticky surface.

"Next time we stop, this is yours," Jim said, knowing Sam would disregard the lint.

A gunshot echoed through the woods, faint, barely audible, and certainly coming from miles away. Jim reined Sam still, listened for a second shot, but heard nothing.

Unexpected gunfire in the wilderness was usually as simple as someone sighting in a rifle, taking a shot at a coyote, or target practice.

Jim's lungs tightened as he waited for a second shot. An unsettling feeling radiated from his belly and throat as memories of Desert Storm flooded his mind. The stench of burning petroleum stuck to his nostrils like sludge from an oil slick. His forehead stung, remembering how his helmet ground the Kuwaiti sand against his skin. His shoulders ached under the weight of Kevlar and canteens. His feet throbbed from days spent tromping through the desert as a newly-enlisted grunt.

Sam shook, whisking Jim back to Wyoming, where he was angry that a single and unsuspected shot could still transport him back to the worst moment of his life.

Jim got off Sam.

While he dawdled, the horses munched the tall grass on the side of the trail. The hunger pangs forgotten, he looked for something to delay returning to civilization. The last horse in the string had tossed a shoe. He retrieved the tools from another packhorse, picked dirt from beneath the hoof, rasped the hoof flat, and nailed on fresh iron. The mare was due for re-shoeing that week, so he decided to set all four hooves in the cool mountain air, rather than back in the heat of the ranch.

With sweat beading on his brow, Jim returned the tools to the pannier. He took his time. Re-shoeing the horse and inspecting all the other animals took an hour and a half.

Duke approached, barking and bouncing up the trail.

"Where you been?" Jim rubbed the dog's ribs and realized he hadn't seen the dog since stopping. "Where you been?"

A rumble from his stomach reminded Jim of the candy so he

took it from his pocket, picked as much lint from the surface as he could, and slid it into the corner of Sam's mouth.

"Let's get some real food." Jim petted the horse's neck, the gunshot now forgotten. "You're due some oats, and I want a burger."

NINETY MINUTES INTO THE HIKE, Larry was breathing in gasps. Marcus and Simon, both older and heavier, looked haggard, their clothes now sweat-soaked and dirty. Johnny hadn't spoken since leaving the parking lot.

"We do him right here!" Marcus wheezed, the tone serious but lacking in volume. From the small of his back he pulled a revolver, pressing the barrel under Larry's throat. "Soon as he talks, we're back to golf."

"I'm down," Simon agreed, sweat dripping from his nose and chin. "We can get rooms in town and take turns watching the trailhead for a month."

The men lasted longer than Larry expected. Loose softball-size rocks and gravel made the footing more like a dry riverbed than a trail as it zigzagged up the wooded mountain.

"Don't you guys want to get him off the trail?" Johnny asked.

"Kid's gotta point." Simon shrugged.

"Who's to see us?" Marcus asked, waving the revolver around like a half-eaten candy-bar. "It's not rush hour, for Christ's sake."

"Do I really need to be here?" Johnny asked.

"You like Porsches for Christmas?" Marcus responded with his own question.

Johnny nodded.

"When a truck-load of our cash goes bye-bye, we look 'til we find it." Simon eyed his nephew for a few seconds.

"How do we know this guy stole it?" Johnny pointed at Larry. "And how do we know the accountant is even in Wyoming."

"Because we know." Simon's tone indicated the conversation was over.

"See this through," Marcus encouraged. "We'll tell your old man you done good."

Larry's strength dissipated, weakening his knees. Like soldiers who found God in their foxholes, his mind turned to his maker:

If God saves me, I'll live better; if not, I'll die brave.

A warm wind caressed Larry's skin. His nostrils took some of it in, but with it came the odor of pine trees and trail dust. A shove and he stumbled, as Simon pushed him from the trail, and then yanked on the leash. They walked into a shallow ravine, startling a small bird into flight. Lodge-pole pines and dumpster-sized granite boulders dotted the forest thickly enough that there wasn't a clear line of sight longer than fifty yards. They came into an aspen grove a few minutes later with a single pine tree close to the middle. After looking around in every direction, Simon picked up a limb, and walked toward Larry, who stood half a foot taller than his attacker.

Simon swung the branch with both hands. It snapped into three pieces, ripping an agonized shriek from Larry as it struck his knee.

"Tee-time!" Marcus said.

Larry fell, clumsy and twisting, the pain radiating all the way to his hip and toes.

Johnny grabbed an even larger limb, stepped over Larry, and handed it to Simon. Larry curled up in the fetal position, but with his hands bound behind his back, he couldn't protect his head. A shoe heel smashed Larry's lips into his teeth.

Shapes and blurry images appeared through his left eye as though he was underwater. *I'm not scared*, he thought and the warm wind returned.

Marcus wound up, telegraphing a kick to the chest. Larry rolled into it, taking the blow with his shoulder.

"Ready to talk?" Simon asked.

Larry spat blood on the ground. His mouth refilled and he spat again. A clump of grass prickled his cheek so he lifted his head to better see his blurry attackers. "You pussies can't kick."

"Talk," Johnny said. "Just tell them."

Adrenaline fed the fire roaring in Larry's belly, removing some of the pain, but instead of spitting he swallowed, and the flames sputtered.

3

Duke stood at point, studying a spot in the trail as Jim rounded the corner. A bark, not happy or angry, but intense told Jim he was onto something.

"What you got, boy?" Jim tied Sam and the first horse in the pack string to the limb of a deadfall tree, then walked up to the energized dog. Duke often alerted him to deer or elk tracks, and Jim paid attention. It helped create a working knowledge for later in the year when the big game hunters came visiting.

Instead of animal prints, he found footprints. Four sets of tracks—two of dress shoes and two of athletic—marked the trail. The tracks headed into the woods, but stopped, turning down a shallow gully.

Someone's got sore feet. Jim thought about the three miles to the parking lot, as he traced a dress shoe imprint with his fingertips.

Curiosity insisted he investigate. Not wanting the dog to get too far ahead, Jim decided to take Sam. The slip-knotted lead-rope undid easily from the tree, and he swung into the saddle.

"Let's take a look," he said, reining the horse to follow the tracks into the gully.

Two hundred yards further, Jim came around a boulder at the edge of a clearing. Three men stood there. Two were dressed in knee-length shorts and golf shirts, and one looked like a skater. The three loomed over an enormous black man, bound and bloodied. The two golfers carried handguns tucked into their shorts at the small of their backs.

Jim's mind raced, and his eyebrows dropped into a scowl.

The victim's hands were fastened behind his back. The largest man was winding up with the club like a woodchopper splitting firewood. Duke's growl stopped him.

"What the fuck?" the man said, spinning around.

"Stop right there!" Jim shouted.

"Who the fuck are you?"

"Step away!" Jim ordered.

The men didn't move.

The man dropped his club. "We found him here." The tone was friendly. "Do you have a first aid kit?"

"I said, step away!"

The man responded after looking at his two companions. "I was offering the stick to help him up."

"With the club above your head?"

The other man—the one on the side opposite the tattooed skater—spoke for the first time. "The only way this turns out good is if you turn around and forget this."

At least they aren't bullshitting me anymore. "What about him?" Jim nodded at the man on the ground.

"What about him?" The tattooed young man puffed out his chest. "He'll be okay."

Both golfers turned to look momentarily at the tattooed young man as though he'd thrown ice water in their faces.

"His bloody clothes and messed up face don't say so." Jim's neck itched, but he refused to scratch.

"He's fine, you fucking hick." The young man stepped forward. "Leave while we're in a good mood."

"Every litter has a runt," Jim muttered to himself.

"What did you say?" the young man demanded.

Jim didn't respond, his eyes moving across the men's hands, making sure not to focus for too long on any one thing.

"You have no idea what this is, you—" The man used a combination of words Jim hadn't heard since boot camp.

"His tattoos are scarier than the language." Jim pressured his stirrups to make sure Sam would stand. Blood pulsed through his temples and eyelids. His nose twitched and adrenaline sped his heart to twice its normal speed, but Jim focused on his military training: *Watch their hands. Project strength, and if you're lucky, they'll back down.* Under closed lips, Jim's jaw hung loose, and he exhaled through his mouth.

He decided against drawing his pistol, thinking it would make things worse.

Duke growled, baring his teeth as his hackles rose, then lunged forward with a bark.

"Call off the mutt!" the tattooed man yelled.

The man on the left grabbed his pistol, but before he could take aim, Jim drew his own weapon and fired. The bullet tore through the man's heart.

Duke charged. The two remaining men drew, but paused, watching Duke leap on the falling body. Correcting, they brought their weapons to bear on Jim, but his second shot shattered the second golfer's skull.

The tattooed runt shot in the same instant, missing Jim but hitting Sam high in the chest between the horse's front legs with a dull thud that vibrated up into the saddle.

Another bullet whizzed over Jim's head as Sam staggered. Leaping from the horse, and landing on his feet, Jim stepped toward the runt, who backed up with a fearful look. The young man shot from his heels, missing to the left. Jim shot, and the young man clutched his chest and fell sideways, his tattooed arms beneath his lifeless body.

Jim stood for a moment. He exhaled and re-holstered his pistol before dropping to his hands and knees. His stomach convulsed and he vomited his scant breakfast into the dirt. Drunk with adrenaline, the earth reeling beneath him, Jim gritted his teeth, refusing to pass out. Thinking about Sam, and Duke's barking drowning out the ringing in his ears, he stood.

Duke growled, bolting between the three bodies, his hackles still on alert.

Sam lay on his side, head resting on the grass. The horse's great bellow-lungs moved air through his nostrils, wiggling the stems, but as Jim sprinted toward him, it slowed.

Sam was going to die. Tears sprang to Jim's eyes as he collapsed next to the horse.

Duke nosed the horse's lip. After smelling his breath for several seconds, he whimpered. The scent of internal blood told him Sam would soon be gone, and he curled up next to the horse's neck.

Jim sleeved away the tears and took aim at his dying friend; his fourth shot seemed louder than all the other three combined. Gun to his side, he wiped his eyes with his free thumb, the tears soaking into calloused, dirty skin. He remembered sleeping in the barn to witness the birth. A perfect buckskin coat surprised him coming from a brown-bay, quarter-horse mare and a jet-black, Arabian stud.

Sam was the best horse Jim had trained. Capable of running for miles, the gift of endurance from Arabian ancestors mixed with the pleasant disposition of a quarter-horse mother.

Ten minutes ago I was headed home, and now Sam and three men are dead? He wanted to wish the reality away, and yet the ugly truth surrounded him.

Jim re-holstered the pistol, and stepped over Sam's neck, the fury growing in his stomach projected onto everything in view. He hocked then spit some of the vomit residue from his mouth as he approached the man.

"Thanks for helping me," the man mumbled through split lips. The words came out slowly, scarcely more than a whisper. "You saved my life."

Jim untied the leash from the man's swollen hands and cut the zip ties. Returning to Sam's side, he yanked to free the saddlebags from beneath the horse's body, which came free in a tug-o-war lurch. From the bottom of the bags he pulled his first-aid kit containing peroxide, bandages, antibiotic ointment, and latex gloves.

4

"What hurts beside these cuts?" The cowboy was speaking as he scrubbed at Larry's chin.

"Everything."

"Did you black out?"

"I remember it all."

"You know what day it is?"

"Sunday."

"And the time?"

"Early afternoon—maybe one thirty." Larry's soft response seemed loud in the quiet woods.

"Does it hurt to breathe?"

"A bit." Larry stopped short of a full breath. "Not too bad."

"I'm Jim."

"Larry."

Jim placed his palm on Larry's ribs, feeling for deformities while the dog watched, his ears pointed forward, studying like an interested child watching a parent.

"This is Duke."

Larry nodded.

"Breath in as deep as you can, then exhale slowly."

Jim put pressure on the quadrants of Larry's abdomen. "What hurts the worst?"

"My knee."

"Did he club it with that tree limb?"

"Yeah."

"Can you move your foot and your leg below where they hit you?"

"You a doctor?" Larry wiggled the foot.

"Volunteer first responder." Jim took Larry's shoe off, and removed the sock. "Push down with your foot." Larry did what Jim told him. "Now pull it back up."

Duke shuffled a few feet away, yawned, then lay down, resting his head between his paws as Jim sorted through some bandages.

"Some of your cuts need stitches, but I think you'll live." Jim paused. "You wanna say where you're from?"

"L.A."

"Long way to come to die."

Larry looked directly at the cowboy.

"Eyes forward," Jim instructed as he closed a deep cut on Larry's forehead with a butterfly bandage. "Why'd they wanna kill you?"

After a few breaths, Larry responded. "You don't wanna know."

"The hell I don't." Jim removed the bloodied latex gloves, carefully turning them inside out and placing them in a zip-lock baggy. He squirted a pool of hand sanitizer into his palm and handed the bottle to Larry. Jim stood, vigorously rubbing his palms and fingers together.

Even though the cowboy's eyes were on him, Larry chose to be silent. After cleaning his hands as well, he tossed the sanitizer back to Jim, who caught it one-handed without looking away or changing his poker-faced stare.

The same knee Simon hit with the tree limb had been destroyed in a college football game a decade earlier. It was the only time Larry remembered being hurt this badly, and now he was disconnected from everything. There had been a delay between the cowboy scrub-bing an open wound, and feeling the pain. It was hard to focus on any one thing now that Jim had stopped asking questions, and Larry's mind settled on the most miserable thing it could. *If my momma saw me like this, I'd feel even worse.* The next thing Larry thought about was almost as bad. *They didn't kill me today, but it won't be long.*

The cowboy spoke to him again. "Feeling any better?"

Larry nodded.

"I've got more horses up at the trail," Jim said. "I'm going to put you on one."

"I can't ride."

"Can you sit?"

"Yes."

"Then you can ride."

Before leaving, Jim gathered the unused first-aid supplies and the remnants of bandage wrappings. Duke didn't follow, but came over to lie beside Larry. In spite of his reeking breath, the dog's warmth was a nice contrast with the cool mountain air.

He licked Larry on the chin and whimpered.

5

arry was sitting up and petting Duke when Jim returned with the
horses. He knew he shouldn't move the dead men, but leaving
them didn't seem right. The sheriff was an old friend who would
need someone with animals to pack the corpses out of the woods,
and his horses were available. With thickets of raspberries, bears
would be close, and Jim worried about them dragging the bodies
into the woods.

He went over to Larry and felt his wrist while watching his chest
rise and fall.

"Your vitals are normal," Jim pronounced after a minute.

"Vitals?"

"Pulse and breathing. You feeling any better?"

"Yeah."

"Can you hang on for ten minutes if I load the bodies?"

Larry nodded.

Jim wrestled the runt on top of a horse from the uphill side.
Then, using his lariat, a packhorse, and a thick tree limb, he hoisted
the two bigger men off the ground. Hanging there, they looked like
enormous, bloody piñatas. After leading packhorses beneath them,
Jim lowered the bodies onto the horses' backs, marveling as they
accepted their gruesome cargo.

It was mid-afternoon, and they could still make it to the sheriff's office by dark. Jim's truck and horse trailer were parked at a trailhead about five miles from the Cooper Ranch, about twenty miles from town. The local hospital was around the corner from the sheriff's office, and his cell would catch a signal close to the trailhead.

Jim stuffed his extra gear into two empty panniers and put his riding saddle on his best packhorse—a mare named Beatrice—for Larry to ride.

Larry groaned, limping on his injured knee. Jim helped him into the saddle, then jumped over another horse's bare back. He nudged the horse forward past Sam's body, where a thick cloud of flies already pestered the bullet holes. Part of the fishermen's gear was a shovel, but even with the tools, Jim couldn't spare the two or more hours it would take to dig a grave in the rocky ground.

"Sorry, Sam." Jim blinked his eyes against the returning tears. "I'll be back and do this right."

Larry rode in front on Beatrice so Jim could keep an eye on the injured man while leading the pack string. Some of Jim's trail horses were naturally slow walkers that would get in a rhythm of falling twenty to thirty feet behind, and then trot to catch up.

In the world of horses, Beatrice was steady and smooth, but Jim doubted Larry appreciated her talent.

LARRY'S HEAVILY MUSCLED LIMBS HAD taken most of the blows, and now everything ached. He could move his arms and legs without difficulty, but the bruises throbbed painfully when he did so. He wanted to walk, but his knee wouldn't take it, and to fall from the horse would be worse than being clubbed.

"Put some weight in the stirrups," Jim's voice said. "Push down like you're standing up."

Larry did as he was told, even though it hurt his bad knee.

"Now lean back and put your feet forward. Hold onto the saddle horn like you're doing, but lean back."

After a few minutes, the cowboy spoke again. "The reins aren't a car brake. Only pull if she goes too quick or you want her to stop."

As Larry got a feel for what Jim told him, he became less worried and replayed the scene.

Even though the horseman looked tough, Larry had wondered what he could do with three gangsters. Then out came the pistol and Jim became a precision machine, killing his targets with brutal efficiency. Larry had witnessed a few gunfights in Los Angeles where people mostly missed because would-be-bad-asses shot from their heels while running away. The cowboy, on the other hand, had moved forward while his enemies cowered at his aggressive posture. Whoever Jim was, he understood the psychology of a gunfight.

Larry smiled, reopening his split lips. His stomach lurched in laughter at the memory of Jim telling them Johnny's tattoos were scarier than their language. The humor quickly subsided, and Larry shivered when he thought about Michael Faletto avenging his son's death.

As his horse's hooves scattered the loose granite pebbles in the trail, Larry became determined to repay Jim. The sensation began in Larry's heart, as if there was a heater inside him, radiating outward into his arms and legs. The warmth consumed his body and took away the pain. As it spread, he half expected to be lifted from the horse on a cushion of warm air. Larry remembered praying. *God saved me.*

fter riding for about half an hour, Jim spotted a group of people coming toward them. From a distance, it looked like day-hikers with binoculars around their necks and small backpacks on their shoulders. They were fifty feet away when Larry turned around looking like he was about to go over Niagara Falls.

"Might get a little awkward," Jim acknowledged.

The people stepped aside, giving right-of-way to the pack-string, but they didn't fully realize what moved toward them because they were petting Duke, who had run ahead to investigate.

As the line of horses approached, a lady turned, shading her eyes with one hand for a better view. She started to wave with the other hand, but dropped it as her mouth fell open, and her eyes bulged at the sight of Larry's bandages and the dead bodies.

"Oh my God!"

"Sorry," Jim called out as his horses rumbled down the trail, motioning over his shoulder with his left thumb. "These guys tried to kill us when I stopped to help him." Jim nodded toward Larry. "So I shot first."

"What?" the lady stammered. "Why would you kill someone?"

Jim ignored the question and called out to Larry. "Lead us down the trail."

"Stop!" a man standing at the edge of the group ordered.

Jim would have ignored the man's command as he would a speed bump, but just then the horse carrying the largest corpse brushed against a pine tree. The dead man's head was caught by a thick, broken branch, twisting him grotesquely and unbalancing him from the top of the horse. The crowd of hikers gasped and groaned, their faces contorting unpleasantly; most turned away from the grisly sight.

"Shit! We're gonna lose cargo." Jim said.

Larry turned around, and pulled back on Beatrice's reins.

As Jim slid from the gelding, the man who had spoken walked toward the badly out-of-balance load.

"I'll give you a hand," he said. "But we need to talk."

"Lift and I think we can get him back on his perch." Jim grabbed a fist full of hair and pulled as the man wrapped his arms around the corpse's legs, helping lift it into place.

"Dead bodies are tough to handle," the stranger said.

"You a mortician?" Jim asked.

"You're packing three dead guys and want to know about me?"

"Is that an answer?" Jim didn't look up as he retied the carcass to the packsaddle.

"I'm a retired cop, and you're an idiot."

Jim's eyes widened, but he ignored the statement.

"Why would you disturb a crime scene?"

"Crime scene?" Jim removed his hat. "It was self defense."

"Even so, it's a crime scene if they tried to kill you."

Jim finished hitching the body over the saddle before responding. "Not much of any kind of scene if a bear drags them off."

"If an animal disturbs them, so be it."

"I had the horses." Jim shrugged. "Sorry."

"Sorry?" The retired cop's incredulous tone matched the look covering his face. "You shit on a crime scene, and say you're sorry?"

"Enough talk." Jim turned away.

"I need to report this to the police."

"Come with us and we'll do it together," Jim said over his shoulder.

"Someone needs to make sure you don't do anything worse." The retired cop pushed past Jim down the trail to retrieve the backpack he'd left in front of Beatrice.

Jim saw it coming. "Don't!"

The man looked up just as Larry's massive fist smashed into the man's face, knocking him to the ground.

Larry wagged his finger, glaring down through swollen features and bandages. "He saved my life!"

Although the man was bleeding, he was still conscious and moved toward the backpack. It was within reach, but Jim jumped ahead, snatching it a moment before the retired cop could put a hand on it.

"Kinda heavy," Jim unzipped it far enough to see a Ruger .44 Magnum. "You almost became number four, and I'm the idiot?"

After adjusting it to fit his larger frame, Jim shouldered the backpack and led his horse over to a stump to remount, while the cop-turned-bird-watcher sat in the trail pinching his bleeding nose.

"Move," Jim said. But the man looked up, blood oozing through his fingers.

"You don't want to steal my property," the retired cop said, rather too forcefully. "Put the backpack down and we'll talk."

"Collect it from the sheriff."

"You've just added theft and assault to everything else." The man looked up at Jim from the middle of the trail with hard, angry eyes.

"Maybe," Jim responded. "Or a guy claiming to be a cop tried to pull a gun from a backpack. For all I know, you're with these guys." Jim nodded in the general direction of the three corpses.

The man said nothing.

"Move," Jim said again.

"There's room to go around." The man's eyebrows dropped in a scowl.

"These horses don't understand traffic signals."

The man said nothing.

"Suit yourself." Jim boot heeled the gelding into a walk. The man remained, playing a game of chicken with the pack string. The first two horses gave a wide berth, but the third didn't. In the instant before impact, the man moved back to avoid being crushed beneath the horse's hooves.

The group looked on at expensive golf clothing, worn by corpses slung over horse's backs, as the caravan disappeared into the dust.

They descended a rocky, winding trail, switch-backing down a mountain thick with pine trees and aspens. As they rode, the air became considerably warmer. They arrived at the parking lot within twenty minutes of leaving the hikers. A tan Cadillac Escalade with Nevada plates was parked next to Jim's pickup and horse trailer.

"That how you got here?" Jim asked, looking at the SUV.

Larry nodded.

Jim noticed a single cigarette butt behind the Escalade. Urging the horse closer, he got off and placed the trash in his shirt pocket to dispose of later. He was about to tie his horse to the trailer when a broken golf tee also caught his attention, so he picked it up and placed it with the cigarette butt.

The limp bodies thudded into the truck's bed as Jim dumped them from the horses. A few minutes later, a horsefly the size of a bumblebee bit the rump of the animal Jim was unsaddling. The horse struck at the pain with its hind leg, denting the Cadillac's front door.

"Nice." Jim petted the animal, then looked at the deep dent and scratched paint. "Kick it again."

Sweat drenched Jim as he continued unsaddling the animals and stowing the gear; it gathered at his earlobes, nose, and chin before falling to his clothing or blotting the dry ground.

Jim was about to load his first horse in the trailer, but was distracted by a sparkle. One of the dead men's hands stuck out between the truck's bedrail and an Indian-style horse-blanket. He wore a wedding ring encrusted with dozens of small diamonds. A twinge ran through Jim's chest; unlike himself, the man had a wife to mourn him.

Jim swallowed and went back to work.

After loading the horses in the trailer, he found Larry sitting in the gravel, leaning on the passenger-side rear tire. A dirt devil spun in the gravel twenty yards away, sending a gust in their direction. Jim buried his eyes in the crook of his elbow, but particles stung the skin on his neck.

I'm so damned dirty, my eyelids stick to themselves.

To exhaust some of the trapped heat in the cab, Jim opened the passenger door. He looked at himself in the mirror; his blue eyes and white teeth shone back as the only clean things in view. Dirt covered his face, and everything itched. He wanted to plunge into a glacier-fed lake.

His threadbare jeans were smeared with fish guts and manure. Loading the dead bodies made his old white dress shirt looked like a modern artist had used it as a canvas, blotting the fabric with human blood, and then rolling him in the dirt.

Jim looked down at Larry's bandaged face and swollen features. "I'm not sure who looks worse."

"You do."

Jim laughed.

Larry chuckled at his own joke, but stopped abruptly, rolling to the side, and placing his palm to his ribs against a spasm of pain. When it eased, he laughed again.

"I'm killing myself here," he said, and Jim laughed harder.

"Let's get you to a doctor before something makes me uglier."

"Like that will happen." Larry's smile broke through his messed up face like a sucker hole in a weeklong storm.

After moving a box of fencing nails from the front passenger seat and sliding it back as far as possible, Jim helped Larry into the pickup. Jim turned the key and the truck grumbled to life.

"Helluva punch."

"We need to talk," Larry said.

Jim didn't respond, thinking the giant could say whatever he wanted on the way to the hospital. After a few sharp turns to get out of the parking lot, Jim dug the phone from his pocket and thumbed it on.

"Hold up a second," Larry said.

"For a second." Jim raised his eyebrows. "But I will call the sheriff."

"You asked why they wanted to kill us."

"I'm listening." Jim set the phone on his thigh.

"I could use your help, if you wanna get rich."

7

Jim's pickup rattled into the hospital parking lot with eight horses in tow. Duke stood proud on the pile of saddles in the bed of the truck. As the truck lurched to a stop, he barked at the approaching medical workers, like a king instructing peasants from the top of his throne.

"Shut up," Jim yelled at the dog through his open window, and then turned to Larry. "Looks like the sheriff made some calls."

"You got any black people in this town?" Larry asked.

Jim paused to look at Larry's expression. "After today, your complexion has you worried?"

"I saw what you did with that rope and tree."

"You serious?"

"Nah—but damn, you gotta lot of white people around here!"

Jim chuckled and shook his head. "These Mormons are as color blind as the horse you just rode. Those who aren't don't work at the hospital. I'll be back later."

A nurse asked him about the blood on his clothing before Jim could walk around his truck to help.

"It's not mine. Go help him."

The medical staff opened Larry's door. They checked his pulse and listened to his breathing with a stethoscope. Jim helped them ease

Larry into a wheelchair and watched as they whisked him through the emergency room doors.

Before Jim had considered his next move, the local mortician, who also ran the morgue, and his son approached. Dressed in dark suits and ties, they looked like they'd just left a funeral. "The sheriff said you were bringing in some bodies?"

"In the bed," Jim responded.

The father and son walked over and peered into the pile of gear. They lifted the saddles, touching the leather delicately between their fingertips to avoid soiling their nice clothing. Their morbid curiosity satisfied, the father spoke.

"We'll change and be right back."

The men hurried away, and Jim heard a familiar voice from behind.

"You made quite an entrance." The sheriff, Albert Johnson, walked up to Jim and they shook hands.

"Where'd you come from?"

"I been watching from over there. You okay?"

Jim nodded.

"Was Kuwait really eighteen years ago?" the sheriff asked.

"Will be this fall," Jim responded.

Albert gave Jim an appraising look. "You think someday we won't count?"

"The years or what happened?"

"Both."

"Maybe." Jim rolled his eyes. "Until today I thought so."

"Walk with me, Jimmy." Though polite, the sheriff's tone made the invitation an order. Jim followed Albert to the far end of the parking lot, adjacent to an empty field. Albert spoke in a hushed tone. "I need it straight here, Jimmy. Was today like Desert Storm? Did you go off?"

Jim turned his palms upward. "I acted in self defense."

For a few moments the two stood, staring at one another.

"Okay, the whole story from the top."

Albert listened as Jim told him everything, exactly as it took place.

"Why do you think they were so stupid?" he asked after Jim concluded.

"They tossed the F-bomb like parade candy, hoping I'd get stupid and want some. No way was I gonna look away, and they had no idea who they were dealing with."

Albert chewed on a toothpick. He removed it from his mouth and shook it to emphasize his words.

"If the black guy stands up, we'll be okay, but why move the bodies?"

"We'll?" Jim asked. "As in *we?*"

Albert stepped forward and paused before whispering, just loud enough for emphasis. "It's always been 'we' from grade school to Kuwait!"

Jim got chills as Albert stepped back and continued, "Why move the bodies?"

"Already had the lecture," Jim responded.

"When and by whom?"

Jim took a deep breath.

"There was this retired cop on the trail calling me an idiot. He threatened to come with us."

"Then why isn't he here?"

"The guy I just brought in caught him with a haymaker."

Albert's eyes bugged out and a look of grief crinkled his face. "That huge black guy punched a retired badge? Is the cop okay?"

Jim nodded. "He'll be coming for his backpack, and to make sure the small-town sheriff does his job."

"Could you be a bigger pain in the ass?"

"Evidently not," Jim responded. "Look, I told him, for all we knew, he was with the guys I just shot, and we weren't taking chances."

"That's a good angle, but he's right."

The words and Albert's tone worried Jim. "What do you mean?"

"You're a volunteer first responder. I could explain moving the bodies for someone else, but they can prove you knew better."

"My mind wasn't in Wyoming." Jim looked at the ground, wishing he was part of the pavement. He removed his hat and scratched his scalp through the still sweat-soaked hair. The appraising look returned, and Jim knew Albert shared his torment.

"After I got done shooting my horse and patching up the bleeder, I wanted to clean up the mess." Jim continued. "You know how Kuwait was. I hate this shit."

"I know." Albert placed a hand on Jim's shoulder.

Duke growled, standing guard against the morticians who were trying to unload the carcasses.

"Hold up, guys," Albert ordered. "I need some photos."

"Here, boy," Jim called to Duke.

The dog jumped from the truck and trotted in Jim's direction, but continued trying to growl the morticians away as he crossed the parking lot.

Jim petted him. "It's not a deer or elk, Duke."

Albert shook his head and walked over to the truck.

"Next to me, that dog's your best friend." As they unloaded the pile of gear from on top of the bodies, Albert spoke again. "You buried these guys pretty good, Jimmy."

"The first thing off the horses went to the bottom of the pile, just to piss you off."

"Like I said," Albert muttered as he lifted a saddle to the ground. "A pain in the ass."

Jim stepped away and watched as Albert took pictures with a digital camera, and then helped the morticians put the corpses in body bags, load them on gurneys, and take them into the hospital. It gave Jim time to reflect on the conversation before Duke's interruption.

"I need to see your pistol," Albert said.

Jim lifted his shirt and removed his forty-five from its holster, handing it grip first to the sheriff, who turned the gun over, admiring its workmanship.

"What'd this set you back, about a grand?"

"Does that matter?"

Albert removed the magazine and the bullet from the chamber, making a count of the remaining bullets.

"How d'you carry? Is there a round ready to shoot all the time?"

"Cocked and locked—like they taught us in boot camp. All I need to do is swipe the safety with my thumb before I shoot."

"We aren't in the army anymore," Albert said matter-of-factly. "And I always worried about shootin' my balls off."

Jim wanted to kid his old friend about needing to aim to hit anything so small, but decided against it. Instead, he asked, "When do I get it back?"

"When the state crime lab says so. Where's the firearm that was fired at you?"

Jim pointed. "In those saddle bags."

"Well, I can't see 'em from here. And fetch the retired cop's backpack."

Jim retrieved the items, and handed them to Albert. The sheriff looked in the saddlebags. "I'll need to take these."

"Can I keep my toothbrush?"

"Aisle three at Ernie's," Albert said, referring to the town's favorite convenience store. "I'm going out to get the plate number from the Escalade. I can't search it until we tie it to those you shot. You'll need to take me to the scene in the morning."

"I intend to take care of my horse."

Albert paused before responding. "I'll give you a hand."

Jim began reloading the pile of gear into the bed. Albert pitched in, and within a few minutes, the parking lot was clear again.

Jim slipped into his truck and shut the door. "I can stick around, but I'd like a shower and some food."

"Go ahead, but I ride Beatrice in the morning," Albert bargained.

"She'll be saddled. Riding'll be up to her."

The truck's diesel motor ignited with a twist of the key. Jim shifted it into first and eased the clutch, the truck and trailer lurched forward, creaking as the horses shifted and stomped. The sheriff turned around and came toward him. "Did you see the vehicle the retired badge was driving?"

"There was a white passenger van with a luggage rack and Oregon plates at the trailhead."

"Get a shower, Jimmy. I'll see you in the morning."

8

ichael Faletto stood beside a puddle of green engine coolant in the parking lot outside his cousin Ralf's repair shop. Michael pushed send on his phone and held it to his ear. Nearby, a semi hit its Jake-brake to stop for a red light, and Michael plugged his other ear to block the noise. The call went directly to an operator's voice. "You have reached 702—" Michael ended the call before the voice finished repeating Simon's number and invited him to leave a message for the seventh time—that hour.

The next number belonged to his brother, Marcus. Michael listened until the female voice said, "You have—"

He lifted the phone like a football player about to spike the ball, thinking he'd grind any un-shattered pieces into the asphalt with his heel for good measure. A ring stopped him. Turning to the east, and cupping his hand to shade the screen from the evening Nevada sun, he pushed accept and even smiled.

"Thanks for the limo, Mike. I'm at dinner with your mother."

Even though Spencer Faletto had been in Boca Raton for several years, it was the first time Michael and his brothers hadn't flown to celebrate their father's birthday.

"You're welcome, Pops. Sorry we couldn't make it out this year. There's been—"

"Don't wanna hear it." Spencer's elderly but robust whiskey tenor voice stopped Michael mid-sentence. "I'm sure you have reasons."

"Hey, Pops?"

"Yeah."

"You hear from Marcus or Simon today?"

"Their wives called. Johnny texted me this morning."

"What time?"

"About eight-thirty."

Michael thought through the Nevada-to-Wyoming-to-Florida time conversion. *Johnny must have texted a few minutes after when I last spoke to them.* "You haven't heard from Marcus or Simon though?"

"Not yet. Things okay?"

"They'll call as soon as they can," Michael answered.

"The limo was a nice touch."

"Happy birthday, Pops. Enjoy dinner."

Michael ended the call and then held down his son's speed-dial number. There was no ring, just Johnny imitating Johnny Carson's night show announcer, Ed McMahon. "Heeeeeeeeere's Johnny! Leave me a message."

He'd heard the same cheerful invitation over twenty times that day, but it still made Michael smile. *God, I love that goofball kid.*

The circumstantial evidence tumbling in Albert's head indicated Jim told the truth. His friend could have killed the three men and the black man and hidden them in a million acres of wilderness to be scavenged by bears. The other undeniable fact was that Jim would never do anything to hurt Sam.

He did wonder if the three dead men accidentally shot the horse, causing Jim to retaliate. If that were the case, Albert figured it served them right. He'd borrowed Sam several times and had never ridden a finer horse. Still, he wondered: why would Jim bring the bodies in if that were the case?

Albert got in his SUV and drove until he found what he was looking for, two miles out of town. He turned on the flashers, flipped a U-turn, and pulled over a white passenger van with Oregon plates.

The driver's hands were high on the steering wheel, communicating that she wasn't a threat. Through the unrolled window a man, wrinkled and gray, leaned over from the passenger's seat. Tufts of blood-soaked tissues protruded from each nostril, and the small slits of blackened eyes indicated how hard the man was hit.

"I'm glad you stopped us," he sniffled. "I was assaulted."

Albert held his hand up with his palm out in the Indian-peace-sign, while tonguing the toothpick from one corner of his mouth to the other. Then he walked to the rear of the vehicle as the passengers rubbernecked to check his movements.

"I clocked you at eighty in a forty-five," Albert said, returning to the window. "Do you have your license and registration?"

"I'm a retired police officer," the man stated.

"Several of you weren't wearing seat belts, and you have a blown tail-light."

"I'm a retired police officer!"

"Sir," Albert yawned. "I need you to step out."

The retired cop did as ordered. Albert motioned to his patrol vehicle and opened the passenger side rear door. "Sit here while I make a call. Don't touch anything."

Albert shut the retired cop inside and called the morticians as cars passed, sending gusts that made his pants wag like a downwind flag.

"Learn anything yet?" Albert asked when he had the mortician on the phone.

"I'm telling you, Sheriff," the mortician said. "This was precision shooting. Two got it through the heart and one between the eyebrows."

"Any powder burns?" Albert asked.

"None. Jim must have been at least ten feet away."

"That's what I expected." Albert paused. "Listen to me, Tom. You don't know anything about anyone named Jim, understood?"

"Understood."

The mortician hung up, but Albert continued to pace and wave his free arm in an imaginary conversation.

Any minute now.

The retired cop pulled out his cell. Albert pocketed his own phone, palmed his Glock and threw open the door.

"Out of the car! Drop the phone!"

The retired cop did as ordered.

"Hands on the car and spread your legs." Albert patted the man down. "Who were you calling? You got a buddy you want to come shoot me?"

"No."

"Then who were you calling?"

"The hospital to let them know I'm coming. We went for a day hike and we saw this guy packing dead bodies."

"There may be danger to anyone around the hospital," Albert interrupted.

"I need medical attention."

"Try Jackson or Soda Springs."

"The only danger around here is the idiots who killed three men, and assaulted me!" the retired cop said from the spread-eagle position, his hands still on the police vehicle. With the cuffs from his belt, Albert ratcheted the man's left hand then right behind his back. With one hand gripping the cuff-chain and the other on the crown of the man's head, Albert pushed the retired cop inside.

Albert retrieved the backpack Jim had given him from the back of the vehicle and tossed it onto the man's lap.

"Recognize this?" Albert climbed in. "Gotta permit for the revolver?"

"I have the right to file a complaint."

Albert removed the toothpick and shook it at the ex-cop. "But who'd listen?"

"I could talk to the circuit judge or the county attorney," the retired cop said beneath the tissues.

"And I could cite you for no permit, the speeding ticket, a half-dozen seatbelt violations, disobeying a direct order, and the van could be impounded until the local shop opens up to replace your blown tail light."

The two men locked eyes for a several seconds.

"Uncuff me and we'll head for Jackson."

Albert opened the door and flicked the toothpick into the weeds at the side of the road.

"Forgetting something?" he asked as the man rotated toward him to have the cuffs unlocked.

"You won't see me again."

Hands free and eyes watering, the retired cop pulled the packing from his nose. No blood gushed, but the tissues had been hiding a swollen upper lip that protruded like a purple balloon about to burst. No doubt, the man needed medical attention, but the injury was far from life threatening, and the last pistol shot Jim Cooper placed between someone's eyes had saved Albert's life.

Blood dripped from both nostrils, blotting the man's yellow shirt. Reaching over the SUV's rear seat, Albert snagged the first-aid kit and offered him several packets of gauze.

"Tell me again how this happened?" Albert asked as the man repacked his nose.

"I fell on the trail."

"Jackson then?"

"Jackson." the retired cop nodded.

"I'll call ahead." Albert smiled. "Good hospital there. They'll be waiting for you."

10

The horses stomped their impatience as Jim stopped at Ernie's where, sure enough, he found a toothbrush on aisle three. He also bought two hotdogs, a cup of coffee, and a bag of chips. At the edge of town, he was pouring the remaining chip crumbs into his mouth when his phone rang. About to let it roll to voicemail, he reconsidered—it might be Albert. Arching his back and straightening his thighs as much as possible, he dug the phone from his front pocket.

"Hello?" he said after swallowing.

"Jim, it's your mother."

"Mom?"

"Are you okay? Betty called from the hospital." Jackie Cooper, Jim's mother, lived with his sisters in Newport Beach, California. With the small-town grapevine enhanced by nationwide calling plans, the surprise wasn't that she already knew, it was why she had taken so long to call.

"I was just gonna call you."

"Don't bullshit your mother."

Jim paused for several seconds. His mom rarely swore, and when she did it was usually to cut through the word she had just used.

"Sorry," Jim responded.

"Don't be sorry, just truthful."

"Hold on a sec." Jim put the phone in his lap to down shift as he started up a steep, winding two-mile stretch. A red Corvette flared its brights on him, apparently thinking it was easy to pull over a truck and trailer full of horses and resume on a steep grade. Jim dropped another gear, causing the truck to belch exhaust, as the Corvette's flashing headlights caught his eye through the fumes in the rear-view mirror.

"Still there, mom?" Jim asked after picking up the phone.

"I'm flying home tomorrow."

Jim liked it when his mom referred to the Cooper Ranch as home, even though she hadn't lived there in two years. "I'm not sure it's safe."

"Why wouldn't it be safe?" Jackie demanded.

"What did Betty tell you?"

"When you explain what happened, I won't have to rely on her version."

I've already practiced with the sheriff, Jim thought. He told his mother exactly what had happened, concluding with, "They may retaliate."

"I see. What did Albert say?"

"Not much. I think we were both thinking about Kuwait."

"What happened today has to be a lot like when you two were in the army."

"Nothing was like Kuwait, Mom."

A virtual avalanche of traffic barreled toward him on the winding road, mostly Utah and Colorado plates that Jim guessed were speeding home from Jackson Hole and Yellowstone after the weekend. The Corvette's Nevada plates caught his eye as the road straightened. His phone landed on the passenger seat next to the empty bag of chips, and he wondered how long the state crime lab would keep his pistol. He reached into the extended cab's rear seat to push aside an assortment of tools, jackets, and old horseshoes and grabbed the hunting rifle he kept to ward off coyotes on the ranch.

The Corvette tried to pass and Jim swerved, forcing the car onto the gravel shoulder. The sudden acceleration that brought the car alongside and matching speed seemed impossible. The tattooed and pierced passenger leaned outside the vehicle and yelled something about people from Wyoming being good for nothing but driving slow and molesting sheep. Jim thumbed the window all the way down and pointed the barrel of the rifle into the open air.

The Corvette was a quarter mile down the road and still disappearing in the distance by the time he returned the gun and picked up his phone.

"Mom? You still there?"

"What's going on?"

"I'm headed home to unload the horses."

"Not that. You cut me off."

"There was a bee in the truck," Jim said nonchalantly.

"Do I need to swear again?"

Jim shook his head and smiled. "I'd love for you to come home but let me call you first."

"What just happened?"

"Nothing really." Jim shrugged. "Some guys in a fancy car had a little road rage."

"Now, how was killing those men today different from what happened in Desert Storm?"

"Albert and I came home from Kuwait." Jim waited for a second. "Guarding our best friend's casket." He took the phone from his ear, swallowed the lump in his throat and then continued. "I know Albert and I were both a wreck back then, especially me. Today was different."

"Promise me you'll be careful, and keep me posted."

"I will, Mom. Love you."

"I love you, too."

Jim wished his mother could see his smile as he ended the call. *Killing people in Kuwait led to my best friend's death. But today, I saved Larry's life.*

11

After unloading the horses and gear, Jim looked west. A few clouds floated across the darkening sky, and the setting sun stained them amber and red.

Sunsets were best enjoyed with someone else, and it hurt to think how long he'd lived in isolation. Jim turned away and walked into the barn to take care of his horses, Duke by his side.

The picturesque house and barns sat about a mile from the main road, with the nearest neighbor about three miles to the northwest. The ranch held six thousand acres of good pasture and hay, with about four thousand more of rocky foothill rangeland that was mostly full of sagebrush. The home sat in the middle of pine tree-ringed pastures, affording views from every angle.

The house was large and tidy, with six bedrooms and four bathrooms. Its center was the kitchen where a big wood-burning stove stood. The place was well kept, though it wasn't Jim's doing; a local lady came to clean up each week. While he'd been gone, she'd made him a plate of fresh cinnamon rolls in addition to cleaning up. Taking a huge bite out of one of the rolls, Jim decided she definitely earned a generous tip beyond the agreed-upon sum for cleaning and straightening the house.

Jim tossed his clothes in the trash and hustled to the shower where he watched the swirling blood and dirt disappear down the drain. As he toweled himself dry, he thought of Larry sitting alone in the hospital.

Larry had had nothing with him beyond the shorts, tank top, and shoes on his feet—all of which were torn and bloody. Jim went to a spare closet to see if he could find some things that would fit Larry. Lots of the guests were larger men, mostly big city types who didn't get nearly enough physical activity to burn off the rich food and drink they apparently couldn't live without. He stuffed a few old t-shirts, pants, and socks into a couple grocery of bags, and left for the hospital.

Just inside the main doors, Jim tried to coax the room number from Betty at the information desk.

"We have a new standard called HIPA. I can't give you any information," she said.

"It's been a long day."

"I cannot confirm or deny anyone is in the hospital. That information needs to come from the patient."

"Does this new set of rules—what do you call it?"

"HIPA," Betty said in an authoritative tone.

"Does HIPA include talking to my mother in California?" Jim asked.

The muscle tone left Betty's sixty-something-year-old face.

"She told me about your call," Jim continued. "Wanna give me the room number?"

Betty looked around before whispering, "Twenty-four."

"I didn't hear it from you," Jim whispered back.

Jim made his way through the dark hospital halls, eyeing the room numbers as he went. He was nearing a corner, not paying much attention to anything but the room numbers, when Sally Strobel, his old high school flame, surprised him. Before he knew it, he found himself reliving their courtship, right up to their breakup and her wedding to one of his friends. He thought he'd come to grips with it . . . hell, he was their best family friend; Sally's kids all called him "Uncle Jim" and her oldest son, Skinner, was one of his ranch hands. But standing there, looking in her eyes, he couldn't help wishing things had gone differently.

"I saw you pull in." She smiled, and his pulse quickened. "I'm glad you weren't hurt."

"Where's the man I brought in today?" Jim asked, anxious to keep moving.

"He's sleeping, but I'll take you."

"Thanks."

Instead of walking, Sally looked Jim in the eyes. "Are you okay?"

"No."

"Is there anything I can do for you?"

Jim struggled, knowing he shouldn't say what he was about to, but it came out anyway. "Not unless we can go back in time twenty years." It was more of an honest sentiment than he'd spoken to her in the same amount of time, and Sally's face showed surprise. "I'm sorry. It's been a long day."

Sally put a hand on his forearm, and Jim froze, holding his breath. She must have sensed his discomfort because she removed her hand after only a second or two.

"Let's take you to where you were going."

WAKING UP IN A STRANGE room, Larry panicked for a moment before remembering where he was and why everything hurt. The blurry vision of an attractive nurse and the lifesaving cowboy—minus the straw hat—hovered before his eyes.

"We meet again," Jim greeted him.

"You're cleaned up. Now I look worse." Larry's right cheek was too swollen for him to smile. "Thanks for keeping us alive."

"Brought you some things."

"Thanks . . . didn't expect that."

As Jim placed the care package next to his bed, the simple decency of the gesture struck Larry's conscience.

"How long they keeping you?"

"He's being held overnight for observation," Sally answered. "The doctor was worried about a head injury. If all goes well, he should be released in the morning."

"Will you excuse us?" Jim asked. Larry thought he heard an irritated tone in Jim's voice.

"Of course." Sally walked out and shut the door.

"She do something to piss you off?"

"Long story." Jim sat in the chair beside the bed.

"I told the sheriff it was self defense, and they would have killed me if you hadn't come along."

"Happened fast." Jim glanced around the room. "Did what needed done. I'd do it again, but I'd leave my horse a good distance away."

Larry touched his swollen lips with his fingers tips. *No wonder my words sound funny.* "Sorry about that."

"Me, too." Silence settled over the room for a moment before Jim continued. "How bad's the danger? These people's family won't like today's results."

"Have you thought about what we talked about?" Larry asked.

"Might make sense to help you, but I don't care about getting rich. I just want life to continue—unchanged."

"Rich or not, we're in deep shit." Larry sipped water through a flexible straw. The paper cup felt ridiculously small in his hand. "There's no place they aren't connected. They'll learn who killed their family and friends, and they'll come for you." Jim didn't respond and Larry sensed he was upset. "If you don't want to help, can you leave here fast?"

A grin came over the cowboy's face. "So no good deed goes

unpunished." After a long breath Jim spoke again. "I ain't runnin'. In the morning, I'll take the sheriff to the scene. My hired man'll be by to pick you up."

"Pick me up and take me where?" Larry cocked his left eyebrow; his right was inhibited by a steri-strip that held down a gauze patch.

"My place. You'll be safe for now. We'll figure it out when I get back in the afternoon."

They shook hands in an awkward arm wrestling grip, and Jim left.

Larry lay in bed, head spinning. Hopefully, Jim was more than a onetime answer to a desperate prayer. It would be several days before he could move quickly. He needed a place to chillax, and while the country sucked, it might be the best place to hide. Besides, the events of the day demanded some serious contemplation. He would at least go to Jim's and try to convince him to be his partner. He needed help, and Jim was certainly capable.

Larry's instincts had always kept him out of trouble—until he'd ignored them and nearly been killed. And now, everything told him to make the Marlboro man his partner.

Leveling with Jim about the danger seemed the right thing to do. If nothing else, it was an honest response to an honest question. Though he had gotten used to telling half-truths and outright lies as he'd gotten older, the truth took away some of the pain as he drifted back to sleep.

Larry's sobering words itched like a mosquito bite in Jim's head as he got ready for bed. Being on the run from the mafia would have seemed preposterous as he woke up on the horse-blankets that morning. Now, the prudent thing to do was to take Larry up on his offer, but the lack of alternatives angered him. The only other thing he could think of was to sit at home and wait for the hit men to show up.

Jim wanted to shoot them all, but he knew he was already lucky to be alive. He'd been stupid to get involved in the first place; these men had no scruples about torturing someone or killing in cold blood. As he replayed the scene in his mind, it was shocking how little regard they held for life. To them, killing Larry and himself was no big deal, like making a phone call, or using the rest room.

Hollywood movies were literally Jim's only window into the world of organized crime—and probably not the most accurate window at that. He remembered watching *The Godfather* and *Goodfellas* and hating the characters—bedazzled with jewelry and tailored suits, they seemed like overdressed clowns.

Jim undressed, brushed his teeth, and tried to sleep, but he couldn't stop thinking about the day's events. They would find a way to kill him if he stayed on the ranch, and he doubted anyone from the community—other than Albert Johnson—would help.

Jim wasn't Mormon, which was the predominant religion in the area. He'd lived among them all his life, except for his four years in the army, and he'd always felt like an outsider. If someone was speaking at church and he wanted to hear, he would attend. He'd also go to some of the social functions, where some well-meaning neighbors invariably tried to talk to him about his beliefs; and he would politely decline. Sally had invited him to listen to the Church's missionaries after high school, but the spiritual awakening she prayed for never quite materialized. The Book of Mormon didn't accomplish what the missionaries promised it would—give him an overpowering spiritual witness of the faith's authenticity—and he'd read it twice.

Deep inside, I'm a skeptic.

He'd realized that fact about himself in high school. He'd gone to see a hypnotist with a few of his friends. The hypnotist had called several people up on stage and told them to extend their arms. They counted down from the number ten, and with each descending number, their arms would feel twice as heavy. As it became unbearable, it would be okay to drop them.

"Ten, nine, eight, seven . . ." Strange music played in the background while they were told to breathe slowly, but nothing got heavier. If anything felt different, it was simply fatigue. Jim heard other people's arms slap their bodies.

Because he was the only person with arms still extended, the hypnotist whispered in Jim's ear, "This isn't working for you, is it?"

"No." *What isn't working for me?*

The hypnotist dismissed him to sit in the audience as nine of his friends became mindless pawns, their dignity sacrificed for the performance. They danced like Michael Jackson, walked like ducks, and screamed for their favorite horse at a race. Feeling left out, Jim approached the hypnotist after the performance and asked why the spell hadn't worked. The explanation was unexpected.

"You have a literal mind," the hypnotist had said. "Most people believe what they're told, but you don't. As I counted backward, you checked to make sure your arms were the same. The difference between you and the others is you prove things to yourself first."

Jim had wondered through the years what the hypnotist meant. It made him think about organized religion and the crazy things people did: drinking poisoned Kool-Aid, crusading to reclaim the holy land. And it wasn't just Christians. Muslims flew airplanes into buildings.

What a bunch of stupid bastards, believing whatever they're taught or told.

Did the men who drew their guns on him today act on a belief system?

When the Mormon missionaries said he would feel all sorts of wonderful impressions, he waited, only to be disappointed. Maybe he was spiritually dead, or inept. Or maybe he wasn't influenced by their power of suggestion.

Their advice had been simple: pray more and pray harder.

It seemed obvious then, and had ever since, that what they meant was: "Trust us. Your arms are getting heavier. They really are. Even if they don't feel different, they are."

Twenty years later, Jim knew how the experience shaped his life. At the same time, he discovered a connection in the poetic lyrics of a favorite song. "No, his mind is not for rent, to any God or government." Rush's song resonated, speaking to his bone-deep pragmatism.

I definitely need to dig through my old music stash.

Jim switched gears and thought about the few spiritual impressions he had had. The closest thing to a faith-promoting tingle came when he'd helped or received help from other people.

The words of his favorite hymn, *A Poor Wayfaring Man of Grief,* played through his head. He felt good knowing he'd saved Larry's life. Maybe the song had it right. "These deeds shall thy memorial be. Fear not, thou didst them unto me."

The hymn was sung at Bradley's funeral after the Gulf War. Whatever God was, Jim hoped deeds done by pistol might count.

With the long day over, and the adrenaline gone, he finally drifted off to sleep.

He dreamt of riding through the mountains with Sam. Sam's thundering hooves powered them across a meadow. The wind pushed across his face, tugging at his shirt and making his eyes water. They galloped into the woods, jumping over deadfall trunks, weaving around boulders at a reckless pace. Sam leapt into a stream and charged out of the woods through another meadow and around a sagebrush hill.

Jim bent low, moving his weight over the horse's neck. His cowboy hat flew off in a gust of wind, its string tugging at his neck, wagging like an out-of-control kite caught in his tailwind. Together they ran for miles, pushing for something he couldn't quite recall, moving because they could, driven by instinct, heading wherever felt right.

They came to the end of the world, a great precipice, where birds flew beyond the edge toward an eclipsed black sun. Its light cast long shadows with rainbows trimming the edges, as though viewed through a prism.

Jim dismounted.

"Thanks for the ride."

He wrapped his arms around the horse's steaming neck, feeling heat and perspiration stain his shirt. Sam's ears were strained forward. He stood gazing fixedly out into nothingness, perhaps hearing something meant only for the souls of horses.

Sam bent down, looking at the abyss. Then a great snort and a stomping front hoof sent small rocks tumbling over the edge. Sam relaxed as Jim petted him.

They stood for a long time, both confused by the edge of nothingness.

13

Before the sun was up the next morning, Jim woke up his hired man, Brody, who also lived in the ranch house.

Brody was an old time cowboy well into his seventies. He was steady and helpful, knew how to run a ranch, take care of horses, cows, and machinery. He was also a passable carpenter, and even knew quite a bit about plumbing and electricity.

Jim trusted the old man, allowing him to come and go, and charge on his accounts at stores. The two rarely spoke. When they did, Jim usually learned something new.

"I need you to go to the hospital this morning," Jim said from the door of Brody's bedroom.

"And do what?"

"Pick someone up."

"A guest get hurt?" the old cowboy asked, squinting into the day's first light.

"Big guy named Larry. He's beat to hell. Call Sally Strobel and make sure he's cleared. I want him on the sofa this afternoon."

"He knows I'm comin'?"

"On the sofa." Jim shut the door, but then reopened it. "There's a leftover cinnamon roll on the table."

DUKE GREETED JIM IN THE kitchen, sniffing upward as Jim poured himself a tall mug of coffee. Normally he'd fill a thermos, but this morning he stood looking out the window above the sink at his cows in the north pasture. Duke rested easy against his leg as Jim sipped. The coffee was black and hot. The ceramic mug warmed his hand. Jim remembered his father using the same mug. It was man sized with a handle big enough for his hand—not just a few fingers. Outside, the ridges to the east lit up with amber and yellow trimmings like the continental divide had the morning before. He bent to pet Duke.

"What a difference a day makes," Jim said to the dog and the empty kitchen.

Duke looked up in response to the words until the creaking floor drew their attention—Brody going to the bathroom. Jim finished all but the last ounce, filled the mug half full with water and swirled to rinse before setting the mug in the sink.

Duke nuzzled into his leg, and Jim crouched to take the dog's head between his hands. Then he pulled the dog close in an encircling bear hug.

"Let's go take care of Sam."

JIM WATCHED FROM THE BARN as Albert pulled into the Cooper Ranch. A plume of dust billowed behind the vehicle as Jim walked to the trailer, where he had Beatrice and a gelding named Terence saddled and loaded.

Albert got out of his SUV.

"Been up all night, Jimmy," he said, "and I want you to know, soldier to soldier, I'm sorry about yesterday."

"I appreciate that," Jim replied, locking eyes with his old friend.

The moment grew heavy with sentiment as neither man spoke. Their focus increased until Jim looked at the sky and Albert the ground.

"That's enough of that," Albert stated.

"I was worried you were gonna hug me," Jim said. Duke trotted up from behind the barn and growled at the sheriff.

"Where'd you come from?" Albert asked. The dog was now at Jim's side eyeing the sheriff.

"Atta boy, Duke. Good dog!" Jim said.

"You're going to encourage this?"

"He thinks you're evil," Jim responded.

"So, after growing up and going to war together, I'm evil?"

"Duke must've had a bad dream. We both know I could've made the bodies vanish. Could've shot Larry as well, and done the same to him."

"Larry?" the sheriff asked.

"You not get coffee? Larry. Big black fella, got the shit beat out of him yesterday."

"He wouldn't give me his name."

"What did he say?" Jim asked, doubting Larry would offer much to the sheriff.

"Said he's one lucky minority."

"Anything about those I shot?"

"Claimed ignorance. It don't matter. I'll know who they are by end of the day. Ever seen this guy?" Albert pulled a paper from the dash of his vehicle.

Jim recognized the mug shot immediately, with the graying sideburns and heavy man's face. His reply came in a quiet tone as he looked away from one of the men he had killed. "That's the second one."

Albert nodded and placed the paper back on the dashboard. "In addition to catching your bullet, he owns the rig with the horse-kicked door at the trailhead. I'm gonna have it towed."

After Albert got off the phone, Jim was anxious to get moving. "We ridin' or you waitin' on breakfast and coffee?"

"Since you lack hospitality, we'll ride."

"Hospitality's given to those who pay," Jim said as he opened the door of his pickup.

Albert climbed in the passenger side. "Beatrice has probably missed me anyway."

"Like a hemorrhoid."

"Whatever. That horse loves me," the sheriff insisted.

Jim smiled. "She's about as particular as the girls you dated in high school."

"You said the young kid shot at you three times?"

The change of direction surprised Jim, but he knew Albert was his friend first and sheriff second. "That's right. He hit Sam with the first shot, the second whizzed over me as I jumped, and the third missed after I landed on my feet."

"You sure?"

Jim waited for Albert to look at him before responding. "I been wrong twice my whole life."

"Now I know you're lying," Albert said raising an eyebrow. "The .357 the kid fired at you had three spent casings in the cylinder, but the Glock .40 from your saddle bags was missing a round."

Jim thought about the gunshot he heard while riding down the trail. "Just up-trail from the conflict, there was a shot."

"And you failed to mention this because?"

"Didn't think to," Jim said. "I got off my horse to listen for a bit. A mare had kicked off her iron. She was due for re-shoeing, so I reset all four."

"Fair enough," Albert scratched at his chin. "Then what?"

Jim shrugged. "Rode to where Duke introduced Josey Wales to the bad guys."

Albert's jaw dropped.

"The shot could've been anything."

"Maybe, but I won't abide blasphemy." Albert's stern voice

sounded like Jim was caught with the idol worshippers as Moses returned from Sinai.

"Blasphemy?"

"I'll help you through this," Albert emphasized each word. "But don't claim you're Clint Eastwood."

"Duke was right to growl at you."

The two men shared a chuckle.

They drove in silence until they came across a car broken down on the road a few miles from the ranch. Jim levered the blinker and pulled the truck and horse trailer ahead of the car as Albert's irritation surfaced. "Now what?"

"Maybe we can help."

"Oh no you don't. Did yesterday not teach you anything?"

"Isn't there a lawman's oath?" Jim asked. "Give me a hand."

"When exactly did we become friends?"

Albert made a call from the truck while Jim hopped out to help a teenage girl fumbling with the jack and spare tire. Within five minutes, he had the tire changed. Explaining the process, Jim had her tighten the lug nuts. "Next time you'll know what to do."

"Thanks," she responded with an admiring look.

She was cute, but *far* too young. Jim caught a vibe, but said good-bye and walked back to his truck. Most of his adult life may have been lonely, but he wasn't stupid.

"You have to be about the damndest, do-gooder I know," Albert said before Jim could fasten his seat belt. "Is there anyone you don't help?"

"You're just urinated over having to work. You'll be back to the doughnuts and coffee routine by next week. And you're welcome."

"For what?" Albert asked, his body reclined in the seat that was still moved to its limit to accommodate Larry.

"For giving you something to do." Jim checked the blind spot, turned on the blinker and pulled onto the road.

"I don't need your help, and I don't drink coffee. I'm Mormon."

"A Mormon who accused me of blasphemy," Jim growled. "The gallon jug of Mountain Dew you fill at Ernie's three times a day ring a bell?"

"That's different." Albert yawned.

"Carbonated coffee if you ask me." Jim shifted the manual transmission and the truck picked up speed.

"I didn't, and you just proved my point. Only you would kill three people then twist it into helping me."

"Pretty pathetic for me to shoot someone just so the local sheriff can earn a paycheck."

"Three people's more than someone. Every day I do you a favor."

"You'll need to elaborate."

"I get up, put on this badge," Albert tapped the star on his uniform. "I keep the community safe, so you can hunt and fish. Someone does the heavy lifting, and it ain't you."

"Is that why the county bought you the new SUV with the automatic?" Jim mocked. "They're worried about your arm wearing out from the stick shift?"

"Partly. I need a hand free to drink the carbonated coffee. That gallon gets heavy. Where the hell d'you come up with that one anyway?" Albert asked.

"Same place you found blasphemy and Clint Eastwood."

"Stop!" Albert yelled as they pulled into the trailhead parking lot. Jim stomped the brake as hard as possible without sending his horses through the front of the trailer. Albert jumped out of the truck, ran ahead ten feet, and got down on his knees. "Jimmy, there's a duffle-bag behind the seat."

Jim retrieved the bag and handed it to Albert. The sheriff rooted through the bag until he found a digital camera. He took several pictures from both sides of a shiny spent shell casing, then shook open a zip-lock bag.

"Maybe we just found the brass for the shot you heard. Saw it shining in the sun as we pulled in." Albert tweezed a single .40 caliber casing then labeled the zip-lock after dropping it in.

"Hey Inspector Callahan, come take a look."

Albert stuffed the evidence inside the duffel and turned his attention to Jim. In front of Jim's foot, about thirty feet from where Albert found the casing was a golf ball sized mound of gravel with a straight groove leading up to it.

"Looks to me like someone shot a bullet here in the parking lot," Albert stated.

"That it does."

"Give me a minute." Albert scratched the earth, gently moving gravel and dirt away. He produced a bullet, and placed it carefully into another bag.

"I told you I've only been wrong twice," Jim said.

"Yes you did." Albert stood. "We'll send it to ballistics with the pistol to see if we have a match."

Jim got Beatrice and Terence from the trailer, and took them to a watering trough at the side of the parking lot. A small seep fed water through a pipe into a barrel. The parking lot was already hot, and the trail would be almost as warm until they reached the tree line. Additionally, between the parking lot and the site of the shooting, it would be dry.

Neither horse drank.

As they rode up the trail, Albert commented on Jim's mount. "He's a big one."

"Wanted to see how he'd do."

"He got a name?"

"Terence."

"Where the hell d'you get 'Terence?'"

"Can't name a horse I like Albert."

"Too embarrassed to tell me?" the sheriff baited.

"Client I packed in two days ago scolded me because the trough ran dry. I filled a five-gallon bucket. His eyes bugged out when

Terence drained it. The guy says, 'I saw people funnel beer at fraternity parties, but that was awesome!' Terence sounds like the name of a frat boy, don't it? Terence the guzzler?" Jim rode in the lead, and he turned to smile at Albert.

"Good hell you're bored."

"Here's the best part," Jim continued. "'What's a gelding? And how is that different from a mare?' this guy asks. So I tell him, 'A gelding's a boy and a mare's a girl.' So he asks, 'If you cross a mare and a gelding you get a colt, right?' 'No. If you cross a mare and stud, you get a colt.'"

"Can we play the silent game?"

"The guy puzzles over it for about two breaths, 'So what's the difference between a stud and a gelding?' he asks. And I answer, 'Brain surgery.'"

"What the hell are you talking about?" Albert asked.

"Brain surgery sets the male horse's mind free. You could say it totally changes his personality."

"What?"

"He figured it out quicker than you, dumb ass—castration?" Jim said.

"A city dude figured that out?"

"The guy set a record. Some'll go days, and once they finally figure it out, they can't understand how a stud might ruin the day for the person riding the mare."

Albert's eyes rolled. "When did you last contribute to society?"

They rode, but the mood turned somber as they got close.

"After you sheriff through the crime scene, I'm dragging Sam a long way off. I don't wanna smell him when I ride this way."

"Shouldn't be a problem," Albert replied. "I'll need to take some pictures, and get an idea from you as to where the bodies fell. If it all makes sense, I'll help you do it."

Jim didn't respond and Albert continued, "Mostly it needs to make sense to me. I need to know it all if I'm to ride shotgun for you on this one."

Jim recommitted to show Albert exactly what had happened, because he knew, once convinced, there would be no backing up in the sheriff.

The truth was about to set him free. At least with the law.

As Jim turned off the trail, he thought about Larry walking the green mile a day earlier. Duke started down the draw. Speaking as he rode, Jim retold the events as they happened.

Sam was there.

Flies buzzed around the dead body of the once magnificent horse, and Jim blew his nose, wiped his eyes, and told every detail—where the men stood before dying, where Duke was, and how Sam fell.

"What a shit storm," Albert said, looking at the depressions in the grass where the bodies had fallen.

Jim nodded.

"Thanks, Jimmy. Take the frat boy up the trail a few miles. Give me an hour or so."

Jim needed to leave. Terence shied as he tried to mount, a rookie behavior common to most beginning horses. Pulling on the left rein, Terence circled Jim twice before standing still. Placing a foot in the stirrup again, Jim swung himself up into the saddle.

"Got some big shoes to fill," Jim said, petting the gelding's neck.

Coaxing the horse into a canter, Jim moved rapidly away from Albert, Sam, Larry, and Kuwait. Duke whimpered next to Sam. Then he growled and barked three times. His eyes focused on the clearing as he sniffed the air, possibly remembering the violence. He growled again and bolted up the trail, catching Jim and Terence in less than a minute. He slowed up, looking at Jim on the horse. Duke ran at their side shadowing the horse and rider like a concerned parent.

14

As Albert looked over the crime scene, it all made sense. He found four spent forty-five caliber shells on the ground from Jim's gun, making the number of total shots an exact match with Jim's testimony.

He put the spent shells into evidence bags, labeling them with a sharpie. There were big depressions in the grass, and blood stains from the dead bodies. Ultimately, there was nothing to condemn his friend, and he took digital pictures of everything to verify the findings.

Jim's boot marks were randomly strewn about, along with lots of horse tracks and a few size fourteen basketball prints.

Looking at a spot under the tree that had been tromped down by Jim and several horses, Albert pictured his friend loading the dead bodies and putting them over the packhorses. If Jim hadn't done it yesterday, Albert knew he would be doing it today. Then again, this was Jim Cooper, forever considerate—unless you were shooting at him.

AFTER JIM AND TERENCE LEFT Albert, the trail leading into the backcountry opened up for several miles. They traveled through meadows and open stretches of trail where he could let the young gelding run.

The horse showed him some surprising things. Up to that hour, he'd mostly ridden Terence at a walk, and was pleased with how nicely the horse would move into a faster gait.

If not pushing cows, Jim hated to sit a trotting horse. Ideally, his horses would move from a fast walk into a nice easy canter without much urging. And then a flat out, ass hauling, Kentucky Derby gallop was the finishing touch to the perfect mountain horse.

Terence crossed several streams and also negotiated some rough spots in the trail without much hesitation.

Sam would be proud.

Life went on.

As Jim moved through the woods on the horse, Duke followed like a shadow, always keeping enough distance from the pounding hooves to keep from getting stepped on.

The horse and Jim were in-sync. If the trail opened up enough to gallop, he turned the gelding loose with just a squeeze from his legs. As the trail closed up, or got tight from going around a rock, or into the trees, the horse would instinctively slow.

I think this was better for me than the horse, Jim thought, but almost as soon as it had begun it was over. They arrived back at the scene of the shooting, where Albert was still studying the ground and taking pictures.

Jim waited to speak until Albert looked at him. "Well, am I the guy you've known all your life, or am I Charlie Manson?"

"Well, at least you don't think you're Clint Eastwood."

Jim dismounted. "Done some honest 'sheriffing,' I hope?"

"They call it police work," Albert responded. "Spent the last hour looking for a reason to make an arrest. Other than your friend in the hospital, you killed my witnesses. The rocks and trees won't speak, so it looks like you're clear."

"Feel good to earn your paycheck?"

Albert was fumbling with Beatrice's saddlebags. "Not as good as having a ranch as your birthright."

"I was kinda looking forward to giving it all up—spending life in prison. Now's your chance."

Jim put a lariat around Sam's back legs and dallied the horn on Beatrice's saddle.

The corpse scraped the ground, leaving bits of Sam's fur on the rough edges of rocks, bringing Jim's anger back to the simmering point. Remorse whispered to him for killing the two older men and practically screamed at him for killing the tattooed skater. He realized from the moment it happened, the mouthy runt was showing off. If only they hadn't drawn, Sam would be home in his stall; and they would be playing golf or skating or whatever it was they used to do.

Jim and Albert found a rocky spot further down the gully to leave Sam. Between the bears, the coyotes, and the birds, the wilderness would quickly dispose of the horse's body. Very little went unused in a remote area. The rocky patch was out in the open, and the ultraviolet rays from the sun would break down the tissue as quickly as anything.

This wasn't the first horse Jim would miss. Even before riding Terence, he realized Sam wasn't going to be the last exceptional horse he'd train and own. His herd of horses was about twenty head total.

His father had called the herd his "congregation." Several noteworthy members had received "sainthood" and were given hero's burials. A row of pines behind the barn marked the graves of those revered horses, ones that had worked, lived, and died on the Cooper Ranch. Sam deserved to be buried with them. He should have his own tree, and it added to Jim's anger.

Before leaving, Jim used a pair of old hoof trimmers to remove Sam's shoes. He planned on making a plaque for his wall with them and maybe a picture of him on Sam.

The men rode back to the trailhead in silence, each man thinking about what they had to do the rest of the day. After about fifteen minutes, Jim called to Albert. "I'll be quiet if you wanna speak."

"For once I believe you," Albert said.

"About being quiet, or this whole thing?"

"Both. I'm contemplating. The owner of the Escalade's a convict. If the other two are as well, chances are the feds or anyone taking an interest'll figure you did society a favor. I'll need to sort all this out with the county attorney and medical examiner, but I'm not worried about the outcome."

"Thanks," Jim responded.

Jim's mind turned to Larry, and being deliberately quiet about what he knew regarding the crime family in Vegas, and his advice to flee.

There was no sense worrying too much about what might happen until it did. If the Vegas Mafia came looking for him, he'd give them a warm welcome. But Jim's next thought turned his blood to ice water. *I won't see them coming. I'll be dead without knowing how it happened.*

Jim was straightforward and expected anyone who had a problem to confront him directly. Yesterday's conflict was direct because he took away their deceit, tackling the problem head-on. He remembered the way they insisted he ride away, and it poked at his anger.

They wanted to shoot me in the back.

What would be the best way to deal with these people? How could he handle someone who would try to kill him before he even knew they were there? Here one moment—gone the next.

He could be difficult to find. *Let them look for me in the mountains.* It would work until snow flew, but eventually he'd need to live near a furnace. Besides, the thought of running tasted bad. He could ask for Albert's help, but the law couldn't watch out for him constantly.

I've been a civilian too long.

Back in his army days, he'd have gone after them instead of waiting around to die. He wouldn't have to kill them necessarily, just let them know he was as dangerous to them as they were to him.

Shattering a plant on a porch with a precise shot, just as the gangster walked out the door would be an easy message to send. It had been a long time since he'd been to Las Vegas. Perhaps there was a trip there in his near future.

15

Brody followed orders, calling Sally at the hospital to make sure the patient in question was good to go. Upon arrival, she waved from the entry door. Though Brody seldom talked to other men, a pretty nurse was an altogether different matter.

"Seems I'm Jim Cooper's limousine service today," he said by way of greeting.

"That's what I understand," Sally replied. "When you get done running errands for Jim, you can swing by and give me a ride home." She smiled and raised an eyebrow.

The old ranch-hand cracked a rare smile. It cheered him thinking, if only for the moment, she thought enough of him to flirt.

Brody doffed his Stetson. "If I ever picked up a gorgeous thing like you, the last place I'd take her would be home to her husband!"

"Let me take you to someone you're supposed to pick up." She took two steps, but then paused and looked like she was going to speak, but stopped.

"What?" Brody asked.

Sally coughed into her fist and then hung her head.

"If you have something you wanna say, I got no place better to be," Brody nodded to a man in a shirt and tie, who walked past talking on a cell.

"Does Jim ever talk about me?"

Brody smiled. Sally's marrying while Jim was in the army had surprised some, but not Brody. He'd known when Jim didn't saddle up to Mormonism he'd lose Sally.

"Jim hasn't said anything in years. But every time Skinner comes around, he asks in his own way."

"What to do you mean?"

"Jim asks how his family's doin'. It ain't your daughters or your husband Jim wants to hear about."

Sally nodded her head, then smiled and offered Brody her hand. "Let's go introduce you to Mr. Lyons."

Larry was sitting in a wheelchair with bandages on his head when they opened his door. His knee was wrapped, his foot elevated.

"The doctor cleared him. No broken bones. Just lots of cuts, scrapes, and bruises. He needs to rest, but in a few days should be okay. Here's a number if you need anything."

Brody looked at Larry and was shaken. Even in a wheelchair, the giant looked like he could pummel a whole gang of bikers.

It's been a long time since I've been around a black person.

His first impulse was to run, but he knew how pissed Jim would be. Jim rarely gave direct orders, but the boss expected those he gave to be followed.

Sally made introductions. "Larry, this is Jim's hired man, Brody."

You old fool. You've been alive for more than seventy years, and you're scared of another human being because of his skin color?

Sally helped wheel Larry's chair out to the truck. Brody thanked her politely and climbed into the driver's seat. Neither man spoke.

16

Larry's discomfort exceeded Brody's. Kidnapped, hauled to Wyoming, beaten, saved, hospitalized, and driven to God-knows-where by a crypt-keeping, cowboy-booted, Stetson-wearing redneck.

Now, here he was, a long way from anyone or anything familiar, and he hurt like hell. The décor was western, with pictures of cowboys and cowgirls. Black and white photos of horses and old tractors hung on the walls. Spurs, ropes, and various mystery gadgets were displayed like museum pieces on the shelves.

Then something caught Larry's eye. On the coffee table was a picture of Jim in a football uniform, wearing number 54, a helmet to his side and a big smile on his face. Jim looked younger; he had a teenage exuberance, now replaced by a weathered adult capability and some gray hairs. In the frame was stenciled, *James Owen Cooper 1987.*

Sounds of the geezer rustling around in the kitchen caught his attention. Then the door creaked open, latched shut, and the screen door slapped closed, telling Larry he was alone in the house.

This sucks. Breathe out. But as he tried to exhale away the worry, the sense of isolation increased. Out the window, there was a long gravel lane joining the public road the redneck had driven to get here. There were no other houses in view.

Why would anyone live like this? Even if it meant dying, Larry wanted to leave, to go somewhere with people.

He tried to stand, but everything hurt and he collapsed, creaking into the couch. He closed his eyes against memories from the hospital, the X-ray room, and the staff whisking his gurney in and out. A salty old doctor, who could have been Brody's older brother, stitched up his cuts and asked why he was still alive.

"You have strong bones. It's rare seeing the kind of bruising you've got with no fractures. You'll still hurt for a few weeks. Get moving and it should help," the doctor had said.

No shit it hurt. Mafia spooks are like a pack of dogs. None of them would try a beating like that alone. Larry needed rest, but his swirling thoughts pecked at him, keeping him awake and tense. Hopefully it would take a few days for Faletto or his goons to find him. For the time being, his family would be safe, and most importantly, he still knew where the money was.

Eventually, narcotic-induced lethargy and the thought of wealth took over, and he slept.

After several hours, he woke up startled. Momentarily disoriented, it took a few a seconds to focus on Jim, who was sitting across the room in a chair reading a sheaf of papers.

Jim hadn't looked toward him yet, and Larry studied the cowboy. Rugged. Tough. Even though the t-shirt was loose, it showed a strong upper body, and if it weren't for the graying blonde hair and a few wrinkles, Jim could still pass for the kid in the football picture.

Larry rolled, creaking the couch, and Jim snapped to attention.

"Howdy."

Larry tried to sit up, groaning and holding his ribs.

"Feel like talking?" Jim asked.

Larry shifted to several positions, but couldn't find a place that didn't hurt.

"Take your time," Jim said.

"I appreciate you bringing me here, but why?"

"Because I can." Jim set the papers on the coffee table. "Yesterday I wouldn't have imagined someone like you would be in my living room."

"You mean someone black?"

Jim looked Larry in the eye. "I spent four years in the army. Some of the best soldiers were men of color. But you're right, we rarely see black folk here."

He kept his uninjured eye focused on Jim. The cowboy's stare held an intensity Larry had only shared with his mother and a handful of coaches. "I appreciate that. Most of the people at the hospital got whiplash."

"Drummed up some business for the local chiropractor, huh?" Then Jim changed the subject. "Yesterday you offered riches if I helped you retrieve the money you stole. I don't mind cash, but what I really want is to live."

"Your best shot at that will be helping me."

"Why cut me in? You could split and leave, never to be seen again."

"Two reasons." Larry paused. "First, from where I sit, you were an answer to my prayer."

"Stop." Jim's rolled his eyes and looked away.

"Yesterday, before you came, I prayed for help."

"I'm not the answer to anything," Jim said with a deepening scowl.

"I'm just telling what happened."

"God isn't in this and that," Jim snapped. "If he's so involved, why not save you the ass-kicking, me from killing three guys, and keep my best horse alive?"

"What would you want God to do?" Larry asked, surprised by Jim's outburst.

"Three lightning bolts."

"Maybe that's what he did."

"What? Out of my pistol?"

Larry shrugged.

Jim's eyebrows relaxed as his head shook. "How do you know it wasn't coincidence?"

"Because, right after you told me to put my weight in the stirrups and lean back, I felt something I can't describe."

"I didn't say that."

"You told me, 'lean back and put your weight in the stirrups.'"

"No I didn't."

A loud knock interrupted the conversation, and Larry jumped.

"If they're coming already, we might as well give up," Jim said casually.

Whoever it was knocked again, louder this time.

"I'm more worried about the redneck old man returning with some friends and a rope."

"Brody?" Jim's face relaxed into a smile. "Why worry about him? Just say a prayer."

17

A third knock on the door within ten seconds meant someone really wanted to get in. Jim opened the door to see two of his Mormon neighbors carrying arms full of food. Jill Smith and Sarah Bott were from the local congregation. They'd brought more food than Jim, Larry, and Brody could eat in a week, and Jim wished he had more fly fishing guests coming to eat it all. There were baked beans, potato salad, ham, chicken, Jell-o, coleslaw, and a few mystery casseroles that all smelled good, even if they didn't look it. On a second trip through, the ladies brought two apple pies and a chocolate cake as they tried not to stare.

After putting her food in the kitchen, Sarah Bott strode into the living room, hand extended.

"Hello. I'm Jim's neighbor, Sister Bott. Welcome to our community."

Larry looked shocked but took her hand. "I'm Larry."

In her early thirties, Sarah bubbled enthusiasm like a never-ending Alka-Selzer. "Where are you from?" she asked.

"Los Angeles."

"No kidding! Where exactly?"

"Some rough places."

"Southwest or East?"

"Neither. Close to downtown," Larry responded.

"I spent a year and a half of my life on the east side on my mission. I'm always telling my family about southern California. The summer barbecue is Friday evening at the church. Will you come?"

Larry stammered through his hydrocodone and pain-induced lethargy. "I don't know where I'll be . . . I . . . I don't have a way to get there."

"We can pick you up, or Jim can bring you," she said, her already high-pitched, chipper enthusiasm overmatching Larry by several multiples.

"Not me." Jim avoided the trap. "I'm retrieving guests from the mountains. Let's let Larry rest, ladies. If he's still here, he can hitch a ride with Brody."

"If I'm still here, I'll ride with you," Larry said to Sister Bott.

"I can't wait to tell my family that I met someone from where I served my mission!"

"If there's anything you need, let us know," Sister Smith said as they moved toward the door. "You'll be in our prayers."

"Thank you," Larry acknowledged from the couch. Jim rolled his eyes.

Jim thanked them for the food as they walked out on the porch. Shutting the door behind them, he looked at Larry and exhaled like someone who had been underwater for too long.

"Who were they?" Larry asked, the bandages, and swollen features did little to conceal his astonishment.

"They're Mormons."

"And they pop in with dinner whenever anybody's hurt?"

"Pretty much. You hungry?"

Larry nodded.

SITTING IN THE KITCHEN AMID piles of food, Jim was impatient to get answers to his questions—though he certainly didn't want to resume the divine intervention conversation.

"Yesterday you told me I could get rich. But all I care about is those I killed have families who will try to kill me. So why don't you tell me exactly what the hell is going on."

Larry swallowed a mouth full of potatoes, took a drink of water and cleared his throat. "Three days ago, a couple of partners and I stole a truckload of cash from the Las Vegas mob."

"Why?"

"Greed."

The honest answer made Jim shake his head in amusement. "Okay, but why steal from the most ruthless folks on the planet?"

"We weren't planning on getting caught."

Jim chewed on a chunk of honey ham. "You have a dollar figure?"

"No idea. But man that truck was full. We're talking hundreds of duffel bags, Jim."

"And Wyoming fits into this how?"

"My partner came up here fly fishing. He's an accountant. Typical smart-as-hell nerd. He figured out how the Mafia smuggles their cash. They kept me alive to get to him. But then they got sick of hiking."

"Why come here to fish? Why not high tail it to the border?"

"Where better to lay low? It's why the plan was so perfect, a truck that big will be seen. So we hid it back in Vegas in a storage bay less than a mile from where I jacked it. The plan was to move the cash from there one trunk-load at a time."

Jim realized what had been staring him in the face all along. Chris hiring him on short notice, and paying him five hundred per guest to be spot packed was part of staying off the radar after the heist. "Is your partner Chris Cobb?"

"You know him?"

Jim shook his head in disgust. "He helped me saddle up yesterday before I met you."

"That's the dawg."

Larry was right about Chris's smarts. Some clients became friends, but Chris Cobb was aloof, an observer, the guy who would sit back and study the situation. Jim remembered teaching him things once. Things like saddling and bridling a horse, and how to set up a tent and make a fire. Jim loved low maintenance guests like Chris.

Jim buttered a roll and smeared it with raspberry jam before eating it in two bites. "You said there were two reasons for wanting my help. The second one better not involve God."

"After saving my life, the least I owe you is the cash to run away," Larry started. "And . . ."

"Just spit it out."

"Let's say you're in the NFL, and you've bet it all on winning the Superbowl." Larry moved his fork like a conductor stick as he spoke, emphasizing his words. "Your game plan's perfect, but you're getting your ass kicked. It's so bad there's no hope, and out of nowhere, a player you've never seen walks onto the field, and throws three touchdown passes in a row."

"I'm the new quarterback?"

"You got game." Larry shrugged.

"If they're gonna try and kill me, the money would give me options," Jim said.

"You in then?"

"Until I find a better solution." Jim scratched at his stubble. "I'll take my share as payment for my horse."

"Alright then!" Larry smiled.

"So where did the cash originate?" Jim asked.

"You name it. They have legal and illegal shit going down in and out of Vegas. Even the legit businesses only claim a fraction of what they make."

"So, the cash collects and they move it all at once?" Jim asked.

"You got it. They take it to a private dock where it's taken out of the country."

"So how did you and Chris meet?"

"An old friend from college. She introduced us."

"She?"

"Her name's Sheila. She got answers for us about details."

"So is she an item with you or Chris?'

"I wish. More of a business association."

"You were her pimp."

"Nah." Larry paused. "Sorta. She gets rich guys to give her shit. Cons 'em into emptying their wallet." Larry gave Jim a half smile "If they get possessive I step in."

Jim chuckled inwardly thinking of Larry scaring off some middle-aged executive who wouldn't leave a pretty young lady alone. Jim let Larry swallow another forkful of potatoes before he asked the next question. "So they see you and decide to cut and run."

"Something like that."

"So this gal . . ." Jim paused.

"Sheila," Larry stated.

"Right. She introduced you and Chris. What will they think about you bringing in another partner?"

"They'll do it if I say so."

Jim nodded and chuckled again, wondering, other than the Mafia, who would want to argue with Larry.

"Sheila's not in it for the money anyway," Larry continued. "She got beat up by some Mafia guys a while back, and has wanted payback ever since."

Jim had heard of Mafia-owned ranches used to launder cash. How do you account for expenses on a ranch that's tens of thousands of acres? When it came to verifying loss of crops or livestock, it would be impossible.

While he was fairly honest and tried to keep accurate financial records on his own place, Jim didn't report the cash tips guests usually left at the end of their stay. Most of his clients tipped him at about ten percent of the trip cost. He always reported the fee his clients paid to the outfitting company, but any cash went to pay for diesel in his pickup and daily expenses.

"So Chris is in danger and doesn't know it?"

"Is there any way we can call him? Cell phone maybe?" Larry asked in response.

"Not unless he has a satellite phone."

"Damn, you people are off the beaten path."

"Are any of the other guests I packed in involved?"

"No. He told me he was going fishing for a week with some buddies."

Jim leaned back in his chair. "So Chris puts his friends at risk, as long as he's around."

"Oh, yeah."

"How long until they send someone up here?"

"Now." Larry's tone was matter of fact. "In the real world, cell phones keep these guys talking, and those three haven't been answering since the star quarterback jumped their shit."

"How'd they know where Chris was?"

"No idea. I told them nothing by telling them Chris knew it all. They load me in the Escalade, and we drive straight through. Came within seconds of pissin' my pants. Then that trail kicked our asses. Huffin' an puffin', they was yakking about poppin' a cap in my ass. I said my prayer . . . and you came along."

Jim rolled his eyes. "I'll get Chris first thing in the morning."

"I need to call my little brother and my mom."

Jim stood and moved toward the door. "Even though we're not in the real world, you should call your mom first." He reached in his pocket and tossed Larry his cell phone, and then went outside. Passing Brody, Jim mentioned the Mormon sisters had brought food.

"Saw them coming," Brody responded, and headed into the house.

Jim worked through the barnyard. He straightened out the tack room, fed the animals, and geared up for his morning ride. After retrieving Chris from the mountains, if it all still made sense, he would help get the cash away from the Mafia, and then the chips could scatter.

Jim racked his brain for other options, and his inability to find any pissed him off. Adrenaline surged and he found himself hoping his new partnership wouldn't bring more conflict.

He thought about Larry. The man obviously grew up in circumstances far away and different, but who hadn't? Not that many people were born and raised on a ranch.

He'd always thought Wyoming was perfect, but who was he to say? If he'd been raised in the inner city and had to live Larry's life, would he be any different?

Was he an honest rancher by choice or circumstance? His Mormon neighbors, who had been, for the most part, kind and nice his whole life, lived squeaky clean. Growing up around such people, he'd naturally adopted their sense of values, conduct, and social graces, even if he didn't accept their faith. How was Larry or the Mafia any different?

Brody walked up just as Jim was finishing sweeping out the barn with a big push broom.

"How long we keepin' the spook?"

There was no shortage of racists in Wyoming, but even so Jim was still surprised by Brody's words. He considered jumping down the old man's throat, preaching the surly old-timer a sermon about skin color. Instead, he tried conversation.

"Larry's my friend," Jim began. "He can stay as long as he wants. Like you and the rest of the horses in the congregation, the duration depends on behavior."

"Will he pull his weight or sit around eating my Mormon groceries?"

"Your Mormon groceries?" Jim burst out laughing. It started low, his voice echoing in a deep and resonant tone. After a minute, Jim was doubled over with his eyes watering. He tried to draw a breath, but he thought about what had tickled his funny bone, and the laughter chased itself like a dog and its tail.

"You wanna explain the amusement?" Brody stomped around, his face beet-red.

"Those Mormon sisters've proselyted you for years, and guess what? There's a new potential convert!"

Jim's eyes watered.

"Have your shits and giggles. I work 'til I'm too tired to move every day for years, not asking more than beer money and a dry place to sleep."

"Must've broke your heart," Jim paused, his wind spent in more laughter. After a clumsy minute, he continued. "Probably some chocolate cake left."

The laugh had done Jim a lot of good. He felt noticeably less tense and much more optimistic; it was like waking up after a good night's sleep.

They walked back to the house with ten feet between them. Jim considered teasing Brody about how Larry hadn't eaten everything, but decided not to rub it in.

Neither Larry nor Brody acknowledged each other's presence. Jim pulled out a bottle of whiskey and three shot glasses. After filling each to within a millimeter of the top, Jim lifted his glass. "To new friends, punishing horse killers, and to the Mormon Relief Society."

Brody wrapped his gnarled old knuckles around the shot glass. "I'll drink to the last two."

"I owe you. I'm your man," Larry said, lifting his glass toward Jim. He gulped his whiskey, and before he could reach for the bottle, Jim poured him another shot.

Brody often took a drink at the end of a long day to help him sleep. He went for the bottle, but before he could grasp it, Larry gripped the base.

"What're you, the bartender?" the old man grumbled.

"Damn straight." The two locked eyes and Brody pushed the glass forward and Larry poured.

"Thanks for the ride from the hospital."

After watching Larry and Brody throw back a few more shots, Jim slipped into the living room to continue his paperwork.

"Pour me another shot, barkeep," Brody said in an almost cheerful tone.

After a minute the ranch-hand continued. "You know, the more I drink, the less black you get."

"Any other day, I'd kick your ass."

"But this ain't no ordinary day is it?" Brody's slurred words made Jim wonder if he should return to the kitchen and insist they go to bed.

"Neither was yesterday. Your boss saved my life."

"I'll drink to that," Brody said cheerfully. "That's Jimmy. Nice to everybody. Wher' d'you says you's from, barkeep?"

"California."

"'Bout time I met someone I liked from that state," Brody stated in as cheerful a tone as Jim could remember.

Larry chuckled and Brody continued. "We got this California transplant neighbor. Lives three miles down the road. Bastard has Pasofino horses. You know what a Pasofino horse is, barkeep?"

Jim guessed Larry shook his head "no," because he didn't hear a response before Brody continued.

"Worthless. Ever' Goddamn one of 'em. Prancin' 'round like ballroom dancers, picking up their feet every which way. Jim's nice to the guy! Lets him ride his worthless prancing ponies all over the ranch. Leaves gates open, the bastard does. No-pride, belt-buckle wearin' Californian!"

"Enough!" Jim yelled from the other room. "I like the guy!"

"Well, nobody else does!" Brody hollered back.

Jim got up and walked into the kitchen. "He's my neighbor."

The room was quiet until Larry smiled. "Well, I promise to shut all gates and not ride horses."

"That's good, barkeep." Brody raised his glass. "You're a credit to your state."

Jim walked from the room. While brushing and flossing the whiskey and dinner from his teeth, he overheard the two men continue laughing. *Best friends,* he thought. *Until the bottle's empty.*

18

Michael hung up and zombie-walked toward his bedroom, marveling at his wife, Francesca, with whom he had just spoken. She had urged him to finally rest. Francesca always knew best, and after a week with little sleep, his body screamed at him to obey.

She had witnessed a few minor crises over their twenty-eight years together, mostly petty stuff—somebody opening up a competing business or someone being called in to meet with the boss—but there was the week five years ago when Michael had a snitch locked in the spare bedroom, and all he had to say to his wife was, "Ya don't wanna go in there."

With no other explanation, Francesca understood the code. "Ya don't wanna go in there," meant exactly that, but it also meant. "I know you'd never rat me out, sweetie, but if you open the door and see a guy duck-taped to a chair with some missing fingers, you may have to lie for me."

Francesca responded, "I was thinking I could take the kids to Maui for a few weeks," to which Michael smiled and said, "That'd be nice, I'll call soon as things slow down around here."

When Francesca got home with the kids and the forbidden room had new carpet and paint, she kissed Michael's cheek. "Love what you did with this room!"

Two hours after the cash-truck was stolen, Francesca was on a plane, headed for the family condo in Maui with their teenage daughter.

That was a week ago, and Michael was running on nothing but coffee. He'd almost taken a hit of meth for the first time, just in case Johnny or one of his brothers called, but decided against it. Finally, too exhausted to worry or ignore his wife's suggestion, he face-planted into the mattress and fell asleep without resting his head on a pillow.

The doorbell rang in Michael's dream. It was teenaged, free-spirited Johnny with a skateboard in his hand before all the ink, like God had sent him with clear ivory skin. The door rang again, and it was Johnny as a little child with a ball mitt asking to play catch in the backyard. Francesca waited with food, but the doorbell rang again and again. His brothers, Simon and Marcus, walked in, a combined six hundred pounds of loyalty. Each time the doorbell rang, someone he knew was there: a neighbor, a former mistress, bouncers from the club with strippers on their arms. Some he turned away, others he let in, but the doorbell kept ringing.

Everyone I know is here. Who could it be? Someone kept pushing the doorbell. The dream even had a soundtrack—the Paul McCartney and Wings song played in the background: *Somebody's knocking at the door, somebody's ringin' the bell. Do me a favor, open the door, an' let 'em in.*

The dim light coming down the hall into the master bedroom burned his eyes, so he snapped them down and in an instant was dreaming about drops of Visine while standing on a glacier.

The door chimed again, loudly, finally drawing Michael out of his near-coma. Michael groaned and looked at the clock. It read 3:45 a.m. That had to be a lie.

Michael rolled to his feet. A head rush almost toppled him back to the mattress. He shook it off, took a deep breath, and waited for his heart to speed up enough to pressurize his vessels. The doorbell rang again in the hall, and again as Michael walked past the fountain in the front foyer.

Without looking in the peep, Michael slid the chain from the keep and unbolted the latch. He cracked the door open just a bit, only to find a badge shoved in his face.

"Michael Faletto?" a voice called from somewhere behind the badge.

Michael nodded at two men in dark suits and white shirts.

The Feds. Think fast!

"Told you guys I wasn't interested," Michael tried to shut the door, but the younger and larger one put his foot out as a stop.

"Ya not selling me somethin'?"

"No, Mr. Faletto," young-and-brawny said. "We're the FBI. I'm Agent Benson and this Agent Schmidt."

The older and smaller agent took over.

"I regret to inform you that your brothers, Simon Paul and Marcus Paul, and your son, Jonathan Michael Faletto, have been killed."

19

U p before dawn, Jim prepared to ride the same trail for the third time in three days. Saddling Terence for himself and Beatrice for the accountant, he loaded them in the trailer and drove away from the barnyard, Duke riding in the bed of the truck.

He hoped to be back by dark, but made plans for spending the night in the backcountry, just in case. It took six hours with loaded horses to ride into where he had left the fishermen. If they had wandered off and he had to run Chris down, they would spend the night and come out the next day. Either way, Chris's trip was over.

At the trailhead, Jim noticed the Escalade was gone, and a group of boy scouts was preparing to head out. With Duke at his heels, Jim bridled Terence, tied his saddle bags, and climbed on board, hoping to beat the group up the trail, but one of the leaders approached.

"Excuse me, sir. Are you familiar with the area?"

"Sure am." Giving the man some directions would be better than getting called out with Search and Rescue in a few days.

"It's been ten years since I've been here. We're headed for Tombstone Lake. As I recall, the trail's obvious, and the lake is visible after about four miles."

"You're not suffering from Alzheimers."

"What?" the scoutmaster asked.

"You got it. Where'd you camp last time?"

"On the far side between the lake and cliff," the leader answered.

Terence shifted, and Jim reined him still. "That's the best spot. If it's taken, go up the stream a quarter mile. On the west side, you'll find another campsite."

"Thank you. Is there any other advice you can offer?" the leader asked.

"Only feed boys who follow orders."

The scoutmaster stifled a laugh. "That's not what they tell us in leadership training, but it sounds practical. Have you worked with scouts before?"

"I've taken some groups where you're headed."

"Is it a local troop?"

"Yeah, it's part of the Mormon ward I live in." Jim already knew what the leader would say before he said it.

"My name's Brother Coleman. We're from Utah. You're a member then!"

"No 'Brother' for me. Just Jim. I said the *ward* I *live* in."

"That's kind of you to pack them in if you're not a member," Brother Coleman replied after a pause.

"They paid me." Jim smiled. "Normally, the closest I get to Mormonism is a shot of whiskey with their Jell-o salad."

Brother Coleman chuckled. "Does whiskey make it taste better?"

"No. But a few shots'll make it bearable." Jim sensed Brother Coleman appreciated the humor so he continued. "Does putting Jell-o around an apple make it taste better?"

The scoutmaster removed his cap and rubbed his forehead. "I guess not."

"Then you folks put vegetables in it," Jim continued. "Don't get me started on mixing carrots in that crap." Jim shuddered and his mouth puckered, so he leaned over and spat the imagined taste onto the gravel.

Brother Coleman laughed. Obviously, Jim sitting on his horse being brutally honest about the Mormon diet struck his funny bones. They visited for a few minutes about fishing, and then Jim said, "Gather your troop, and I'll make your job easier."

"Absolutely. Boys, come here. This man has something to tell us!"

The young men numbered about a dozen, and they hurried over.

"At this point things are friendly." Jim paused until the last scout and leader straggled in. "Right now I like you guys, so I'll bring candy and root beers on Thursday when I pass through. If, however, I see one speck of lint, or Brother Coleman informs me of any bad behavior, you won't get shit. Understood?" His words came out with all the polish of a drill sergeant teaching the waltz.

Each scout nodded, seeming both excited and nervous about this gruff stranger visiting, bearing gifts in a few days. Jim suspected that, for most of them, the closest they came to camping was slow room service, or a non-working television.

The thought made Jim glare more than he intended, but they returned his intensity with somber expressions. One thing appeared certain: they thought it better to have him happy when he visited their camp in a few days.

Jim turned his horse and rode away, breaking quickly into a canter as Beatrice ran along the side of Jim and Terence at a smooth, ground-covering gait.

The other leader, who had walked up with the boys and hadn't met Jim, turned to Brother Coleman. "So, do we use that guy as an example of bad language or how to be kind to strangers?"

20

"We need you to answer some questions." Agent Sorenson removed his foot from the door, and Michael instantly slammed it shut and twisted the dead bolt.

"Talk to my attorney!" Michael yelled before collapsing on the cool marble.

Muffled voices came through the solid mahogany door, then chuckling, followed by retreating footsteps and a car starting and driving away.

For ten minutes, Michael's body refused to obey him. Crippling sorrow became spasms that overtook everything.

Who killed my family? Who killed Johnny?

Michael's lungs wouldn't expand through the grief. He focused against the panic, but collapsed. His body writhed on the marble with the fountain's running water in the background. Instead of inhaling, air went the opposite direction. It reminded him of heaving from food or alcohol poisoning as his breath was cut short with stomach seizures that forced involuntary groans through his vocal chords. It was as if his body was trying to vomit the toxic sorrow of losing his child and brothers.

Sweat beaded on his brow. Michael rolled to an elbow but passed out from exhaustion and suffocating anguish. Once unconscious, his body took over and he slept for several hours.

Cool tile and the trickling fountain brought Michael back to his senses. As he focused on breathing, the agonizing spasms in his gut gave way to a more constant, knife-sharp pain.

Rolling onto his back, he began pushing himself toward the circular pool at the base of the fountain with his legs. The grouted gaps between the tiles bit his back, but he kept pushing. When he made it to the pool, he gripped the top edge, pulled himself up, and rolled in. The shock of the cool water expanded his lungs, making it easier to breathe.

Michael leaned back and moved his arms up and down, like a child making snow angels. With his ears beneath the surface, all was silent except for the splashing of the fountain. After a few minutes, he stood up and looked at his phone for the time, only to realize it was ruined. His Rolex, however, was still ticking, its hands pointing to 9:10.

9:10? He thought, confused. He looked at it again, not believing he'd been unconscious for six hours.

Stepping out of the pool, he tried to think. He needed to talk to his cousin Ralf, but without his cell, Michael couldn't remember the number. There was nothing else to do but drive out to Ralf's body shop and talk to him in person.

Twenty minutes later, Michael pulled into the body shop's open door and blared his horn. Cigar in hand, Ralf Faletto emerged from the office at the back of the shop.

"Mike? Wasgoin' on?"

Rolling the window down, Michael cleared his throat, tried to talk, but his voice only came out as a strangled squeak.

"It's okay, Mike." Ralf rested his palm on the boss's shoulder. "Take your time."

"They're dead."

"You don't mean?"

"Johnny, Simon, Marcus. They're fucking dead!"

Ralf knelt next to the car, leaned in and kissed Michael's cheek. "Tell me what you need from me, boss."

"Ya know the bouncer. Keeps askin' to do more?"

"Sure. Don, the Jarhead."

"My house, with him and two others we trust, in an hour."

"I'll be there in thirty."

After leaving the body shop, Michael swung by a cellular store he owned through a shell company. As he approached the counter, the young man behind the till snickered and asked if he'd gone swimming.

"Leave," Michael whispered.

"What?"

A lady came from the back room. Middle aged, buxom, compensating for too much sun with too much make-up. "Apologize for laughing at our customer," she snapped at the young man, "and then take a break until I call."

The apology was offered and the lady escorted the young man to the front door.

"A new phone, just like my last one."

"Unregistered and prepaid?" she asked, flipping the sign in the window from open to closed.

Michael nodded, and put his old phone on the counter. The lady worked at the casing with a box cutter. Within a couple of minutes, she had the memory card out and transferred it to a new, identical phone.

"Plug it in to your car charger," she said at the door. "The battery sucks straight from the box."

Sliding into his car, Michael plugged in the phone, as instructed, and scrolled to an Italian restaurant's number to order a catered lunch.

"Still working from home, Mr. Faletto?" the voice asked.

"Got some planning to do."

"It'll be there within the hour."

Rather than go home, Michael drove the nearby suburbs to place a call to his attorney, who expressed condolences and promised to find out by day's end any details surrounding what he called "the Wyoming incident."

A decade or more had passed since inviting anyone outside the family to join the organization. If three bouncers were to be brought in, his performance would need to be perfect. And no performance could be worth a shit without the right entrance.

Within minutes, Ralf called. "We're here, boss."

"Have 'em out of the car, but in the driveway when I get there."

Three men, two in their mid-twenties and one in his thirties, stood next to Ralf. The oldest had the start of a belly, but all three looked like they could lift a gym. Michael parked beside them, got out, and headed for the front door.

"Shut that," Michael said to Ralf, who was the last man to walk in.

"This place is amazing." Don, the oldest, scanned the mansion.

"Shut up and listen." Michael waited for more than two minutes before continuing. "The next time I'm silent will be your last chance to walk out—no questions." Michael held up the key-pod for his Cadillac. "I'll even give you my car."

The silence only lasted a few seconds before one of the two younger men spoke. "I just got accepted to medical school. I . . . I don't need your car, Mr. Faletto. I'll call a cab."

"Med school? Where?" Michael asked.

"Georgetown. I start next fall."

"You'll need wheels to get there." Michael handed him the key-pod.

"Thank you, sir." The young man didn't make a sound as he shut the door and left.

"Smart kid, that one," Michael said as he eyed Don and the other young man who exchanged nods.

"I can speak for both of us, sir. We're ready for this."

An hour later, Michael reopened the dead bolt as the two well-fed bouncers—and newest family members—paused to kiss Michael's cheek before leaving for Wyoming.

Michael shut and locked the door.

"Whatever it was killed Johnny and your brothers may not be easy to bring back," Ralf stated.

"Why'd you think I'm sending new guys?"

Ralf nodded.

"You're headed there, too," Michael added.

The tip of Ralf's cigar dropped several inches.

"In a few days," Michael continued, "to bring back Simon's Escalade."

Ralf didn't saying anything. He looked at Michael curiously for a moment, then nodded and left.

Alone again, the pain in Michael's gut returned, but not as sharp and biting. He showered and dressed in fresh slacks and a summer shirt. He went to his den, where he pushed papers around on the desk. After what felt like years, his attorney called and told him that his family had been killed by a solitary Wyoming rancher. Michael smiled as he got off the phone, thinking about the two men who were already on their way. Picking up his phone again, he called for a cab to take him car shopping.

As the cab drove, the mansions of Henderson gave way to suburbs, and then businesses. Michael exhaled when his chest and belly contorted. By the end of the ride, he was able to picture his brothers' dead bodies and exhale the pain before it got too intense.

The rear door squeaked as the cabbie opened it for Michael to step onto the curb at the Cadillac dealership.

"Getting a new ride today, sir?" the cabbie asked.

"Keep the change," Michael responded as he paid with a crisp century-note.

The cab pulled away and Michael pulled out his phone and scrolled to Johnny's number. In a moment of hesitation, he almost didn't press send. But he took a deep breath and pushed the button.

"Heeeeeere's Johnny! Leave a message."

Pain shot through his chest. Sharp. Michael staggered to a nearby bench, but then didn't sit, proving to himself he could handle the heartache.

In through the mouth out through the nose, he repeated to himself.

A salesman pushed open one side of a double glass door. After a few minutes inside the air-conditioned lobby, he realized he was breathing the chilled air pain free.

A half-hour later, Michael sat behind the wheels a new Eldorado, identical to the one he'd given away that morning, right down to the light grey leather interior.

The salesman wore a huge smile, no doubt buoyed by Michael's writing a check for full sticker price.

"Have a nice day, Mr. Faletto."

Michael nodded through the open window.

"Headed for a night out on the town?"

Michael levered the window up in response. In truth, he wasn't sure what he wanted to do; checking in with Ralf, going by one of the clubs, finding a poker game were all possibilities, but Michael knew he couldn't postpone the inevitable any longer. It was time to get really drunk, and then call Francesca.

21

On the trail, Terence reminded Jim of what he liked the day before, and Jim let him run for a while. The young gelding was smooth and strong.

None of his horses had special gaits like the Fox Trotter or Pasofino horses that Brody hated. There were some impressive Fox Trotters Jim thought could stand up to the day-to-day riding he required, but the Pasofino horses were small, and he doubted they could be packed every day.

In contrast to Brody, Jim liked the California transplant, who had ridden through the ranch one day. Wanting to be friendly, Jim accepted an invitation to climb on the horse. As the pony moved into its gait, Jim was amazed at how smooth and quickly the horse traveled.

That winter, Jim was in the local tavern on a blizzard night, having a burger and beer with Brody, when the neighbor approached. Naturally, he wanted to talk about his horses, so he listened as the well-meaning Californian, who had enjoyed too many beers, went on and on about how Jim should sell his herd and replace them with Pasofinos.

"They have so much heart and determination. Think how quickly you could get your clients into the mountains moving at that ground-covering gait."

Jim wasn't going to change, but it didn't hurt to be friendly. As the man continued, Brody fidgeted and then finally exploded.

"If I wanna ride something that small, I'll beg her to accommodate me," he'd said, pointing at a cute young waitress named Wendy Frandsen, who had been walking past their table. The mouthful of Budweiser Jim had spit in his hand marked the end of the conversation. When they bumped into each other around town or in the mountains, the subject of Jim converting his pack string to something different never resurfaced.

Regardless of the breed, the art of horseback riding was anticipating where the horse was going before he went. Terence wasn't spooky, and made good decisions. He also didn't care about what the mare was doing behind or beside him. Often, trail horses would lose focus because they weren't getting along with the animal to the bow or stern. It was hard to concentrate and keep all four feet where they needed to be, if they were preoccupied about one of four things: kicking or being kicked, and biting or being bitten.

The best trail horses didn't want to kick or taste each other.

Jim had owned several that were good as a single horse, but were lousy trail horses for this reason. He had one mare in particular that was splendid to ride alone, but was downright dangerous in the mix of the herd. He found a buyer who needed a single horse, and she and the new owner had gotten along ever since. Jim regretted signing the brand inspection to transfer ownership. He raised her like the others until she was old enough to ride, but he couldn't abide the kicking and biting, especially with guests who paid hundreds of dollars for their time in the mountains.

Brody summed it up one day. "You know, Jim, there are enough good ones you don't have to put up with the bad ones."

It bothered Jim when folks, or horses, couldn't get along. Even though he and the California transplant liked different breeds, they both liked to saddle up and ride.

The hours passed quickly, and being alone in the woods elevated

Jim's spirits. With any luck, he would find Chris and be home to talk things over by evening.

Without the pack string, he made good time. Leaving the trailhead about seven, his watch read ten-thirty, when he came into the campground where two of his guests—Mark and Landon—sat beside the fire.

"Hello, the camp," Jim called out.

"Hello, yourself," the closest man spoke for both of them with a look of astonishment, "What's going on? We didn't expect you for a few more days."

"You guys have been here three weeks. Pack up. It's time to go."

"We all wish we could stay three weeks. The fishing's been great." He returned Jim's teasing.

"I'm here for Chris Cobb."

"Why?"

"He's got problems in civilization."

"I think he's up the stream working the hole in the bend. Is everything okay?" the man responded with a concerned look.

"Don't know. Need to get him out of here. If I don't ride back, it means we're down the trail. I'll be back Friday."

The two guests nodded.

"Thanks, Mark. Thanks, Landon."

"You remember our names?"

"Customer service," Jim said, turning the gelding toward the stream with Beatrice and Duke following.

The big bend the men mentioned was about half a mile from camp near the trail Jim had ridden moments ago. The creek wound its way through the forest, turning at a sharp angle as it flowed from the woods into the meadow. The water was more than ten feet deep at the bend. A sandy beach lay across one side of the stream from a boulder, making a nice place to cast a fly, or swim on a hot day.

Jim directed Terence upstream where Chris casted from the bank.

Conversation usually came easily, but Jim worried about how to start. He assumed Chris would cooperate, like Larry, but what if he didn't?

"Mornin', Chris."

The accountant's line went slack as he stopped mid cast. "What are you doing here?"

"Sunday, I killed three men who were after you. I stopped them from killing a guy named Larry. I can't have you near my guests."

A look of fear clung to Chris's face for a few seconds, but then, like a mime, his expression went stoic. "I'm sorry for putting anyone in danger," he said and then reeled in his line.

"I'm not sure apologies count. Get on the horse."

Chris looked toward the camp. "What about my things?"

"Got your wallet?"

"Yes."

"Leave your pole behind the tree and I'll get it with your stuff when I come back on Friday."

"It'll only take a minute."

"Get on the damn horse."

Jim bridled the mare and Chris climbed on as Jim released the lead rope. They took a shortcut back to the trail.

"In half a mile is another creek with some grass by it. These two worked pretty hard. Let's take twenty before pushing out of here."

The horses didn't really need rest, but Jim hoped it would give Chris a chance to tell him a little about what was going on. He believed what Larry told him, but was eager for the any insight Chris might offer.

The horses stepped into the water. With the late morning sun directly above, they drank for over a minute, lifting their muzzles from the stream in a drizzle, then dropping to take more.

After getting off the gelding on the other side, Jim stripped Terence's saddle, blanket and bridle to make the horse more comfortable. Just then, Chris heeled Beatrice into a gallop down the trail.

"Are you kidding me?" Jim quickly re-bridled Terence and hurled himself on the horse's bare back. With a fistful of mane and his legs squeezing the horse's brisket like a ju-jitsu submission hold, Jim was twenty lengths behind within seconds.

Chris bounced like a scarecrow in the saddle as he tried to rein the mare with his hands above his head. Jim leaned over Terence's neck, squeezing with his legs. In a few lunges, he was in-sync with the thundering animal, and comfortable enough to release the mane.

With the horse's hooves pounding down the trail, Jim urged Terence up alongside Beatrice, who was giving less than a Kentucky Derby performance—no doubt frustrated by her inept handler. Jim reached over and grabbed Beatrice's left rein and stopped both horses in a small meadow.

Swinging his leg over Terence's neck, Jim slid off and landed on his feet between the two horses. Chris blocked the sun that shone around him like a full eclipse. In the accountant's hand was a metal canister.

"I'll use this!"

"Use what?"

Chris pointed a canister of pepper-spray at Jim's face.

Jim's regular carry gun was still wherever the sheriff had sent it, but he had an older model 1911 Springfield concealed in a holster beneath his shirt. Beatrice dropped her head to graze. Jim leapt and grabbed two fistfuls of Chris's canvas fishing vest. Beatrice shied from the commotion, taking a quick step that helped Jim topple her rider. Chris landed with a thud and pepper sprayed mosquitoes and the mountain air as Jim pushed the canister away. Then Jim knocked Chris unconscious with a solid punch to the nose.

After a few seconds Chris woke and gingerly touched his nose, which wasn't bleeding, but looked broken.

"Do I need to hit you again?"

Chris shook his head.

Jim handed the canister back to the accountant. "Pepper spray's like Jell-o Salad," Jim said. "Tastes like shit, but won't kill you."

Jim gave Chris a minute to stand and then jumped on the gelding and watched as Chris mounted Beatrice.

"I love a horse race, feel free to try again."

"I won't," Chris responded, his face now swollen from Jim's punch. Jim heeled Terence to the trail as Chris followed to where the saddle lay near the stream. The lush grass beckoned and the horses munched, tearing away foot-tall sections that disappeared into their mouths a few inches with each chomp.

Chris wasn't talking as Jim re-saddled Terence. In Jim's opinion, he'd lent the man plenty of time to collect his thoughts, and his reticence wore on Jim's patience.

"You tell me everything you know if you want to ride that horse."

Chris didn't respond.

"You wanna walk?"

"Is Larry okay?"

"Should be. Spent the night before last in the hospital."

"You say you killed all three of them. Do you know who they were?"

"Don't play stupid. You and Larry stole their money."

Chris sucked in a bellyful of air. When he spoke his voice cracked. "If he told you who we stole the money from, do the police know what you know."

"I haven't told anyone."

"Either way, he was stupid," Chris stated in a tone of half anger, half panic. "He shouldn't have told you anything."

The smugness tormented Jim like a swarm of bees around a grizzly. He knocked the ball cap from Chris's head. Grabbing a handful of hair, he flicked Chris's nose with the middle finger of his free hand.

"Ow! Shit! Don't!"

Jim let go and Chris gently touched his nose, blinking away his watering eyes.

Duke growled.

"Larry owed me the truth for saving his life, and now he's stupid? We can get the money without you."

Chris stood, brushing the dust from his clothing, as Jim offered him the canteen from his saddle.

"What are you, good and bad cop all at once?" he said after taking a drink.

"My worst compares favorably to those you stole from."

Chris swished a mouthful of water and spit it on the ground. Then he took several swallows, and gave it back. The sky was building to a gully washer, coming from the west, and Jim doubted they would make it to the truck dry.

"Let's ride. We can talk on the trail," Chris suggested, a worried look creasing his features.

"Looks like you have us riding into a storm, Chris."

22

Headed toward civilization, Chris confirmed what Larry had told Jim. How he had gotten the idea, meeting Sheila and Larry, and eventually hijacking the truck. The plan had been to hide the truck and lay low, then move the cash from the hidden truck in small amounts.

"Where is it now?" Jim paused and looked at a hawk in the sky. "It's tough to hide a delivery truck."

"Your asking means Larry didn't tell you."

"Could be I wanna compare your answers."

As Chris rode, he knew that his plan had been delayed. He was smitten with Sheila, but didn't envision sharing anything with Larry or Jim. He'd offered Larry an equal share, but once the money was safely out of the country, he'd never see a red cent. He was dreamily picturing himself on an island, salt-water fly fishing in the surf, while Sheila sipped a drink in a sun chair, when Jim suddenly interrupted.

"You guys stole the money and thought you had gotten away with it. You're up here. Larry's back in Vegas. How'd they find him and know about you?"

Chris was quiet.

"It'd be good to know where the leak is before we fire the pump."

Jim's words made sense, and Chris thought about them for several minutes before responding.

"I'd love to blame it on Larry. But my secretary probably squealed. She called in sick the day we stole the truck. We did most of the planning meetings in my office, and she must have overheard us."

JIM RODE IN THE LEAD, worrying about what to do. This was all too strange. Living life in the Rockies, he was no stranger to conflict and didn't hesitate when it came his way. But stealing big money from the Mafia was like stumbling upon creepy green monsters in the woods, creatures with oversized eyes, bulbous heads, and long skinny limbs.

In his small community, there was rarely theft of any kind, and most donated time or goods to neighbors. Freeloading was despised and hard work garnered respect more than money.

Jim remembered the spring his father died. It was a wet, rainy week, and he'd fallen behind on the ranch work. Guests were coming in for some early fishing, and he hadn't been able to cut any hay. Brody was recovering from hernia surgery. The hay would have to wait until after he was done with his guests. But when he got home, after being gone for a week in the mountains, he found the barns stuffed with hay. The farmers and ranchers, who were still working on their own hay crops, were the ones to thank, but they all denied involvement.

Later, he learned that it was a concentrated effort by many of his Mormon neighbors. It was planned in church by the ward's bishop. Even though he doubted he would ever join their religion, they came through in a moment of need.

Living in a community like this made him wonder how trucks full of cash turned people into such assholes.

The storm broke loose. The horses showed their indifference, continuing their steady walk as rain bounced from their necks and shoulders. Jim pulled a slicker from his saddlebags for Chris and they dismounted momentarily. The sky grew dark even though it wasn't yet evening. Chris slipped into the slicker and Jim decided to ride in a poncho instead of his too-warm oilskin coat.

"So, you killed three gangsters with your pistol?" Chris asked from underneath the hood, the rain bouncing off of the waterproof plastic.

"Yep," Jim replied as lightning lit the sky, the thunder booming a split second later.

"You must be pretty good with a gun."

"Is there a point?"

"Were they totally outmatched, or were you just lucky?"

Jim stared him in the eye for a few breaths before answering. "Don't fuck with me with a gun in your hands, or you'll die."

Chris shivered and then looked away. His Adam's apple bobbed up and down, and the exposed skin on his neck and hands had goose bumps. Coming from the Mafia, "fuck" was white noise. Coming from Jim Cooper in the cold pouring rain, the effect was chilling. The words had conveyed the effect Jim wanted.

The two men got back on their horses, and Jim looked down from the saddle at Duke's sad brown eyes looking up, a whimpering sound coming from inside the shivering animal. "Come on up."

Jim's rain poncho draped from the gelding's neck to his saddle-bags and the horse's rump. The second Jim peeled it back, Duke leapt into his lap.

"Duke is smart," Chris observed.

"Smarter than me. Now I get the wet dog smell all the way to the truck."

It was still raining hard as they got to the trailhead. They hurried Beatrice and Terence into the trailer and themselves into the truck. Neither of them spoke until they pulled into the ranch.

Brody was in the barn waiting for them as they came. Before Jim could get out of the pickup, the curmudgeon had unloaded the first horse. The two quickly unsaddled the mare and gelding, while

Duke ran on top of the stack of hay. Although he had ridden under Jim's slicker on the trail, he rode in the back of the pickup from the trailhead to the ranch. Now soaked, he nestled down into the warm, dry hay to wait out the storm.

Putting the horses into some stalls, Jim noticed fresh hay in the mangers. If Brody wasn't the best help he could hope for, he wasn't sure where to find better. Jim and Brody walked into the house.

Jim was surprised to see it had been put back together from the previous night. Someone had vacuumed the rooms, and mopped the tile floor by the back door. In the kitchen, he found Larry wearing an old apron. He was up and about and hobbling on his sore leg. His lips and one eye were still swollen, but he looked better.

"That apron hasn't been worn in ten years," Jim said by way of greeting.

"Hope you don't mind, I thought the place needed some help— What happened to you?" Larry asked as he noticed Chris's black eyes and swollen nose for the first time.

"He ran into my fist."

"What did he do?"

Chris stood head down at the room's edge.

"Tried to steal my horse."

Larry looked at Chris. "You got off easy."

They were all hungry. Chris, Jim, and Brody quickly set the table as Larry pulled leftovers from the fridge.

Larry stopped them as Brody grabbed a roll. "It's not my place to say, but my momma wouldn't let me put food in my mouth without first saying grace."

Jim couldn't remember any words said over a meal since his mother lived there. "I agree, and since you're the one bringing it up, it would only be fitting if you would be the one to say it."

"Make it quick." Brody's tone did nothing to mask his irritation.

Folding his arms and bowing his head, Larry started, "Dear Lord, as we gather around this table, we want to thank you for all of our many, many blessings, Lord. For the safety we've had, and for the goodness of this day. We pray, Lord, that at this time we might ask a favor—no—two favors. Bless this food we're about to consume and secondly, as we all have a common adversary, with the exception of Brody, help us to get through this trial in our lives, unharmed, unscathed, unmolested, scraped, marred, lacerated, scuffed, scarred, contused, broken, or traumatized, and if it comes to be that we must use force, Lord, help us prevail upon our enemies as Jim did the other day, putting an end to any altercation quickly, decisively, and expeditiously. This is our prayer, Lord . . . and please help Chris to be smart enough to not make Jim angry again, Amen."

The four men ate, and Jim had to think that, whoever the Lord or God was, a little prayer couldn't hurt. He had just pushed himself away from the table when the phone rang.

"Jim, this is Albert, I understand you have the black man out there."

"That's right."

"How's he doing?"

"Good enough to say grace. Come see for yourself."

"Might later, I just wanted to tell you what I know. I've been on the phone with the FBI all day and an organized crime unit out of Vegas. They're worried about you, Jimmy. Seems you killed some bad guys the other day. Two of them have done time, and are suspects in lots of bad stuff. That's good for you because they haven't pushed me at all on your innocence. They all think you did society a favor with your pistol. In fact, they all want to meet you. Seems to me a few of them may be jealous and wish they coulda' taken the shot. The worry is that those guys might have friends who'll find out who it was killed their kin. They're already talking protective custody."

"I won't live in a subdivision."

"That's what I told them," Albert responded. "Either way, they'll be up here day after tomorrow, and will want to talk to you."

"You know where to find me," Jim said, thinking the conversation would be over.

"Jim, I know what you're thinkin', but by refusing their help, they'll think you might be involved in some way. I know it sounds ridiculous, but it will look a bit suspect."

"I understand."

"They'll ask some tough questions. Be honest like you have been with me, and it'll be okay."

Jim went back into the kitchen, and noticing Brody had drifted from the room, told Chris and Larry about the conversation. "Seems we're in this together. I didn't steal anything, but they want me dead. So, what I'm asking is simple: you two figure this thing out. I don't care how. You both were smart enough to steal a truckload of cash and hide it. Now be smart enough get them off our backs."

Chris had been quiet ever since they arrived, but now he was the first to speak.

"The Mafia hates two things: losing their own, and being robbed. I don't know which they hate the most, but unless we can get some leverage, we need to run."

"Leverage?" Jim asked.

"I've heard of people who negotiated to be left alone. If they have financial records or anything incriminating, they arrange for it to be turned over to authorities if or when something happens to them."

"I'm not following."

Chris continued, "If we knew bank account numbers, or had pictures of them in illegal activity, surveillance tapes or things of that nature, we could turn them over to an attorney some place, with instructions to turn the material into the cops if and when one of us meets an untimely fate."

"Do we have anything like that?" Jim asked.

"Some, I think. In order to steal, we had to know how they moved the cash and where it's held, but my guess is they've already changed how they get their cash out of Vegas."

"What we really need are cell phones," Larry said. "And that's where I can help."

"How?" Jim and Chris said in unison.

"Remember, Jim, how they shot your horse, and then you had to walk back to the trail to get the other horses?"

"Sure, I was gone about five minutes."

"I was hurting, but while you were gone I stole their cell phones."

"Let me get this straight, you stole all three of these guys's cell phones?" Chris asked a smile coming over his lips.

"Damn straight!" Larry replied.

"I still don't see how it helps," Jim said, perplexed.

"You really are a simple country gent," Larry said. "It's like this: I bet those three got dozens of messages from their bosses, wondering what in the world's going on. Is the job done yet? When will they be back? Have they found the stolen goods? Even if there's nothing too incriminating, they won't remember everything. What text messages and voice mails they might not have deleted. All we have to do is make the Vegas crime bosses believe that these phones have incriminating things on them."

Jim thought about what Larry was saying, and although this was new to him, it made sense.

Brody had excused himself earlier, and while he was sure the old man suspected something, Jim was sure he would say nothing. For the next two hours, the three of them sat around the table, talking about their worries. Larry had spoken with his brother and Sheila, who were still safe and hiding in an apartment in Henderson. Chris had no family and was sure it was his secretary who tipped off the mob.

Larry and Chris told Jim how they rented a truck-sized storage garage only a few miles from the place they stole the truck. They hoped the truck was still safe. They all agreed that they needed to get the money out of Vegas.

As the conversation wore on, Jim found himself inadvertently assuming the lead in their plans. As it grew dark, he drew the informal meeting to a close, frustrated that he'd come up with a lot more questions, and only a few answers.

"I think we can sleep on this for a night or two. We have the cell phones, and you two know where the loot is. I don't know how involved I want to be. I have a great life here, and even though the thought of big money is as attractive to me as the next guy, I'd be happy if all this went away. I have an idea how to get the money out of Vegas, and where we can store it. Let's talk about all this tomorrow night."

23

As usual, Jim was up at the crack of dawn. Terence needed to have his shoes reset. Jim was driving the nails in the fourth and final shoe when the squeak of the ranch house back door told him one of the others was up. A moment later, Chris stepped into the barn. Both eyes were now slightly black, but his nose was less swollen.

"I'm scared, Jim," he said without preamble. "We'll have Mafia here any minute. They knew where to find us. We needed to get out of here."

"Does the worry come with a plan?"

"You can meet us in Vegas, but until we cut a deal with these guys, we need to be moving targets. Larry and I will get cell phones in town so we can stay in touch. It will be easier for you to answer the FBI questions if we aren't here."

"Okay."

"You mentioned last night you had some ideas about how to get the truck out of Vegas?"

Jim set the last nail and, turning off the sharp end with the claw of his shoeing hammer, he set the hoof down. He petted the gelding for behaving so well while being shod.

"I don't have any guests coming next week, so hopefully we can meet up down south. We need to move the money in broad daylight. Drive past the place you stole it from and draw them out. They'll follow, and with what I have in mind, they'll regret it. If it all works, we can bring the truck to a place on the ranch where they'll never find it."

"Sounds good," Chris responded.

"Once we have the money, we can worry about cutting a deal. Brody's moving some irrigation pipe, so let's go get some breakfast and talk it over."

Larry agreed with what Jim and Chris discussed.

"I flew into Jackson Hole and rented a car. The Mob won't know the car, and they could be waiting in Jackson for me to come back to the airport," Chris continued. "Let's take the rental to Vegas. It'll take a few days, and we can figure things out as we go. I can turn it in to the rental agency in Vegas."

"Once we get there, we can lay low with Sheila and wait for Jim," Larry said.

"I'll pack my guests out on Friday morning. I'll play the game with the FBI, and then head south."

"Won't it be kinda strange? You being gone for a whole week?" Larry sounded a bit worried as he asked the question.

"Nah. I disappear in the mountains for weeks. Nobody to miss me, not even Brody."

"Cool!" Larry shot back. "Tell Sister Bott I'm sorry I won't make the picnic on Friday." Jim had forgotten about the invitation, and could sense some sincerity in Larry's words.

"If we all live through this mess, you can visit any week of the year and the Mormons'll be doing something we can plug you into."

"So let me get this straight." Larry paused to collect his thoughts. "Was she one of those, you know, people walking around with a name badge, knocking on doors?"

Thinking about his own experience with the Mormon missionaries earlier in life, Jim responded, "Pretty much. She would love to talk to you about it."

24

That afternoon, Jim was headed out to the barn to climb in his pickup when Brody came at him from the side.

"Don't know what the hell's going on, boss. I try to mind my own business, but this stinks like corn-fed-cow-shit."

Jim jumped back. "Speaking of shit, you just scared mine right out of me! Where were you hiding?"

"Hiding? I was where I am now. Plain as day. Think I snuck up on you? Damn fool. You don't know if you're afoot or horseback. No wonder I think whatever is going on's a bunch of shit! Either you're going blind, or something on your mind ain't right."

Jim was caught flat-footed, and had nothing to say. The old man called it as he had seen it and, as usual, Brody was right. For a few seconds both men stood. It was Brody's agenda, and he spoke next.

"All I ask is you stay alive so I can keep my job. I may not be city educated, but I'm smart enough to see when someone sets their teeth into something. Whatever it is you're up to is none of my affair, unless it harms you, and my future employment. Far as anyone's concerned, I don't know nothin'. But I'll be looking after you."

It was the most Jim remembered Brody saying all at once. He was embarrassed that he hadn't seen him standing there, and knew he couldn't be so unfocused on the here and now, and come away alive.

For the first time since his father's death, someone older and definitely wiser had his best interests at heart. Brody could be trusted.

"Thanks," Jim said as he walked to his pickup.

25

Several old friends buzzed past in the oncoming lane as Jim drove into town. As usual, he waved at everyone he recognized and anyone else who waved first.

Several people pretended not to see him, and his sixth grade teacher, Mrs. Munson, didn't even smile. Perhaps she was deep in thought, as he had been when Brody surprised him. Jim wasn't offended, but at the grocery store people acted strange. Folks who usually greeted him looked the other way. Finally, Darren Wyatt, one of Jim's oldest (if not closest) friends, jogged all the way down the aisle.

"Hold up, Jim. We gotta talk."

Jim waited as Darren came up to him and continued, partially out of breath. "You gotta lay it out for me, dude. Rumor has it some folks from Nevada fucked with the wrong cowboy."

Jim smiled. Darren worked winters as a ski instructor in Jackson, and also as a waiter in one of the fancier restaurants. When he wasn't on the slopes or waiting tables, his life was anchored to a pot smoking habit. Several hits on the bong must have lowered Darren's inhibitions. Jim thought about people's reactions and realized they all must feel awkward.

Jim remembered feeling like he carried a contagious disease after his father died. People avoided him for months, probably not want-ing to intrude on his personal space. Analyzing it, he couldn't blame them.

How the hell do you approach someone who just killed three people?

"Come on, man. Tell me how it went down." Darren tucked some hair behind his ear, and Jim thought that even after hundreds of sunburns, his old friend looked much the same as he had twenty years ago.

"Patience, Grass-Smoker," Jim said, trying for an oriental accent.

"Don't give me that kung fu shit. You can't just leave me hangin' here, man."

Jim shrugged and raised his eyebrows. "Not much to it, really. Sunday I stopped on the trail after taking some customers into the mountains." Jim paused as people, who moments before pretended not to see him, gathered close. Even Frank Smart, the store's custo-dian leaned on his broom to listen.

"Judas, Jim. We don't care about the customers. Get to the good part," Darren urged.

"Anyway, I thought my dog was on to some game down a draw. So I went a few hundred yards from the trail and found three men beatin' on a big black guy. I ask 'em to stop, and the next thing I know, they're drawing on me—I think everyone knows the rest."

Silence hung over the crowd like mist over the ground on a frosty morning, but soon Darren spoke. "Damn dude . . . That's serious. Had you ever seen these guys?"

"Never." Jim suddenly wondered. "How did you know the guys I shot were from Nevada?"

"Come on, man. You know how things buzz. Everyone in town knows about the Escalade with Nevada plates at the impound yard."

"I heard they shot your horse?" one man asked.

"He caught a bullet meant for me."

"Got what they deserved then."

Jim was pinned to the spot as neighbors he'd known his whole life asked questions, and he gave them answers. The townsfolk left, one at a time, as though waiting their turn in a reception line. Their curiosity satisfied, they gave words of encouragement. Most of the women hugged him, while the men shook his hand and slapped his back.

Alone again, but no longer feeling shunned, Jim and Darren stood in the beverage aisle. Jim bent over to pick up a case of root beer, only to be needled.

"Why are you buying root beer?" Darren asked. "You know, there's no *beer* in that."

Jim exhaled and shook his head, not wanting to explain.

"Did you convert? The least you coulda' done was tell me so we could have one last party before they dunked you."

Jim smiled at Darren's jibe. "Me goin' under would be bigger news than killing people."

"Good man, 'cause sometimes I feel like a loner."

You're not the only one.

The two made small talk while Jim shopped. True to his reputation, Darren was in no hurry to be anyplace or do anything, shadowing Jim like an abandoned pup.

"You still haven't told me who the Mormon beverages are for," Darren said as they reached the checkout register.

"Some potential clients I met at the trailhead, a group of boy scouts out of Salt Lake."

"So what are you gonna do? Tell 'em next year you'll pack all the root beer they can drink for a fee?"

"Something like that," Jim responded.

"You could at least give 'em a chance to say no."

"You think they'll take the bait that easy?"

"It'll be like giving me a free ounce."

Jim laughed. "I don't want 'em to fall in love with me."

Daren rolled his eyes. "I'm just sayin' there's a bottle of whiskey for every Indian."

The two men loaded the groceries into a shopping cart, and Darren followed Jim all the way to his truck.

"Do you remember I lived in Vegas for a while, Jim?"

"Sure. It was while I was at college. You came back to ski over Christmas."

"I'm not tellin' nothin' ya couldn'ta figured out, but a brother gettin' FUBAR'd by the Mafia stinks like weed."

"Yeah?"

"Oh, yeah. Never seen a Mary Jane scene like the one in Vegas back then. The Mafia let people run it through all their businesses for a cut. Strip clubs, restaurants, you name it. Wherever you worked, you could distribute the herb."

The thought settled into Jim's mind. From what Larry and Chris said, the Mafia smuggled money they made legitimately out of the country to avoid taxes, but what if there was one collection place for all the cash? Was the money from the legitimate businesses and illegal operations mixed? It made sense, and if it was true, there might be more money in the truck than they'd originally expected. Oddly, the idea of stealing dirty money settled better in Jim's stomach.

Jim offered Darren his hand and they shook. He opened his truck door, climbed in, started the motor, and waved at his stoned friend who stood in the parking lot, probably wondering what to do next.

Jim was excited about the cash truck, but as he drove he wondered, *How can I kill three people, sleep like a baby, and then make plans to steal their money?* He looked at the floor of his pickup where Sam's horseshoes rested in the foot-well. He remembered Sam dying, the horse crumpling beneath him, and then dragging the carcass the next day into the woods.

"I killed those bastards in self defense," Jim growled to a fly buzzing around the cab. *And whatever I steal is payment for Sam.*

Jim passed three people on the way home. They each recognized him and waved, but got no response.

26

Thursday afternoon Jim headed up the trail for the fourth time that week. Accompanying him were Duke, Terance, and eight packhorses with an assortment of hard and soft panniers slung over sawbuck packsaddles. As planned, Chris and Larry had left for Las Vegas, and as soon as Jim was done talking with the FBI, he would join them. But first, he needed to get his remaining guests home safely.

Tucked in a pannier was a care package for Brother Coleman and the scouts. True to his word, they wouldn't receive a thing if they hadn't kept a clean camp.

Hopefully, he could reach Tombstone Lake, find the troop, and distribute the root beer and candy. He wouldn't sell the guiding business too hard, but would let them know that, for a fee, their next fishing trip to Wyoming could be less strenuous. If it wasn't too late, he'd continue on to his clients' camp eight more miles into the mountains. If not, he'd stay near the scouts and get up early the next morning.

What the hell am I thinking? I might be dead or fighting strangers next year. The thought developed. *After I get the cash, they won't have to look for me, I'm gonna stay right here in Wyoming.*

A young mare in the middle of the train kept wrapping

trees—walking on the opposite side of the tree as the horse in front of her. Jim took her out of the line and made her the caboose.

Keeping peace in the herd was a constant frustration. One horse would jump through a stream and pull the head of the horse behind, who was unaware to a certain degree what was happening in front. The trailing horse would often retaliate with a bite or kick to the animal in front or behind. It made Jim the clergyman for all disputes great and small among his equine congregation.

Then one day, he had a vision. He drove to the hardware store and bought a spool of half-inch bungee cord and fed it through flexible plastic pipe as a way to join the horses. The stretch worked miracles. When one horse jumped unexpectedly, the trailing horse wouldn't feel like they'd been beheaded.

Rearranging the lineup as he came up the trail cost him time. But as the caravan rattled and thumped through the woods, thoughts of Larry, Chris, Las Vegas, and the Mafia faded into the background. Oddly, he was looking forward to driving to Las Vegas. It was definitely going to be dangerous, but maybe there would be an hour to relax. He'd been taking other people on their vacations for so long, he looked forward to going on one of his own.

As they came around a bend to the south, Tombstone Lake appeared over Terence's ears. The lake was about a half-mile long and a quarter of a mile wide. The far end was fairly deep, producing some good-sized trout. There were two islands. Jim had swum to both of them, but preferred to do so on a hot day. The lake was eighty-nine hundred feet above sea level, and the winter's ice usually wasn't fully melted until the middle of June.

As he came through a thick stand of lodge pole pines mixed with some bus-sized granite boulders, he got the view he was waiting for. The scouts were in the camp they'd wanted. Riding steadily, he reached them in fifteen minutes. Jim coaxed Terence up to the fire pit and looked around to see several young men approaching from different directions. The camp looked clean. He looked hard, but couldn't even see a speck of lint.

Jim dismounted and a young man of about sixteen was the first to greet him.

"I told them you'd come. I knew you wouldn't say you were going to visit and then not show."

Jim nodded at the boy. "I keep my promises."

"So do I!" the boy said enthusiastically.

Jim looked around at the gathering scouts. "What's your name?"

"I'm Blake Daines."

As the natural leader of the group, Jim guessed it was Blake as much as Brother Coleman who had pushed for the clean camp. "You've done a commendable job. I bring clients here, and there's been a few times the group before left it messy."

"Did you bring us the candy?" one boy asked. "What about the root beer?"

"Yeah, but I need the go ahead from your leader."

"But you said—"

"Fu-crying out loud! Is this a scout camp or a nursery?" Jim scolded the whining boy, just barely keeping his tongue in check. "I'll break out the goods when Brother Coleman gives me a good report."

"You have it."

Jim spun on his boot heel to see the scoutmaster carrying a fishing pole and a few nice-sized trout. He walked up, set the pole down, and extended his hand. "They've been great young men, thanks to your encouragement."

"Looks like you've done good," Jim commented, admiring the fish.

"Really good. I'm lucky to work with these fine young men."

"They're lucky you're their leader," Jim said, admiring Brother Coleman's attitude.

"Well, in that case we're all lucky. I'm not sure who enjoys these outings more, me or the boys."

"I owe you some groceries." Jim walked toward the packhorse that was carrying it for him. "Form a line and I'll hand it out."

The boys stood a dozen deep, except for one scout who snuck back to his tent. Puzzled, Jim made a mental note to ask what was going on. *Had the boy been bad? Was he a diabetic?* Jim hoped not. Diabetes was tough, but he figured it must be the situation. The rest of the scouts accepted the root beer and candy with eager hands and eyes. As the boys dispersed, Jim turned to their leader. "You look straight arrow, but I brought you something anyway."

A quizzical look came over Brother Coleman's face.

"It's not whiskey for chasing Jell-o." Jim reassured him. "Most Mormons I've known—straight and Jack, allow for grey area when it comes to caffeinated pop."

"You're kidding me." Brother Coleman's eyes got bigger.

Jim reached into the pannier and brought out a six-pack of Diet Coke. "The local sheriff gets urinated when I call this carbonated coffee."

Brother Coleman took it with a big smile. "I've had a caffeine headache since the hike in. Thank you!"

Jim smiled.

"You are a kind man. Manna from heaven, as the Old Testament says,"

"So what's up with the exile?"

"Exile?" Brother Coleman's puzzled look returned.

"The glasses-wearing little guy. Did he want quails instead of candy bars?"

"Sorry. His name's Vincent Packer. Great kid. A little small for his age. Blake looks out for him."

Jim considered the words. "Is he a diabetic?"

"That might be easier." The scoutmaster let out a lengthy sigh. "Vince has parent problems."

"Parent problems?"

"Last year, the Packers went nuts over nutrition and diet. They banned processed sugar, won't even bake with it. Fruit and honey are okay, but anything processed is out."

"You shittin' me?"

The scoutmaster shook his head. "I got into it with Vince's mother when she tried to get me to go sugarless for a camp."

"What'd you tell her?"

"That it was a great idea, but since I was pressed for time, her suggestion meant she'd volunteered to rewrite the menu and come cook for us."

"Did that end it?"

"I wish. After that, Vince's father got in my face about how I was setting his child up for a target.'

"What'd you tell him?"

"That making Vince the reason the rest of the troop couldn't have sugar would make him the biggest target of all." Brother Coleman paused. "I feel for Vince, but I won't punish the rest of the troop with some idiotic parent's rule."

Jim laughed, and Brother Coleman stood by, probably hoping it wasn't him.

"Mormons who volunteer for less fun? Don't smoke, don't drink, don't take drugs, don't fish or ride horses on Sunday, and now some hate sugar? What the hell?"

Brother Coleman chuckled as well.

"What do you call Mormons like that?" Jim asked.

"Maybe we should call them stupid."

Jim liked the scoutmaster. He was definitely devout, and lived and believed it from appearances, but he wasn't a fun hater.

It was late in the afternoon, and Brother Coleman invited him to stay for dinner.

"I have a Dutch oven and fixings for peach cobbler," Jim answered.

"Boys, we have an honored guest for dinner!"

Several scouts followed Jim to his horses. Showing them how, they quickly stripped saddles and put the animals out to graze in the meadow with a picket line and stake for each horse. Jim had each of them pick up a branch or two of firewood as they returned.

At camp, dinner preparations were underway. He brought his fourteen-inch Dutch oven up to a big stump that would work as a passable table. Most of the scouts came to help, but Vince Packer stood by himself, milling about on the fringes. A friendless kid trying to be tough, hoping someone would take notice.

How long will he wait? Then Blake approached him and Vince smiled.

"You two come give me a hand."

Blake and Vince jogged to Jim and the Dutch oven.

Struggling for friends, and no sugar? What kind of asshole parents would do that to a kid?

Jim asked Blake and Vince to finish opening the cans of peach pie filling, then took three strides toward his gear before turning around. "But wash your hands first!"

Jim continued to his saddlebags where he probed through the contents. Dry flies and lures, mixed with personal items poked at his hand. *These bags are worse than my sister's purse.*

In the bottom, he felt what he was looking for. A few years earlier, Jim had several custom knives made by a local manufacturer. Stainless steel blades, rosewood grips, and brass buttressing at the pommel and forefront made great gifts. On the middle of each grip and on the leather scabbard, was stamped the Cooper Outfitter logo.

After cleaning the knife of saddlebag crumbs and lint, he went to Brother Coleman to make sure the Packers didn't have any stupid rules forbidding folding knives. And then Jim called Vince over.

The boy approached.

"I'm Jim."

Vince pushed his glasses up on his nose and shook Jim's hand.

"I heard of your family's sugar rule. Takes guts being different, but you've caused a problem."

"I'm sorry." The boy looked like the last thing he wanted was to hear what Jim would say next.

"I promised to reward everyone who kept camp clean."

"Okay." Vince's voice cracked.

"So, since you're parents won't let you have sugar, I want you to have this."

Both boys gasped, and Vince's eyes widened under his glasses as he took the gift. Jim turned to look at Brother Coleman, who smiled his approval. The other scouts, bristling with excitement, gathered close to Vince and his prize.

A cool wind rippled the lake and blew through camp as the group ate a trout dinner and the cobbler. Jim and Brother Coleman talked. The scoutmaster inquired about a guided trip the following summer, and thanked Jim for being kind to his young men.

Duke stretched out beside the fire and rose when Jim did.

"Where are you going to sleep," Brother Coleman asked. "Do you have a tent?"

"Don't like tents. Can't see the stars." Jim paused. "What's your first name? I hate calling you folks Brother and Sister."

"I'm Allen."

Jim nodded across the fire.

"That was a nice thing you did for Vince."

The past had been on his mind, and Jim almost didn't respond. "The patrol leader, Blake?"

"Sure. What about him?"

"Seeing him mother Vince." Jim nudged the end of a log further into the fire with his boot. "It's how it was with my best friend." Jim took a breath, held it then blew through pursed lips.

"What's your friend's name?"

Jim cleared his throat. "It was Bradley."

"Was?"

"We went to Desert Storm together. He didn't come home."

Allen paused. "I'm sorry. I didn't mean to pry."

"You weren't."

"He was lucky to have a friend like you."

"Not really. He shouldn't have been there. Goodnight." Jim walked into the darkness, the temperature dropping with each step from the fire.

"Good night."

The horse blankets on pine needles made a fine bed, and his straw hat was the perfect container for his wallet, hunting knife, and pistol. As he stretched, the soreness in his muscles eased. Jim pulled his old oilskin coat and a tarp up to his chin.

A waning sliver of moon crept over the cliff's edge. The lakeside camp, with horses snorting in the distance and scouts chattering in their tents, was the center of Jim's universe with stars stretching to every horizon.

Duke stretched out by his knee, the dog's warmth soaking through Jim's Carhartts in the crisp mountain air.

"Have a good night, boy?" Jim asked, reaching out from under his makeshift covers, to pet the dog. "We need someone who likes the trail and the wide open spaces, but looks twice as good as you."

Jim tried to scrape the thought away.

Two Mormon girls had broken his heart when they married men of their own faith. The first was Sally Strobel. Even though he knew it wouldn't have worked, Jim couldn't help feeling jealous at times. The Mormon religion was everything to Sally, and he couldn't pretend conversion.

Or did I miss the boat?

Why not compromise? Live the Mormon or any religion for someone he loved. Perhaps there was still time.

The perfect girl might come to the mountains for a guided week. She would be athletic, pretty, smart, assertive, friendly, and love to sleep under the stars, ride horses—and have no religious convictions. Hopefully, she would be a better cook than Brody.

Minus the religious part, his mother had been all of the above in spades. His dad had been lucky. *Maybe someday I will be as well.*

Almost asleep, his mother's words when Sally married while he was away at boot camp came to him, "Just worry about being the best you can, and eventually the right girl will find you."

He had been honestly in love with Sally. Word of her marriage came two days before the end of basic training. It no longer hurt, but if there was someone out there, she needed to kick it in gear.

He drifted off to sleep to the smell of the campfire and horses. The night sky wove itself into his dreams as the stars transformed into the glittering lights of Las Vegas.

27

Allen Coleman helped Jim saddle the pack string under the light from their headlamps. He told Jim that several of the scouts' parents were wealthy, and that with his recommendation, would be happy to pay the professional fee for a guided trip the following summer.

Jim got to his guests' campsite at about eight in the morning. The group was rolling up tents and gear as he rode into camp. All were curious about Chris, and why Jim came in earlier in the week to take him back. Jim deflected their questions, saying it was a personal matter, and then asked them about their week.

Without exception, they were all happy. It had only rained one day, and the fishing had been phenomenal. The guests gave him tips, totaling two grand, mostly in hundred dollar bills.

As he stuffed the bills into his vest, Jim decided to take the cash to Vegas, to avoid leaving a credit card trail.

I'm already thinking like a criminal.

Back at the ranch, the guests packed up and left fairly quickly. With the last car out of sight, Jim's cell rang.

"Hello."

"Jim, it's Sheriff Johnson. You still got the black fella?"

"Nope," Jim responded, thinking Albert had never used his title.

"Brody?"

"At the church picnic," Jim responded.

"I'm here with a pair of FBI agents who need to talk to you." Albert paused. "Immediately."

Jim looked at the sky, wanting to join the hawk hovering overhead, riding the updrafts above the pasture. "Bring 'em out. I'm about to shoe a horse."

"They'll wanna visit in the house."

Jim hung up. He suspected the agents would try to catch him off balance, hence the invasion of his privacy. Nothing was set in stone, and even if he went to Vegas, he wasn't obligated to do anything.

Even though it was evening, it was still ninety degrees, so Jim went to the fridge, poured a glass of ice water, and drained it in a few gulps. He guzzled two more glasses, and took the last one with him to the barn. He set it on his workbench where he kept his shoeing tools. He fastened some farrier chaps over his Carhartts and waited in the shade until the rotating flashers of Albert's SUV came into view in the distance.

Heading out to the corral, he retrieved an old mare that was always a handful to shoe and half-hitched her lead rope to the rail. With the front right hoof between his knees, he picked dirt from beneath the hoof as Albert and two men in dark suits and sunglasses got out of the SUV.

"Jim, this is Agent Benson and Agent Schmidt. They need to ask you some questions."

Jim nodded.

"Can we go inside?" the older and smaller Agent Schmidt asked.

"Don't have the time." Jim looked up from the hoof. "I'd shake hands, but you'd be exposed to the corral."

The mare lifted her tail, and defecated. Constantly eating given the chance, horses moved lots of grass, making it likely her tail would lift again before the shoes were set.

"Shit!" one of the agents said.

"Not shit, manure," Jim explained, putting the hoof down and walking between the agents, who separated like the red sea before Moses. He grabbed a garden rake hanging on the barn wall and used it to pull the mess away to where the agents had been standing.

"We would prefer to do this—"

"Why?" Jim said, cutting him off. "If this needs done indoors, it'll have to be Monday." Jim talked as he strode to the table and picked up an old set of hoof trimmers while the agents looked at each other.

Jim worked the trimmers between the mare's hoof and worn metal shoe. It had been two months since her last shoeing, and the hoof had grown about half an inch. The mare flinched, staggering Jim before the shoe released, the twisted nails that once held iron to hoof protruded like the burnt remnants of a sagebrush beyond the metal. Jim stood and handed the shoe to the agent.

"Souvenir from Wyoming," Jim said.

The agent accepted it, though he only pinched it between his forefinger and thumb, before setting it on the ground.

Jim was under the opposite front hoof before one of them spoke.

"You killed three men last Sunday. How is it you weren't harmed?"

Jim didn't respond or look up, but suspected it was the bigger, younger Agent Benson.

"Do I get an answer?"

"I'm better at shooting a pistol than pulling horseshoes." The second shoe came free. "They say these are lucky," Jim said, handing the second shoe to the agent.

Before picking up the mare's right hind hoof, Jim slowly ran his left hand down the horse's rump and leg. She un-weighted, and let him take it. Stretching the leg behind her, he rested the hoof on his lap and went to work as he had done on the front hooves.

"How did you get so good with a pistol?" Agent Benson asked.

"Boot camp." The mare flinched, jostling Jim, his feet digging into the ground to steady the thousand pound animal.

"Ever shoot anyone before?"

"Yep," Jim responded without looking up from his work.

"Where?"

"Kuwait."

"How many?"

"He killed seven people during Desert Storm," the sheriff answered for him.

"Is that true?" Agent Schmidt turned from the sheriff to Jim, who ignored the question.

"So, how did it go down this time?" Agent Benson asked.

Jim finished pulling the rear shoes and gave the agents each a second prize. He looked them both in the eyes and told his story as a smile, fairly faint, crossed the lips of both agents. Pretending not to notice, he walked to the tool table and picked up the newer hoof trimmers. Returning to the mare, he lifted the first hoof and trimmed about a half inch from the mare's foot.

"So you're telling us you just happened to be in the wrong place at the wrong time?

Jim waited until he was done trimming the second hoof before saying, "Yep."

"You just happened to be there?"

"If anyone 'happened' it's the dead guys and Larry."

"That's right. Tell us about Larry Lyons," the agent ordered.

"Steady girl," Jim grunted as the mare shifted. "Met him Sunday." The mare shifted again. "I said steady! Didn't know his last name 'til now."

"You didn't know his last name, and you let him stay here?"

Jim was done trimming the third hoof. The excess came away cleanly, leaving a nice flat area to rasp and set nails through. Duke rose from the bale of hay where he was lying and snatched up the trimmings from where Jim had tossed them.

"Caviar," Jim said, smiling at the happily chewing dog. "Larry . . . what did you say his last name was?"

"Lyons," Agent Benson said, sounding irritated.

"He left night before last."

"Did he say where he was going?"

"Nope."

"Do you have any ideas?"

"Home, I guess. Yellowstone maybe." Jim didn't like lying, but thought it came out fairly well, so he continued to work in silence. He began sweating like a leaking irrigation system, the moisture cooling him as a breeze swept through the barn.

"I'm still not sure why you would let a total stranger into your home without knowing his last name."

"I'd board FBI guys if they needed it," Jim said as drops of sweat blotted the ground in penny-sized circles.

Jim walked past them for the rasp, a horseshoe and nails, grateful that he had worked as a farrier after returning from active duty. By necessity, he'd learned to talk to his clients while working.

He was just driving the nails into the first shoe when Agent Benson spoke.

"Why are you sweating so badly?"

Jim rolled his eyes in disbelief. The mare flinched again.

"Do we make you nervous?" the agent asked.

"No."

"Then why are you sweating?"

"It's hot," Jim said as the horse leaned forward. "Stand," he scolded the mare, who swished her tail at the flies pestering her flank.

"We need to talk to Larry. We aren't sure why he or the three men you shot were here. As we piece this together, we may need to talk to you again. Don't be hard to find."

Jim pounded another nail through the hoof. "Never am." Jim thought about being gone the next week and added, "Sometimes I take guests into the mountains. My hired man knows my schedule."

"Look, this all seems transparent enough. Are you sure you've never met any of these people before?" Agent Benson asked.

Obviously they were looking for something that just wasn't there, some connection to explain the bizarre circumstances.

"There's one thing I suppose," Jim offered.

"How about you stand up and tell us instead of hiding under the horse," Agent Benson demanded, his temper rising.

Jim ignored the command and continued driving nails into the second shoe. "I usually don't speak badly toward the dead."

"Go ahead," Agent Benson said.

Jim finished pounding the nails. "The first two I killed were assholes."

"How so?"

"Arrogant." Jim walked to the tool bench for his nail clincher. "But the young one was out of place."

"How so?"

"Like he'd never held a gun before."

"Then why did you kill him?"

Jim clinched all eight to the hoof before answering. "Out of place or not, he was shooting at me."

"Are you sure you didn't retaliate because he shot your horse?" Agent Benson's tone had grown accusatory.

To avoid speaking for a few minutes, he used his mouth as a nail holder instead of the magnet embedded in his chaps. Taking one nail at a time, he pounded them through the hoof, twisted them off and then clinched all eight. With his mouth now empty, he answered the question.

"I shot to avoid ending up like my horse." Jim walked to his workbench to shape the hind shoes over the anvil. Agent Benson took the opportunity to ask the stupidest question yet.

"Are you sure the kid was shooting at you?"

"Asked and answered by my dead horse." Jim's anger flashed. He wanted to be coherent, but had no problem with letting them know how ridiculous they were being.

"Asked and answered? That's a legal term. Where did you learn that?"

Jim ignored the question.

"We need to make sure not to miss anything," Agent Schmidt said. Compared to his younger partner, his tone was pleasant.

Jim made them wait as he set the last two shoes. The mare's constant jostling and the nails in his mouth helped.

"The truth always comes out the same," Jim said as he put the final foot down. "Forward, reverse, or sideways."

"Do you have a permit to carry a concealed gun?" Agent Schmidt asked.

"I taught his class." Albert spoke for the second time since making introductions.

"Why would you feel the need to carry a gun in the first place?"

"Because it's the wilderness," Jim responded, his eyes bugging out slightly under his raised eyebrows, thinking it was almost as stupid as asking if he was sweating because he was nervous.

"How did you get Simon and Marcus Faletto on a horse? They both weighed over three-hundred pounds."

"Good girl." Jim patted the mare's neck, then stood back to admire his work. The nails were at uniform depth and the hoof angles were perfect.

"How did you load up two three-hundred-pound dead guys all alone with Larry Lyons hurting so badly?"

Jim took off his hat and sleeved sweat from his brow.

"He hoisted the bodies with a rope, a tree, and another horse," Albert grumbled. "I told you guys this already."

"Why do you think Jonathan Faletto, missed all three times?" Agent Schmidt asked.

"People shooters kill target shooters."

"What do you mean?"

"After seeing me kill the other two, he shit himself and shot from his heels."

Agent Schmidt's face relaxed into a knowing expression, and he extended his hand toward Jim. "You're an honest man."

"All the evidence points to his innocence," Albert stated.

"I think we have a clear picture," Agent Schmidt said and started walking to Albert's SUV.

As they got in the vehicle, Albert glanced back and rolled his eyes like he was glad the interview was over. Albert was a good sheriff, and it probably made him sore to have his conclusions second-guessed like that.

Alone again, Jim returned the mare to the corral. She trotted, ears forward toward the herd. Jim laughed. Unbuckling the chaps, he returned them to their hook near the anvil and shoeing tools. Before walking into the house, he looked at where he'd raked the manure that was already drying in the evening heat. It would be as inert as an old piece of leather within hours. He kicked the pile then went to the workbench and chugged the water, chewing on the only ice cube that hadn't melted.

Duke nosed his leg.

"What d'you think, Duke?" Jim asked as he petted the dog. Duke barked twice as he wagged his stubby tail.

"I agree." Jim continued to pet his best friend. "I'm glad they're gone, too."

AN HOUR LATER, AGENTS BENSON and Schmidt sat in their hotel room talking about the interview.

"He sure didn't give us much," Agent Benson remarked. After thinking for a few seconds, he continued, "I think he gave us exactly what he wanted, a couple of horse shoes and a pile of shit."

"Sometimes a spade is a spade," Agent Schmidt responded.

"What's that supposed to mean?"

"That it happened like he said it did. Our old friends from Vegas fucked with the wrong cowboy."

"Cliché, cliché, old man."

"He was where he was supposed to be, doing what he does, and the three dead goons had no idea a decorated soldier was coming toward them." Agent Schmidt decided to change the subject. "Tell me you wouldn't want to be there to see him kill those three. First, he kills Simon, and then Marcus goes down. Johnny had to've shit his pants."

"It would've been cool," Agent Benson agreed. "Michael Faletto will take this personally. The sheriff told us Cooper wouldn't do protective custody, but he should."

After a few minutes, Agent Schmidt responded. "Do we care?"

"We're supposed to."

"The guy doesn't want our help." Agent Schmidt slipped off his loafers, flinging them from his toes toward the corner. "He has no wife or kids—and when they come, Mr. Cooper may take some with him."

28

After bidding farewell to the law, Jim showered and gathered his things, hoping to leave first thing in the morning. As he was stuffing his toothbrush and paste into a duffel bag, he thought of his old horse trailer and realized it would be a great way to smuggle the cash away from the delivery truck.

He smiled, thinking of leaving Las Vegas with a manure-stained, rusty old livestock trailer full of cash. Once, as a young soldier stationed in San Diego, he took a weekend trip to Vegas and promptly lost his entire month's pay. Young and foolish as he might have been, he never repeated that particular mistake.

Several years later on a trip to Vegas for a hunting and fishing exposition, Jim walked through some of the casinos and realized just how counterintuitive it was that people thought they would actually win money. The opulence of buildings, with their marble floors, fine carpets, chandeliers, and mirrors, conveyed a message of money, but it was wealth gained from people like himself as a young soldier.

The hustle and bustle and sightseeing contrasted so brightly with a life spent in undeveloped parts of the world. The only place that compared to Las Vegas in terms of overdevelopment, in Jim's mind, was Newport Beach. His sister lived on Lido Island, and he loved strolling down the boardwalk, or taking a sea kayak to see all the houses crammed within inches of one another. He'd tried to explain to Brody how close houses were by saying that your next-door neighbor could hand you a fresh roll of toilet paper through a window if you needed one. The old man just couldn't fathom it.

"Well I'm glad it's there and I'm here," Brody had grumbled.

Even though he'd started the day in the wilderness and he'd worked till sunset, he knew it would be hard to fall asleep, so he continued packing the things he would need for a week on the road. He could live from his truck to avoid detection. There was also a place he wanted to spend the night, in memory of Bradley.

Jim dressed the part of the modern cowboy while on the ranch, but around town he preferred sneakers over cowboy boots. Like any lifestyle, there were always wannabes. Brody said it best one day when they saw the California transplant neighbor.

"Big boots, big hat. No cattle."

Jim threw a sleeping pad, as well as a few blankets, a pillow, and a five-gallon jug of water down next to his duffel. Next, he went to his gun safe. He normally carried a pistol in the waistband of his pants under his shirt, but the plan for getting the truck out of Vegas called for firepower.

As a younger man, he'd spent a lot of money on guns, and as a hunting enthusiast he held an impressive collection. Years earlier, he'd bought a single-shot fifty caliber, bolt-action from a client. It weighed close to thirty pounds, and literally kicked like a packhorse.

It would be perfect for what he had in mind.

Next, he grabbed his M-4 assault rifle and an old sawed-off, pump-action shot gun.

With a box of ammunition for each weapon and his gun cleaning kit, it took three trips to lug all his equipment out to his truck. He locked it all inside the toolbox behind the cab.

To the east, the headlights from Brody's return bounced up the road. Jim's mind reeled like a fish with whirling disease as he tried to come up with a convincing lie. He decided to tell Brody he was going to the mountains for a week. He'd load up Terence and a pack horse, along with all his camping gear, then leave the horses at the far end of the ranch on a pasture of fresh grass, with a free-flowing spring for them to drink. He doubted Brody would go there, and if he did, Jim would claim he changed his mind, deciding to hike into some places impassable to livestock.

It was likely the old-timer would know it wasn't the truth, but Jim thought by offering a story, all Brody would need to do is repeat what he'd been told.

As Brody's old pickup pulled into the barnyard, Jim walked out from the barn.

"How was the social?"

"Ate too many baked beans. It's probably a good thing I don't have a roommate."

"Roommate hell, it's good you have an outdoor job."

Brody ignored the words, and walked toward the house, so Jim continued. "In the morning I'm gonna take a few horses to the mountains to check on some camping spots. We don't have any guests until next week." Then Jim added, "You might want to go to the grocery store; I may be gone a week."

Brody stopped, took a deep breath and looked up at the stars. "I can keep a better eye on the horses if you leave 'em. If the law asks, they won't know two extras from twenty. Far as I'm concerned, you're unavailable."

Jim wasn't surprised. "Thanks. I'll see you when I get back."

"I'll be seeing you, but will you see me?" Brody paused, and Jim's hair stood on end, as he pictured Brody viewing him in a casket.

"Call if you get in a pickle."

Jim walked into the house, brushed his teeth, and climbed into bed, but didn't sleep. Lying was wrong, especially to someone who had been honest and upfront his whole life.

Jim fought the urge to get up and drive, thinking he needed to rest, which only made sleep even more elusive.

The truck was loaded with everything he might need. Thinking about his guns, he hoped he wouldn't need everything he'd packed. At five a.m. he breezed through the shower, ate breakfast, brushed his teeth, and scratched at his stubble but decided against shaving. Putting on a pair of flip-flops and shorts, Jim looked at his pasty white legs and feet.

Leaving through the back door of the ranch house and climbing into his truck, he backed up to his horse trailer where Brody appeared in the side mirror, waving directions.

The ranch-hand was already plugging in the light and trailer-brake harness to the bumper of the truck. Jim stepped on top of the rear driver's side tire and climbed up into the bed in one fluid motion. He secured the trailer hitch around the ball, then fastened the safety chains to their latches inside the bed. As he looked up, Brody's stare caught him off guard.

"I'm not from here," the old man said, somewhat enigmatically.

"What?"

"I was born in Chicago. I came west at seventeen."

Jim processed the words and realized Brody wasn't speaking with his usual Western Wyoming drawl.

"I'm all ears."

Sloping shoulders and lines in the old man's cheeks, and around his eyes, masked Brody's size. He was big, and looked every bit the weathered old ranch hand.

Brody cleared his throat and, staring at the ground, kicked at a rock. Although he wasn't looking directly at Jim, his voice was clear; obviously the salty old-timer intended Jim to hear. The words sounded unnatural, precise, and unaccented.

"I was born in 1933. My father was a postal worker who got killed on his route when I was four. The depression was on, and after my dad died, we struggled. We had no family, and if it weren't for some of the people at the local Catholic Church, me, my mother, and sister would've starved. I grew up poor, never having much to eat or wear. Mother kept us in school, but nothing came easy.

"When I turned ten, a rich man from the church hired me to work on his place in the stables. Mother sent me, knowing he could feed me better than she could. It was a big country spread outside Chicago, and I never saw my family again because they died when their apartment building caught fire. The people I worked for took me to the funeral. It wasn't much of a service, but the church members paid for the burial plots and a few flowers.

"I grew up fast, working hard, doing about what I do for you now. Eventually, I came to know the people I worked for, and not knowing better and wanting a pay raise, I got involved in the family business.

"A business I suspect is much like that of the three men you killed."

Brody stopped, but the words had already chilled Jim to goose bumps. Jim hoped Brody would tell him more, and after a few breaths, the story continued.

"I ran west, ended up here. When the family gave me a chance to work outside the stables. I should've refused. I carry guilt for killing people who didn't deserve it.

"I know the other night you thought I belonged in a white sheet. This Larry is a nice guy. When I left Chicago, they sent a big black man after me, and I've been hiding all these years. The folks who wanted me dead are likely gone now."

Brody paused. "They kill. No mercy. They only respect power and strength if it's used ruthlessly. Be damned careful. My guess is, when they drew on you, it was abrupt. They would've watched you die, then carried on like it never happened."

Brody walked away then stopped,

"I'll load us up with supplies." The cowboy accent returned. "What're you gonna do with Duke?"

"Huh?"

"I can kick a pig in the ass and get more than 'huh.' What're you gonna do with Duke?"

Jim's mind wouldn't leave Brody's story to focus on what the old man asked.

"Never mind. Here boy." Brody patted his leg. Duke reluctantly left Jim's side and went to Brody. "You'll stick here with me." He bent to pet the dog and playfully fold over his ears.

Jim was tired, but after Brody's speech, he didn't dare rest. At the very least, he wouldn't coffee-up before noon. The story explained things about the man, Brody's reluctant friendship with Larry, and his quiet, observant manner. It was clear that, like himself, there were parts of Brody's life he only revealed out of necessity—even to Jim.

Brody, Duke, and the ranch buildings shrunk and disappeared from the rear-view mirror as he drove away.

29

L eaving the ranch before daylight Saturday morning, Jim traveled west into Idaho, then south on interstate fifteen. By nine he was within five miles of the Utah border. Driving gave him time to listen to his classic rock collection. He'd been raised by a ranching family, but he came of age in the eighties when hard rock music ruled the airwaves. He loved the riffs of AC/DC, VanHalen, Rush, Metallica, and just about anything his father dismissed as loud and obnoxious.

It gave him a kick to think that the younger crowd loved eighties rock. Sally's son, Skinner, was a classic rock aficionado, telling Jim things he didn't know about his favorite bands. The stereo blasted Metallica as he drove until, between songs, his cell phone rang.

"Hello, this is Jim." The number was from the Wyoming area code, but he didn't recognize the number.

"Good hell, I been calling like twenty times," Larry's voice answered. "Did you go deaf?"

Larry sounded strong, more succinct, no doubt the man was healing.

"Sorry, the stereo's been cranked. Where you calling from? The area code's Wyoming."

"Before we left, we bought phones, remember. Look under the seat, and you'll find yours. Turn it on, and I'll call in five minutes."

Before Jim could respond, Larry hung up.

What? Why would they buy me a cell phone?

Turning on his right turn signal, Jim moved the truck and trailer off the highway. As promised, he found a box with a cell phone and an adapter for his cigarette lighter. The phone had been opened, but the packaging for the adapter could survive a bunker buster and Jim had to cut it open with his hunting knife. Turning the phone on and setting it on the dash, Jim was looking over his shoulder to see if the highway was clear when it rang. The ring tone was Garth Brooks's "I Got Friends in Low Places."

"Hello, this is Jim."

"This is Larry."

"Why do I need a new phone?"

"Your new phone is pre-paid for five hours. I have one. Chris has one, and you have one. We shouldn't talk on any phones that are in our names. This is an untraceable phone."

"The ring fits."

"'Friends in Low Places' refers to Chris." Larry chuckled. "You on your way?"

"Like a southbound bird. How you been? Any problems with our friends?'

"None yet," Larry answered. "The funeral for all three is in a few days."

"Which day?" Jim asked.

"Tuesday." Larry coughed and then continued. "We have an apartment in Henderson. As far as we can tell, the cash is safe, but we're having a helluva time trying to figure out how to move it. Chris and I feel good about our agreement. If you'll help us, you're in for a fourth. And there's one other problem."

"What's that?"

"Their cell phones have been scrubbed. We've got no leverage.

We're betting they own a cellular store because the things are dead. You can't even place a call."

A shot of adrenaline accompanied Larry's words, making Jim a little light-headed as his heart sped. It was the feeling that propelled him into the army twenty years earlier. It spoke to him now, pushing him into action. Even if there were no money involved, he would have helped his new friends in the name of adventure.

In the past, his instinct had always been to turn and leave, but defying instinct brought the adrenaline high. It was that way in Kuwait, or when someone brought a rough horse to train.

He knew he could get hurt or killed, but that made the moment more alive. It defied common sense, but Jim related to mountaineers and thrill seekers who found meaning in risking everything. The ultimate rush came when he prevailed over whatever he shouldn't be doing. Someday, though, he knew he'd find a match for his skill.

The thoughts went through his head in seconds, but it was long enough to make Larry wonder if a solar flare had severed the connection.

"Jim? You still there?"

"Sorry, I think I can help us out. We'll need to talk it over and make sure we all agree."

"Chris and I will listen to whatever you have in mind,"

Larry gave Jim directions to the apartment in Henderson. Jim estimated he would be there in about seven hours and promised to call as he got close.

He closed the new phone, and thought about the conversation. Obviously, Larry and Chris had saddled something they couldn't ride, and needed his help.

Brody's warning was the roadmap. He wouldn't expect mercy under any circumstances.

He wanted to be aggressive. It made more sense to hunt than be hunted, to preserve his life and his lifestyle. He wanted to protect his friends, and if he could make himself rich at the same time, he was stupid not to try. It might mean dying, but if he didn't attack now, he'd never get another chance and eventually he'd get killed.

The horizons changed with the passing miles as the truck and trailer rattled down the highway. Many people held visions of going to Las Vegas for wealth. Without picking up a card, or even walking into a casino, he might realize that dream.

He figured he would use the money to do some of the things he'd always wanted around the ranch. He could use the cash for all his incidental expenses and funnel all his ranch money into some of the things he wanted. He also thought of setting up a retirement account for Brody, and maybe a disability and dental plan as well.

As he traveled, he thought about the men he'd killed. They would have families, with children and wives who were, right now, grieving their loss—a loss caused by him in a fateful instant on the trail to Tombstone Lake.

30

With Jim gone, Brody ate in town at the diner while looking for anything out of the ordinary. Tourists on the way to Jackson or Yellowstone bustled in and out, but nothing presented itself as anything but friendly. He drove past the motel. Maryland, California, Utah, Nevada— most of the license plates were from out of state so he decided the best way to guard the ranch would be at the ranch. And there was always work to do anyway.

While driving back, he noticed a few fishermen casting into the streams, their vehicles parked at the roadside, but nothing out of the ordinary.

Another cup of coffee would hit the spot, so when he got back to the ranch, he filled the pot, thinking he'd coffee up after checking on the calves on top of a nearby mesa. Duke greeted him on his way to the tractor, so he let the dog into the cab and drove up the access road.

Halfway to the top he saw something.

Even though the SUV was shorter than the surrounding corn, the morning light reflected through the stalks. The mesa's grass would feed the hundred or so yearling calves for another month, but Brody decided to drop a one-ton bale of alfalfa at the mesa's edge so he could eye the reflection without being too obvious.

Duke whined to be let out of the cab.

"In a minute," Brody said and the dog was quiet. After spiking a bale with the tractor's front tines, Brody tied Duke to the fence with an old piece of wire.

"Be back soon as I can." Brody petted the dog for a minute before returning to the cab. He drove the tractor across the mesa top to the opposite edge, with the calves following—no doubt happy to eat anything other than their usual ration of field grass. Brody levered the hydraulics from inside the cab, and the bale slid from the tines and landed with a thud. He hopped out and drew his Cooper Outfitters lock-back knife. The tensioned strings popped as he cut them one at a time. Brody re-sheathed his knife and rolled the strings into a neat bundle. Several of the calves gnawed at the bale as Brody stepped away for a pitchfork that he kept in a pipe sleeve near the tractor's rear tires.

The barn, house, and out buildings were more than six hundred yards away, so he didn't worry about looking their direction as he forked the hay near the mesa's edge. It took him twenty minutes to spread the hay so the calves wouldn't tromp the field to death from eating in just one place. He returned the pitchfork to its sleeve and drove the tractor to the other end of the mesa, where it would be out of sight to anyone looking up from the ranch house. Even before Jim's run-in with the men, Brody carried his Winchester .30-06 in the tractor's cab or in his old truck, so he snagged the gun, patted Duke again, and walked back toward the calves.

The line of sight below the mesa broadened with each step, and when the house and barnyard came into view, Brody dropped to his belly and inched to the mesa's edge where he slid between two knee-high boulders. The scope's amplification went to fourteen, so he twisted to the maximum and seated the rifle butt against his shoulder.

The shadow line creeping eastward told him he had about an hour until the sun rose over the pastures below. The cornfield, where the SUV was located, was a half-mile beyond the house and backed up onto forest.

Shaking corn stalks drew Brody's attention. For five minutes, he scoped the shaking stalks as someone moved in a straight line toward the SUV. Someone opened the rear hatch that reflected sun toward him from nearly a mile distant. The hatch was shut and three men got in the SUV and drove off.

Twenty minutes later, gun in hand, Brody got out of the tractor near where the SUV had been parked.

Damn vandals, Brody thought as he looked at corn that had been crushed by the SUV's tires. Three sets of boot tracks, leaving and returning to the SUV were easy to follow as Brody pushed through the cornfield. The tracks spread out in the woods, but weren't hard to follow to where they stopped, less than fifty yards from the barn. Cows grazing the pasture between the forest and the barn made tracking slower, but a boot print here and there took him to the corral, where three men had stepped through the fence and walked into the barn. In the barn's center was a ladder leading to the loft. Brody slung the gun over his shoulder and made his way up the rungs.

Modern one-ton bales made the loft impractical for storing hay, so it had become a catchall for old gear and equipment. Rather than disturb anything, Brody dropped back down the ladder and returned with a flashlight. Nobody had been in the loft for weeks, so the three sets of tracks on the dusty floorboards were as clear as someone walking in an inch of fresh snow. Now that he knew the men's hiding spot, Brody made tracks of his own as he crossed the loft.

Three hanging bear-traps were spiked through their anchor chains to one of the barn's rafters. They hadn't been used since Jim's dad had trapped a calf-killing grizzly more than fifty years ago. Brody slipped the chains from the spikes, then slung the rifle from the same spike before carrying the traps down the ladder to a workbench where Jim kept his anvil and horseshoeing tools.

The spray bottle of WD-40 ran dry before he had removed the rust from the first trap, so Brody left and came back with a gallon milk jug of used oil. *This beats recycling,* he thought, *pouring oil over the first trap.*

An hour later, with one foot on each spring, the jaws of the third trap fell open, and Brody set the trip-pad. Careful to remove his hand, he stepped off the springs and the mechanism held. The broom handle Brody had used to test the first two traps had been broken too short to use for testing the third, so he grabbed a piece of firewood from the porch and returned to the barn. His first and second lobs bumped the trap but didn't trip the mechanism. Brody stepped closer for the third try and lobbed it like a softball pitch. The jaw's snapped shut and splintered the log. Brody put a foot on each spring and the jaws fell open again, but before he could remove the splintered log, his cell buzzed.

The screen was easy to read in the barn's dim light. "Howdy, Jim."

"Everything okay?"

"You're either in a windstorm, or you need to roll up the window," Brody said, hoping Jim would end the conversation.

"Everything okay?" Jim repeated.

"Far as I can tell."

"Make sure to check the calves on the mesa."

"Already did." Brody used his free hand to remove the firewood and reset the trip-pad.

"Skinner should be there tomorrow night."

Brody stepped from the springs. "I'll put him to work when he gets here." Then he moved several feet away and lobbed the beat-to-hell chunk of firewood at the trap, which sent splinters all the way to the ceiling.

"What was that?"

"Bucket of tools fell over. Better go clean 'em up." Brody flipped the phone shut and slid it into his pocket, then retrieved the rifle from the loft. On the way to the house for a cup of coffee, he realized something was missing.

Better go get Duke. Almost left him in all the excitement.

31

Michael sat in an enormous leather chair, sipping his fourth tumbler of fifty-year-old imported bourbon of the morning. Across the freeway, some idiot free fell from the Stratosphere before the bungee cord slowed his descent and slung him back skyward. A vagrant walked across the parking lot below Michael's window as noontime traffic buzzed up and down Western Avenue. None of it held Michael's attention for longer than two breaths.

His exquisitely appointed office resembled an attorney's, with solid cherry wood cabinetry and granite countertops, all of it concealed within a dilapidated old building that he refused to remodel. The paint peeled from the siding, and the weather-baked shingles crinkled in the hot Nevada sun. The stench of burning carpet fibers from his cigar's fallen ash reminded him it was still between his fingers. He chewed on the end, took a puff through pursed lips, then blew out through his nose. The smoke failed to tingle his nostrils, indicating the alcohol had numbed almost everything.

Being tanked separated conscious thought from grief, like a missing bridge between landmasses. The awareness of losing his only son and two brothers was still there, but the pain was gone for the moment.

The FBI had no shame, beating on his door at three a.m. He could sense them gloating behind the door as he lay in crippling pain.

Michael's attorney had hustled, paying off authorities in Jackson Hole to learn the killer was thirty-eight year old James Owen Cooper, a wilderness guide, rancher, and decorated Gulf War veteran. At least Johnny's death wasn't at the hands of a rival; he could kill a rancher at his leisure.

He'd sent an underling, one of Ralf's body shop guys, to watch over the newer bouncers. They'd called, telling him they were outfitted to fight in Somalia, but Michael counseled them to wait for the right opportunity and then kidnap the rancher and bring him back to Vegas. Meanwhile, he worked in a drunken haze to plan a hero's funeral for his son and brothers.

When his family was laid to rest, he would focus on Wyoming.

The stolen money meant almost as much as the deaths. The cash in the truck was minuscule, pennies compared to the mountains of cash he'd never need, but losing anything through theft challenged his authority.

In the last few years, he made cash like a boomtown's sole merchant. Aided by a robust economy, Michael had tripled the family's cash flow in five years. Like an octopus with tentacles throughout southern Nevada, Michael used illegal cash to open legitimate businesses—collision repair shops, laundromats, storage rental facilities, cellular stores, and the always-expanding strip clubs and restaurants created a cash problem.

With the amount of money he smuggled the growth of the shipments forced Michael to weigh the risks and benefits of moving more cash less frequently, and he ultimately chose to go with two large shipments per year.

Each time, the truck was loaded and a contract driver hired. Nobody followed the truck. The driver worked for a shipping company that was unaffiliated with the family's businesses. The trucker never knew he was moving tens of millions of dollars. If he was caught, absolute deniability would be the truth. Each time a new driver was hired, a company was set up to pay him. As soon as the shipment was made, the paying company was dissolved. Michael's perceived brilliance fed his ego, knowing he'd found a way to have innocent people smuggle.

Then someone stole the truck.

By sheer luck, he'd learned the thief's identity from the accountant's secretary. Michael rallied the family. The accountant was fishing in Wyoming, and Michael dispatched his two brothers to retrieve Chris Cobb, kidnapping Larry Lyons first to ensure they got the right man.

Johnny had been an afterthought, preferring to ride his skateboard or dirt bike to being involved in the family matters. Even though Johnny's interest hadn't surfaced yet, Michael knew it would in the right time and place. The theft of the money was exactly what Michael wanted. A chance for Johnny to return victorious; earning respect by returning the money and killing the thieves might ignite some interest in the boy.

But now it didn't matter.

After the funeral, he'd make things right, devote every thought and moment to revenge. Just picturing it relieved his grief, in the short term, more effectively than alcohol. James Owen Cooper would watch while he beat Larry and Chris with a ball-peen hammer, smashing their fingers and toes so everyone would know what happened to those who stole from him. Then he'd stuff their mouths with wads of cash and wrap their heads with duct-tape so they'd suffocate to the taste of money.

He would do the rancher last with all his men watching. It would be ceremonial, solemn, spoken of only when those attending gathered in hushed conversations, a moment his men would contemplate with reverence.

Michael's focus grew, knowing soon the rancher's blood would permanently cure what alcohol only partially made bearable.

And it would be easy. Even though he'd told the bouncers to wait for the right opportunity, he expected a call any second. They would be eager to make an impression.

Michael finished his drink, and then dripped the last few ounces from the crystal decanter into the tumbler. He stood. A moment of vertigo angered him, and he threw the empty container into a mirror, shattering both in an eruption of shivered glass.

He stared at the glistening pile on the floor.

The rancher will soon be in as many pieces.

Michael ignored the mess, and sat back down. He swore the chair was surging on hydraulic levers, shifting and rocking as he leaned back. Then there was a moment of panic when he wondered if he'd topple backwards as the chair reached its limit.

He swiveled the chair side to side, his toes barely touching.

The ceiling tile drew his attention. The pattern became a pumped skyward blood splatter from the rancher's carotid artery, sprayed on the ceiling to mark Michael's moment of vengeance when all would watch as Michael severed Jim Cooper's head.

32

By late afternoon, Jim arrived at a truck stop in St. George, Utah. It had only been three years since driving through, and it surprised him how much the city had grown. Condominiums and golf courses squeezed between box stores and restaurants now stood where he remembered sagebrush and open space.

As he pumped diesel into the tank, he noticed everyone was tan, and he half expected a wisecrack about needing sunglasses to withstand the glare from his legs. Pants were an option, but being the only person not in shorts would make him even more of a "turd in the punchbowl" as Brody was fond of saying

The asphalt's heat waves and the dry desert air refreshed his flip-flopped feet as he walked toward the store to pay for the fuel and get some coffee.

"This place got busy," he said to the lady behind the counter, who looked to be in her mid-fifties.

"Which pump you on?"

"Nine."

"It's the damned retirees mostly. Every Mormon with money wants to die next to a golf course. Saw the license plate on your truck and trailer. What part of Wyoming you from?"

"Southwest of Jackson. I'm headed to Vegas. I'm gonna pick up some horses on the way back through." Jim thought as he talked.

"Where you picking them up?"

"Fillmore," Jim lied.

"When you coming back through?"

"Later this week."

"You could park it out back. Plenty a space. It don't make sense to pull that thing all the way there and back."

Jim was wondering what to do with his trailer. The plan he had in mind was to bring the cash truck out of Vegas, and then transfer the contents to his horse trailer somewhere in the desert. Ditching the gooseneck would be convenient. "I think I'll do that."

"Park it so the big rigs can pull alongside to the left and right."

"Thanks. It'll be gone by next week." *Or I'll be dead.* "Do you sell locks? I might run a chain through the wheels."

Where the old trailer wasn't stained with manure, it had rusted, and Jim knew what the cashier was thinking before she said it.

"Anyone wanting it is too honest to steal."

Jim smiled. "Darn thing won't die. Looks like hell, but it's tough and never given me a moment's trouble."

"Sounds like my first husband. I never should've traded him in for the fancier model."

Jim laughed. "Sounds like two lucky guys to me."

With the trailer back at the truck stop, nestled between two semis, Jim skirted Las Vegas toward Henderson. Larry gave him final directions, and within an hour of seeing The Strip from the freeway, he was at Canyon Vista apartments, knocking on door number five of building H.

Expecting his gigantic friend or Chris, Jim was momentarily speechless when the door was opened by the most gorgeous woman he'd ever seen. She wore a miniskirt, a tank top and sandals. Her hair was black and lustrous, hanging below her shoulders. Dark eyes and flawless olive skin hinted at some Asian ancestry. "I hope I'm in the right place."

Reaching out and taking him by the wrist, she tugged him into the apartment.

"I'm Sheila, and you're Jim. Larry hasn't shut up about you." Jim shut the door and Sheila continued. "Larry told me how you saved his life. I've never met somebody with this much buildup. He didn't say how handsome you are though."

She released his wrist, and Jim wanted the soft hand to touch him again. Then he caught himself eyeing her figure. The snug tank top revealed voluptuous cleavage and a tiny waist, while the mini skirt hinted at curvaceous hips above toned athletic knees, thighs and calves.

Be a gentleman you idiot. Look her in the eye.

He realized that she'd just given him a compliment that lifted his mood but also made him squirm.

"Once you get to know me, I'm sure you'll find me ordinary enough, I'm sure," Jim said with conviction, only to feel foolish at repeating himself.

"Trust me," Larry's enthusiastic voice boomed from down the hallway. "This dude is anything but ordinary!" The giant limped into the room, arms extended. He bear hugged Jim off the ground and set him down. "How's the drive?"

Since Jim's mother left the ranch, few people seemed happy to see him. The greeting from Larry and Sheila alone made the long trip worthwhile. Like the desert air between his toes, the warmth of camaraderie washed over him, and he realized they had anxiously awaited his arrival. "The drive was good."

"Can I get you something?" Sheila smiled. "We have cold beer."

Jim nodded.

At the fridge she grabbed three bottles of Budweiser and returned with a smile. She handed one to both Jim and Larry, and they all sat.

Larry opened his beer in an easy twist between his thumb and fore-finger, while Sheila struggled. Jim twisted the cap from his bottle and handed it to her.

"Thanks," she said, sliding her original bottle to him.

"Where's Chris?" Jim realized he hadn't seen the accountant.

"For the most part we've been stuck waiting for you to get here. The Mob knows us, and Chris is nuts. He goes out to run after dark. It's risky, but he's been bouncing off the walls, and we're sick of his ass."

"Hoping they'll kill him?" Jim joked.

"Sometimes." Larry and Sheila nodded at each other.

"How about the two of you?" Jim asked. "Either of you been out?"

"Doesn't bother me. I been sleeping mostly, healing up. They have no idea who Sheila is. So it's just Chris and me who need to lay low."

Jim swallowed a mouthful of beer. "How about your brother? Didn't you call him from Wyoming?"

"He's safe with our momma in Seattle," Larry said. "I brought him in, and I got him out."

"Having a brother like you would've been nice back in Wyoming."

"You need help?" A smile broke over Larry's face. "Shit! I seen some bad asses, but nothing like you! Art with a pistol, dawg. Art with a pistol."

Jim drank, and his beer was mostly gone, his empty stomach warm with a slight buzz. Usually he'd shrug off the compliment, but in Sheila's presence and also feeling her gaze combining with the alcohol made his cheeks hot.

"You're making him blush," Sheila said, skewering Larry with a glare from across the table.

Jim took a deep breath and considered his father's words from years earlier. It was before he shipped off to boot camp, and the message was clear: "Even though you're from a ranch in Wyoming, people are the same everywhere. Just be yourself."

Jim exhaled and smiled big, he looked at Larry first and then at Sheila. "It seems this pilgrim has found a soft place to land."

"Damn straight!" Larry said, raising his bottle. "I'll drink to that."

Standing up, Sheila put her hand on Jim's shoulder as she slid past on the way to the fridge. Her electric touch sped his heart, and he thought maybe she let it linger for a moment. Bringing another two beers back, she rested her hand on his shoulder again. He twisted the tops off both beers and looked at her.

"Thank you." She was sitting several inches closer to him. Then her leg touched his beneath the table.

"You're welcome."

He moved away on reflex, trying to be a gentleman to allow her room, but as his leg moved, hers maintained the contact. Sage hens instead of butterflies exploded in his stomach. It had been a long time since a beautiful woman intentionally touched him. Not knowing what to do or say, but keeping his leg against Sheila's, he sucked down some Budweiser.

"So, you've figured out a way to get the money out of here?" Larry asked.

"Maybe." Jim cleared his throat. "On the phone you said the horse killer's funeral is Tuesday?"

Larry raised an eyebrow. "You thinking about moving it during the funeral?"

"Unless someone has a better idea."

"Sounds good."

Jim's back was cramping from his long drive. He wanted to stretch, but moving might risk losing contact with Sheila's leg. He decided his back was okay.

"After I come back in the morning, let's go over the details with Chris."

"You're not spending the night here?" Larry asked, surprised.

"Me and an old friend camped on a beach at Lake Mead before shipping out for Desert Storm."

"Did he die?" Larry asked, a look of understanding crossing his face.

Jim nodded.

"I know all about buddies dying—not as soldiers, but I know."

Sheila's shin was still pressed against Jim's, and he felt like a teenager again, both worried and hopeful that he wasn't misreading any signals.

He planned on camping, but his mind raced, thinking maybe he should stay. He knew he needed to sleep, and if he stayed in the apartment, he was sure he wouldn't rest. His mind sped down the track like a jockey-less horse as he thought about the girl next to him.

I've been lonely my entire adult life, how many chances does a rancher get?

Here, right now, was the prettiest girl he could imagine, and it seemed she might be interested. The stakes grew. If she didn't want him, he would move on. It had happened before. His life lent itself to recovery from heartache because there was always so damned much to do and so little time to fret, but living in a Mormon community where most got married before twenty-five made for a lousy dating scene.

Even though they'd only met less than an hour ago, he made up his mind to tell her he wanted to get to know her better, letting the chips scatter. But right now he needed sleep and he would never rest in the apartment with people coming and going.

"I'd love to see Lake Mead." Sheila's tone was nonchalant and uninterested, as though they were talking about a barbershop or convenience store, but Jim took it like she wanted to accompany him to the world's seven wonders.

But then her face was hesitant. Maybe she wanted to take it back. Jim hadn't moved his leg. He felt foolish and pulled it away, and as he suspected, she didn't follow. Why in the world would a big city girl be interested? It was going to be another lonely night. She looked awkward now, acquiescing. *Have I already screwed up?*

"I'm sorry," she said. "You probably want to be alone."

Maybe she was thinking about how a country boy could never be interested in a city girl. *She doesn't know you haven't been on a date in ten years.*

"I'd love some company," Jim said.

"Are you sure?" Sheila's tone didn't contain her enthusiasm.

"Wouldn't have invited you if I wasn't."

"I'll get my things." She stood and headed down the hallway, but turned as Jim spoke.

"I have an extra sleeping pad, but you'll want some blankets and a pillow."

"Just one damn minute!" Larry cut in. "You two are stranding me with Chris?"

Neither of them answered.

"You two are leaving me with Chris?"

Neither of them answered.

"This is my friend, Sheila! He saved me in those bad ass woods, not you."

Jim was about to tell Larry to quit *bellering* like an un-mothered calf, but Sheila beat him to it.

"You big baby. It's not like we're dropping you off in the middle of nowhere." Her voice came from down the hallway as she moved between rooms in a flurry of activity.

"That happened! Just last week, Jim's hired dude picks me up, hauls my black ass out to the ranch. Leaves me alone for hours. I hate being alone!"

"You won't be alone." Sheila was back at the table carrying a suitcase and some pillows and blankets. "You'll be with Chris."

"Like I said, I hate being alone."

Jim stood. "Let me help."

"We'll be back first thing. I promise," Sheila said as she walked toward the door behind Jim.

"Hang on." Sheila handed Jim the bundle of blankets and pillows. "I forgot something." She disappeared down the same hallway and came back with a small cooler. The remaining beers clanked together as she took them from the twelve-pack carton and placed them in the cooler.

"You're taking the beer?"

Sheila shrugged. "I left one for you and one for Chris."

"No. You left me two."

As Sheila walked up to Jim and Larry, who were now standing near the door, Jim caught a whiff of perfume that he didn't think she'd been wearing before.

Jim pointed at his truck. Sheila made her way in front, turning and smiling as she reached the driver's side door. The warm desert breeze carried a pleasant moment of déjà vu.

Noticing the expression on his face as he unlocked his truck, she asked, "Okay, what's the smile about?"

"Just a memory of a pretty girl I went for a ride with."

"How long ago was that? This past week?"

"Add a decade and you'd be closer," Jim said, not wanting to admit it was two decades.

"Sounds like you need to get out more."

"That's for sure." Jim opened the door, and Sheila slid in.

"So, who was the girl? An old high school flame?"

Jim climbed in and shut the door. Sheila did exactly what he hoped for by climbing in the driver's side and scooting just enough to give him room to drive. She leaned into him, and a bigger flock of sage hens erupted in his stomach while adrenaline buzzed all the way to his capillaries. "We were an item in high school. She's a nurse now. Her oldest works for me."

"So why didn't it work out?"

The starter motor whined like a toddler and then the diesel rumbled like a choir's bass section. "Religious differences."

"Religious differences?"

"We didn't belong to the same church."

"What church do you belong to?"

"The church of pick-up trucks, horses, and wide open spaces."

Sheila moved her knees as Jim pushed in the clutch and shoved the stick over and down into reverse. Then he shifted into first gear and they pulled out of the parking lot. Without thinking, Jim shifted up through the gears, ending in fifth as the truck picked up speed. Sheila's soft hands touched his forearm and then slid up to his hand.

"So where are we spending the night?"

"Down the road and east into the desert." Jim paused. "But first I need to do something."

"What?"

"Go to an ATM, take all the money I have, and find a roulette wheel."

"Why?" Sheila asked.

"It seems like this is my lucky night."

"You're that sure of yourself, are you? I bet lots of girls go for rides in your truck." Jim wondered if she didn't believe him. He gave her hands a gentle squeeze and then a gigantic smile worked its way up to his face. For too long things had just happened. The sun came up, the grass grew, his calves got fat, and he was lonely while years frittered away wishing.

"I want to get to know you. Growing up with two pretty little sisters, I'm a protective grizzly bear." Jim cleared his throat before continuing. "I'm happy as hell just being here."

33

Leaning on the apartment doorway, Larry watched them drive away with Sheila like a teenager in the shotgun seat.

Sheila camping? Larry's belly bounced at the thought.

Through ten years of friendship, he'd watched Sheila pick her marks. Usually middle-aged, rich types with enough ego to believe a gorgeous young lady would still want yesterday's news. She'd pluck them from the verge of Viagra. They'd wine and dine her, lavish her with gifts in exchange for hearing how their gray hair was distinguished and their pot bellies success symbols.

It usually took less than two weeks before she had enough new jewelry to take to an appraiser, who already had buyers lined up for the Cartier or Tiffany pieces.

Then, if needed, she'd slip Larry a percentage to pose as her partner. Somehow, the swinging-dick middle-aged Charlie Sheens lost their mojo when they saw him at her apartment.

The way she treated Jim had been different. Beer from the fridge and Sheila as host was hysterical. She didn't even like beer; and if Jim were her next victim, he'd have been on his way to buy her eighteen-dollar cocktails served by pretty boy bartenders behind the velvet rope at the Foundation Room or Studio 54. The camping thing and the dented old truck clinched it; she'd never get into anything but a

European sedan to go anywhere, unless she thought the driver was the full on total shit.

He swirled the half full beer to a head, pressed it to his lips, and took a swallow, then shook his head.

Larry Lyons the matchmaker.

He hadn't seen it coming, would've bet against it, and might've even mistakenly warned Jim off.

I still owe you Mr. Marlboro Man, bullets-flyin', git'r done cowboy. But the gap is closing.

CHRIS RETURNED FROM HIS FIVE-MILE evening run as the couple got into Jim's truck. Even from fifty feet away, her body language fairly screamed the attraction. Her fingertips lingered on his forearm as he opened the door. A sharp pain in Chris's belly doubled him over, stealing his breath and forcing him to sit on the warm sidewalk. After a few minutes, Chris stood and walked to Larry, who was leaning against the open doorway.

"Where did those two go?"

"How's the run?" Larry responded, his tone nonchalant.

"I asked a question."

"In my line of business, when a man and a woman go off together, the less I know the better."

"This is different. Where did they go?"

Larry didn't respond to Chris's agitation, taking his time he swirled the beer to a head again before drinking the last of it. Then he turned his head away and covered his mouth to burp.

"I think they wanted to be alone."

"Do you even know where they went?"

"They're camping by Lake Mead."

"Camping?" Chris's sounded like someone just told him money wasn't green.

"Chill," Larry responded, still leaning against the doorway. "Jim wants to move the money to his ranch during the funeral."

Chris stared at Larry. "Chill? With millions in a truck ten miles from here! What if they take it and run?"

"She doesn't like you, Chris. They aren't running anywhere." Larry stepped outside the doorway and handed Chris the empty bottle. "Toss that in the trash."

Chris stormed into the apartment, but still made sure to set the bottle upright in the garbage so drips wouldn't spill. In the bathroom, he looked in the mirror while brushing his teeth, the anger of his own reflection making him more upset. He spun the shower knobs and waited as the water got warm. After shampooing, he shut off the hot water and resisted the urge to jump out of the way as the cold pelted his torso. The initial shock took his breath, but his anger didn't cool.

They can all go fuck themselves in the gutters and sagebrush they came from—as soon as they get my money out of Vegas.

34

After taking guys for cash and jewelry for the past decade, Sheila found herself wondering how to work a guy that she didn't want to work.

Jim might be a man she could begin to trust, a man who still wanted to get in her pants, but wouldn't try to buy, coerce, or force his way there.

She slid away, turning to study him. As she moved, Jim took his hand from her knee, but she reacquired it, sandwiching it between her hands.

He turned to meet her gaze. "I'm attracted to you, and I don't know anything to do except be an idiot and say it."

"That was direct."

Jim shrugged.

Sheila paused, exhaling through her nose, was about to speak but bit down.

"A man of my word?" Jim asked.

"What?"

"I'm an idiot."

"You," Sheila emphasized the word, "are the first guy in years I'm genuinely interested in."

"Really?" His response sounded like the roulette wheel actually did hit his number.

"I wanted to get to know you as soon as I opened the door."

"I think it was me who was amazed in the doorway," Jim responded.

Sheila smiled in spite of herself. It was a typical male line, but sitting next to him, holding his calloused, sand-paper-rough hand, it made her smile.

"I'm catching something here," she said, "but we hardly know each other. Tell me everything!"

"Like what?"

"What you like and don't like, what your favorite food is. What kind of music you listen to."

"My favorite—"

"And what your favorite book is," she continued. "Your family and pets. Have you always been a rancher?"

Jim laughed.

"Kind of a long list?"

"Not really." Jim checked the rearview and both side mirrors.

"Then what's so funny?"

"Right now."

After hearing Larry rave about Jim's pistol skills, how he stared death in the face with icy precision, she expected a hardened cowboy from a spaghetti western.

"Do you always enjoy the moment this much?"

"No." Jim switched on his blinker before pulling his truck off the highway and heading down a dirt road into the sagebrush. "I love T-bone steaks, Metallica, my dad's dead, my mom lives between my sisters in California, I have eight hundred cows, twenty horses, a dog named Duke, my favorite book is *Huckleberry Finn,* and I was four years active duty army out of high school." Jim glanced her a smile. "Your turn."

"You were taking notes." She slid closer. "But you forgot to tell me what you don't like."

"Have been since the doorway. Let's stick with what I like. You're gonna love this place." The truck bounced down the dirt road, and Sheila decided to redirect the conversation because, for all she knew, she might hate where they were going even though she was definitely interested in Jim.

"You don't get off that easy." Sheila tugged on his arm. "Give me one thing you don't like."

"Zealots."

"Me, too."

Lake Mead came into view, a dark pit where the cliff's end marked by water's beginning. The full moon's reflection sent long shadows across the lake and over the desert landscape.

Twenty minutes after first glimpsing the lake, Jim recognized the campsite where he had stayed before Desert Storm and pulled over. The lake's level was considerably lower than he remembered as he pulled the truck down a small canyon that ended at the water's edge. Jim killed the motor and set the truck's parking brake.

"Let's look around." Jim shouldered the door open.

A few steps to the edge and the warm desert wind with wisps of desert mesquite pillowed against him. It was mixed with moisture from the lake and caressed his nostrils and lungs as he held a deep breath. Rising goose bumps on his arms and neck matched the chills that zipped up and down his spine.

He remembered the dream.

The tingling continued as old friends, Bradley and Sam were close. It lingered as the warm wind made him part of the desert. For a second Sam stood beside him breathing, the horse's presence warming Jim's core. It clung, but at the moment he wanted more, it dissipated from his grasp like clinching fine sand.

"What's on your mind?" Sheila asked.

Jim waited a swallow before speaking. "Dead friends. Let's find a way to the water."

Returning to the truck, he grabbed a flashlight. To their right, a ramp-like path of sandstone led down to the water. Sheila followed him back to the truck.

"What are you doing?" she asked.

"I need a bath."

"Trying to get me to go skinny dipping?"

"I'll leave my shorts on. I can get your bed situated, or if you want, you can join me."

An impulsive gleam flickered in her eyes, then she smiled a big smile and nodded enthusiastically.

"I'm in, but you first." The cheerful tone of her voice surprised him.

"You'll love this!" Jim grabbed a duffel with a bar of soap, shampoo, and a towel. "Let's go!"

Holding hands, they hurried to the water's edge. Gentle waves lapped against the sandstone where he set the bag near the shoreline. He pulled his t-shirt over his neck and tossed it next to the bag.

"Do you live in the gym?" Sheila asked, looking him up and down.

"What?"

"You're ripped!"

"A ten-thousand acre gym, I guess," Jim responded, kicking free of his flip-flops. He dove in, surfacing twenty feet away. He spun to look back. Sheila stood, her athletic curvy figure accentuated by a bra and g-string. She tested the water with pointed toes.

"Stay there a second."

"Why?"

"Taking a mental picture."

She smiled at the comment.

"I was wondering when you'd notice more than my eyes."

"I thought we established my note taking."

"Can I dive in now?"

Jim nodded.

"Here goes nothing!" The dive barely rippled the water. After coming to the surface and swimming toward him, her arms wrapped around his shoulders and neck as she pulled herself close.

"Wow," Sheila said. "Look at the sky!"

"Pretty cool, huh?"

"You were right; I love this place."

The stars stretched to the horizon in every direction, their constant beauty looking down at Jim like they had for years as he wondered if he'd ever be anything but worn-out and alone. A montage of lonely nights, reaching back to boot camp, stampeded past him and out of view. He shivered, then his heart filled and poured into her. In a rush, every positive emotion he held for anyone, long stored away or wished for, surged between them. Their breathing was in-sync.

"You're wrong," Jim teased.

"About what?"

"Here goes nothing doesn't fit."

"What does?" she asked.

"Here comes everything."

35

arly Saturday, Skinner Strobel rode home in the back seat of the team bus from Laramie. He pushed the latches inward, dropping the window to let in more air. Sagebrush and diesel fumes blew in, mixing with the stench of dirty, week-old teenage laundry.

"Open the windows," he ordered. "This bus reeks!"

His teammates scampered, opening all of the windows even though the morning air was still cold.

On the back of Skinner's forearm, he traced his favorite bruise, the mesh pattern of some opposing player's jersey.

I should get it inked. His first tattoo would be the perfect way to remember football camp, and thinking his dad would shit his church clothes at seeing his only son tattooed made Skinner chuckle.

Apart from his forearm, most of his body ached, each bruise a reminder of a running back he'd tackled or an offensive lineman he'd blocked. Though none of them had hurt at the time, now the pain helped him relive the collision; and the coolest part was that in three days his seventeen-year-old body would be mostly healed.

Wolverine has nothing on me, Skinner thought, as he looked at the plaque resting in his lap, naming him the camp's outstanding linebacker. *I can't wait to show this to Jim.*

As fun as the past week had been—anticipating the snap count or thinking about formations—it all left his mind as his best friend, George Peterson, plopped down in the other backseat.

"Brought you something, bro," George said, tossing him a Red Bull.

"Right on." Skinner popped the top and chugged half. "Thanks."

"You workin' out at Jim's next week?"

"I hope my mom'll run me before church tomorrow."

"Like that'll happen." George teased. "She say any more about what went down Sunday?"

"Just what I told you, dawg." Skinner covered his mouth, forcing the Red Bull burp through his nostrils to enjoy the tingle. "She said Jim dropped by the hospital to see the black guy."

"You think Jim'll talk to you about killing those guys?"

"Doubtful." Skinner shook his head. "I asked him once about the Gulf War."

"No way, bro. What'd he say?"

"He pretended not to hear me."

Skinner chugged the rest. The miles flew past while he thought about the scout camp four years ago where Jim came to help with his horses. After helping wrangle animals and gather firewood, Jim made him an offer.

"Interested in a job?"

Skinner had worked hard to make an impression, and he was proud to be the one scout out of a dozen who got Jim's nod. On his first day at the ranch as a thirteen-year-old, he struggled to lift a single bale of hay. Now he could snatch one in each hand and toss them twice as high as his six feet.

Jim taught him what needed to be done and paid him fairly, and Skinner liked working at the ranch so much he almost quit sports until Jim talked him out of it.

"Wrestle and play football now. I'm glad I did. You can work your whole life after high school."

Skinner soon grew stronger than most adults, and he began

challenging Jim to the occasional wrestling match—always unsuccessfully. The first time he tried, Jim pinned him in under a minute. After all, Jim was his boss, and it was uncomfortable being as aggressive as he would be with someone the same age.

"I don't give head starts," Jim said as he extended a hand to help Skinner off his back.

The next time, it took several minutes, but the result was the same.

"Gone all week then, bro?" George's whining brought him back to the present.

"Wish I could go straight there and miss church tomorrow."

"Not happening with your ol' man, bro. That guy's got religion on the brain."

"One more year, and I'm out of the house."

"Think the wrestling scholarship will come through?" George asked.

"Hope so," Skinner responded. "That or football at a Junior College."

36

The horses pushed and shoved for better position at the grain bucket in Brody's hands. He let each one take a mouthful as he turned in a circle to distribute the mixture of corn, oats, and barley. The yearling stud-colt he wanted had yet to make his way forward, no doubt weighing his desire for the sweet smelling grain against his instinct to flee from any threat.

"You're not stupid," Brody told the horse. *I'm a predator in a predatory mood.*

When the colt finally came, Brody shooed the other horses away to let the animal eat alone, while he slipped a halter over its nose. Before the colt realized what had happened, Brody had buckled the halter above its ears. The half-grown horse pulled back, but Brody was ready. His boot heels skidded a few feet in the dirt, then the colt stopped and took a step forward to eat more oats. With the grain bucket in hand and the horse haltered, he led the animal to the barn, where he intentionally locked the colt in the middle stall. Brody emptied the oats into the manger and forked in some hay, but the yearling wanted none of it and started to prance and whinny.

"That's the way," Brody told the horse. 'Stay noisy all night."

The whinnying and prancing, along with an occasional banging hoof against a board, followed Brody until he shut the house door and went to the kitchen for lunch.

After a sloppy Joe and some cookies, he went to get his guns. The cylinder in his .45 Colt Peacemaker spun with an easy rhythmic click. He checked to make sure he had five rounds loaded, leaving the hammer over the empty cylinder. Beneath his bed was a Winchester double-barrel twelve-gauge shotgun. The gun was unloaded, so Brody put in a pair of number four rounds he used for goose hunting. Revolver in his waistband and shotgun in hand, he made his way back to the barn, where he deposited the shotgun in the stall next to the jazzed up colt—which hadn't slowed one bit.

On his next trip, Brody brought in an old army cot and pillow, then returned to the house for a canteen, his winter Carhartt coat, and a wool blanket. He broke open and spread a half-bale of straw at the bottom of the ladder.

After feeding Duke, Brody took him to the basement and locked him in the cement room beneath the porch. Back in the stall, the cot looked inviting, and Brody sat. Guilt wouldn't let him lay down, so he found an old horse-blanket in the tack-room and took it to Duke. The dog's whine and prancing meant he needed to be let out, so Brody let him run to the corral to take care of business.

Brody called him back to the house and the cement room, where Duke stretched on the old blanket. Brody smiled before re-locking the door and returning to the stall with the noisy yearling stud-colt neighbor. Even though the colt's separation anxiety was still in high gear, Brody dozed until dusk, with the horse constantly prancing and calling to the herd.

Brody woke a half hour before three men entered the barn through the corral. Over their shoulders were assault rifles tricked out with all sorts of gadgets Brody didn't recognize. In spite of the firepower, Brody figured their mission was to kidnap, or Jim would have been dead already. They looked the part of military, but their clothing sounded new and stiff. It reminded him of Jim's buddy, the big boots, big hat, no cattle, California transplant.

Skinner would call these three "posers." Trained soldiers would never risk congregating in one place.

Rain and thunder started around ten-thirty. The colt, who had calmed down to some degree, started to whinny and pace the stall as the rain echoed beneath the tin roof.

"Horse is noisy," somebody said.

"I could shoot it."

"And risk being heard? Don't forget, this guy killed three men."

With the rain and the colt covering any sound, Brody slipped from the stall and set the first trap at the bottom of the ladder. The other two he placed a few feet away in spots they would walk as they came to rescue their friend. He covered the rusty, makeshift land mines with straw, and slipped back in the stall.

He rechecked the shotgun and the Colt Peacemaker.

For three hours an occasional muffled whisper, fart, or sneeze broke through the rain. A floorboard squeaked and a voice spoke.

"Let's go warm up. Looks like Cooper lives another day."

Brody eyed the ceiling as footsteps moved above and dust settled through ceiling cracks that glittered in the light from outside lamps. A foot descended through the trap door to the top rung. Five steps down the ladder, the man came fully into view, a rifle slung over his back, and a pistol on his belt.

From the lowest rung he turned and stepped directly into the trap. Straw flew as the trap sprang shut with a loud pop. The man groaned as his broken leg collapsed, causing him to face-plant into one of the two remaining traps. There was another metallic snap and then silence as the jaws crushed his neck.

Brody didn't blink, swallow, or look away.

"We have a situation!" a man yelled, climbing down three steps before jumping. The mercenary landed on his feet but fell forward, his hand tripping the third trap. His enclosed forearm swung freely below his crushed elbow, and he screamed like he'd just lost his arm to a chainsaw.

Brody threw open the stall door and shot him in the head with the shotgun.

"Your two friends is dead!" he yelled. "Drop your weapons and clothes. Come down naked."

"Not gonna happen," the voice came back.

"I'll turn out the horse and torch the barn!"

"Only heard one shot. How do I know you killed both?"

"Use your flashlight, but shine it on me and I'll shoot.

A scuffling on the floor sent more dust through the floorboards and a beam shone on the bodies.

"I'm not coming down naked!"

"The fuck you won't."

The colt stopped pacing.

"I ain't strippin'!"

"Naked or I'll shoot." Brody's breath cycled in and out. "Now!"

The yelling made the horse forget its separation anxiety and it started eating from the manger.

To Brody's surprise, a boot landed in the straw. A rustling above and the next boot fell, as did the socks, pants, shirt, underwear, pistol, and rifle.

"Come down, and you'll live." Brody eyed the trap door.

"Do I have your word?"

"Now." Brody watched as the naked man descended, and then stared at his two dead companions.

"Over there." Brody motioned with the shotgun.

"I'da never given up to you. I thought—I thought you was Cooper!" the man stammered.

"You wanna' insult me again?"

"Not with that shotgun, old timer. Just give me my boots and pants. I'll vanish."

Brody stepped toward the pile of clothing, and the man spoke his relief.

"Thank you. You'll never see me again, I promise."

Brody unsheathed the man's silenced pistol and the bargaining went into high gear.

"I did what you said. I came down naked. You said I'd live!"

With the shotgun in his right hand, Brody aimed the pistol left-handed and shot the man two inches below the ribcage. The man fell backwards, blood oozing between his fingers like chocolate syrup in the dim light.

The man drew an agonized breath and Brody decided against a humane bullet. After resting the shotgun against the wall at easy reach, and placing the pistol in his waistband, Brody pulled the can of Copenhagen in his back pocket. A pinch of nicotine would counter-act the adrenaline even though partaking wasn't Brody's regular habit.

"Shit," the man sobbed. "Look at me!"

After bottoming the chew in the crevice of his lip, Brody spat. "Who sent you?" He reseated the tobacco and spat again.

The man's pupils relaxed and all muscle tone and the tension vanished as life slipped from his body.

Without even blinking, Brody strode from the barn and returned driving a backhoe. He killed the motor and rolled the bodies into the front-end loader. He forked the bloody straw over them, then bleached the floor where blood had pooled. After the bleach he poured on hydrogen peroxide. The effort went unappreciated except for the colt, who finally stopped pacing to watch a master resurrect dormant skills, as the bubbling elixir fizzed away the blood splatters.

Rifling through the dead men's pockets, Brody found the keys to the SUV. The intermittent rain dampened Brody's coat as he walked to where the vehicle was again parked in the cornfield. He took it to a place surrounded by willows near a public fishing hole. The spot was often used, but the vehicle wasn't visible from the road, and Brody figured it would be weeks before anyone found or worried about it. The straw cowboy hat on his head was like a sieve as raindrops ran down his cheeks during the four-mile walk back to the barnyard.

The weapons and gear, including three bulletproof vests, were hidden in a dried-up storm drain, and Brody was on his way to dig a grave.

As he rounded the corner past the house, he thought again about Jim. It was good the boss didn't know what just happened.

Some decisions weren't meant to be made by committee.

Then he thought of Skinner who would be coming the next day.

Good to have some company. I bet he takes state in wrestling this year.

The backhoe creaked and the diesel engine rattled as he drove through the pine trees behind the barn and up an old access road toward a meadow. At the desired spot, Brody dumped the bodies and straw, dropped the outriggers, and began digging the mud on the downhill side of a trough, where the excess water soaked the ground.

The rain began again in earnest as he worked. It smacked the windshield as mud, manure, and diesel fumes seeped into the cab. Brody dug to the machine's limit of twelve feet. Without leaving the cab, he scraped the bodies and bloody straw into the hole with the mechanical shovel.

Dead people look stupid, he thought.

Then he levered the door open, stood on the step outside the cab, and lobbed the SUV's keys on top of the bodies before backfilling the hole.

He drove away, knowing that, within a few days, the cattle would tromp through the area, covering any tire tracks that weren't already erased by the storm. It made him think of where the SUV had been in the corn, so he drove to the spot and rolled the backhoe tires over the crushed stalks.

Rain swirled in the headlights, as he came into the barnyard. He parked inside the Quonset and stepped into the rain where he fumbled in the dark to get a hydrant's hose attached to a pressure washer. After a thorough spraying, he poured on peroxide and scrubbed everywhere the machine might have been in contact with body parts, then rinsed everything again.

The backhoe's never been so clean.

He thought to check his phone. Sure enough, there was a text from Skinner. "B there tomorrow night, unless you need me sooner."

Skinner had been teaching him how to text, but it was clumsy. Brody pushed buttons for a few minutes before he had the screen for a response.

"Will avoid that trap not yor excus to mis chruch"

Within seconds the response came. It was four thirty in the morning. "Church sucks. I'd rather dig post holes."

It took Brody just over a minute to text back. "then yer stupd why up this early?"

"Not early. Late. Mom and dad fighting. What's your excuse?" came the answer, almost instantly.

After fumbling for three minutes Brody chuckled before pushing send. "Boss is gon so i party lik tenagr got 2 little time 2 waste it being old."

"U D man dawg! Way to roll. Remind me 2 show you T9 tomorrow"

T9? Must be some video. Damn, that kid's fast.

Brody's stomach grumbled. The pickup fired after pumping the gas pedal. He drove into town to the all night diner, and ordered pancakes, bacon, scrambled eggs, toast and hash browns. For the first time in days, he deserved a respite.

In spite of several cups of coffee, the food and warm building made him drowsy. The sun was peeking above the valley's eastern mountains as he walked in the backdoor of the ranch house. He slipped his boots off on the porch. In his bedroom, he shed his clothing down to his thermals, and collapsed with the Peacemaker at hand under the covers.

It's been fifty years.

A muffled whimper came from Duke. Grumbling, Brody threw back his blankets, got up and headed downstairs. The basement's cold cement floor stung his bare feet as he let the dog out and grabbed the horse-blanket to take to the barn later. Duke ran up the stairs.

His claws clicked across the kitchen floor as he squeezed through the pet door.

Duke must need to visit the corral.

A pillow between his knees helped his sore hips, and the Peacemaker hidden beneath the cool sheets hastened his slumber. Exhaustion shut down his senses. With no smells, sounds, sights, and the numbness almost complete, a final thought followed Brody into hibernation.

Some things are like riding a bike.

37

The sun broke over the red rock landscape to the west of Lake Mead. To the northwest, undulating sandstone formations curved and dipped as though God poured a hardening sandstone batter over an uneven surface. Sheila lay curled up beside him, her head nestled in the crook of his shoulder, her shin resting between his knees.

Under the moonlight they swam, talked, kissed, and snuggled, but her reluctance to go further was obvious, and Jim didn't push. He woke up throughout the night, each time realizing their breathing was in-sync. Her body next to his brought a clear-headed intoxication, a connection beyond physical attraction. His mind raced ahead, jumping to the possibility of unfulfilled dreams. He felt foolish, like betting on an unseen horse. But the harder he tried to bridle the wishful thinking, the more it raced undirected toward the end of his life as a bachelor.

ALTHOUGH SHEILA KNEW JIM WAS awake, she said nothing. With her head on his chest, she listened to his heartbeat, strong and steady, a resolute rhythm beating life through his body. She wondered how long she could laze, pretending to sleep.

Could time slow down? Could she will it?

Her actions the night before were a calculated test. Each thing she said and did was a question, an examination she'd dreamt of giving to the right man. For the past five years she'd hoped to find the right guy to put through the paces—Jim had passed with flying colors.

If she were ever to trust a man, he'd have to do the one thing she had never dared try. He'd have to be willing to wait. The guy she could tease to the brink of sex, who could control himself, would be a true protector. Making Jim think he had a sure thing, and then reneging showed her everything about his self-control. In the world of men, last night proved everything Sheila didn't think possible. Jim obviously wanted her, but didn't even pout when she got him wound up and stopped.

As the sun inched higher, Sheila raised her head and looked at the man she never thought she'd meet. He looked back at her, the smile on his face genuine, like he had never been so happy.

38

Skinner attended church with his family, and in the evening he packed his stuff and his mother drove him to the Cooper Ranch.

"Your dad lectures me about the Sabbath Day, which is fine, but I'm the one who takes you out here at O-dark-thirty," she said as they got in the car to leave.

As they pulled into the barnyard, Duke growled a protective warning until Skinner unrolled his window, called the dog to the car and petted him. Sally grabbed his arm as he leaned into the door to open it. "We need to talk."

"What?" Skinner was in a good mood, and the worry in her voice surprised him.

"Your father didn't want you coming out here."

"He doesn't want me to earn some money?"

"It's what happened. Jim brought the toughest-looking man I've ever seen into the hospital."

"Right, the black guy. Sister Bott, the Robot, went on and on in Sunday School."

"Enough with the nicknames. Did she teach a lesson?"

"She talked about Jesus walking on water and Peter sinking. Then she told us about the black dude."

"Did she tell you how badly he was hurt?"

"Just that when she brung food with the Relief Society he was pretty fu—" Skinner stopped himself mid-word. "Messed up."

Hopefully his mother would give him credit for catching himself before completing the F-bomb.

"Brought food, not brung."

Skinner smiled. "Right. Brought. I got it."

"I've never taken care of someone like that."

"Really?"

"I'm sure Jim saved his life." Sally paused. "There are rumors floating around about these people coming to take revenge."

"And Dad's worried about me getting mixed up in it somehow." Skinner rolled his eyes.

"He wants what's best for you."

"As long as what's best involves church." Skinner knew he had crossed the line.

Sally paused. "He's being protective. Promise you'll be careful and call if there's any trouble."

"I will, Mom. Tell Dad thanks for letting me come."

"You need tell him yourself."

Skinner leaned over and gave his mom a rare kiss on the cheek. After opening the door and grabbing his duffel from the back seat, he looked back through the open window.

"Thanks for driving me out here, Mom. Love you!"

"Thanks for the kiss. I won't tell the guys." Sally backed up then came forward in a three-point-turn around. She waved and blew him a kiss, and then she pulled away slowly, as if looking for something.

Skinner was on the porch turning the knob when Brody hollered from somewhere in the barnyard.

"Stow yer shit. I need a hand."

Good to see you, too. Skinner grinned.

After chucking his things in his usual bedroom, he tromped from the house without shutting the back door. Then he followed Duke to where Brody's boots were sticking out from beneath the swather in the Quonset.

"I thought we had all the hay in," Skinner said.

"Jim wants to cut the high meadows instead of grazing it out." Brody's reply was partially muffled beneath the machine. "Wants to sell some hay to the California transplant."

"Makes sense."

"Up to me, I'd let the winter starve him out." The old man's legs kicked like a running back at the bottom of the pile, but Skinner had no idea what he was fixing.

"Hand me the end wrench from the table."

Skinner placed the wrench in Brody's greasy palm.

"No. The five-eighths, and climb yer ass under. God gave you my third hand."

Skinner did as Brody told him. The old man was working on tightening up the belt drive that ran the swather's blades and turned the crusher as the hay was cut.

"Belts started slipping last time."

"So where's Jim?"

"Gallivantin', trainin' horses, and lookin' at some forest service land where he holds grazing rights."

"When's he get back?" The belts were tightened, and Skinner slid from beneath the swather.

"Few days. More maybe."

Brody was still beneath, and Skinner was glad because it kept the old man from seeing his disappointment over not being able to tell Jim about being named outstanding linebacker.

"So, has Jim talked about killing those three guys?"

Brody inched out and Skinner extended a hand to lift the old man to his feet.

"Not much. If the boss wants, he'll speak. Otherwise, leave him be."

"I won't bug him," Skinner replied.

"Didn't figure you would." Brody stepped forward and pressed a gnarled old finger into Skinner's chest. "You need to tell me if you see someone snooping."

"You think they'll try to get revenge?"

"I don't think, boy. I know."

Even though the boy reference chafed, Skinner listened to the old man like an Eminem lyric. He has already dismissed his mother's worry as routine, but Brody's stare lingered, putting emphasis on his words.

"Promise me, boy. Anything outta the ordinary, high tail it and come find me."

"I will," Skinner lied. "Anything else you need tonight?"

"Na," Brody responded shaking his head. "Let's hit it first thing in the morning." Skinner tried to return at normal speed to the house and the backdoor he'd left open. If anyone came snooping, he wouldn't need a third hand, and he wouldn't feel any bruises until the next day.

Maybe some things are as exciting as football.

39

Skinner breakfasted with Brody at daybreak.

"Fence by the road needs fixing," the old man muttered into an oversized coffee mug. "We'll winter the cows there."

"Makes sense, it's closer to the house."

"Don't talk with your mouth full," Brody grumbled. "Load a spool of barbed wire and the tools in the bucket of the old tractor. I'll find you something else when you finish."

After three bowls of cereal, a toasted peanut butter sandwich, and two slabs of ham from the fridge, Skinner grabbed a cookie and slipped out to the barn to gather the supplies. At the public road bordering the ranch, he turned the tractor west to start at the end of the fence and work his way east.

After stretching wire for almost four hours, the sound of a diesel engine slowing to a stop caused Skinner to look up. A flatbed wrecker with no name on the door panel pulled partially off the shoulder. The driver put an unlit cigar in his mouth before opening the door and walking forward.

"How far's Afton?" he asked without removing the cigar. A short-sleeved mechanic's jumpsuit with 'Dan' in the name-patch covered the man's barrel chest and protruding belly. A balding dome contrasted with thick hair on his oversized forearms and chest.

"Fifteen miles," Skinner said. "Where you from?"

"It's quite the place. Who owns it?"

Skinner looked at what the man was so impressed with. In the distance, the ranch house and buildings sat atop a knoll, looking down over a thousand acres of pasture, all bordered with aspen and pine trees.

"Not sure," Skinner replied, snagging a hammer from where he left it in the grass. "I work for a fence contractor."

Sunlight reflected from a gold rope necklace nestled between the man's jumpsuit and chest hair. His sunglasses, gold rimmed and mirrored, looked expensive, but the black, heavy soled work boots fit what mechanics wore, and the jumpsuit had several grease stains.

"About fifteen miles?" Dan extended his hand, a powerful grip that reminded Skinner of Jim's, minus the calluses. In his other hand, he twisted the cigar in his clean fingertips.

Poser for sure, Skinner thought considering how much grease his nail beds caught in a few minutes under the swather with Brody.

Dan returned to the still idling wrecker and pulled away. The Nevada license plate caught Skinner's attention "like a turd in a punchbowl" as Brody would sometimes say.

All the grownups he knew would urge caution. Their collective voices rang in his head, especially his father's. "Violence is only called for as a self defense measure."

If I were as tentative on the football field or wrestling mat as adults tell me to be at everything else, we'd never win a game, and I'd never win a match!

Skinner snatched the phone from his pocket and held down number two.

"George?"

"Wassup. Thought you was at Jim's all week."

"I'm on the main road. Bounce out here and get me."

"Cool! What're we gonna do?"

"A guy just came by that could be Tony Soprano's brother."

"Really? Don't shit me."

"You gotta be my wheels, but keep it quiet!" Skinner insisted.

"What's the plan?"

"Spy on him, I guess. Find out if he's really who I think he is."

"Be there in a minute."

As the biggest kid in the school, George liked confrontation almost as much as Skinner. In his haste, he had probably left the TV on and would drive twice the limit. *I hope he doesn't get busted for speeding.*

Skinner slid the phone back in his pocket, and took a long drink from a water bottle then sat on the tractor's front tire. Movement caught his eye, and he looked up to see Brody driving in one of Jim's old trucks.

Shit!

Skinner quickly stuffed his hands back into his heavy leatherwork gloves, and was crimping the stretcher to the top rung of barbed wire as Brody drove up.

"I'm headed to town." The old man got out of the truck, sauntering over for an inspection.

"When I'm done, I'll reset the gate on the north pasture," Skinner said, hoping the old man would pick at his ass and leave.

"The tools are scattered from hell to breakfast." Brody scowled at where Skinner had dumped the hammer in the grass next to some pliers and wire snips.

"I'll pick 'em up." Skinner scanned the horizon for George's car.

"You looking for something?" the old-timer asked.

"No." Skinner pounded a fencing nail over a strand of wire, securing it to the wooden post, then looked up to see Brody returning a can of Copenhagen to his rear pocket. "When did you start chewing?"

Brody spat. "The boss'll shit himself sideways if he sees these tools."

Jim's never said an angry word to me. Skinner wanted to say it, but bit his lower lip.

"I'm headed to Soda Springs for alfalfa seed. Be back after dark."

Brody looked down the fence line. "Messy or not, you're doing good here."

Skinner smiled at the first complement he'd ever heard the old-timer offer.

Brody spat again before climbing in and starting the pickup. As the truck lurched forward, he barked through the open window. "Surprise me. Don't forget the tools."

Within minutes, George pulled up, the passenger door flying open before he stopped.

"How we gonna find this guy?" George asked as Skinner slipped in.

"He's drivin' a flatbed wrecker."

"So?"

"So we find the wrecker we find the guy."

"Where we gonna look first?" George asked.

"Where would we go for lunch—if we were old enough to get a beer?"

George's eyes widened as the realization came to him. "Marty's!"

Down a side street in town, Marty's Bar served the few non-Mormons and the rest of the Jack Mormon population. Jim and Brody had taken Skinner there for dinner once after working all day. Skinner hadn't told his folks, but he did tell George, only to be twenty-questioned about everything from what the waitresses wore, to how good the cheeseburger tasted. Skinner patiently answered, knowing that, roles reversed, he'd want to know everything about a place so forbidden by their parents.

"Pull us down the alley around back. I bet you anything the wrecker's there," Skinner said as they got close.

"No way. My folks'll kill me if I get caught."

"Tell 'em I needed to find Brody." Skinner shrugged.

It was only a few minutes after one o'clock when they rolled down the alleyway and into the parking lot. Several dusty pickups were parked close to the rear entrance.

"Maybe he wasn't really a gangster," George suggested.

"I'm sure of it," Skinner insisted, but he suddenly felt deflated. He'd been sure this was going to turn into the most exciting thing to happen all year.

"Let's cruise past Janice and Shelly's." George smiled. "They might be sun bathing."

"Go for it," Skinner said, not really interested.

At the road in front of Marty's, George turned right, making for the homes of the two prettiest girls in town. But when they were still three blocks away, the Nevada-plated, flatbed tow truck came into view, signaling a left turn at the curb of Johnson's wrecking yard. Perched on the wrecker's deck was a tan Escalade.

"Shit! That's our boy! Roll past, but be casual," Skinner said nervously, hoping the man hadn't seen him behind the mirrored sunglasses.

"What do you want me to do?" George asked.

"Go around the block." Skinner whipped his head right then left to keep from losing sight. "And tail him slowly."

George followed Skinner's suggestion then a few seconds before Marty's, the wrecker signaled and pulled down the alleyway.

"Park down the block," Skinner suggested. "Looks like our boy's hungry."

After pulling to the curb a block from the bar, George dropped the car into park and turned to his friend.

"What're we gonna do if he pulls a gun on us, like they did Jim last week?"

"Relax, we're just gonna go check it out." Skinner pulled the latch and shouldered the door open. The afternoon sun warmed him as he looked down the street toward Marty's. "Come on. Let's go check out the Escalade before he finishes lunch."

As the teenagers approached, the aroma of frying burgers wafted toward them.

"Smells good, I'm hungry."

"Me, too," Skinner responded over his shoulder as he trotted twenty yards ahead. At the alley, Skinner sprinted behind the bar. The same trucks were parked close to the back door, and in the back corner of the lot, a few feet from the fence, the sun reflected from the Escalade's chrome wheels like a boy scout signal mirror. Gravel crunched behind him as George lumbered down the alley, sweat beading on his brow.

Standing next to Skinner, George bent over, putting his palms on his knees.

"I can lift the weight room," George huffed. "But run a block and I'm a tub of lard!"

"Come on." Skinner loped like a deer across the parking lot.

Skinner stood on the wrecker's running board to look in the cab. A few papers were scattered across the dash. A large bag of chips sat in the passenger seat, the opening turned toward the driver. In the cup holder near the floor was a large coffee mug.

"Check out the rims. This baby's tricked out!" George's voice came from behind.

Skinner turned to look at his friend who was studying the Escalade's wheels next to the passenger-side rear door.

"These low profile tires . . ."

Suddenly, the door flew open, smashing into George's forehead. Skinner took a step forward, but didn't get there before George fell forward, his head kinked unnaturally under the wrecker's rear tire.

"George!" Skinner took another step, but a pistol barrel peeked out from behind the Escalade's open door.

Skinner dove beneath the wrecker's deck and rolled to his feet on the other side. One step forward and he vaulted the six-foot picket fence at the edge of the parking lot, landing in a ditch flowing with cool irrigation water that immediately topped his boots.

Was it a gun barrel, or just a cigar?

"Your friend's hurt." The voice was too quiet. The man obviously didn't want anyone but Skinner to hear. "Come back and we'll talk."

Skinner couldn't see over or through the fence. Where he stood, the ditch ran next to the fence line, but a plank was missing ten feet upstream. After sloshing upstream as quietly as possible, he took a baseball-size stone from the streambed and looked through the opening.

Marty's back door, which had glass from top to bottom, was at least forty yards away, and he doubted he could jump high enough to make the throw over the fence and hit the door.

From the other side of the fence, the wrecker door opened and closed and the diesel motor ignited. He thought of the truck's rear tire crushing George's head, and a wave of panic propelled him back onto the fence, but his soaked boots and the stone in his right hand slowed the ascent.

Clearing the fence, he wanted to vomit as the truck lurched forward. He landed in a stumble and heaved the stone through the driver's side window, shattering it into thousands of small pieces, but the truck kept moving. Another step and he leapt on the running board, reaching through the shattered opening trying to yank the wheel. Dan glanced a punch off Skinner's face, then hit his throat directly and stomped on the breaks, sending Skinner air-born.

Skinner's lungs whined like a kinked vacuum hose as they expanded, trying unsuccessfully to pull air past bruised and contracting throat muscles.

He stood. The ground heaved beneath his boots, the same direction at first and then like Jell-o. In his periphery, things became bluish then black as the edges got bigger. He looked for George with reverse telescope vision.

Did the water feel like this when Peter walked to Jesus?

A tipping sensation and the cheese-grater sharp gravel against the exposed skin of his arm and cheek made him aware that he'd fallen. A wisp of dusty air slipped into Skinner's lungs, but it wasn't enough.

George?

The gravel against his face was losing its sharpness, another thought of Peter sinking.

Oh, Skinner of little faith.

The thought brought a smile. He thought he heard a horn blaring as the gravel became a pillow, welcoming his unconsciousness with cold indifference.

Twenty seconds later, he woke, neck relaxed, and breathing. The sun, directly above, burned his eyes, reminding him of The Brian Regan Comedy Routine.

I might have just won the sun stare!

Somewhere to his left, he heard the unmistakable sound of a shell being pumped into the chamber of a shotgun.

"Get out of the car!" Marty Junior stood shoulder-to-shoulder with several bar patrons.

The man stepped down from the wrecker, hundreds of glass particles either clinging to his clothing or falling to the ground. He tried to brush off, but Marty stopped him.

"Hands in the air!"

"These teenagers attacked me. He threw a rock through my window!"

"You okay, bro?" George walked over and helped Skinner to his feet.

"I'm just glad you are."

"He's gotta be one of 'em," a man said, his palm resting on the handle of his thigh-length bowie knife. "We all know who owns that Escalade."

"Let's beat his ass!" the man beside him yelled.

"Nonsense!" Brody's voice cracked like a whip.

The crowd turned in unison to see him standing twenty feet behind next to his truck, which was blocking the alley. "He'll go after I have what I want."

The crowd parted like a pack of wolves for the alpha male as

Brody walked between them and stood eye to eye with the wrecker driver.

"One quick move and he'll shoot you." Brody motioned to Marty, who stepped closer and pointed the shotgun at Dan's head from five feet away.

Brody rooted through Dan's front pockets, producing a cell phone, and wallet. After placing the phone in his own pocket, he rifled through the wallet.

"Let's take it all. Split up his money!" someone from the back of the crowd suggested.

"We ain't thieves!" The thick fury in Brody's voice made everyone in the crowd step back. The glare under his cowboy hat left no doubt who was in charge.

"I agree, but what are you doing with his wallet?" Marty asked.

"He'll leave when I know who he is." Brody removed the man's driver's license then dropped the wallet in the gravel.

"All right, mister?" Brody squinted as he held the license as far away as he could. "Ralf Faletto?" Brody asked like a first grader who just sounded out his first word. "Or is it Dan?"

Silence.

"You wanna leave here in one piece?"

"My name is what the license says."

"I think he had a gun on me," Skinner croaked, the words tickling his throat. He hacked and coughed for thirty seconds or so as Brody opened the wrecker and found a Kershaw knife and Beretta pistol under the front seat. He walked over to Ralf, shaking them in the gangster's face.

"If I'da found you first, you'da lost more than your driver's license and some weapons."

Ralf moved his eyes to stare back at Brody, but said nothing.

Brody drove his boot heel into Ralf's knee with a sickening crunch. As the big man crumpled, Brody kicked his head. Ralf rolled over, dazed but conscious as Brody pressed the confiscated pistol into his upper lip.

"Tell whoever sent you that the road runs both ways." Brody took a step back, but kept the pistol aimed between the gangster's eyes. The mobster stood, unsteady and leaning a bit then limped backward toward the wrecker.

Ralf brushed some of the glass away before sitting, and Brody kicked the door closed without dropping aim.

"Someone move my truck!"

"Where's the key?" the bowie wearer asked after climbing in.

"It don't need one. Just twist."

As Brody's truck moved forward, the wrecker tires rolled past, crunching the gravel. The crowd yelled threats while Brody tucked the Beretta in his waistband and walked to stand between Skinner and George.

Marty Junior stood at the gate to the parking lot.

"Don't ever come back," he said, shotgun in hand. Then he latched the gate and faced the crowd. "Inside to talk this over."

As the people began filing in the back door, George and Skinner looked at each other, not believing they had been invited.

"That means both of you." Marty waved them toward the doorway.

"I thought we had to be twenty-one," George replied.

"Only if you're not accompanied by an adult, and we're gonna be officially closed while we talk anyway."

Once inside, Marty racked the shotgun in a pair of elk antlers behind the bar and turned to his employees.

"Serve burgers and fries for anyone who wants 'em. Slide the tables together. Grab the first aid kit, and let's take a closer look at Skinner and George."

Twenty-two-year-old Wendy Frandsen may not have had Barbie doll looks, but at just over five feet tall, her fit, muscular body and clear complexion turned most men's heads. She disappeared behind the bar for a second, reemerging with a first aid kit, and walked over to Skinner, who had some deep scrapes from hitting the parking lot. His upper lip was split and his ribs and neck were bruised.

"You smile at me in church," she said, her breasts inches from his face, "but I can't get you to hold still long enough to talk."

Skinner blushed as Wendy smeared a Band-Aid with Neosporin and put it over a scrape above his cheek.

"You need to say hello to me, okay?"

"I will." Skinner nodded. "Thanks for patching me up."

As Wendy walked back to the bar to put the first aid kit away, George kicked Skinner in the side of the leg under the table. Then Marty brought a towel full of ice for George to place over the egg-sized lump on his forehead.

"This is how I see it," Marty started. "Jim's our friend, and we sent a message that we'll look after our own."

Everyone at the table nodded.

"Hell, yeah," bowie man said as he raised his glass.

The waitresses brought beers and a platter of cheeseburgers and fries to everyone—George and Skinner had to settle for quart-sized mugs of root beer.

"All I'm suggesting is that we be Jim's eyes and ears," Marty continued. "Put his number on speed dial, and call him if you see anything."

"We aren't talking about maybes," Brody said from the head of the table. "Jim killed men with families."

"Gotta suggestion?" Marty asked.

"What you said and more. Alert each other—every one of us—the minute someone comes, and confront them together."

Marty unfolded his arms. "Not much happens I don't hear of. Any of you can call, and we'll stop everything."

Everyone in the room mumbled their agreement.

"Let's reopen in a half hour."

George and Brody got up and went to the men's room while

Skinner remained, opening and closing a fist he hadn't realized was bruised from skidding into the parking lot. Some of the patrons left or went to the pool table. Wendy smiled as she tugged the beer lever to refill someone's mug. She tippy toed to get another mug, filled it, and turned around to gaze at Skinner. As she brushed past him, she leaned over, the smell of perfume or scented shampoo clearing his short-term memory.

"Following that guy for Jim was brave," she said.

"I like it in here," George said, coming back from the restroom. "Let's stay for dinner."

"Skinner needs to gather the tools he left in the grass."

The two young men and the elderly cowboy walked out of the bar, saying goodbye to the remaining patrons.

"Thanks for lunch!" George hollered to Marty, who raised a hand in response.

As George pulled away, Brody turned to Skinner. "You're a pain in the ass."

"So are you!"

Brody's eyebrows dropped into a scowl as he stood a little straighter. Skinner braced for a punch or a backhand, but Brody's words caught him off-guard.

"D'you learn anything?"

Skinner touched the band-aid on his temple. "Those assholes fight dirty?"

"And?"

"I should ask for help next time."

Brody tilted his hat back. "I'd have done the same at your age."

As they pulled out of the parking lot, Skinner's hand bumped something hard on the seat beneath an old jacket: a cocked Colt Peacemaker and a pair of binoculars. Skinner palmed the gun and opened the trap door to make sure it was loaded. "Alfalfa seed in Soda Springs, huh?"

"The gate at the north pasture still needs resetin'."

The pickup rattled and Skinner rolled his window down to scoop the air with his bruised right hand. His neck reminded him of a nasty case of laryngitis in third grade since even a light touch or swallow ached.

"Saw the wrecker from the hillside," Brody said. "Un-cock that for me."

Skinner placed his thumb between the hammer and the gun's frame before pulling the trigger. He slipped his thumb out to let the hammer rest, and set the gun down. Brody set the Beretta next to the Peacemaker, then he arched his back and pulled the Kershaw knife from his pocket and tossed it to Skinner.

"Thanks," he said, examining the knife.

Brody pulled to the curb, put the transmission in neutral, and extended his hand. Chills ran down Skinner's spine, and his belly grew warm as the calluses and the gnarled old knuckles pressed against his palm and fingers.

"Partners," the old man informed him.

Skinner wanted to say something, but he coughed as the outside air tickled his throat.Brody got out, and dug for something behind the seat.

"Medicinal purposes," he said, tossing a flask that landed in Skinner's lap.

After twisting open the cap, he took a sip that made him cough for a few seconds, but then the burning went numb and his throat muscles relaxed. The second sip swallowed easier than the cheeseburger or icy root beer.

"What is this?"

"Jack Daniels."

"Want some?" Skinner asked.

Brody took the flask and Skinner watched as the old man took a couple of swallows and handed it back.

"Keep it handy," Brody said as he checked the rearview mirror before pulling onto the road. "It'll help heal your throat."

40

"How'd you sleep?" Jim asked after their second night on Lake Mead.

"Better than in a long time."

"It must've been the beers after swimming,"

"Or the company," Sheila said.

She kissed him gently. It was lingering, but not passionate or erotic. He pulled her close, wanting more, but she didn't reciprocate. They'd spent the previous night and the day together, waiting for the funeral to risk moving the money. Talk came easy, and so had the quiet moments when just being together was the most pleasant thing Jim had ever experienced.

"Whenever I sleep under the stars, I always wish there was someone to share the view with," Jim said, to no one in particular.

"When was the last time you slept out before coming here?"

"Last week," Jim said, recalling his night with Allen Coleman and the boy scouts.

"I'd love to see where you're from."

"You will. The plan is to head to my ranch."

"Really? Why there?"

"A ten-thousand acre gym to hide the money."

"Sounds good." Sheila paused, tucking her hair behind her ear. "Are you cool with us not going all the way?"

"That was a change of subject."

"I need an answer."

"Yes."

"You weren't disappointed?"

Jim smiled. "You and disappointment don't go in the same sentence."

The wind blew her hair free, so Sheila took a hair tie from her pocket and sat up to pull it into a ponytail. "Talk to me. I need to know what you're feeling."

"Right now is enough."

"What do you mean?"

"Being here with you is enough."

Sheila put her index finger over his lips, then kissed him with growing passion.

After a few moments, she stopped and nuzzled into his neck and cheek. It made Jim laugh.

"What's so funny?"

"It's what my horses do when they want some affection—my dog, too, for that matter."

"So now I'm a horse or dog," Sheila teased, pushing him in the shoulder.

"That sounded bad . . . I hope you're my girlfriend."

"After two nights together, I hope it's obvious."

"While we're changing the subject, we should talk about something."

"What?"

"As we leave here with the money, we'll split up. I'll send Larry and Chris in the stolen truck, and I want you with me. I think I can do this without much violence, but if anything goes bad, I need to know where you are."

"I understand."

"One more thing." Jim paused. "Before it's over, you may see me take charge. I like Larry and Chris, but the platoon does better with one Sergeant."

"I'll do whatever you ask."

Jim needed to move, thinking about what was coming up sent adrenaline through his blood. They both stood. About to pick up his clothes, he reconsidered, ran down the beach and dove in for a last-minute swim. As he surfaced, Sheila smiled. He dripped his way back to her, palmed his hair back, and put on the dry clothes over his wet body. After threading his toes into the flip-flops, he rolled up their sleeping pads, blankets and pillows.

"Damn. You look good in those shorts and tank top," Jim said as he lifted the bundle.

Sheila smiled.

"Let's go get some breakfast," Jim suggested.

Sheila turned at the truck door giving him a big hug. She wrapped her arms around his shoulders. The sudden move surprised him as she pulled his head down, to whisper something in his ear.

"Thanks for being cool for two nights in a row. You passed."

"I passed what?"

"You'll know soon enough. Why didn't you tell me about your friend?"

My friend? "You mean Bradley?"

The euphoria drained from Jim's body, replaced by a churning in his belly, like an over zealous cement mixer. He hadn't thought of the Gulf War since the moment at the cliff's edge the night before last. "I was going to, but we were having such a good time . . ." His words trailed off.

"Whoa. Hey there," Sheila said empathetically. "Don't vanish on me." She rubbed his chest like she was trying to unthaw something frozen.

"I'm sorry. What?"

"I said don't vanish on me. I've never seen anyone do what you just did. You're a different person, right down to the color in your face. You were hugging me and your arms just dropped."

Jim shook his head like a wet dog, and forced a smile. "I got strangled for a second."

"I can tell. So his name was Bradley?"

Jim nodded.

"If you want to tell me, I'd like to know." Her tone changed to enthusiasm. "But right now I think we should change the subject."

It was an obvious attempt to cheer him up, and Jim reciprocated, trying to match her enthusiasm. "I'm in, but you start."

"Do you know what I liked most about last night?" Sheila asked as Jim opened the truck door and slid in after her.

"You want me to guess?"

"Sure. Tell me what you think it might be."

"Okay," Jim responded as he put the key in the ignition and started the truck. "Was it . . . the moonlight?"

Sheila shook her head no.

"How about skinny dipping? Sleeping under the stars? My farmer tan? The beer?"

Sheila continued to shake her head.

"I give up."

"Even though I totally dig your farmer tan in the moonlight," Sheila teased. "It was how you scooped me!"

"I did what? I scooped you?"

"After we fell asleep, we drifted apart but I could sense you trying to bring me back to you. You reached over and pulled me into you like spoons."

Jim recalled doing exactly what she said. He remembered waking up a few times, and when she wasn't touching him, he reached out and pulled her into him with a thud.

"It didn't startle you?"

"I loved it! It was like you knew where I belonged. It felt comfortable. I felt protected."

Jim knew he'd been the fool. How could thinking about Kuwait be an option when right now was so much better? He decided to make the million-dollar statement.

"When we get back to the ranch, you're welcome to stay with me as long as you want."

"I'd like that."

"There's one other thing."

"What?" Sheila asked.

"You and I could just leave. Get on a plane."

"Where would we go?"

"I don't care. We could tell Larry and Chris the money's theirs. I can't promise anyone my plan will work. At least we'd be safe."

"Do you really want to do that?" Sheila asked.

"If I can leave with you."

"Do you have family?"

Jim's idea fell like it was dropped from a cargo plane. His dismay must have shown on his face.

"Then we stay," Sheila said firmly. "After the last two nights, I'd love to disappear, but they'll go after anyone to get to you. Our best bet will be to get away with the money and try to bargain."

"Why are you involved in this?"

"Because I hate them," Sheila replied.

"Can I know why?" Jim waited for her response for several seconds as the truck bounced down the dirt road.

Squeezing his hand, she spoke in a hushed tone. "The men you killed were the brothers of the boss, Michael."

Anger rose from a dark place like a grizzly from a cave. He hoped she wouldn't say what came next.

"I worked in their strip club. One night, they cornered me in the dressing room." She didn't say any more, but she didn't need to.

"I'm glad I killed them."

"Me, too."

Jim looked at her, a tear surfacing in her bottom eyelid. He was glad she spoke next. "There it is, Jim. You know more about me than anyone but Larry. I hope you still like me."

"Why wouldn't I?"

"It doesn't bother you?"

Jim shook his head. "Does my killing eleven people bother you?"

Sheila pulled back, her look a mixture of surprise and appraisal "I thought there was only three."

"Three last week and eight during Desert Storm."

Silence hung between them for several seconds. Their eyes met, dropped, and met again. When they spoke it was in unison, talking over each and lurching to a stop.

"Ladies first."

"I think we make the perfect couple."

"Damn right we do." *Damn right we do.*

41

After stopping for a take-out breakfast at a local restaurant, Jim and Sheila pulled into the apartment parking lot an hour after sunrise. Jim carried several Styrofoam take-out boxes in plastic bags, and Chris opened the apartment door before Sheila could knock.

Chris's eyes were still slightly black. Jim wondered how much of it was his punch or maybe Chris hadn't slept.

"Mornin'." Jim strode past him to put the food on the dining room table.

"Breakfast!" Larry's booming voice echoed from down the hallway. "Be there in a minute."

In contrast to Larry's enthusiasm, Chris didn't say a word, or even make eye contact. Jim wondered what it might be. Brody was an arthritic badger before coffee. Hopefully Chris would cheer up with some caffeine and breakfast.

"You da man, Jim!" Larry walked into the dining room, his limp almost gone, and opened the Styrofoam containers. "Right on. Let's eat and figure out what we're doin'. The three of you. Sit. I hate eating in front of people, and I'm not about to wait."

Jim, Sheila, and Chris all sat down and started on pancakes, and assortment of fruit and some scrambled eggs.

"So, how's my man Brody doing?" Larry asked as he scooted his chair closer. "I was thinking about him last night. I'm not sure when I was more scared, heading into the woods with the guys you killed, or riding out to your ranch with *that* guy. I tell you what though. By the time I left, Brody and I was friends."

"I'm glad, because we're going back to the ranch."

"What about the money?" Larry asked, after swallowing a forkful of pancakes.

"It's going with us. The ranch is over ten thousand acres and borders National Forest or wilderness on several sides. Do you worry about them finding it down here?"

"Shit, yes. It's hidden under their noses. It's all in a big storage garage that we rented." Larry paused. "From them."

"Okay," Jim responded.

"The problem now is: how to get it out of the city. Up and down the street are several more businesses that we think these guys own. We see them coming and going, and they all know what the truck looks like."

"So assuming we can get it to your ranch without getting killed, what do we do with it then?" Chris asked, speaking up for the first time.

"I thought my share I'd keep there. You all could leave yours, or take it whenever you want."

"I'd rather have mine in Wyoming than worrying they may find it," Larry said in agreement.

Jim looked at Chris, who took another sip of coffee before he spoke.

"We can't transport it a little at a time without being noticed, and moving the truck all at once invites disaster."

"We will move it all at once," Jim placed his hands on the table. "Tomorrow before the funeral. I think they'll only chase us with a few cars. Once we're on the freeway headed north, they won't do anything to keep us from rolling along. They'll wait until we stop."

"Okay, so we're safe going down the freeway, but what happens when the truck stops?" Chris asked.

"They won't be there." Jim waited until they all looked at him. "I can tell you how, but it might be better not knowing—so you can deny involvement in case someone gets hurt."

Larry put his fork down. "I trust you."

"So, do you plan on taking the truck all the way to your ranch? It's still hard to hide." Chris was thinking ahead, and Jim liked that.

"How big is the truck and how full is it?"

"It's a delivery truck." Larry said. "It has one big axle with dually tires, but it's full. And I do mean full. The gym bags of cash aren't all the way to the ceiling, but they're piled at least six feet."

"It'll be tight, but I want to transfer it to my horse trailer in the desert. Hopefully they won't know my truck and we can take all the back roads."

"You brought your horse trailer down here? Where?" Sheila asked.

"At a St. George truck stop. I'm betting we can get most or all of it in there. If not, we can always come back and make two trips."

"What do we do if the cops pull us over?" she asked.

"We don't. We drive the speed limit and stop at all the stop signs."

"Do you have your own car here?" Jim asked Sheila. Then he thought of something else. "And we're sure they aren't looking for you?"

"They don't know about Sheila. The bitch that ratted us out only saw Chris and me in his office when we made the final plans."

"Let's leave that word for those I shot and pregnant dogs." Larry didn't respond, so Jim continued, "We all need to be on the same page."

Larry and Sheila nodded. Chris sat like a statue.

"Get everything together that you'll be taking. We leave the apartment at dark, and spend the night with the truck. In the morning, Sheila and I will leave at around six, which allows me time to get into position to stop any chase vehicles. The two of you will leave when I call. It'll probably be around eight thirty or nine.

"If they follow, I'll take care of it. If nobody follows, so much the better. Drive down Western, get on I-15 and head north for St. George. Now here is the important part: drive slowly. Come along in the slow lane and make sure you know exactly who, if anyone, is tailing. Call and let me know how many cars there are.

"There's a dirt road before you get to St. George. Turn right and it will take you into the desert toward Grand Canyon. We'll meet to transfer the money to my horse trailer. Then we take back roads to Wyoming, where Brody and Skinner will have breakfast ready."

"Who's Skinner?" Larry asked.

"A kid who works for me in the summer when he isn't playing football."

"I don't like it." Chris stated. "It sounds too easy."

"Do you have a suggestion?" Jim asked before pushing away from the table.

"No," Chris said petulantly. "It just sounds too easy."

"Let's get something straight." Jim raised his eyebrows and stared at Chris, who dropped his eyes. "Unless you're ready to make a suggestion, we go as planned."

"Sounds good to me." Larry slapped his hands together and stood. "Do you have some extra sleeping pads for the garage?" Larry asked. "It's been a long time since I didn't sleep in a real bed."

"I'll pick a few up. I need to get my truck serviced. The last thing we want is to be headed down the road and have a break down on the highway, then have a well-meaning officer try to help."

"No shit there. What do you need to get done?" Larry asked.

"Tires, and an oil change. I put new rubber on my horse trailer a month ago, but I'd hate to have a flat on my truck."

"Don's Tire and Lube is on tenth as you're leaving Henderson. They'll treat you right."

"Do you want me to come with you?" Sheila asked.

"Sure, but I'll be gone for a few hours. Will you have enough time to pack?"

"If you give me a hand."

Without saying anything, Chris stood, pushed his chair over, walked into the bathroom, and slammed the door so hard, Jim's eardrums throbbed. Sheila's dumfounded look matched his. From the bathroom, the ruckus continued as the shower curtain rolled back, water ran into the tub, and a toilet lid thudded closed.

Larry's raised eyebrows and a puppy-dog expression indicated understanding.

"Do you know what the hell that was all about?"

Larry exhaled and nodded yes to Jim's question.

42

"What crawled inside him and died?" Sheila asked.

Larry motioned them closer and answered in a hushed tone. "The love-at-first-sight stuff was cool and all, but Chris's been beside himself for the last two nights. The dude is bright green jealous."

Jim and Sheila both sat up a little bit straighter.

"I thought he was mad over my punching him, or splitting the money another way," Jim said.

"Look. The second I could sense the collision, I was happy as all get out. You're perfect for each other, but Chris don't think it's so cool. Just don't flaunt it and I'll try to chill him down."

Both Jim and Sheila nodded before Larry continued. "We still need him to help negotiate, so let's give him a little bit of time to get used to the two of you."

"I don't trust him." Sheila stated in a matter-of-fact, hushed tone.

"I agree," Jim started stuffing breakfast containers in the trash. "He tried to run from me in the mountains—and steal my horse."

"That makes three of us," Larry whispered. "Let's all keep an eye on him and cut him loose as soon as we can."

Larry, Sheila, and Jim communicated their agreement with glances.

In the parking lot, the mid-morning heat was already promising a scorcher.

"This feels good," Jim said. "It's probably already about as warm as it ever gets where I'm from."

"I like cold weather," Sheila replied. "I've been in Las Vegas for too long."

"You aren't from here?" Jim asked.

"I grew up in Oregon. We had a change of seasons. Fall into winter and winter into spring. It gets cold in Wyoming?"

Jim laughed. "You have no idea. I bundle up, but don't like the early sunset because I run out of daylight."

"It sounds like you need to find something to do after the sun goes down."

"I was hoping you might help."

"Larry told me about your horses," Sheila said, in a not so subtle change of subject. "It scared him riding one of them."

It had to be his fault she redirected the conversation. In spite of what she claimed, Sheila seemed less than enthused about spending the winter on his ranch. And who could blame her? Wyoming's miserable winters could freeze any romance.

"The trail's rough where I found Larry. I didn't have much choice but to put him on my best horse and let her babysit him home."

"What's your best horse's name?"

"It was Sam."

Sheila's eyes squinted slightly. "Larry told me about what you had to do. I'm sorry."

"Maybe Sam was pointing me down a new trail that day."

"That's a good way to think. I like that." Sheila said, with some understanding in her voice.

"So, who's your best horse now?"

"Beatrice."

"Is Beatrice the horse I get to ride when we get to your ranch?"

"Absolutely. Have you ridden before?"

"A little bit. Does Beatrice love to run?"

"Like a scalded dog,"

"This is pretty cool." Sheila smiled. "You're sure she's your best horse?"

"I think I'd know."

"Good, because if we're going to spend the long nights of this winter together, it only seems fitting that you let me ride your best horse."

After Jim and Sheila had Jim's truck serviced, they stopped to fill it with diesel at a truck stop. Jim had an extra thirty-gallon fuel tank installed beneath the bed several years earlier. Hopefully, they would make almost all the way to Wyoming without refueling. Before they moved out, Sheila suggested they return and get her car and fill it as well.

Jim dropped Sheila at the apartment to pack and fill her car, and then set about planning the next day, approaching it like he would a pack trip with his guests. Once his horses left the trailhead and were in the wilderness, it was a pain in the ass to turn around. His mind worked steadily, planning for any unexpected incident that might come up.

At the Henderson Wal-Mart, he bought heavy-duty, outdoor garbage bags, thinking they should stuff the gym bags into them, before putting them into his horse trailer. It would keep the cash dry in case of rain, and a trailer full of garbage bags might look less suspicious—like bagged up leaves. He also bought sleeping pads for Larry and Chris, and an extra five-gallon gas can for Sheila's car.

At the apartment, he thought of one last item. Walking to the kitchen, he opened the door to the fridge and found a gallon of milk with a few ounces left in the bottom. Opening the top, and smelling the contents first, he drank the remainder.

"They make glasses and cups for that sort of thing." Chris's somber expression hadn't improved since storming off earlier, but Jim smiled at him in embarrassment.

"My mom used to get pretty worked up over me drinking from the jug."

"It's not like you're putting your germs back in the fridge. The garbage is under the sink." Chris pointed in the general direction.

"I might use this on the way home," Jim said shaking the jug like a tambourine.

"For what? To make a bomb?"

"Could be. I'm hoping once we transfer the cash to my trailer, we can drive straight through."

"I'm with you, a pee jug."

"Remember when we talked about studs and geldings and brain surgery?" Jim asked.

"Sure." Chris actually smiled. "Castration causes a radical change in personality. It caught me off guard when you put it that way, but I laughed."

"Some of my guests never figure it out; for most, it takes a few days. You figured it out in record speed." Jim's words held the tone of a genuine compliment.

"Really?"

"I respect your smarts, Chris. Right now I'm doing my best to plan for any eventuality. It's why I have a pee jug and why I just put new tires on my truck. If you can think of anything else, let me know."

"Hey, Jim, can you put this in the trunk of my car before you fill it with gas?" Sheila emerged from the hallway, her suitcase rolling behind.

"Sure."

"The key is on the counter."

Jim took the suitcase and looked around the counter for a set of keys. After a minute he set the suitcase aside, wondering if he was missing something.

"It's right there. It says BMW."

Jim picked up a small oval piece of plastic. "This?"

"The car unlocks as you get close," Sheila explained.

"Really?"

"Trust me," Sheila said over her shoulder. "And pull it a little closer if there's a spot."

Jim took the remote with no key in one hand and lifted the suitcase with the other. At the doorway, he looked across the parking lot at a metallic blue BMW. Five steps from the car, he heard the mechanism unlock. He found the button to open the trunk, and after stowing the luggage, stared like an Englishman attempting to read Greek at the car's dash.

After several minutes he pushed the start button and the car fired to life.

I'll be damned.

As the afternoon wore on, Jim hauled Larry's things out to the parking lot while Chris and Sheila packed them in the back of the truck. Then they loaded Sheila's things into the trunk of her car. None of them had much, which made Jim happy; he worried about having enough space in the back of his truck and trailer to haul the cash. They all agreed to ditch their belongings in the desert if needed to make space for the moneybags.

As the sun went down, they left the apartment and went to the south end of Western Avenue, where the truck was stored inside a big garage. Larry sat in Jim's truck in the front seat. Sheila followed behind in her car and Chris sat in the cramped rear seat of Jim's extended cab.

As they got to the garage, Larry handed a key to Jim. "Once you open the door, I'll pull us in. I think we can get your truck and Sheila's car in alongside the delivery truck."

Taking the key, Jim realized Larry didn't want to leave his truck even for a minute for fear of being seen.

Jim slipped out, unlocked the man door and quickly released the lever that locked the huge rollup door. The chains rattled as Jim pulled them through a block and tackle system that raised the door high enough for the vehicles to clear.

With everyone inside, Jim lowered the garage door. Sheila got out of her car, and hurried over to him while Larry, who was still moving slowly with his stiff knee, got out of Jim's truck.

"I just wanted to give you a squeeze before Chris gets out."

"I don't care what he thinks." Jim returned the hug.

"I agree, but let's not get him too upset before tomorrow."

There was enough ambient light coming through some high windows in the building, and they decided to leave all lights off, for fear of attracting any unwanted attention. Petroleum and rubber smells filled the garage. Not unpleasant, but certainly different from the fresh mountain air.

A twinge of doubt ran through Jim's belly. He missed Duke, Brody, and the ranch. Skinner would be itching for a wrestling match. In forty-eight hours, Sheila had changed everything. He'd come to Vegas for lots of reasons; there was the adrenaline, the money, the opportunity to help new friends, and the need to get the Mafia off of his back. Now, his mind fixated on her. In his world of dead friends, war memories, good horses, fluctuating cattle prices, and rusty old tractors, he would carve her place.

A wink from Sheila told him she was only putting her bag away from his to keep from upsetting Chris as they all spread their sleeping pads out in the space between the BMW and truck.

Jim looked at his three partners. "Any last worries?"

"Let's do this," Larry responded.

Jim looked at Sheila and Chris, whose somber faces expressed the reality of coming danger.

"Let's get some sleep then," Jim said as he lay down on his mat, adjusting his pillow under his head. Sheila, Chris and Larry all did the same.

"What time do you want me to set the alarm on my phone?" Sheila asked.

"Your phone has an alarm?"

"Everyone's phone has an alarm," Chris answered like Jim was the stupidest hick from the stupidest place in the universe.

Chris was lying on his side, facing away from the group. Larry caught Jim's eye and made an exasperated expression that Jim understood to mean "don't worry about this asshole."

"I'll probably wake up, but set it for five-thirty." Jim smiled at Sheila.

Before Jim's muscles relaxed, Larry's snoring reverberated through the building in an awful rhythm.

"He sure fell asleep fast," Sheila grumbled as she slid out of her bag, pillow in hand, about to chop down on Larry's noisy head.

"Hold up there, Brutus." Jim opened a pocket on the outside of his sleeping bag and took out three small cardboard packets.

"Earplugs. Thanks," Sheila said.

"I always take these to the mountains. If I don't, I hear my horses stomp and snort all night."

"It seems you are the guy who thinks of everything." Sheila smiled.

"We'll know tomorrow." Jim tapped Chris's shoulder, who took the plugs without offering thanks. Jim compressed his earplugs by rolling them between his fingers before putting them in. Something bounced off his sleeping bag and landed on the floor. The cardboard packet he'd given to Chris. The sleeping bag's pocket was still open, so Jim returned the packet. The plugs cut Larry's snoring in half, and diminished the noise from outside traffic, but Jim couldn't sleep. Five minutes later, Chris stood and jogged around the garage.

Jim thought about punching Chris in the face again, or tripping him on his next lap, until Sheila slid toward him. Jim pulled his plugs out. Larry's rumbling snore, Chris's feet on the cement, honking cars, and un-muffled motorcycles outside the garage, contrasted with Sheila's silent movements. He remembered her dive into Lake Mead the first night, then pictured Larry doing a cannonball.

Duke barking, Brody grumbling—pistol shots. My life is too loud.

He helped her position her pillow and sleeping bag over the pad and Sheila laid down beside him.

Chris quickened his pace.

Her fingers found his bicep and slid to Jim's left hand. She rolled away and placed his palm on her belly. Her back thudded into his torso as he scooped her close. She nuzzled into his face, and the scent of petroleum and rubber tires gave way to coconut scents and sweet-smelling flowers. Her soft breathing eclipsed all noise, syncing with his as Jim fell to sleep with his earplugs on the floor.

43

A t the end of Sally's shift, she punched the time clock, walked
through the hospital's front doors, and jogged toward her car
at the far end of parking lot. She rummaged the keys from
her purse, and chirped the car open with the remote.

More than anything in recent memory, she looked forward to
going home to a quiet house. Her two daughters, ages fourteen and
twelve, were away at girl's camp. Skinner was at the Cooper Ranch for
a few more days, and her husband was working swing.

Her phone rang before she had clicked into her seatbelt. Checking the number to make sure it wasn't a family member, she declined
the call.

Hopefully, they won't leave a message.

She inserted the key, twisted the car to life, and shifted into drive
when her phone chimed. After shifting back to park, she retrieved
the message.

"Sally, this is the ward executive secretary, Brother Baggett.
Bishop Fawson wants to meet with you tonight at eight in his office.
If I don't hear from you, I'll tell him to plan on you being there."

Sally groaned. Her favorite television show was on at eight, and
for once she could watch it without a house full of noisy teenagers, or
her husband waiting for an opportunity to decry the evils of modern
media because of one or two racy moments in an hour-long show.

Bishop Fawson probably wanted to give her a new calling within the church. As an active Mormon, it could be anything from arranging the flowers on the podium, to teaching the five-year-old Sunday School class. The perfect assignment would be something that involved her daughters or Skinner, so she could spend time with her kids while she was on the Lord's errand. Instead, she usually got assigned to work with the elderly or pre-school kids.

She parked the car, but before walking into the house, picked up the paper and looked at the lawn. The grass had grown long and shaggy with Skinner gone for almost two weeks to football camp and the Cooper Ranch. Her weed-filled flowerbed begged for attention. She looked at the homes across the street and next door with their neatly trimmed lawns bordered by flower beds that were bursting with marigolds.

She had quit trying to get her husband to do anything with the yard years ago. Unlike Sally, who viewed attendance as a nuisance, Charlie was a church-aholic, filling his free time with meetings and volunteer service.

Frustration over her husband's church dependency wouldn't cut the grass, so she decided to mow it. The evening was pleasant, and the exercise would be enjoyable. Better yet, she decided to put on running shoes, shorts, and tank top, and go for a run afterward.

To Charlie's dismay, Sally argued that staying fit was godly and part of the religion's healthy lifestyle. He would invite her to stay and study the scriptures as she pulled on her running shorts. After returning home, he would look at her woefully, probably wondering why his apostate wife insisted on such nefarious behavior. After a few minutes of silence, he would ask about some church task she had neglected. In return, Sally would elaborate about her exhilarating run.

With nobody home to guilt her into wearing a more modest t-shirt, she stepped outside wearing a tank top, the late afternoon sun warming her shoulders.

After mowing the lawn and running, Sally went inside, showered, and got ready for her appointment. She turned on the television, made a sandwich, and wondered again what the bishop had in mind. If it was something awful, she could always say no. She never had before. If nothing else, it would irritate Charlie.

Sally walked the four blocks to the church, arriving at a few minutes before eight. She expected a wait, but was greeted by the bishop just inside the front door.

In addition to his ecclesiastical duties, Bishop Fawson taught high school English and coached the varsity football team, so it surprised her to see him dressed in a suit and tie.

"Thanks for coming, Sally." He unlocked the door to his office and offered her the chair across the desk from his. "How's Skinner? Did he enjoy football camp?"

"You know Skinner. It made his whole year, being named the top linebacker."

"I only made it the first day," Bishop Fawson said, leaning back in the chair.

"I appreciate everything you do for Skinner, as coach and bishop."

"I'd rather just be the coach," Bishop Fawson said, a hint of weariness embedded in his voice. "People come to me with problems, and I feel inadequate."

"You do a fine job," Sally said, wanting to end the pleasantries. "Why did you call me here?"

"Before I start, I want you to know that nobody's in trouble, and that what we talk about will be confidential. I'm your friend."

In all the years she'd known him, he always had people's best interest at heart. "I understand, Bishop. Have I offended someone? Did Skinner do something?"

"No. It's not that at all. Remember my first year as head football coach? Your senior year?"

"Sure. 1987."

"I was only twenty-five." The bishop paused to lean forward, resting his arms on the desk. "Anymore it runs together, but a head coach never forgets the first year—the players, how he puts that first team together."

Sally nodded, and the bishop interlocked his fingers.

"During your senior year, you and Jim Cooper were an item."

Sally's heart sank. The biggest regret she had was not marrying Jim. Before the bishop took the conversation further, she worried about the wisdom of opening a painful memory.

"Is that why you called me here, to talk about my high school love life?"

"It is, Sally, but this is strictly between us. And no matter what you think, you aren't in any trouble."

Sally nodded. Growing tears in each eye blurred her vision. Bishop Fawson unlocked his fingers and pushed a box of tissue toward her.

"Last summer, watching Skinner on the football field, I realized he was the spitting image of someone who played for me that first year." Bishop Fawson paused. "Skinner has your features, but the way he plays football is a carbon copy of Jim Cooper."

Sally had learned how to keep her emotions in check as a nurse, but Bishop Fawson blindsided her with something she thought was hidden away forever.

Her mind screamed, demanding she leave or yell, *What business is it of yours?* She knew that members could be excommunicated or otherwise disciplined for fornication, but such actions were the bishop's decision. She also trusted his confidentiality.

With the secret etched in her soul, carrying it was as much a part of her as mothering her children. She stood to walk out, but then sat down again—surprising herself more than the bishop from the look on his face.

"I'm here to help," he offered.

"I'm glad you called me here." Sally tugged a tissue free and blotted one eye at a time. "Jim and I made love in his old truck the night before he left for boot camp—I got pregnant."

Bishop Fawson squinted at an empty spot on the wall then looked her in the eyes. "Why didn't you marry Jim?"

"Before they'd let him date me, my parents made Jim take the missionary discussions. It didn't work for him, and I can understand. If I hadn't been born Mormon, I wouldn't join."

Sally paused, blinking her eyes like a fan against the avalanche of tears threatening to burst through. Bishop Fawson removed his glasses and set them on the desk. Without them, the concern on his face and in his eyes appeared even more focused, but Sally doubted he would speak because they both knew she wasn't finished.

"We planned to elope after boot camp, but then I found out I was pregnant. My parents hated Jim for not joining the church."

"Why?"

"They refused to believe anyone investigating Mormonism could decide against it. Jim did it all, reading and praying. But he wouldn't commit to something he didn't believe in." Sally's eyes dropped to her lap. The Hawaiian floral print dress had always elevated her mood, but now the garish colors seemed to mock her.

"My parents hoped Jim would die in the army," she said without looking up. "They even blamed him for Bradley Salveson's death."

"I remember." Bishop Fawson exhaled. "We all mourned Bradley. Especially Jim. I wasn't the bishop then, but he came to talk to me about it."

Sally was surprised, but not shocked. To Jim, Head Football Coach Fawson would have been someone he would have trusted, just as she did.

"I understand all this, but why marry Charlie?" Bishop Fawson asked.

"My parents adored him, mostly because he took church so seriously. My family didn't have insurance, and Charlie was insured through his job with the city. I got married six weeks after Jim and I were together." Sally paused and wiped at brimming tears. "Everyone thought Skinner was a honeymoon baby born three weeks early."

"How do you feel about it now?"

"I should have moved to the Cooper Ranch. Jackie and Hank would have welcomed me.

"But I can't imagine life without my daughters." Sally sniffled. "Even here, now, I feel like I made both the right and wrong decision."

"Has Jim ever suspected Skinner was his son?"

"Not that I know of, but sometimes I wonder, the way those two have taken to each other the last few years."

Bishop Fawson put his glasses back on and leaned back in his chair. "Do you feel okay about me knowing?"

"I do," Sally said, her composure returning.

"Was it a secret you were going to keep forever?"

"I've wanted to tell both Jim and Skinner at some point."

"And your husband?"

Husband. The word belonged in a hospital bedpan. "I can't imagine living with Charlie if he knew."

"Why?"

"He nit-picks everything. If I'm a minute late to church, I get lectured about being worthy of the Lord's kingdom."

"Do you understand that it's really his controlling personality?"

"I do." Sally sighed. "It would be easy to blame religion, but I know it would be something else making him uptight if it wasn't church."

"Have you ever sought marriage counseling together or separately?"

"I've mentioned it."

"And?"

"He says the answer to all of our problems is to be more righteous."

The bishop leaned back in the chair and pressed his fingertips together. "If I prepare a lesson for the brethren on listening to their wives, that if they ever ask them to get counseling, it means they should do it without asking questions. Would he go? Or would it just make things harder?"

"I think he'd go if it came from you," Sally responded, her tears now gone.

"And don't feel too bad. Charlie isn't the only man in the ward who needs to hear what I have in mind."

"Do you think I should tell Skinner and Jim?"

"They should know, but let's not do anything until you think Charlie can handle it. If we can't get him to counseling, you should consider just telling Skinner and Jim, but I think we would need to consider it very carefully."

"There is another option."

"What?"

"I decided a long time ago that, once my girls were raised, I'd leave if Charlie doesn't treat me better. I could tell Skinner and Jim then."

"I hope it doesn't come to that." The bishop leaned forward again. "I'll do whatever I can to help Charlie change."

"Control freaks don't change."

The bishop was about to speak but then stopped for a moment. "My wife would disagree. We went to therapy."

"You went to counseling, Bishop?"

"The Head Football Coach in me takes over. Controlling every move eleven athletes make—I used to go home and do the same to my family. She says I'm better."

When they'd finished, Sally left the church building, the sunset making her shadow long across the church lawn. Her mind drifted to where it always did, when she thought about being single: with her family raised, what would stop her from divorcing Charlie and reigniting her relationship with Jim?

44

The chirping bird alarm on Sheila's cellphone shocked her out of a pleasant dream. She looked over to see Larry and Chris rolling over, but Jim was gone. Within five seconds, her mind went from panic to knowing that without him she would still find a way to get the money out of Las Vegas. Then her worry left knowing that Jim wouldn't abandon her.

Several times during the night she'd stirred, and he was the first thought on her mind. She was glad she slid her pad next to his. Worrying about upsetting someone inconsiderate enough to jog around after bedtime just didn't matter.

After a few yawns, she could hear somebody moving behind and she knew it was Jim. The aroma of coffee overpowered the rubber and petroleum garage smells. He walked up to her and the others without making a sound, and set a bag of bagels and a small crate with four large cups on the floor.

"How long have you been awake?" she asked, reaching for the warm cup with her cold hand.

"Since about five. I thought I'd get us some go-juice and something to eat."

"Thanks." Larry's morning voice was almost as abrasive as his snoring.

Chris sat up and flicked sleepy sand from his eyes.

"Sheila and I will take off in a minute. Are we all set?"

No one said anything.

"This is your wake-up call." Jim's tone was quiet, but held drill sergeant level focus that brought everyone to attention as he looked each of them in the eye. "I'll risk my life today, and, if necessary, kill to keep us alive. But I won't do anything unless I get a better answer than silence."

"I know you will, Jim. I will, too," Larry said.

The two men nodded at each other. Jim turned to Sheila. Her body resonated like a tuning fork that hummed to life and matched his intensity. "I'm with you."

Then Jim locked eyes with the accountant, who stared back, not answering.

"I won't beg you, Chris. We'll hear it from you right now, or the three of us will toss you out of here."

45

After tolerating Chris's insolent eyes a few heartbeats too many, Jim grabbed Chris's scalp and slid him across the concrete. Still in his sleeping bag, Chris clawed at Jim's hand, struggling to break away. Jim paused at the door, and shook Chris's head. "The army stole my gentle nature. You're in or you're out."

"I'm with you. Let go," Chris pleaded. But as Jim's fingers un-clinched, the accountant's expression darkened.

"I got this." Larry spoke from the same position he'd been in since waking. "You feel me, Chris?"

Chris glared at the group.

"You're my wingman." Larry spoke to Chris while looking at the ceiling. "But if you mess with us, you'll beg for Jim to drag your nerdy ass again."

Larry looked toward Jim. There was a connection with the big man Jim hadn't experienced since Desert Storm, a feeling known to soldiers. The look on the man's face, through healing but still swollen features, conveyed an understanding that it was no longer about money. Or Mafia, or Wyoming, or Las Vegas. It was about dead or alive, and friends taking care of friends.

"Get out of here," Larry said to Jim. "The sooner we get going, the better."

Jim nodded. "It'll be a few hours for us to get into position."

"Leave me your pad. I'll double it on top of mine on this cement." Larry said the last word like sea-meant.

Jim walked to his truck and retrieved his bedding from the extended cab.

Chris stared at the floor and didn't speak as they left.

The door retracted as Larry worked the chains, and Sheila's car followed Jim's truck onto Western Avenue. The heavy morning traffic on I-15 separated them for a few minutes until Sheila slipped her BMW between Jim's northbound truck and a tailgating minivan with a skill worthy of NASCAR.

Jim's phone rang. With all the stress, the number still brought a smile.

"Hello, gorgeous."

"Hello, yourself. How's my drill sergeant?"

"I'd be better if I could figure out Chris."

"What an ass."

"I agree."

"He's lucky you or Larry didn't kill him."

"I was about to, until you slid your bag up to mine," Jim said.

"I couldn't imagine caring about his feelings with him doing laps around the garage."

"Good call," Jim said. "So how far back do you and Larry go?"

"We met in college, and we've been friends ever since."

"Were the two of you ever an item?"

"Nah. We had a class together as freshman. He played football and tried to hit on me. I shut him down, but he stuck around and we became friends. He's that way, Jim. Larry has a huge heart, and once he lets you in, there's nothing he won't do."

"I sensed it just now."

"He feels obligated to you. I've never seen him so determined."

"I'm glad because we're messing with some bad people."

"If anyone deserves to lose, it's them. When Larry told me about you killing those assholes, I knew we'd click."

"It's not too late. We could call the whole thing off." Jim wasn't serious, but Sheila's reaction surprised him.

"Even if we begged and told them where the money was, they'd still come after us."

Adrenaline rushed through him like a flash flood, raising goose bumps up and down his body. He thought about Brody's parting words at the ranch: kill them first.

"Good enough. I'm ready."

"I know you are. Thanks for coming to help us."

"Thank me tomorrow when we're all safe in Wyoming having breakfast."

For the next few minutes they talked, and then agreed to hang up and save their batteries. Las Vegas Motor Speedway appeared on the right as they sped north on I-15.

A hundred miles later, Jim pulled up next to the horse trailer that was exactly as he left it. Sheila parked next to the trailer and hopped in Jim's pickup. "So, where are we going now?"

"Back to the canyon we just drove through," Jim responded.

"That's where you're going to stop them?"

"Yep."

"Do I get to know how before it happens?"

"You'll see the whole thing." Jim dug around under his seat, focused on something other than her question. After fumbling for a few seconds, his hand touched what he wanted, and he handed her some binoculars.

"You're going to be my backup eyes."

Sheila took them from their case and struggled through a few minutes of familiarization. Soon, she was rolling the focus knob between the eyepieces. Then she adjusted the eye relief corkscrews. "I think I have it. I'm ready."

"Good," Jim said. "Keep practicing. Pick out landmarks to focus on."

Ten miles from St. George, Jim turned onto an unmarked dirt road running parallel to the freeway. They traveled southwest for five miles. A cloud of red dust rose behind his truck as the canyon dropped away. He found the perfect spot near the road's end. A stone fire ring and some empty beer cans marked a campground of sorts. Cedar trees shaded some of it. Jim parked beneath the largest one. Nobody would see his truck unless they were in a helicopter. The sounds of traffic greeted them at the cliff's edge as they looked down at the freeway three hundred feet below.

"We're here."

"This is where you are going to stop them?"

"This is where we stop them." Jim's eyes hadn't left the freeway.

"How?"

Jim strode back to his truck, but the key wouldn't twist in the lock of the in-bed toolbox. He tried jiggling it, to no avail.

"What's wrong?" Sheila asked.

"The lock's frozen, and my guns are inside."

"That's not good." Sheila's face tensed.

Jim popped the hood of the truck and extracted the engine's dipstick. The oil level was perfect, which he expected after the garage had changed it the day before. Heading back around to the toolbox, he touched the dipsticks end to the key, letting a few drops ease into the grooves. The lubed key turned like new and the hatch popped open. A long canvas case containing his fifty-caliber rifle was on top of the pile.

Jim pulled the bolt back, opening the gun's chamber. Next he grabbed a box of shells, inserted one, and shoved the bolt forward again, closing the chamber. Jim double-checked to make sure the safety was on, then set the massive gun on his tailgate. From the glove compartment, he pulled out what looked like a smaller pair of binoculars.

"What's that?" Sheila asked, obviously unaware of what Jim was doing.

"It's a range finder." Jim looked down the canyon to a spot where a widened shoulder allowed disabled vehicles to pull off the freeway. "It tells how far away something is. I'm six hundred and twenty yards from where I want to stop anyone from following Larry and Chris.

"A bullet starts losing speed the instant it leaves the barrel. It pretty much goes in a straight line, but because it's losing steam, the trajectory drops." Jim turned away from the freeway, looking west into the desert with the range finder.

"Okay. I get it, but now what are you doing?"

"Do you still have the binoculars?"

Sheila jogged to the truck and grabbed them from the seat. Pointing in the direction he had been looking through the rangefinder, Jim turned to her. "See the lone barrel-cactus in the valley? It's about the same distance the cars will be."

Sheila looked through the binoculars. "I see it."

"Do you still have the earplugs from last night?"

Looping the binoculars over her neck, Sheila dug the plugs from her front pocket and put them in.

"Watch the cactus."

Sheila did what Jim told her until she realized Jim was on his belly looking through the gun's scope.

"Don't look at me, look at the cactus and tell me when you have it."

"Got it."

Jim took careful aim and squeezed the trigger. Even through the plugs, the report of the fifty caliber shattered the desert solitude, and the cactus exploded, obliterated with pinpoint accuracy.

His ear canal tickled as Jim pulled out his own plugs and set the gun down on the truck's tailgate.

"That was impressive." Sheila's eyebrows rose.

"No more than your keyless BMW."

"What kind of gun is that?" Sheila asked.

"It's a fifty caliber."

"Like that tells me anything. Will it blow up an entire car?"

"No, but put a bullet in the right place, and a car won't go any further."

"So you aren't going to kill them?"

The disappointment in her voice surprised Jim, but it wouldn't change his plan. He took the phone from his pocket and dialed Larry's number.

"Hello." It was Larry's sleepy voice on the other end.

"Been sleeping?"

"I'll die well rested."

Jim laughed. "Did you thump Chris?

"Antsy pencil-pusher's been disturbing my laid-back vibe."

"Ready to roll?"

"Give us the word and we're outta here."

"Word."

"We'll be in touch."

46

"Go time, Chris. Open the door!"

Larry climbed in the truck and adjusted the mirrors and seat to his liking. "Didn't have time to adjust much last week when I jacked it."

The truck belched soot, filling the garage as Larry revved the engine. The garage door rolled up as Chris worked the chains before climbing into the passenger seat.

Larry glanced at Chris, who was disturbingly pale. "Damn! You okay, Casper?"

"No! Pallbearers carry people to their hearse. I just ran to get in mine!"

"I plan on being cremated anyway. Shit! Almost forgot." Larry pulled a money clip from his front pocket and removed a hundred-dollar bill. From the cubby in the dash, he took a pen and a thumbtack, then drew a smiley face across the bill. He got out of the truck and pinned the bill to the garage's back wall.

Climbing back in, he buckled his seatbelt and shoved the truck into gear. Grinding gears vibrated up the shift lever, so Larry double-clutched to put the truck in reverse, pulled out of the garage, and accelerated down Western Avenue.

47

Michael Faletto's morning was already in shambles. He had gone to his office to get some urgent work done before the funeral, but when he arrived he found Ralf, fresh from Wyoming, parked in the lot in front of his office. Ralf had driven through the night, coming directly with Simon's Escalade still on the tow-truck's deck instead of going home—which impressed Michael.

In addition to losing contact with the bouncers, Ralf told of being stalked by the teenagers, and practically mobbed by the locals. It seemed the whole town was ready to protect James Cooper.

After dismissing Ralf, Michael worked two more hours in his office, but his mind kept wandering to Ralf's story. No contact with the bouncers could only mean they were dead—or maybe arrested, which would have been even worse. Jim Cooper wasn't going to be an easy hit. A gruesome, ceremonial death for the rancher was the only acceptable way, but kidnapping him from a protective town with only one road coming and going might be impossible.

After working 'til the last possible minute, Michael got up and entered the code to set the office alarm. The scorching Nevada sun glinted from his new Cadillac, which automatically unlocked for him as he drew near. Then, right in front of him, was the unthinkable:

the delivery truck, with Larry Lyons at the wheel and the accountant riding shotgun, was rolling down the road toward him.

"Stop the fucking truck!" Tires skidded and horns blared as Michael charged into the oncoming lane of traffic.

The throaty combustion of the motor increased as Larry leaned over the steering wheel, as if an aggressive posture would make the truck speed up. The giant cranked the steering wheel to the left.

Michael took two steps and dove onto the sidewalk to avoid being squished through a storm drain. Before standing, he reached in his pocket for his cell, pushing the scroll button ten times harder than necessary to find the right number. A ring and a hello and Michael barked at the person on the other end. "You still down the street?"

"Sure, Boss. Paul, Frank, Al, and I were just leaving to get ready for the funeral."

"Listen to me and don't ask stupid questions. In a second, you're going to see the cash truck with the two guys we're looking for coming down the street."

"Really?"

"I said don't ask stupid fucking questions!" Michael could feel his blood pounding in his jugular as he continued. "You, Paul, and Frank, get in your cars and follow that truck! Send Al with his Corvette up here to the office."

"Okay. We're on it."

"Don't do anything stupid that will get the cops involved. Sooner or later, that truck will stop, and I want to know where. Call me back when you know something I don't."

48

hris's entire body shook like he was having a seizure.

"You with me?" Larry asked. "Exhale."

"Do you know who you almost ran over?" Chris asked in a staccato voice.

"When I missed, I should have stopped and beat his ass into the pavement! He's on the phone already," Larry said, looking in his side mirror. "Someone'll be tailing us. Come on, man. Find your backbone and be look out."

"What?"

"I said be my look out. We need to tell Jim who's following us!"

"Okay. I'm with you. Shit! Up there, on the left!"

"I see them."

The truck rolled past a strip mall parking lot where an Escalade, a Mercedes, and a brand new Audi A8 waited. The driver of the Escalade removed his sunglasses to glare as they drove by, drawing his finger across his throat.

Larry waved, smiled, and then flipped them the bird.

"Fuck you!" he yelled with his head and arm extended through the open window. Chris went even whiter, and Larry thought he might pass out. "Okay, Opie. Get it together."

Chris's rapid nod resembled a woodpecker's.

"And don't worry too much," Larry continued. "If I had twenty bucks for every time some wannabe badass threatened me, I wouldn't be driving this truck. Call Jim."

Chris dug the phone from his pocket. Larry blinkered before entering the freeway on-ramp with all three vehicles following them closely. Each time Larry checked the side mirror, the driver of the Escalade drew his finger across his throat.

"Got your poo in a group?" Larry asked.

"What?"

"Is your shit together?"

"Maybe."

"Call and tell Jim we're rolling. Or do I need to drive *and* make the call?

Chris held number three down for a few seconds then put the phone to his ear.

"On your way?" Jim asked.

"It's just what you said. We have three tailing vehicles."

"Are you sure it's the guys we want?"

"Oh, yeah. Tell me something good. Tell me they won't be there when the truck stops."

"Keep driving and it'll be all right. But don't take my word for it. Here's Sheila."

"Hello, Chris?"

"Tell me the cowboy has this thing figured out because from where I'm sitting, Larry and I are dead."

"Just do what Jim says, and it will all be okay before you get to Utah. Trust me."

"We won't stop."

"Chris, this is Jim again. Can you give me a description of who's behind you?"

"There's a white Cadillac Escalade, a green Mercedes—I'm not sure the make—and there's a red Audi A8. They all look new."

"Good. Keep Larry in the slow lane and call me when you get to Mesquite."

"Okay. Mesquite. I will."

49

J im turned to Sheila. "I'd say we have a nervous accountant."

"Larry will get them here," Sheila said with confidence.

The shaded truck beckoned and Jim walked from the cliff's edge to sit on the tailgate. Not yet ten o'clock, and it was probably close to a hundred degrees. Sheila came over to sit next to him.

"So now we wait," she said.

Jim looked at the sun before checking his watch.

"Why do you do that?"

"Do what?" Jim responded.

"Look at the sun before checking the time."

"Old habit, I guess. How should I do it?"

"Most people just look at their watch. Or cell phone."

"Guess I'm not most people," Jim shrugged. "It's ten minutes to ten. I bet they call at about eleven and they should roll through about eleven thirty."

After ten minutes, Sheila strolled to the truck for a water bottle. She took a small swallow, and handed it to Jim who gulped half before stopping.

"Thirsty?"

"Do most people drink slower?"

"I need you to do something for me."

"Sure."

"When we get to your ranch, I want you to teach me how to shoot."

Jim smiled. "That's easy."

50

The morning's events dragged on Michael Faletto like dead weight at a tractor pull. His Superman-like dive onto the sidewalk had left him with a sprained ankle and bruised knee. There were scrapes on the palms of his hands and elbows from the pavement, and his brand new, freshly starched and monogrammed dress shirt was ruined, as were his silk Italian slacks. The tailored clothing had been made for the funeral, and he swore bitterly, thinking that he had only worn it once.

Michael walked back into the building, stripped to his underwear and threw the pants and shirt directly in the trash. Then he turned on the water in the bathroom sink adjacent to his office.

"Fuck!" Michael yelled as the running water stung his raw skin. The soap stung even worse, stoking the fire of rage in his chest.

Nobody tries to run me over on the day of my son's funeral!

His phone rang on the desk where he'd set it. Striding from the bathroom and snatching it up, he pushed the button to accept the call.

"You better be following them!"

"We are, boss. We're all three tailing like you asked. They're headed north on fifteen."

"Follow them to wherever. Let me know when the truck stops. No witnesses."

"Got it. We're wondering what you'll do about the funeral?"

"I've already delayed it four hours. We'll have it tomorrow if we have to. Just don't lose that truck!"

"They sent me down here." Al Litizette walked in his office.

"Are you ready to stand next to me?"

Al looked at Michael for a few seconds before kneeling and bowing his head. "Nobody can replace your brothers, Mike."

"You ain't nobody."

"My car's out back." Al looked up. "The motor's running."

"Good." Michael walked to a closet where he always kept a change of clothes. "We're going for a ride."

51

While looking down at traffic, Jim tried to describe to Sheila the culture of his local community by explaining how strangers were scarce and neighbors lingered for decades. His cell rang. "It's our friends in low places," Jim said as he pushed accept.

"We're north of Mesquite, a few miles from the canyon."

"Have they tried to stop you?"

"No, but the driver slits his throat with his finger when we look."

"They're waiting until you stop. You'll lose cell service through most of the canyon. You'll get signal for a few miles in the middle; call when you do."

"I will."

Jim returned to the truck and pulled an old horse blanket from his toolbox. He walked between two boulders at the cliff's edge and spread the blanket on the ground. Back at his truck, he grabbed the rifle and five fifty-caliber shells. He laid the bullets down next to the gun in a neat row. They looked like five medium-sized flashlights. He dropped to the blanket, lying on his belly.

"In about five minutes they'll call. Two minutes later we should see the truck. Watch with the binoculars and tell me when you see them. Don't forget your earplugs."

"I'm ready."

Jim rolled to stare up at her.

"What?" she asked.

If she was scared, it didn't show. Her breathing and color were normal, and her posture was relaxed, like someone watching a parade.

"So where's the ice in your veins from?"

"Normally this would freak me out, but I know you'll take care of things."

"How do you know that?"

"After the cactus, the cars will be easy," Sheila responded.

Unfortunately, she was only partially right. Shooting downward into a canyon, across traffic at moving targets would be tricky. The vehicles might be out of position or blocked by a semi-trailer or bus. Making Larry drive in the slow lane would hopefully keep the tailing cars behind the cash truck, but nothing was certain. Even if he had a clean shot, the gun could malfunction, or he could miss.

"And you're not most people." Sheila bent over and kissed him.

How could he doubt? According to his father, Jim's mother's support made his dad better at everything. Jim wondered if he was already experiencing some of it.

The phone rang.

"We just went under an underpass." Chris hyperventilated into the phone. "There's a campground on the right. Can you see us?"

"A few sec—I got you." Through the rifle's scope, the truck came into view. "Stay in the slow lane, and tell Larry to slow."

"Jim says slow down!"

Jim handed Sheila the phone. "Got 'em both?"

"Got it," she said, sandwiching the phone between her shoulder and ear while looking through the binoculars. "Here they come!"

Behind the truck, the pursuers came into view—three vehicles clustered close together. Jim let out a long breath through his mouth. *A little closer* . . . The crosshairs marked the spot he wanted, leading the moving vehicle just enough to smack the Escalade's grill. He squeezed the trigger, and the recoiling rifle smashed his shoulder. Not wasting time to check if the shot hit home, he worked the bolt to eject the spent shell. Less than a second later, he had a fresh round loaded into the gun and fired at the Mercedes. Repeating the process the third time, he aimed the rifle and fired directly into the Audi's engine compartment, but instead of hitting the radiator and engine block, it must have hit the latch because the hood flew open and the car swerved into the left lane, clipping a minivan that started fishtailing.

Jim worked the bolt to eject the spent casing, eyeing the scene through the scope. The first two vehicles were slowing down, belching steam from under their hoods. The delivery truck was now moving away instead of closer. The Audi driver must have been able to see beneath the hood covered windshield, because instead of slowing it sped toward the delivery truck.

"Dammit!"

"Shoot it again!" Sheila said in a too-enthusiastic tone.

Jim placed the fourth bullet in the gun and took aim at the accelerating Audi. He remembered the Audi having no passengers so he aimed for the left side of the trunk, hoping to pierce the gas tank, and pulled the trigger. The car still didn't slow, so Jim chambered the final shell and shot the right rear tire from more than five hundred yards. For a split second, he thought he'd missed again, but the car slammed into the protective roadside barricade and burst into flames. The driver jumped from the car, his back covered in fire that looked like a downwind flag.

"Drop and roll!" Jim growled, still eyeing the scene through the crosshairs. The flames grew as the man fled the burning Audi. But then he dropped and rolled side to side, and the flames dissipated. The traffic backed up behind the Audi, partially blocking one lane as drivers-turned-spectator condensed to a single lane to view the carnage.

"Tell 'em to take the dirt road."

Sheila ran to the truck, relaying the orders as she went. Jim picked up the horse blanket and shook it clean before wrapping it around the rifle. He placed the gun back in the toolbox like a baby in a cradle. He gathered the spent casings from the ground, all the while scanning for anything left behind.

"I cleaned up, except for the bullet thingies that came out of your gun," Sheila said as she threw open the driver's door.

"Bullet thingies?"

"You know, the things that pop out after you shoot."

Jim leapt behind the steering wheel. He'd left the key in the ignition on purpose to hasten the getaway, but as he twisted, the motor didn't crank.

Jim groaned.

"What's wrong?"

"I left the key on." Jim noticed Sheila's concerned expression as he opened the door to get out. "Slide over and drive. We'll roll start it."

"We need to hurry," Sheila said. "The cops will be coming any second."

"Just scoot over here and drive!" Jim hurried to the front to push the truck backwards with the small of his back against the bumper. Heaving like an ox, he pushed the truck in reverse for several feet in the first stage of a three-point turnaround.

"Stand on the brake until I jump in," Jim yelled over his shoulder. "I can't let go until you have your weight on the brake!"

"I'm pushing with both feet."

Jim relaxed, but his boots plowed through the gravel. His thighs burned, and the bumper and grill dug his back. "Are you sure?"'

"The pedal's all the way to the floor."

What the hell? She's pushing the clutch. "Try the middle pedal."

"The middle pedal?" Sheila sounded like the idea was as abstract as a quadratic equation.

"The gas is on the right! The clutch is on the left!" Jim grunted as his boots lost traction, slipping over the ball bearing like gravel.

The truck was picking up steam. His feet would catch and then the truck would roll over him. Perhaps he could get low enough the axles would clear his body. But could he avoid being crushed by the even lower hanging front differential and transmission? And Sheila would still be in the runaway truck.

"Oh—Okay. Got it," Sheila's voice exclaimed over the sound of his skidding boots. The brakes squeaked and the truck stopped.

Jim exhaled a breath he was sure had more adrenaline than air, then relaxed and the truck held. He ran back to the driver's door and slid in under Sheila, whose body was arched from pushing on the pedal.

"Slip over to your seat."

"I will in a minute."

Jim laughed.

Sheila's feet came off the brake and she sat on his lap. Jim reached both arms around, cranking the steering wheel. The truck picked up speed, and the gears made an ugly grinding noise until he double clutched and dropped the lever into third. With his arm around Sheila's belly, Jim dumped the clutch. The truck almost stopped, but because he was braced, they didn't smash into the steering wheel.

"You just scooped me again," she said, a happy, teasing note in her voice. The truck burped black diesel soot into the desert air. The motor's familiar rattle accelerated as he pushed on the gas.

INSIDE THE ESCALADE, THE DRIVER saw a streak from above and the bullet struck the grill, radiator, and engine block with a thud. Billowing steam from under the hood eclipsed the road. The driver stomped the gas to the floor, but the car refused his demand as coolant fumes flooded the cab. Mercifully, the shoulder was wide enough for him to pull off and avoid traffic. A glance in the side mirror showed steam rising from the first following car, then the Audi's hood flew up, covering the windshield.

The bright red lights on the dash indicated nothing worked inside the Escalade.

"What the . . .?"

The temperature, oil, service engine, and battery lights all glowed bright red. The sweet scent of coolant filled the cab and the driver got out and slammed the door before coughing and fanning at the steam as he stepped away.

The Mercedes rolled slightly ahead, making it just beyond the Escalade. The Mercedes's driver was tangled in his seatbelt. He stepped through the webbing, grasped the buckle, and threw it back, taking a chunk of paint as it bounced off the post between the front and rear door.

"I think someone just shot our cars."

"Tell me something I don't know, you stupid fuck! Let's jack a car and go after them!"

"Okay, Einstein, whoever shot us might still be up there, and if he can hit us moving sixty-five down the fucking freeway, he can put a bullet in your fat ass!"

"He probably left already anyway."

"I'm stupid? You wanna follow when you have no idea where the bullets came from?"

The two arguing men stopped. "The boss is here."

Behind the steaming Escalade, Michael Faletto got out of the passenger's side of a bright yellow, late model Corvette.

"How long you been here?" Michael snatched the sunglasses from his face and scowled at the vehicles. "Where's Frank?"

"His hood flew up but he kept going," the Mercedes driver explained.

"Hope that ain't him," Al Litizette had joined them from the Corvette, and he motioned toward a column of black smoke a half mile up the road.

"Someone shot us from above, boss."

"Really?" Michael's belittling tone made them drop their eyes beneath bowed heads. "Are dumb and dumber listening?"

"Yes, boss," they said in unison without looking up.

"Call Ralf. When the cops show, tell 'em you all had your vehicles serviced at the same place. Unload your wallets if you have to."

"I thought Ralf was in Wyoming."

"Would I say to call if he was in Wyoming?"

"My mistake."

"We'll run these assholes down. And keep your phones on!" Michael said over his shoulder as he strode back to the Corvette.

JIM LOOKED AT SHEILA. HER laugh showed perfect white teeth as waves of long black hair cascaded across her face. She swept the tresses back and wrapped her arms around his neck, smashing two kisses on his cheek. Then she kissed his mouth.

"I knew we'd do it. That was the coolest thing ever!" she exclaimed. "I wish we'd stayed to see their faces."

The plan, aside from missing the third shot and the truck's dead battery, had worked. The third driver would probably survive his burns, and Jim was grateful—he hadn't killed anyone other than in self-defense. All they had to do now was pick up his horse trailer, meet up with Larry and Chris in the desert, transfer the cash to the trailer, and head for Wyoming.

"You okay?"

Jim turned to Sheila, whose smile had become a look of concern. "That got ugly. I should have made the third shot."

AFTER HONKING THEIR WAY INTO the slowing traffic, it only took Michael Faletto and Al Litizette a few minutes in the yellow Corvette to inch alongside the Audi in the stop-and-go traffic.

"Is that Frank?" Al asked, eyeing several people kneeling around a body.

"He's alive. Don' worry 'bout it!"

"How'd you know?"

"'Cause everbody's lookin' at him. If he's dead, they'd be lookin' away."

"Wanna stop?"

Michael didn't speak until they were past the Audi, which still had flames trimming the edges and inside.

"Goddam mess."

"I said don't worry about it," Michael snapped. "Punch this thing. All the cops will be headed this way."

His back sank into the Corvette's seat as the vehicle rocketed forward, buzzing through and around traffic at more than a hundred miles an hour. Soon they were all alone on the freeway.

"Where'd all the cars go?" Al asked.

"They got backed up behind the mess. We should have free sailing for a few miles."

Even though the Corvette was already going forty over the speed limit, G-forces pressed Michael into the seat again as Al punched the gas and the car sped to one-fifty. Sagebrush and cliffs whizzed by for a few miles until they caught traffic. The Corvette's speedometer dropped to ninety, and Michael swore he could get out and crawl faster. They passed three cars, and then Al blinkered to the center lane and dropped to seventy-five.

"I didn't tell you to slow down."

"Right there." Al pointed ahead at the slow lane, where a dented and rusty Dodge Cummins extended cab with Wyoming plates was moving north up the freeway. The passenger had her arms around the driver.

"Maybe." Michael considered the possibility. "But there's gotta be a hundred trucks on the road with Wyoming plates between here and Salt Lake."

"I'll do what you tell me, boss."

"Punch it for a minute. If we don't see the delivery truck we'll come back and follow this guy."

Michael's body sank into the seat again as the Corvette rocketed forward. The white lines on the pavement came toward them like tracks on a runaway train as Al maneuvered between traffic. As they rounded a bend, the delivery truck came into view.

"Tail him from right here."

Al let off the gas. Within seconds, the steep uphill incline slowed the Corvette's momentum to match the speed of the other traffic.

"That Wyoming pickup back there look dirty to you?" Al asked.

"Yeah," Michael grumbled, remembering how the truck was caked in red dust. "I think it came from someplace above where a good shooter could hit three vehicles!"

BEHIND THE CONVENIENCE STORE, JIM and Sheila hooked up the trailer. Sheila tailed the truck and trailer in her BMW as Larry talked Jim to a secluded spot ten miles off the highway that was surrounded by cedar trees.

As they pulled up, Larry came toward them in a limping run, arms extended. Wrapping Jim and Sheila in a group bear hug, he picked both of them off the ground, turned a complete circle and set them down.

"Can you believe it?" Larry threw both fists in the air. "Poof one car explodes, poof goes the next one, and then all three cars are puking steam!"

Larry's infectious energy gushed a few minutes. Jim sensed they all knew it wasn't the end of their difficulties, but a momentary celebration seemed fitting.

"We still need to transfer the cash to the trailer," Chris said. "And first we need to stuff the gym bags into the garbage sacks."

"Aw, man! Why you gotta do that already? Fun police." Larry dismissed Chris's suggestion.

"Let's get back to Wyoming." Jim tried acting as go between. "I'll call Brody on the way to make sure he has a cooler full of beer for tomorrow night."

"Beers with Brody. Now you're talking! I bet he's missed me. He's gonna tell me to shut all the gates again!"

Jim chuckled, remembering Brody's whiskey-induced California transplant tirade.

Larry walked over to the back of the cash truck where a padlock held the lever. He grabbed it and turned to the group. "I hope you have bolt-cutters, Jim."

"Plug your ears." Jim drew his pistol, and shot the lock.

"Or a gun might work." Larry shook his head.

Jim tossed the shattered lock into the dust, twisted the lever, and stepped back as the door rolled up. Several gym bags fell near their feet. Larry snatched one and opened the zipper, while Jim, Chris, and Sheila watched like kids on Christmas morning. A handwritten tally-sheet sat atop of the bundles of cash.

100 bundles $20x100—Total $200,000.

"What do you make of that Mr. CPA?" Larry asked as he handed the sheet to Chris.

"This is perfect," Chris's eyes expanded. "My guess is every bag in the truck has a similar sheet."

Jim unzipped the next bag, and sure enough, there was a sheet of paper with a breakdown of the cash it contained.

"While we're transferring the cash, we should open each up to write down the amount, and we'll know exactly how much we have," Chris suggested.

Sheila jogged toward her BMW, and returned with a pen and a spiral notebook. "We can use the calculator on one of our phones."

"Your phone has a calculator?" Jim asked.

Sheila smiled.

Jim backed the trailer up to the back of the cash truck. The level differed, but it would enable them to make the transfer more quickly.

"Chris, you and Sheila make a record of what's in each bag, and then stuff a few of them into a garbage sack. Larry if you can hand the bags to those two, I'll stack them in my trailer after they're done," Jim ordered.

For the next hour, they worked and sweated like starving miners at the mother lode. The front of the trailer was stuffed with bags floor to ceiling.

Larry and Jim leaned into the rear door to force a few bags back inside as they shut it.

They walked around the trailer to join Sheila hovering near Chris, who was leaned over the hood of Jim's truck, punching at the numbers of a cell phone.

Chris looked up, a smile covering his face for the first time since helping Jim catch horses in the meadow. "There's $29,546,230 in that trailer!"

"How much is one fourth?" Jim asked.

Chris's fingers moved in a blur. "Almost 7.4 million."

Jim picked up the phone from the hood of his truck. He frowned as he looked at the figure. "I'll accept it as payment for the best horse I ever owned."

"That is the stupidest fucking thing I've ever heard."

Two large men stood behind Jim. The one to the right was a bit older than the two brothers he'd killed in the mountains, trimmer and taller, but definitely their brother. He held a snub-nose revolver in his right hand. The man on the left—obviously nothing but a lackey—held a pistol-grip shotgun, rigged with an extended magazine to hold extra rounds.

Jim pulled his pistol and shot the man holding the shotgun in the chest, but before he could move or adjust his aim, the man with the revolver grabbed Sheila.

"Let her go!" Jim snarled as he sighted his gun, trying for a margin near the man's head.

The gangster held his face directly behind Sheila's head as they backed away with Jim matching the steps.

"Push him, Sheila. I only need an inch."

"Shoot him. I don't care if you hit me!"

Jim lowered his pistol and shot the man's foot from ten yards away. As the gangster crumpled, he dropped the revolver to clutch his foot. Jim sprinted, covering the distance to the revolver in four strides. He snagged it left-handed and pointed both guns at the gangster's head.

"Do it," Sheila pleaded. "It's Michael."

A groaning behind them startled the group. The first gangster wasn't dead. Larry lunged at the rolling body, but couldn't get there before the man stood, shotgun in hand, holding them all at gunpoint.

"Drop the guns." The gangster's voice sounded weak, like he'd been horse-kicked in the chest. A Kevlar vest showed beneath the bullet holes in his dress shirt. The man pointed the shotgun directly at Larry.

Jim crouched and set the guns in the dust then backed away.

Michael snagged the revolver with his burly fist and pointed it at Sheila.

"You're mine, bitch," he snarled. "Get in the truck!"

"Ten steps back," the other gangster ordered.

As Jim, Larry, and Chris retreated, Jim fully expected to be shot. At least the scattergun would be quick, but what Michael said surprised him:

"Come alone tomorrow in the Corvette that's up the hill. The corner of Tropicana and Western, your life for hers at ten a.m."

"Why not kill me now?"

"Because you don't get to die quick."

"I'll be there," Jim said, scowling like a thunderstorm.

The lackey walked toward the driver side door of Jim's truck. As the two got to leave, Michael's foot left a bloody trail in the dust.

Jim scanned for a chance to keep them from getting away. Michael winced with each movement, but he kept the revolver pointed at Sheila who was in the truck as ordered. The lackey moved like everything hurt. His breath was shallow, no doubt the result of bruised or broken ribs from the bullet's impact. Their sluggish movements made Jim look at his pistol, which lay ten feet in front of him and to the left.

"Try it," Michael sneered. "I'll spray the inside of your truck with her brains," Michael climbed in the passenger door, the revolver now at Sheila's ribs.

The door squeaked shut and Michael's focus strayed. A clicking noise sounded from under the hood of the truck, but the engine didn't catch.

The dead battery? Maybe the starter motor is fried!

Just as the lackey was trying the key again, Sheila exploded, a manic blur of hair and fingernails inside the cab as she stomped on Michael's foot and fought for the gun. Jim bolted forward and Larry did the same, causing both Michael and his thug to look up. Larry shattered the driver's side window with a single punch, and still had enough power to knock the lackey cold. Larry hit the man again, and opened the door, then flung the unconscious body like a rag doll into the dust.

Jim smashed his fist squarely into Michael's face through the open passenger window. Sheila opened the door and Jim gripped Michael's throat, pulling him to the ground.

"Everyone okay?" Jim called out, never taking his eyes off Michael Faletto. Even so, his tone pleaded for a positive answer.

Sheila slid past him and nodded.

"Larry? Chris? Speak to me!"

"We're good, Jim," Larry blurted from the other side of the truck.

"Let us go and we'll fight another day," Michael's defeated voice cut into Jim's psyche. "Have you no honor? This is the day of my son's funeral."

Jim released his grip on Michael's neck. "At what time."

"This evening. Six o'clock."

The sun and his watch told Jim it was one p.m. "Bring my pistol."

Sheila disappeared behind and came back with the gun.

"Shoot him if he moves." Jim got up to retrieve his first aid kit from the truck's toolbox. "Why won't this work?" Sheila screamed, shaking the pistol in disgust. Her forearm muscles flexed, and Michael shut his eyes and turned away from the barrel, just inches from his face.

"The safety's still on." Jim extended his hand.

"How do you take it off?" She stepped away, refusing to give up the gun.

"Your lesson's coming." Jim stepped toward her and placed his hand on her wrists, then slid them to the pistol as her muscles relaxed.

A sound like an elk or deer carcass being dragged over rocks came from the front of the truck as Larry dragged the gangster he'd clobbered by the hair to his side of the vehicle.

"Same directions I gave Sheila."

Larry took Jim's pistol in one hand and the shotgun in the other.

The fingers of the latex gloves ballooned out when Jim blew in before he put them on. With medical shears, he cut off the bloody loafer and sock, and examined the wound. He dressed the entry and exit holes as best he could while Michael growled. Three rolls of gauze slowed the bleeding, and Jim looked the man in the eye.

"The cash bought my horse," he said. "If I sense your shadow's echo, I'll come killing." The two men locked eyes until Michael looked away. "Sunday, Christmas, or funeral, I won't care the day."

The lackey was conscious by that time, a swollen jaw and red features roared behind his dust-covered face.

"You have no idea who you fucked with," he managed to say through mangled and swollen lips and cheeks..

"You don't!" Sheila picked up a softball-sized stone and whacked him across the head. She lifted it for another blow, but Larry stepped between them as a human shield.

Jim took his pistol and the shotgun from Larry, who grabbed the man's throat.

"Give me your cell phone and wallet."

The man squirmed a bit, but as he ran short of breath, he fumbled the items out of his pocket and handed them over. Larry stood, towering over everyone. Without a word, Michael produced his own wallet and phone. Larry placed both wallets on the hood of Jim's truck.

"We have both their driver's licenses."

A gray rock, about the size of a loaf of bread, sat beside Michael. Sheila picked it up with one hand and dropped it on Michael's bloody foot.

"Fuck!" Michael screamed in a borderline soprano voice. "Bitch!"

Jim hit him in the face. Michael's muscles instantly relaxed and he slumped unconscious to the ground. Dropping the tailgate, Jim grabbed the five-gallon water jug he'd filled before leaving. He poured half of it over Michael, who woke in a start.

"You with me?" Jim grabbed Michael's left ear. Michael nodded. "Apologize."

"To who?" Michael spat blood on the ground.

"To her." Jim yanked up on the ear until Michael stood.

"Okay, okay," Michael paused, but didn't look anyone in the eye. "Sorry."

Jim swept away the shattered safety glass on the driver's seat with an old jacket. Then he wrapped the shotgun and revolver in the jacket and tucked them under the back seat. The truck and trailer were parked on an incline, so Jim opened the door for Sheila and pushed the clutch to the floor. They inched forward, gathering momentum and Jim dumped the clutch to bring the truck to life.

"Thanks for sticking up for me," Sheila said. Jim didn't say anything, but nodded.

The BMW followed the creaking old truck and trailer as hot desert air blew through the cab. At the yellow Corvette, Jim got out without killing the motor. Sheila stood beside him as he sketched a crosshair in the dust on the passenger side window.

"What's that?" Sheila asked.

"It's what a shooter sees through a rifle scope."

They got back in the truck and drove with the BMW following. In a flat spot a hundred yards away, Jim retrieved the fifty-caliber, chambered a bullet, and waited until the delivery truck pulled behind the Corvette. Michael waved off help from his companion and made it in a hopping limp to the Corvette's passenger side. Through the riflescope, Jim watched as Michael paused at the window's artwork. Right then, Jim squeezed the trigger, and the bullet shattered both passenger and driver's side windows into thousands of pieces.

The spent casing fell in the dust as Jim worked the bolt to insert another round, his eyes not leaving Michael.

"Hands in the air!" Jim yelled.

Michael and his companion both reached for the sky as Jim walked forward.

"Want me to come with you?" Larry asked.

"Absolutely," Jim said, still not taking his eyes off Michael Faletto.

"How about me?" Sheila asked. Larry handed the shotgun to Sheila and whispered something to her before walking with Jim.

"What are you going to do?" Larry asked.

"One last chance to make sure we're on the same page."

The Corvette and Michael got bigger with each step until they stood nose to nose. With his index and middle finger Jim made the "I'm watching you" signal to Michael.

Michael nodded but kept his arms skyward.

Jim stepped back a few feet. "I don't miss unless it's intentional."

"I get it." Michael lowered his arms.

The gun grew heavy. Jim set the rifle's butt in the dust but held the barrel with his left hand to keep it upright.

"You'll be watching for me," Michael said. "I get it."

"You better!" Larry growled.

A synapse connected in Jim's head. The bullet fell in the dust as he opened the bolt. Making sure to keep the barrel's tip above the dirt, he set the rifle between them.

"What are you doing?" Larry asked.

"A peace offering." Jim locked eyes with Michael. The 1911 pistol slid from Jim's waistband. He placed it beside the rifle before standing up and stepping back. "What the fuck is he doing?" the lackey asked.

"He's offering peace to your stupid ass!" Larry growled.

From nowhere in particular, a hot breeze kicked up dirt around them. The dusty guns still reflected light in their eyes. Jim extended his index and middle fingers, but instead of pointing at his eyes or at Michael, Jim lifted his hand in a peace sign. "Better get to that funeral."

Chills covered Jim as Michael looked at the guns, then at Larry, and then at Jim before nodding.

The Corvette sped away and Larry helped gather the bullet and guns.

"You know that peace offering shit ain't gonna work, right?" Larry asked.

"I know," Jim paused. "But at least I tried."

Halfway to the truck Jim spoke again. "What did you tell Sheila?"

"I gave her something to do." Larry smiled. "She would have started throwing rocks again if she came with us."

"So what was it?"

"I told her to make sure Chris didn't drive away with the cash."

52

"This man kills my family, shoots my son's foot, then escapes?"

Michael didn't respond to his father's questions because the doctor's examination shot searing pain all the way to his hip. If he uttered anything as the doctor drenched the bullet hole with iodine, it would be heard in basements across the street.

"Do I get an answer?" the old man's anger contorted his features, deepening the crevices of his eighty-four-year-old face.

"Fuck, dad!" Michael screamed. "Can you wait until the doc leaves?"

The doctor had been summoned from the Corvette as Al drove Michael home. He practiced medicine by making house calls for cash. As he put it, he would stop the bleeding and start the breathing—for a steep price. When Michael arrived in his driveway, the doctor was there waiting.

"He knows nothing, hears nothing, says nothing. Am I right?" Spencer Faletto's crackly but strong elderly voice filled Michael's bedroom.

The doctor looked up from where his medical supplies covered the nightstand. "I work better in silence."

Spencer hesitated, apparently unconvinced.

"You heard him, old man. Get the fuck out so I can bleed in peace!" Michael grabbed a pillow and threw it at his father, who stepped aside as it bounced against the wall.

Moving away from the next projectile kept Spencer headed toward the door, but his words came from the hallway.

"Leave him conscious enough to speak!"

Michael groaned, trying to relax into his gigantic four-poster bed. His father had flown in the previous evening from Florida. Along with a carload of luggage, he brought lots of unanswerable questions. But as the doctor examined the foot in earnest, Michael's irritation over the old man's boorish behavior was superseded by the pain.

"Do you have anymore numbing stuff?" Michael begged as he watched the doctor push a latex covered pinky all the way through the bullet hole.

"It's Lidocain," the doctor responded. "And, no, I don't. If you want to keep your foot, you'll do exactly as I say. You need to keep this elevated. Stay in the wheel chair with your leg in the support. You're lucky the bullet missed tendons and only nicked one bone. The bullet punched a half-inch hole through the soft tissue. Do not, under any circumstances, bear weight. Take the antibiotics I'm leaving, and I'll come by your house each night to change the dressing. As always, you don't know me."

"Or you me," Michael responded, looking at his pale, sweating face in the mirror above the bed.

The doctor stitched the top of Michael's foot, but left the bottom open to drain. After twenty minutes of painful prodding and poking, he gathered his medical supplies and left. Michael's father came in almost as soon as the doctor slipped out the door.

"This is a disgrace." The old man shook his head.

"Maybe we could talk later."

"Maybe?" the old man's voice exploded. "Maybe I need to come back to Vegas because my son can't stay sober. Maybe if you weren't so focused on opening up car dealerships, we wouldn't be in this mess. Maybe half my family would still be alive, and maybe I understand payback more than you ever will!"

His father's diatribe sliced through everything. "I will make this right. I will."

Spencer Faletto placed a hand on his son's forehead.

"Next to protecting your own life and those you love, vengeance is your greatest responsibility." Spencer paused. "It's time to protect what's ours."

"What are you telling me?"

"That I'm not leaving until this is finished."

Michael fought down the need to yell. The last thing he wanted was his old man micromanaging the killing of his enemies. His throbbing foot might feel better if he screamed the old bastard from the room, but Michael knew that family loyalty and a shared purpose precluded his father from doing anything other than fulfilling the promise to stay.

In consideration, Michael tempered his response by aiming it toward keeping control. "Fine, but understand you can't waltz in here like this is the fucking thirties and the family still runs whore houses in Boulder City!"

"I understand all I need."

"Understand this: the retirement mansion in Ft. Lauderdale wasn't paid for with rigged slot machines and fixing fights. I make more than your tired brain can fathom, and I sign the checks!"

"And it's not worth two farts in the wind if we don't kill the rancher." Spencer leaned down and kissed Michael's cheek, before walking across the room to straighten his tie in the mirror. He looked back from the doorway before stepping through.

"I'll see you at the funeral."

53

The rising sun refracted through the smeared bugs on Jim's windshield. Larry and Chris followed in Sheila's BMW as they approached the Cooper Ranch's western border. Jim turned into an entrance a few miles from the main gate and called Brody, telling him to get breakfast ready and that he would be coming home with some guests.

Near the ranch's northern border was an isolated mountain meadow bordered by forest service land. Over the years, Jim discontinued grazing cows there because there was better feed in less remote areas, and the unimproved access road beat up his trucks and trailers.

A few years earlier, when mad cow disease scared everyone in the beef industry down to their boot soles, Jim installed a small grain silo at the meadow's edge. If he needed to, it would be the perfect place to quarantine any sick animals. Luckily, he never had to use it, and the silo would be the perfect place to quarantine thirty million dollars in cash. Jim shook his head in disbelief at the thought of so much money. Even one fourth seemed astronomical compared to the four grand Chris paid him only ten days ago—and he'd felt like the luckiest man alive at the time.

They left Sheila's car near the main road, and Larry and Chris climbed into the extended cab. Before starting up the steep, twisting road, Jim yanked the transfer case into four low, and the weary passengers yawned as the bouncing truck shook them to wakefulness. When they arrived at the meadow, Jim backed up to the grain silo and got out, opened the doors to the silo and trailer, and went to work. Sheila was at his side helping, and with Larry and Chris, they transferred the bags from the trailer in thirty minutes.

"Should be safe for the time being," Jim said as Larry placed the last two bags in the silo.

After passing through several gates returning to the main road, Chris had a suggestion. "Can we put a chain and padlock on some of the gates up here?"

"They'll be on by the end of the day," Jim responded.

Larry and Chris got out at Sheila's car and followed Jim to the ranch house where Duke came from the barn in an ecstatic, bouncing run.

Sheila's mouth hung open. "You live here? All this is yours?"

"And the dog. This is Duke."

Sheila bent down to pet the exuberant bundle of fur. "I like him! He's really excited, but he hasn't jumped up on me."

"That's Duke, always the gentleman," Jim said.

"I wonder who taught him that?"

Even though they were only five minutes past when Jim told Brody they would be arriving, the old man emerged, glaring from the back porch.

"Ain't got all day. Come if you want any, for hell's sake."

Proving that his mouth worked quicker than his mind, Brody turned to walk back inside, but did an about face as his brain registered Sheila's presence.

"Brody," Larry yelled. "Come on over here and give your old friend Larry some respect."

"Don't hold your breath. I ain't giving hugs, knuckle bumps, or any such thing to you, you, or you," Brody said pointing at Jim, Chris and Larry. Then extending his hand to Sheila said, "But you can have anything from me your heart desires."

"You must be Brody."

"My fame precedes me."

Jim and Larry exchanged glances and smiles as they shook their heads.

"Happens to him all the time," Jim stated. "How've things been?"

"Quiet," Brody responded.

The enticing odor of bacon, coffee, and fresh pancakes wafted from the kitchen, greeting them at the door. Skinner was putting a platter of pancakes on the table.

"How's football camp, S?" Jim asked. "By the way, this is Skinner, or 'S.' Skinner this is Sheila, Larry, and Chris."

Skinner looked up and nodded.

"You get in a fight?" Jim asked, noticing scrapes on the boy's face, the split lip, and some bruising on his neck.

"We'll talk about it later," Brody interjected.

"Jim tells me you play football." Larry's enthusiasm filled the room.

Skinner nodded.

"He tells me you're damn good."

"I try. I love to play."

"I can see that. Some of the best times of my life were playing high school football. When you go to college it's not near as much fun."

"Where did you play?"

"UCLA," Larry announced proudly, catching Skinner's full attention.

"Cool! What position?"

"Defensive end. Jim says you're an inside backer."

"I was named outstanding linebacker at camp last week," Skinner acknowledged, failing to keep a boyish grin off his face. "We have some passing drills the first of next week. Jim sometimes stops by. You should come watch."

"Definitely. There was a time I lived for that stuff." Larry's wistful words struck a familiar note with Jim.

"Already blessed it." Brody intervened before anyone could say grace. "Good long prayer, too. No need for more."

"Liar," Jim said dryly, pulling out a chair for Sheila.

"Sure of that, are you? I blessed the entire grocery store."

"Why stop there?" Jim asked.

"Expert on praying, are you?"

After everyone was seated and the food had been passed, Jim spoke. "There are plenty of bedrooms. Make yourselves at home. There are some old vehicles around, keys are in 'em. I'll be busy most of the day, so let's plan dinner at six. Lunch is in the fridge and I'll have my phone."

Larry, Chris, and Sheila's sagging eyelids and slumped posture announced quite clearly what they would be doing all day. Jim wanted to crash, but sleeping in the daylight felt as unnatural as a cat swimming for pleasure. When the cows were calving, or if he had a mare due to foal, he would stay awake for thirty-six hours. Today would be no different, and working would only make his more welcome at day's end. Sheila yawned, stretching her hands above her head, and Jim was sure he had never seen anyone or anything so beautiful.

"I think we all need sleep." Larry covered his yawn and his eyes watered.

"Go for it." Jim took a large thermal mug from a cupboard and poured it full of coffee.

After breakfast, Jim, Skinner, and Brody went three different directions to work on fences. Claiming the section of the ranch that held the cash, Jim ran to town and bought locks and chains for the gates.

In a few weeks, he planned on herding some of the cows down from the high country to graze down the pastures. In addition to making sure the fences were fit to hold the cattle, there were water troughs to fix and mineral blocks to put out. Winter and drifted snow wreaked havoc on fences, and the past one had been a humdinger. There were several slouching gates where broken posts needed replacing, and cattle guards that needed to be lifted, dug out, and reset.

By twelve thirty, Jim and Duke were driving back to the ranch house. In the rear view mirror, a plume of dust rose as Brody and Skinner followed along. They still needed to repair more fences before they moved the cows, but several of the pastures were ready.

Jim asked Brody about the next most urgent thing. "Got groceries for our guests?"

"Told you, I blessed it all yesterday."

"Run to town and pick up enough supplies to string a fence through the middle of the southwest eighty, like we always wanted. We may have these guests for a while, hopefully one permanently. Get us a few cases of beer."

"Bottles or cans?"

"Bottles."

Brody nodded.

"S., I'm gonna have you help me gear up for next week—is there a reason you two aren't listening?" Brody and Skinner were looking past him, and Jim spun on his boot heel to catch Sheila sneaking up from behind. "I wondered why you two got distracted all of a sudden."

"This be the permanent guest you mentioned?" Brody asked in his dry raspy voice.

"Hopefully. If you don't put too much pressure on her."

Sheila put her arms around him, and Jim hugged her back.

"Get a nap?" Jim asked.

"I slept in your bedroom. I hope you don't mind."

Brody and Skinner both smiled, and without saying anything, they drifted toward the house.

"Find a place to put your things?" Jim asked.

"I found an empty closet. I really don't have many clothes. I'll need to go shopping for some things in the next few days."

Jim thought ahead. Their small town didn't have much selection. "We can get you clothes for around the ranch locally. Anything else and we'll need to take a trip to Jackson."

"Right now it looks like I'll need some work pants and shirts. What are we going to do this afternoon?"

"Let's go get some lunch, then you can help Skinner and me pull gear for next week's guests."

"Sounds great," Sheila said as Jim took her hand in his and went into the house.

After lunch, Sheila helped Jim and Skinner go through all the gear. Twelve guests were confirmed for the next week. Some of them would need to have all their gear provided while others had some of their own things, but might need one or two items.

It was always a hassle to sift through his email and keep track of who needed what. After watching him work for a few minutes, Sheila stepped in.

"You're disorganized." Rifling through his stack of papers, she began making legible lists for each guest, cutting the amount of time it would have taken Jim and Skinner by more than an hour.

"I can't believe we're done already!" Jim said, genuinely impressed. "We suck, S. There's still time to go through the saddles and horse tack before dinner."

In the tack room, Skinner and Jim had the same experience. Sheila inventoried each horse's needs and made lists for each animal.

"We don't just suck, we really suck," Skinner said as he hung the last bridle over the horn of its accompanying saddle. Jim nodded his agreement.

"It's cooled off a bit," Skinner said as they emerged from the barn. "I was hoping you would give me a shot at the champ."

Skinner's challenge didn't surprise him, but the only thing he wanted to do now was eat and go to bed.

"Think you have it in you?"

"There's only one way to find out." Skinner's enthusiastic response brought a chuckle from Jim, because he honestly didn't know if he could win.

Brody pulled up and yelled into the barn. "I got the goods. Wanna help?"

"Sure." Skinner trotted toward the truck. For the moment, Jim was spared.

"What are you two talking about?" Sheila asked.

"He should be state champion in his weight class this year. We've been wrestling for the last few years."

"And he hasn't beaten you yet?"

"No. But he's getting better—and I'm getting older."

"You've been awake since yesterday morning. Are you sure you want to do this?"

Jim yawned. "I'm sure I *don't* want to do this."

Jim and Sheila helped unload the groceries from Brody's truck. With everything put away in the fridge, freezer, or pantry, Jim and Skinner walked through the house to the front yard and the big grassy lawn. Larry and Chris looked up from their reading on the couches, as the group tromped through.

"What's going on? Larry asked.

"Entertainment time. You'll wanna see this," Brody said as he hurried through the front door.

Jim and Skinner were taking off their cowboy boots on the front porch when Sheila caught up with them.

"You're really going to wrestle a kid who's half your age, after no sleep since yesterday morning?" Sheila asked as Jim stepped off the porch and onto the lawn.

"I'm *more* than twice his age."

"And that doesn't concern you?"

Before Jim could respond, Brody intervened.

"Trust me, if there's someone you should be talking out of this, it's the overgrown rug rat. Jim's been doing his best to teach Skinner something he hasn't figured out yet."

"And what would that be?"

"Old age and cunning always prevail over youth and athleticism. Seriously, just sit here next to an old man and enjoy the show."

The concern on her face deepened, but she sat down on the porch next to Brody. Skinner was rolling his head back and forth while Jim stretched his upper body. Chris and Larry took positions on a bench behind Brody and Sheila.

"This is nice, S. We usually don't get an audience."

Skinner nodded his head.

"Bring it," Jim said and the two walked to the center of the lawn.

Skinner attempted to knock Jim off balance by trying to tie up his hands and get some leverage. While Jim wrestled cautiously, he knew Skinner could run faster and lift more in the weight room—but a lifetime spent shoveling, hammering, and shoeing horses had given Jim forearms to rival Popeye.

Exploding toward Jim like a sprinter from the blocks, Skinner shot in and grabbed both of Jim's legs to take him down. The bluff worked and they landed with a thud in the grass.

Twisting to his belly, Jim realized Skinner was finally doing what he needed to take the next step as a wrestler. He had always been bull strong and athletic, but he relied on his natural abilities. The mental part of wrestling, strategizing and exploiting an opponent's weaknesses, would take him to the next level.

Skinner tried to pry one of Jim's arms. Jim had to sprawl his legs to avoid being rolled. They both knew that eventually Jim would wear down, and Skinner's long sought victory was minutes away. All he needed to do was maintain the top as Jim weakened. Skinner tried to wrench one of Jim's elbows. He was prying it further and further from Jim's ribcage. With the elbow extended far enough, Skinner would slide his hand under Jim's armpit, put the palm of his hand on the top of Jim's head, and roll him over for the pin.

Digging for Jim's elbow again, Skinner had it pried far away enough to make his move. Sliding his hand under Jim's elbow, he was ready, but suddenly Jim's elbow clamped back to his body. Jim rolled like a boulder into the teenager.

Skinner recoiled as hard as he could to free his hand. If he didn't, Jim's roll could sprain his hand and wrist. As Skinner jerked to get free, Jim let go.

Like a tug-of-war team that holds the rope when the opponent releases, Skinner fell backward. As the boy stumbled, Jim snagged a leg with his right hand and hooked Skinner's neck with his left arm. Skinner curled up as he fell and Jim locked his two hands together before Skinner's back hit the ground.

A quick roll placed both of Skinner's shoulder blades on the ground for the pin.

"That about does it," Brody yawned and scratched at his chin

Skinner had a big smile on his face. "Someday I'll know all your tricks."

"No you won't," Brody said, through another yawn like he had never seen anything so boring.

"Yes, I will!"

"He'll make up more." Brody stood.

"We can go again in a few days." Jim helped Skinner stand.

The three-minute match left both breathing heavily.

"I'm not sure if I'm more hungry or tired. Why don't we all load up and go to Marty's?" Jim suggested. Brody and Skinner glanced at each other uneasily.

"What's Marty's?" Sheila asked.

"A local bar and grill. The selection's sparse, but what they have is pretty damn good. Let's leave in twenty minutes."

"I need to tell you something before we get there."

"Sure, S. You wanna tell me now, or on our way there?"

"On the way there'll be fine," Brody answered, and Skinner mouthed, "thanks" to the old man.

Sheila walked up to Jim and put her arm around his waist. "Stop for a minute. I want to look at this sunset."

Jim looked to the magnificent western sky. The setting sun behind the mountains cast long shadows across the valley. The high, wispy clouds glowed shades of red and orange.

"Are all sunsets here this pretty?"

"No."

"When was the last time you saw one like this?" Sheila asked.

"The night I met Larry. It made me feel lonely."

"And now?"

"Don't have the words."

They stood looking at the sky and at each other until Larry spoke from the porch. "I'll bring something back if you want."

"Hold on. We're coming," Sheila replied.

"Who's we?" Sheriff Johnson walked around the porch, and Jim spun in his stocking feet to face his old friend.

"Albert. 'We' would be Sheila."

"Ma'am," Albert said, tipping his hat. "Could you excuse us?" Sheila walked into the house and shut the door.

"Don't worry. I don't care who she is or where you've been the past few days. I'm here to give you an update."

"I'm listening."

"For starters, I've been over the shooting with the FBI and both the state and federal prosecutors. It's been ruled self-defense. The next most important thing is the FBI has filed restraining orders against eighteen members of the Faletto crime family."

"It won't stop them from coming."

"You're right, but it does give me the ability to arrest them on the spot if I see them within ten miles of you."

"I like that," Jim responded.

"Lastly, the FBI got me a federal grant to hire three more full time deputies. The money came from the homeland security act. We only have two roads coming and going in this town. Having the extra eyes could save your life."

"This is all good."

"No, it's not. They think you only have a little while before the hound bites your ass. Apparently the mob boss has an injured foot, and with the restraining orders they figure he'll hire hit men."

"Any idea how soon?"

"A month maybe. Could be sooner. I'll guard-dog our valley the best I can."

"Thanks, for everything—thank you."

"Thank you?" Albert laughed. "That pretty little thing has influence! Gratitude's not a suit of clothes I've seen you wear often."

"How's it look?" Jim responded.

"Not bad. You're almost human."

"I appreciate it. I'm still packin' everywhere, won't go anywhere alone."

"That'd be wise. You can always call me or one of the deputies."

"What if I call during a doughnut break?"

"There he is! I knew you'd surface. In that case, you should call Skinner, Brody, or anyone at Marty's."

"What? Skinner or Marty's?"

Albert walked away with Jim tailing him for an answer. At the Sheriff's SUV, Albert turned and opened his mouth, but his eyes went to Skinner as the boy came through the back door and stood on the porch.

"Skinner," Albert called out. "Come here a second." As Skinner walked over, Albert pulled something from the hatch. "These are yours," he said, handing Jim the saddlebags from the day of the shooting.

"Pistol inside?" Jim asked.

"Reloaded it for you."

"How about my toothbrush?"

"You didn't buy a new one?"

Jim smiled. "Aisle three at Ernie's."

The boy approached looking at his feet. His mannerism was out of character and Jim wondered if the boy held some shame the Sheriff knew about.

"Look at me, son."

Skinner lifted his bandaged head, revealing his scrapes, bruised neck, and split lip.

"I'm gonna leave because you're about to say something the sheriff doesn't need to hear."

Skinner's face lost muscle tone and his shoulders hung like someone caught in a lie.

"It's okay." Albert opened his door to climb in. "I won't arrest you, but the second I shut the door, you tell Jim about the dustup at Marty's."

54

Skinner and Brody told Jim about Ralf the wrecker driver. As they ate dinner, many of the regulars came by and mentioned the altercation. Word of Skinner throwing the rock through the gangster's window had spread, and with word spreading, the sentiment toward Jim grew. Everyone in the town, or at least at Marty's, professed a zealous desire to watch for intruders. The well-wishers eventually cleared away and the food was served. Skinner excused himself to the restroom, and Larry leaned forward.

"Let's talk quick while our outstanding linebacker's gone," he said, keeping his voice low. "Chris and I re-checked the cell phones I stole in the woods, and there's nothing. They've been totally scrubbed. I'm staying, Jim. You're the only reason I'm alive."

"You sure?"

"Look at me! I'm six foot seven and three hundred pounds. I can't hide no matter where I go, and I owe you."

"I appreciate it."

"How about me?" Sheila lifted her nearest eyebrow. "Can I stay?"

"You'll need to pull your weight," Jim teased.

"How about it, Chris?" Larry asked.

"I'm not sure yet." Chris muttered. He did seem to have cheered up a bit since they left Saint George, but Jim still didn't trust him.

"Five of us in the house. It'll be worse than church," Brody grumbled.

Jim told everyone of his conversation with the sheriff, emphasizing the restraining orders and the fact that it would take at least a few days for Michael Faletto to hire hit men.

"We could have one here right now," Brody insisted.

"I've thought about this a ton," Larry offered. "He's gonna take his time. It's part of the code. Jim let him go in the desert when he could have killed him. That little nod he gave us when you put your guns down—"

"You put your guns down?" Brody gave Jim a look like he'd just met the world's biggest idiot.

"Jim backed him down first," Larry continued. "Cutting him lose to attend his family's funeral was huge."

"Bullshit!" Brody growled. "You killed his family!"

"What are you saying?" Jim asked.

"That we should drive down there right now and finish this," Brody said, thumping the bar.

"I wasn't talking to you." Jim scowled at Brody.

"All I'm saying is you had his wheels spinning in the desert," Larry whispered. "Respect among thieves—he knows you spared his ass, and he'll think twice."

"I don't think we can count on that," Sheila said. "He wants to take Jim alive."

"Why?"

"He told you, remember? 'You don't get to die quick.'"

"Listen to the lady," Brody responded. "Remember the conversation a few days ago, Jim."

"How could I forget?" Jim replied. Brody's revelation seemed like months ago.

"They're both right," Sheila said. "They know you're here and they can wait for as long as need be."

Skinner returned from the restroom and Larry asked him about football as though the conversation hadn't taken place. After dinner, they drove back to the ranch. The horses whinnied from the barn. Jim forked the mangers full, then followed the others back up to the house.

That night, Sheila slid into bed next to him. There was no teasing, no testing, just pure passion.

In the morning, while the sun was still just a pale glow on the eastern horizon, Jim had managed to get dressed without turning on the bedroom light. Sheila rolled over and sat up.

"Did I pull my weight last night?" she asked, a coy note in her voice.

Jim smiled. "Sorry to wake you. How'd you sleep?"

"Like a rock," she replied.

"I need to take a ride around the place. Care to come along?"

"I'd love to."

Jim found some of his sister's old riding boots, long pants, western shirts, and even a ladies' size straw hat. "These should fit. I'll be getting some breakfast and then out in the barn saddling the horses."

"I'm right behind you."

Down in the kitchen, Brody and Skinner sat hovering over cereal bowls like weanling piglets at the trough.

"Sheila's going for a ride with me," Jim said by way of greeting. "Let's drop back to fencing until I get back."

Skinner nodded, and Brody spoke. "I'll take the miscreant. We need to dig out a few cattle guards and replace some fence posts. I can use his strong back and weak mind."

Brody had given Skinner at least one nickname for every week he had worked on the ranch, "miscreant" being the most recent.

"Use him while we have him," Jim responded.

Wearing Wrangler brand, boot cut jeans, an old pair of cowboy boots, and a long sleeve western shirt with the top two buttons undone, Sheila walked into the kitchen like a warm breeze in Antarctica.

"How do I look?" She spun around on her boot heel.

Brody and Skinner stopped chewing.

"Amazing." Jim leaned over and kissed her lips before grabbing a bagel from the breadbox. "I'll be in the barn. Breakfast is fend-for-yourself. These two will show you where everything is."

With Duke at his feet, Jim had just finished tying a pair of saddle bags behind Beatrice— loaded with a fencing tool, staples, and hammers—when Sheila came out the back door and walked toward the hitching rail.

"Sheila this is Beatrice. Beatrice, Sheila."

"Good morning, sweetheart," Sheila said, petting her on the neck and gathering the reins. Then she put her foot in the stirrup and stepped into the saddle. Standing in the stirrups, she looked down at her feet, and dismounted. Before Jim could help, Sheila was adjusting her stirrups to length. After finishing on each side, she climbed back on the horse and looked at Jim, who smiled up at her.

"Where'd you learn your way around a horse?" he asked, incredulous but happy.

"I lived in a home for troubled teenagers. We got to ride the horses if we behaved."

"You must have been a good girl." Jim climbed on Terence and they were off. For the next five hours, they rode around the Cooper Ranch. Sheila helped him repair fence lines and move some of the cattle from pasture to pasture. Sheila's natural ability impressed him. She sat with an easy, comfortable balance on Beatrice, and good as the veteran horse was, she responded to Sheila's confidence. Jim took notice.

"That horse has never had it so good."

"What makes you say that?"

"Everything else she carries weighs more, smells bad, kicks her harder, and uses bad language. She's liable to buck Brody off next time."

Sheila smiled at the compliment and leaned down to pet her new friend's neck. "You won't buck Brody off, will you girl?"

"You're a good rider. Can you saddle yourself?"

"I can."

"Then she's yours to ride anytime."

"I want to spend my time with you."

"I think it would be wise."

"I didn't say I need to. I said I want to."

On the way back to the house, they urged the horses into a run. With Sheila riding her, Beatrice was a bit faster than the gelding, and Jim enjoyed watching Sheila bounce up and down on the saddle, her hair flying behind in long, flowing strands as they rounded the corner into the barnyard.

Jim was pulling his boot from the stirrup when he looked to the house and saw a strange car parked nearby. He gripped his pistol.

"Seeing you gallop in here put a lump in my throat," said an elderly woman from the front porch. "I remember watching you do the same thing when you were five years old with your father."

Jim released his grip.

Jackie Cooper had come home.

Heat ran through Jim's cheeks in shame. He hadn't called his mom since the night he killed the three men, but he let his excitement override the guilt.

"Mom! It's so good to see you." Jim left the gelding untied and strode to his mother, arms extended to give her a hug.

"Are you going to introduce me to your friend?"

Sheila stood next to Beatrice.

"I'm sorry. This is my girlfriend, Sheila. Sheila, this is my mother, Jackie Cooper."

Jackie walked up to Sheila and hugged her as well.

"I'm pleased to meet you. Let's go inside and get some lunch."

Over sandwiches, Jim introduced Jackie to Chris and Larry, and then Brody and Skinner arrived. Jackie spoke to everyone.

"I'm glad all of you are here. I'm sure I'll learn the details, but I'm glad to see Jim has some new friends. You are all welcome to stay for as long as you like."

The group thanked Jackie for her hospitality.

"This afternoon I was planning on going into Jackson to do some shopping for the grandkids. Sheila, would you like to come with me?"

"Sure." Sheila fidgeted.

SKINNER AND BRODY BOTH NODDED and walked to Brody's truck. Once inside, Skinner turned to the old man. He wanted to ask him something, but he hesitated, and Brody noticed.

"Got something to say, miscreant? Ain't got all day."

"You think I'll ever beat Jim at wrestling?"

"You already could."

"He kicks my ass every time."

"Just like the wrecker driver, Jim beats you up here." Brody reached over and knuckle-thumped the boy's forehead hard enough to leave a welt. "Last night, you didn't even notice how he took the high side of the lawn with the sun to his back."

Skinner's eyebrows dropped to a scowl as he contemplated Brody's words. "He did, didn't he?"

"Is the Polaroid developing yet, miscreant?"

"What's a Polaroid, and what the hell is a miscreant?"

"Never mind. Has the idea circled the corral long enough to read the brand?"

"Jim beats me mentally." Skinner shrugged. "I get it."

"Kicking your teenage ass is no accident. For three years, Jim's used your elbows and knees to aerate the lawn, and he hasn't looked into the sun once."

"So what else is he doing besides making me sunblind and standing uphill?"

"You'll know when you win."

Wrestling Jim had been an exercise in frustration, like wrestling a tractor with arms. Brody was right. Jim always gave himself an advantage.

Skinner was silent for a few minutes. "Brody?"

"Miscreant."

"How do we wrestle from the high ground with the sun to our backs if the folks from Nevada come back?"

"That, *pardner,* is what you and I are going to work on this afternoon."

55

As the two ladies got into Jackie's car to drive to Jackson Hole, Jim ran toward them before Sheila could shut the door.

"Larry's coming with you," he said as the big man walked onto the porch.

"Girls only." Jackie shot her only son a disgusted look.

"But it's not safe," Jim protested.

"How about I follow in Sheila's car?" Larry asked. "Would that be okay, Mrs. Cooper?"

"Here," Sheila said, offering him the key-pod. Having Larry along would be wise, she thought.

"Be careful. I'll have my phone on all day," Jim said as Larry got into the BMW.

Sheila's nervousness had nothing to do with Mafia retribution. At the moment, being alone with Jim's mother was much more terrifying. But as they drove away, Jackie put her at ease.

"I'm so happy there's another lady at the ranch."

"Thanks. Your home is amazing. I want to pinch myself to make sure it's real."

"One thing's certain. My boy's definitely smitten."

"I hope so," Sheila said. "I know I am."

They drove in silence for a few minutes and Sheila worried again.

All of a sudden, Jim's mother's approval meant everything. It was obvious Jim loved and respected his mother, and Sheila wanted more than anything to get off on the right foot. Maybe Jackie disapproved of them living together or something else, but then she spoke.

"Jim called the night he killed those three men. I wanted to rush home, but something told me not to, so I delayed. I'm glad I did because he found you."

Sheila smiled at the thought.

"Jim killed seven men in the first Gulf War. He wore it like the chickenpox for years. I was worried what happened in the mountains would bring it all back. He's learned to cope, but part of dealing with something awful is hoping we won't have to go through it again."

Jim told me he'd killed eleven people. Eight in Desert Storm plus three. Sheila kept the thought to herself, not wanting to slow down the conversation, or betray Jim's confidence. "I understand exactly what you're talking about."

"I expected to find him wallowing in the past. Then he gallops into the barnyard with a gorgeous young lady and a huge smile. It reminded me how happy he was as a little boy." Jackie paused. "I hope you keep him happy for a long time."

Sheila couldn't contain her smile, and Jackie's matched hers. "I hope to."

"I'll help anyway I can."

"Can I ask you some questions about Jim?" Sheila tucked the hair behind her ear.

"Go ahead," Jackie responded.

"Who was Bradley?"

"Jim told you about Bradley?" The smile dropped from Jackie's face, and the reverent tone and open eyes told Sheila she was surprised, or maybe even astonished.

"He mentioned him once. He said he would tell me eventually."

"But he hasn't yet." Jackie completed Sheila's sentence.

For a minute, Sheila sensed that Jackie was trying to decide how to begin.

"Jim's his father's son. He may never tell you, but I will, because Bradley is my story, too."

The two women looked at one another, and Jackie wiped a tear from her eyelid.

"You don't have to," Sheila said, doing her best to sound empathetic even though she really wanted to know.

"It began about thirty years ago," Jackie stated. "Our community's mostly Mormon. I was raised in a Mormon family, but Jim's dad wasn't, and we agreed to raise the kids without organized religion.

"As an exception, I taught Jim and his sisters something from the Bible once a week. Jim's dad was supportive, and sometimes we would even invite my parents to share something with the kids. One night, I taught the parable of the Good Samaritan. How a man was beaten, robbed, and left to die on the side of the road. As he was suffering, the church leaders ignored him, but then an unlikely stranger comes to help."

"Right, the Good Samaritan takes care of him. I remember," Sheila offered, trying to speed the conversation.

"I can still remember Jim's face. He hung on every word. The questions didn't stop for days."

"Like what?"

"How old was the Samaritan and the man who had been robbed? What did the robbers steal? Did they become friends afterward?" Jackie smiled wistfully. "You name it, and he asked it."

"Jim must have been the cutest kid."

"He looked the same thirty years ago—tough, handsome; he just grew up to be a bigger version. When we get back to the ranch I can show you some pictures."

"Absolutely. I would love that!"

"One day I got a call from the principal. He explained that Jim had been in a fight with two boys, who were both a year older, because they had been picking on a new student."

"And the new student was Bradley?" Sheila offered.

Jackie exhaled. "It was the poor little guy's first day. Apparently the two older boys were holding him down on the playground, when Jim came to his rescue."

"Were Jim and Bradley okay?" Sheila asked, concern filling her belly.

"A few scrapes and bruises, but they were all right."

"I hope the principal didn't kick him out of school," Sheila responded.

"The principal was a good friend and a wise man. After he figured out what had happened, he sent the two bullies home, and took Bradley and Jim into his office, and gave them both a cookie."

"That's nice."

"Bradley's parents died in a car crash. He was an only child who came here to live with his grandparents. He was smart and bright, but not very big or tough. As they grew up, Bradley and Jim became best friends. In lots of ways, I feel like I raised two boys.

"Even back then, Jim wanted to help. When he first brought him home to play, it tore me apart. Bradley's shabby clothes and messy hair made a target for other kids."

"Didn't his grandparents take care of him?"

"They were good people, but poor, and too proud to ask for help. Jim's dad and I did what we could, without being too obvious. We would have the boys do chores and pay Bradley with some sneakers, a new shirt, or a pair of jeans."

"Jim's friendship did more than anything. Occasionally, someone may have teased Bradley, but with Jim nearby, I don't think anyone dared to be very mean.

"We all need good friends, and Jim was one. But looking back, Bradley did as much for us as we did for him."

"Really?"

"Bradley was loyal. He never missed my birthday, and I didn't have to worry about Jim hanging out with bad kids."

"Jim said that they went to Kuwait together, but that Bradley didn't come back," Sheila offered.

"It's not that simple. Bradley was Mormon, but he decided to forgo a mission to join the army with Jim. Our local sheriff enlisted with them, and the three went away to boot camp together."

"I don't understand missions."

"Mormon boys go away for two years. The Church sends them to places all over the world to preach. Lots of Jim's friends went, but Bradley decided to join the army. After boot camp, they went into the infantry together. They were only in for a few months when the Gulf War broke out and their company got called up."

"And Jim lost his best friend there," Sheila stated.

"He blamed himself. He volunteered in Bradley's place, but the Sergeant in charge made them both go. Jim told us a decade later that the Sergeant didn't like Bradley, and intentionally placed him in harm's way."

"Does Jim blame himself?" Sheila asked.

"I think you already know the answer."

"Thanks for telling me." Sheila paused, trying not to sniffle. "Has Jim ever been in love?"

Jackie wiped a tear away. "I think he should be the one to tell you about his love life."

Sheila understood. As she discovered more about Jim Cooper, she found depth and layers to an amazing life. She had layers as well. Living between homes most of her life, she had walked some of Bradley's path. For a minute she thought about pouring it out to Jackie, but then she realized what Jackie had told her about Jim's love life probably applied to her as well.

Pondering an image of Jim as a brave little seven- or eight-year-old, pulling bigger kids off an orphan, she knew Jackie was right.

He was just a bigger version of the same brave little boy, grown to manhood—now pulling Mafia-sized bullies off strangers.

They shopped the day away while Larry's watchful eye stayed close. Millions in the grain silo meant saying goodbye to sticker shock. By the time they headed home, her Wyoming wardrobe included work clothes and summer dresses, exercise outfits, a dozen pairs of new shoes, several jackets, and a winter coat. She even had a half hour while Jackie went toy shopping for the grandkids to sneak into a lingerie department.

When they returned home, Jim met the ladies at their car to help with all the packages. A bag full of lacy items caught his eye.

"Where'd these come from?" he asked as soon as they were alone.

"No peeking until I model for you!"

"Did my mom see you buy these?" Jim crinkled a wry smile.

"I snuck away for a few minutes."

"How did you two get along?"

"Your mother is the kindest, coolest, best lady I think I've ever met."

"What did you talk about?"

"I'll tell you before we go to sleep."

"Are you going to tell me before or after you model the contents of the bag you won't let me see?"

"Not before or after," she smiled. "During."

"It'll be hard to focus on the conversation."

Sheila hugged him from his feet into the bed. "I think you're the best friend Larry or I could ask for."

Before Jim could respond, Jackie's voice echoed through the house. "I'm not cooking tonight. Everyone get ready, we're going to Marty's for dinner."

56

For a few days after meeting with Bishop Fawson, Sally was melancholy, wishing life would speed by, so she decided to go for a run after work. The neighbors' manicured lawns, the flowerbeds in front of each house, weeded and brimming with an assortment of marigolds and sunflowers, all annoyed her.

As she approached Marty's, she smiled at a building with no front yard. Forty feet from the front entrance stood a man she didn't know, along with Jim, Brody, Larry, Skinner, Jackie, and an attractive lady. They looked to be heading into Marty's.

"Hello, Sally," Jackie greeted her. "How've you been?"

"I'm good. It's good to see all of you, and especially you," Sally said as she looked at Larry, who towered over everyone.

"You were my nurse!" Larry exclaimed his astonishment. "You look better out of scrubs. The running clothes make you look fine!"

The compliment made her blush.

There were still bruises around Larry's eyes, but the swelling had receded.

"And you look better than the last time I saw you, too."

Larry laughed, but stopped as Sally turned to look at Skinner, who had a few of his own bruises.

"Skinner Strobel, what happened to you?"

"It got a little rough during a wrestling match," Jim interjected. "He knows if he doesn't mind you, it'll be worse next time."

The last match she'd witnessed had frightened Sally. That time, they'd knocked over a stack of firewood, so it wasn't surprising that one of them would come away beat up.

"Let me introduce you," Jackie offered. "You already know Larry, and this is Chris and Jim's girlfriend Sheila."

Sally extended her hand to shake Sheila's.

Jackie turned to Sheila and Chris. "Sally is Skinner's mom, and I owe her an apology. I didn't feel like cooking tonight and I insisted we take him to dinner."

"Why would you apologize for that?" Sheila stood next to Jim with his hand around her waist.

"Because Marty's serves alcohol," Jim explained.

"But Skinner didn't drink any."

"I'll explain later." Jim pulled her close.

Even with a nurse's iron belly, the new girlfriend resting her head on Jim's shoulder made Sally feel like heaving.

"Let's keep this between you and me," Sally said to Skinner.

"Be man enough to hug your mother!" Brody barked at the boy, who did as ordered, and the affection made breathing easier for a moment.

"It was nice meeting all of you. Call me when you're done working, and I'll pick you up."

"No need. I'll bring him home Saturday night."

Sally thanked Brody for offering and walked to the corner, but as soon as she was out of sight, she took off, trying to sprint the hollowness from her chest.

How did it come to this?

Stopping made her feel like she might implode and sink through the sidewalk cracks. Jim's bachelorhood was as established as Yellowstone's Old Faithful. Over the years, she came to believe it could never be different, and her heart ached over things not said and opportunities not taken.

The hell with this, she thought, and ran even faster for a full block before stopping at the verge of consciousness. Chest heaving, lungs burning, she muttered to herself about an unfair life, about how many years she'd lost, and both pitied and berated herself for having to make life-altering decisions at such a foolish age.

She jogged again without catching her breath, but stopped at a flowerbed, where she kicked the head from a neighbor's marigold. The decapitated flower landed in the gutter, a dirty stream pushing it downhill. As she watched it rush away, she suddenly wanted to somehow reverse the damage.

Perhaps she could buy a replacement to replant, but worried about being seen and having to make an explanation.

She ran from the headless stem, propelled by another thought. Her misery had to be comparable to Jim's when he learned from Bradley Salveson and Albert Johnson at boot camp that she was married.

Too late to change anything; Bishop Fawson had been correct. Jim and Skinner deserved to know they were more than wrestling buddies. Her husband, Charlie, deserved to know as well, and she decided it was time she stood up to his controlling behavior.

When Charlie came home, demanding she get out of bed to pray, he would hear the truth.

57

The third morning back in Wyoming, Jim strode down the hallway, his booming voice rumbling through the house. "Boot camp! Roll out. Pistol practice behind the barn in ten minutes!"

Skinner appeared in the hallway, hair messed up and shirt un-tucked, followed closely by Larry, Chris, and Sheila.

"Where's Brody?" Sheila asked.

"Irrigating. Won't be back 'til afternoon."

As they walked through the kitchen, Jackie greeted the group. "Breakfast'll be ready when you get back."

At the back porch, Jim had an assortment of handguns and ammunition ready as well as several packets of earplugs. "Pack this with me, S. Every morning, we're gonna train."

"Cool!" Skinner grabbed several boxes of ammunition.

"I'm down," Larry said, tucking a laundry basket full of handguns under his arm.

"I thought you'd forgotten." Sheila smiled as she put her hair into a ponytail. "So you'll teach us how to shoot targets?"

Jim looked at her and then at Skinner, Chris, and Larry. It was time to start the lesson: "No. I'll teach you how to shoot people."

They marched toward the back of the barn and into the woods. A hundred yards from the barn was a clearing. Against four trees at the edge stood the silhouettes of four men, etched on sheets of plywood.

Jim pulled his pistol from the waistband beneath his shirt.

"The most important part of shooting a handgun is your grip," he explained as Skinner pushed his way between Larry and Chris for a better view. "A short barrel makes the margin for error critical. Squeeze with your three bottom fingers, push into the grip with the palm of your shooting hand, and lock it in by pulling back with your support hand."

Four sets of eyes focused closely on Jim's demonstration, and then he holstered the weapon.

"Alright, everyone, put in your earplugs."

Facing the silhouettes, Jim took his pistol in the same grip he'd just demonstrated, and shot two rounds into the heads of all four targets in just a few seconds. He dropped the empty magazine, and slid a fresh one into the sleeve.

"Sick," Larry said shaking his head.

"Those holes aren't even an inch apart," Skinner said after walking close to the life-sized targets to examine Jim's work. "And your shots are like one sound."

Over the next hour, Jim coached the eager shooters, instructing them to project energy into the fight by taking their adrenaline and using it for aggression to shoot from the balls of their feet with arms fully extended and elbows locked.

After shooting fifty rounds through a Bersa .380, Sheila was consistently hitting her target's head.

"Right now, you're all better than the three I killed a couple weeks ago. From now on, we pack everywhere. No exceptions."

"This one works for me." Larry picked up a .45 similar to Jim's.

"As for you, S, I hate to do this to you, but today's your last day for awhile."

Skinner's smile drooped.

"Your mom called after we got back from Marty's. Being here puts you at risk."

Skinner's head sagged, his chin resting on his chest. He looked like a pup taken from its mother.

"I wish it was different," Jim muttered in a barely audible tone.

"We'll miss you." Sheila patted his shoulder.

Skinner's head lifted, a devil may care look in his eyes. "At least I tracked the guy to Marty's."

Jim returned the smile.

"Yes you did," Jim acknowledged, slapping his young friend's back. He was about to offer his knuckles for bumping when Skinner enveloped him in a bear hug, catching him completely off guard.

"Watch town for me," Jim said as he awkwardly returned the hug.

"I got your back."

"We'll be at football practice on Monday," Larry said enthusiastically, but it sounded like he'd just offered the losing game show contestant the consolation prize.

"I'm catching a bus this afternoon," Chris announced like he was reciting facts from an encyclopedia.

Jim wasn't shocked to hear the accountant's plans, but he wanted Skinner gone before the conversation continued. "Sorry, S. Why don't you go find Brody."

Skinner nodded and headed back toward the house.

"I'm taking as much cash as I can carry with me in large bills," Chris said. "I'll be back for the rest of my share in a few months, if anyone's still alive."

"Tone deaf bastard! Do you ever feel the beat?" Larry growled. "That kid would give anything to stay here and fight it out, and you can't wait to broadcast your travel plans?"

"A fourth is mine," Chris responded, his tone matter of fact. "And I'm taking it in large bills."

"Ones and fives suit me." Larry shot back. "If anyone wants my black ass, it'll be right here."

"I'm glad you're staying." Sheila said.

"I can't hide. Look at me," Larry said with his palms extended. "What was the name of that horse you put me on, Jim?"

"Beatrice."

"Well, Beatrice couldn't drag me away." Larry tucked his new pistol in the small of his back. "We live and die together."

"Brody'd miss you anyway," Jim responded.

"I'd like my cash this morning," Chris said. His business-like demeanor and poker-faced stare didn't waver.

Jim exchanged glances with Larry and Sheila; by their expressions, they were as taken aback by the accountant's one-track mind as he was.

"What time did you say your bus was leaving?" Larry snapped.

"I didn't say. I'm leaving at two."

"Well, I'd hate for you to miss it."

A smile broke over Sheila's face at Larry's response as she turned away.

Even though Chris's curtness surprised Jim, he couldn't blame the accountant for wanting to disappear.

After a quick and silent breakfast, they all headed out to the grain silo, where they dug through the pile until they found several bags with hundred dollar bills. By taking two large suitcases, Chris would walk onto the bus with 4.1 million dollars.

They returned to the house and Chris ran inside to finish packing. Sheila and Larry followed Jim into the barn to visit as he puttered around in the tack-room. Fifteen minutes later, they heard Chris insisting on limousine service to the bus station.

"I think Brody nailed this guy the other day," Larry whispered. Sheila laughed.

"Must've missed it," Jim said. "What'd he say?"

"That, 'Chris was as useful as sheep shit in a Dutch-oven.'"

"That'd be Brody."

"Let's get this asshole out of here." Larry smiled and led the others from the barn.

Twenty minutes later, Jim's truck parked at the curb. They said goodbye on the sidewalk. Chris shook hands with both men. Sheila extended her arms, but instead of embracing her, he offered a curt handshake and walked like a robot to the ticket window.

Back in the vehicle, Sheila imitated the accountant with an expressionless face and a monotone voice. "Bye, Chris. Hope you make some friends where you're going. It's sure been fun."

Jim roared with laughter and Larry clutched his belly.

"Damn, girl!" Larry gasped between guffaws. "You do nerd really good. That is spot on!"

Sheila broke character, but didn't smile. "We need to move the money. I don't trust him."

"You really think he'd come back and steal it?" Jim asked. As much as he disliked Chris, he couldn't quite believe the idea, even though Sheila's demeanor had already answered the question.

"We need to move the money," she repeated.

"It can't hurt," Larry offered. "And let's just say for a second we're wrong. When Chris comes back, we can always take him to wherever we move it."

Jim thought for a moment, running through the possibilities in his mind. "We'll split it up and move it three different places this afternoon."

OVER THE WEEKEND LARRY, BRODY, and Sheila worked with Jim from daylight to dark, making preparations. While setting a locking gate into the enormous posts at the ranch's main entrance, they watched a brand new sheriff's vehicle go by on the main road every few minutes.

"What happened to you and Albert in Kuwait?" Brody asked Jim for the third time.

"Does it matter?" Jim grumbled before smacking a bolt with a sledgehammer.

"It must" —Brody looked to see if the bolt was through its hole—"the way he mothers you. Hit it again."

Jim hit the bolt through the hole and Brody brushed sawdust from the threads with his fingertips.

"Do I get an answer, Helen?"

"Helen?" Jim growled.

"Helen Keller." Brody tilted his head back. "Stop acting deaf."

"Two weeks ago we never spoke."

"Two weeks ago you weren't interesting."

ON MONDAY MORNING, JACKIE COOPER said goodbye. She hugged Larry, Sheila, and Brody in turn, telling them each the same thing: "Take care of my boy."

"Always have. Always will," Brody answered.

Larry overheard the exchange and wondered how many times Brody might have saved Jim's life over the years.

"Thanks for understanding, Mom. This won't last forever." Jim kissed his mother's cheek. "You sure I can't drive with you? I could fly home."

"Old but not helpless," Jackie said.

Jim nodded in response.

"I'll be back in the spring." Jackie waved as she drove away.

Sheila looked at the three men, her eyes suddenly brimming with tears. "We need to make this right, Jim. Your mother should be able to come and go."

The three men all nodded and Sheila buried her head on Jim's shoulder.

LATER IN THE DAY, LARRY barked at Jim and Sheila to be on time for

Skinner's football practice. Sheila went into the house and came out wearing a summer dress and hat. Jim took her suggestion, changing into shorts, flip-flops, and a t-shirt.

Brody waited at Jim's truck.

"You coming with us?" Larry asked.

"Yep."

Larry nodded.

They stopped for drinks and snacks at Ernie's, continued to the high school, and found seats halfway up the east bleachers.

After the team stretched, Larry refused to sit as Coach Fawson tried to call plays on both sides of the ball as the players scurried, trying to please their coach.

"Where's the other coaches, Jim?" Larry demanded.

"They both have day jobs." Jim sipped his coffee. "They'll be along."

"Both? There's only two?"

"They'll be along." Jim shrugged.

"When?" Larry demanded.

"Do I look like I know everything?"

"No!" Larry yelled as several players jumped offsides. "This coach needs help."

"There's only one way to fix a burr under the saddle." Brody yawned.

The bleachers' aluminum support structure vibrated as Larry descended to the field three steps at a time. At the track, he looked both ways even though nobody was there, and then jogged onto the field. Several of the players stepped back, but Skinner moved toward the incoming giant and took off his helmet to say hello.

"What's your coach's name, Skinner?"

"I'm Coach Fawson," the other man said.

Skinner stepped aside, and the two shook hands. "Nice to meet you, Coach. I'm Larry Lyons."

"Okay, Mr. Lyons, what can I do for you?"

"It's more what I can do for you, sir. I'd like to help coach."

Coach Fawson looked up at Larry, a knowing expression on his face. "Team, take three laps."

The young men left, but turned to look as they moved off the field and onto the track.

"Okay, I'm listening." Coach Fawson cupped the whistle in his palm.

"I played four years, plus a redshirt year at UCLA. I have an education degree, and it's been a while, but I helped coach my brother's high school team to a district championship."

"Where would you like to coach?"

"Anywhere you'll have me. Offense, defense, special teams, but I'd probably like the lines more than anything."

Coach Fawson stood, his arms folded and his feet shoulder width apart in contemplation.

"You won't need to pay me," he offered. "And if it doesn't work out, I'll leave. No questions asked."

"I have two other coaches. I coach the offense while they coach special teams and defense. A line coach would be a luxury."

"I'm your man. I love this game, and it pains me to watch when I know I can help."

"It shows." Coach Fawson smiled. "How long can you stay?"

Larry thought quickly. Even if all the Mafia trouble ended tomorrow, he could stay until the end of the season. "Hopefully the whole season."

"It gets cold here."

Larry knew Coach Fawson was giving him one last chance to reconsider the commitment. "I'll buy two coats."

"There's a big and tall store in Idaho Falls," the coach responded. "I'll need to check your credentials tomorrow and get approval from our principal."

"The answer's yes then?"

"Glad to have you."

Larry wanted to do an end-zone dance.

Coach Fawson turned away and blew the whistle. "Bring it in and take a knee!"

The boys accelerated from a lethargic jog to a sprint as they approached the coaches, who stood between the hash marks on the thirty-yard line. Gathering close, the boys' wide eyes made their flushed pink faces and damp hair nearly invisible.

"Team, this is Coach Lyons. He played college ball at UCLA. If things work out, he'll be with us this year."

A rumble and several gasps came from the team. *Coach Lyons.* The emotions of playing the game stole his breath. Highs and lows, victory and defeat, all swirled through him.

"Did everyone see him run onto the field?" Coach Fawson asked in a commanding voice.

The boys nodded.

"I can't hear you."

"Yes, Coach!" the team yelled in unison.

"Did you see how he came out here and asked me for the job?"

"Yes, Coach!"

"That's why he fits and why I said yes. An aggressive attitude starts with the coaching staff, and Coach Lyons has it." Coach Fawson looked toward his new assistant. "Take a minute and introduce yourself to the team."

Larry looked into the faces of almost forty teenagers. None of them turned away or looked anywhere but at him. He'd never felt so needed. But there was something else, a word that came out as he spoke. "Right now we're strangers, but I promise you this: it will be my *responsibility* to make you better football players than you ever imagined. We." Larry paused. "And I do mean *we* are going to eat, sleep, and breathe this game, and I will not rest until we dominate our opponents on every block and every assignment. You have my word." The team returned his stare. Larry swallowed. From the stands,

Jim and Sheila waved. The boys eyed him, and Coach Fawson shook his hand and patted Larry's back.

They looked each other in the eye.

"Welcome aboard. And welcome to Wyoming!"

A wave of excitement and relief washed over Larry. After everything he'd been through, the simple prospect of coaching football did more to brighten his spirits than all the money they'd stolen. He felt like a long-neglected plant resurrected by the light and water of football.

58

The following Sunday morning with Sheila spooned next to him, Jim's phone rang and shattered his cozy paradise. In the dark, he snatched the phone from the nightstand and held it to his ear. "Hello?"

"Sorry to call so early, Jim. This is Bishop Fawson."

Why is he calling me? Jim wondered. *We haven't spoken in years.*

"Are you there?"

"I'm here," Jim responded, realizing he'd missed his turn. "What's going on?"

"I'm outside on the porch. Coach Lyons gave me a key to the gate. We need to speak." Then the bishop added, "Privately."

"I'll be right there."

Sheila rolled over, squinting into the mostly dark bedroom. "Who would be pulling you from our bed this early?"

"Besides eight-hundred cows?"

She snuggled next to him under the warm covers, hooking one of her legs around the back of his knee.

Jim snuggled back for a few seconds as his eyes adjusted. She deserved an explanation, but he worried about his high school coach standing outside alone, and was more than a little curious about the unsuspected visit.

"It's Larry's new boss, Coach Fawson. He's an old friend."

"Okay," Sheila rose up and squinted toward him. "No secrets, right?"

"I promise." Jim slid into the cooler air of the bedroom and pulled on Carhartts and an old shirt. The pistol rested on the nightstand next to the alarm clock that rolled from 4:47 to 4:48 a.m. *Packing everywhere means packing everywhere.* He tucked the gun in his waistband.

Duke greeted him in the hallway as Jim pre-twisted the knob to shut the door as quietly as possible. The dog trundled ahead, down the stairs, through the living room, and to the front door. Coach Fawson's balding head eclipsed everything through the peephole's distorted glass. Duke wiggled as he sniffed at the threshold and barked, his front paws pitter patting in a happy rhythm next to Jim's bare feet. Jim unbolted the door and unclasped the new chain latch to greet one of his most trusted friends.

"This is a surprise," Jim said as Coach Fawson walked in, wearing a suit and tie.

Coach Fawson extended his arms and hugged Jim fondly. Jim returned the embrace a bit awkwardly. Coach Fawson had hugged him twice before—after his last high school football game, and next to Bradley's casket.

"You're special to your old coach. You know that, don't you?"

Jim nodded as they separated. The coach's eyes studied him. From anyone else it would be uncomfortable, but in the day's first light, it was natural, like an old friend doing his best to find a way to help.

"I'm sorry it's so early. I have to be back at church by five thirty."

Jim flicked a grain of sleepy sand from his eye. "You're always welcome here, Coach."

"I'm here as bishop."

"Sit down," Jim offered, pointing to a couch.

Jim sat, leaning forward in a recliner opposite his old friend. He suspected the visit was meant to buoy up a former player. It wasn't the first time coach or Bishop Fawson had done it for him, and Jim knew of several others he kept floating over the years. Perhaps he wanted to make sure Jim felt okay after killing men in self-defense.

The only thing Jim could think to say came out. "I've always listened to everything you've said."

The bishop paused and tears misted his eyes. He swallowed hard, making his Adam's apple bob. Then he smiled and Jim knew someone he admired had gotten up early to tell him something important.

The bishop cleared his throat. "I'm here to invite you to church today."

Jim sat up straight and chuckled. "You know I'll come, and you also know I'll never join."

"I thought the speaker today might interest you."

"Who is it?" the question snapped from Jim's tongue with earnest curiosity.

"My new assistant." The bishop paused. "Coach Lyons."

Air rushed into Jim's lungs, stealing a verbal response. *Larry?* After a few seconds, Jim mouthed the questions he wanted answers for. "Why is he speaking, and why wouldn't he invite me himself?"

"Coach Lyons told me how he believes God sent you to save him in mountains, and I want him to share it with the ward." The bishop took in a breath. Then he looked forward, locking eyes with Jim. "He also told me you never wanted to hear another word about it."

Jim remembered taking umbrage at Larry for comparing him to a guardian angel. Hypocrite wasn't a word Jim liked, but he wore it now for not allowing Larry his own beliefs. Almost twenty years ago, he refused when Sally's parents tried to plunge Mormonism into his soul when what he wanted most was to follow his own beliefs, free of any judgment.

"I'll apologize," Jim responded.

"Will you come?" Bishop Fawson's eyes hadn't left Jim's. "Sacrament meeting starts at nine."

"I'll be there." Jim chuckled again and thought about Brody, and about Sheila, whose warmth was still on his arms. "A few others will be as well."

By eight o'clock, the house buzzed with activity. The drone of Sheila's hair dryer echoed from the master bathroom while Jim sat in the living room, buffing a shine into a pair of black cowboy boots. Brody emerged from his room in a dark green, three-button suit, a starched shirt, bolo tie, and a handkerchief folded into his breast pocket. He sat next to Jim on the sofa. Larry walked into the room in a tailored grey pinstripe suit, complete with yellow silk tie and matching pocket scarf that Jim guessed must have somehow made the trip from Vegas.

After ten minutes of buffing, Jim could almost use the boots to comb his hair, so he slipped them on, feeling the arch of his ankle slide through the neck as his soles thunked into place. He hadn't owned a tie since his enlistment ended fifteen years ago, so he ironed his nicest snap-down cowboy shirt to wear with a pair of Docker khakis.

The three men sipped coffee in silence for a few minutes until the hair dryer quit. Ten minutes later, they all looked up as a pair of stiletto heels clicked down the stairs and into the hallway.

"I have a good feeling about this," Brody said, grinning like a fox.

Sheila walked into the room. Over her olive skin, she wore a flattering sleeveless yellow dress. An anklet and the high heels accentuated her sculpted calves and knees. As she spun, the four-inch slit up the back caused all three men to raise their eyebrows. To top everything off, she wore a pair of white gloves with a matching bracelet and necklace that hung slightly above a hint of cleavage.

"Lady," Brody said, "no man who sees you today will have a mind for the spiritual."

"This will be hard to compete with," Larry mused.

The dimples in her cheeks deepened as she smiled at the two men.

Jim slipped into a jacket that matched his boots and belt and offered Sheila his arm. As they left, he bolted the door and opened his truck door for Sheila, while Brody and Larry followed in another old pickup.

Bishop Fawson greeted them in the church foyer and escorted Larry to the stand while Sheila sat bookended between Jim and Brody in the middle of the very last pew.

Jim waved at Charlie Strobel, who stood—minus Sally—next to an exit across the chapel. Charlie ignored him. He waved again and Charlie looked away, making Jim wonder if Sally's husband was having the same reaction as the people at the grocery store a few weeks earlier before Darrin Wyatt broke the ice.

Skinner and George Peterson nodded to Jim before sitting on the stand behind the sacrament table. A female organist played *How Great Thou Art* and several hymns Jim didn't recognize as the chapel gradually filled. Many of the members greeted Jim and Brody, who exchanged turns introducing Sheila. After sitting, all eyes focused on Larry, who was seated on the stand a few chairs left of the podium.

"Ever seen a black marshmallow?" Brody asked Jim and Sheila.

"Shh!—We're in church," Sheila whispered with school-teacher authority—the only thing Jim noticed, however, was that scowling also accentuated her dimples.

Bishop Fawson stood to make some announcements and to instruct the congregation about the opening song and prayer. Jim yawned during all four verses of *Come, Come Ye Saints,* then someone he didn't recognize walked to the pulpit and prayed for all the earth's inhabitants, mentioning specifically Bishop Fawson and Mormon missionaries everywhere.

The bishop announced the sacrament hymn, which was sung at what Jim guessed was half speed, the slow ponderous lyrics eating away at his wakefulness. Halfway through, Sheila's alto voice snapped him to attention. She shot him a wink mid-note. Jim leaned forward, until something bumped his shin. A little girl, maybe two, smiled up at him.

Wearing a pink ruffled dress, she stood, arms extended, as her mother noticed she had climbed under the pew to visit the neighbors in the row behind. Before Jim could pick the child up and return her to her mother, Sheila smiled and the girl climbed into her lap. The girl stood, facing Sheila, smiling at her new surroundings. After a few moments, Brody made a long, scary face. The girl giggled and put both palms on his wrinkled skin then pulled on his nose. Brody pulled more faces. Apparently bored, the girl climbed off the pew and squirmed underneath, her legs somehow propelling her forward through a sea of ruffles. A few seconds later she reappeared over her mother's shoulder, where she played peek-a-boo with Sheila, and Jim leaned forward again.

Finally, after the sacrament bread and water was blessed and passed, two youth speakers, another slow hymn, and one adult speaker, Larry Lyons stood in front of a church full of Mormons, his shoulders wider than the podium.

Bishop Fawson pushed a toggle switch and the podium raised nearly a foot, but still seemed too short. It startled Larry, who stepped backward with a look of concern, but then flashed a pearly white smile. He stepped forward again, and wrapped his griddle-sized hands around the podium's corners. Then he spoke into the microphone, quietly at first before raising his voice to the perfect level.

"As most of you know, I'm lucky to be here, but not for the reasons you think. It's true that Jim Cooper saved my life in the woods a few weeks ago. It's also true that I prayed, and because of that prayer, God granted me deliverance. But that's not what I want to talk about today, or why I'm here. Let's be clear. When you're six foot seven and three hundred pounds, nobody forces you to say anything unless you're in the woods and they have a gun."

The crowd laughed and it sounded to Jim like the rehearsed laughter plugged into a sitcom after every joke, even the stupid ones.

Larry continued. "I'm from a place where as a twelve year old, I found my best friend beaten unconscious behind our apartment building's dumpster because some older kids wanted his basketball shoes. My first day here, people brought me clothing, when I had none.

"Growing up, my momma worked two and sometimes three jobs. But we still waited in lines at the food pantry, because there wasn't money some months for groceries after she paid the bills. My second day here, Sister Bott and Sister Smith brought more food than we could eat in a week.

"So I stand here today asking. God granted me deliverance. I get that. But when I ask *why,* I'm not sure. Unless the place he delivered me to matters.

"Last Monday afternoon, Coach Fawson saved me, too. If he hadn't made me his assistant, I'd never get away from Jim and Brody."

The congregation's laughter cut Larry off.

"Skinner? George?" Larry's eyes scanned the congregation. "There you are. You and all your friends are a big upgrade."

Larry smiled as the congregation laughed again.

"It's my privilege to now be an assistant coach at the high school. These are fine young men. I've never been around a harder working, or more coachable team. But the other day I lit into several athletes. Made them run. Made them do pushups. I made them crab-walk the field backwards three times, and then I made them do it all over again. I did this not because they missed an assignment, not because they were lazy, not because someone forgot the snap count or caused a penalty."

Larry raised his right index finger in the air and shook it.

"Badger football is aggressive smash-mouth football of the purest form, and occasionally we do have penalties, jump off-sides, or make a mistake. And I understand this. But what I would not tolerate, what I could not stand, what made me set the team straight was a few players badmouthing their religion."

Larry paused and looked at a quiet audience.

"Aside from no coffee—which I could never do—and no

alcohol—which everyone *should* do—I have no idea what Mormon folks do or do not believe. But what I do know is that when a place brings you shoes instead of stealing them, when neighbors fill your fridge with food instead of mugging your lunch money for drugs, when they invite you to the summer barbecue, when the community unites to protect you, and when I get to work with thirty-seven pasty white teenagers who do everything their black coach asks them, the predominant religion of the community deserves my respect.

"Thank you, Coach—I mean Bishop—Fawson for asking me to speak here today and thanks to all of you for taking in a stranger.

"The place to which God delivered me matters, and I'm lucky to be here."

59

Four months later, on Thanksgiving Day, Jim wiggled his toes deeper into the sand in Newport Beach, California. Dressed in shorts and a Hawaiian shirt—to conceal his pistol—he held Sheila's hand as the surf crept up the beach to the tops of their ankles before receding. The ocean rolled into his nostrils. "I love that smell."

"Me, too," Sheila responded. "Come on, big eater. Let's keep walking."

They slipped back into flip-flops, and Jim patted his belly. "I have some calories to burn off."

"Only three plates of dinner and then dessert," Sheila teased.

At the last minute, they had decided to spend the holiday with Jackie and Jim's sister and her family while Brody, practically begging for some solitude, stayed at the ranch.

Larry flew from Jackson to visit his family in Oregon. After helping coach the football team to a state championship, he had accepted a full time position teaching social studies at the high school.

Duke bounced toward them, carrying a stick. Jim let go of Sheila's hand and heaved the stick end over end into the surf. The dog tore after it as if nothing in the world had ever meant so much. Lunging into the water, he swam through a small incoming wave, seized the stick, and returned.

"I think he likes it here," Jim said as he tossed it again.

"He likes being with you. I like being with you."

Jim smiled. He had never been as comfortable around anyone. Since returning to the ranch, Sheila had helped him pack guests into the mountains, tend cows, mend fences, and fix the machinery. There was nothing she wasn't on the spot to help with, and he loved her company. At first, Jim wondered if she wanted to be around him for protection, and while he knew that was part of it, her involvement in every aspect of his life was complete.

"We like being around each other," Jim said as he tossed the stick again.

"I worry sometimes."

He noticed Sheila's creased brow and concerned expression. "About what?"

"If you'll get sick of me. You were alone so long; I'm surprised how much time you give me."

Jim exhaled and then stretched his lungs to capacity with the salty air. "Before I met you, I moped over dead friends and missed opportunities."

Sheila gave him an understanding look. Jim had told her about Bradley, and about how Sally Strobel "Dear-Johned" him in boot camp. "Do you still? Do you miss them both?"

"I'm always looking to help someone because of Bradley," Jim responded. "But knocking on your door in Nevada changed everything."

"You brought up Sally that night."

"I did?"

"How she was the last pretty girl to ride in a truck with you?" Sheila said, poking him in the chest, pretending to be more jealous than Jim thought she actually was.

"You're prettier. And I love you." It was the first time. He'd wanted to say it since the moonlit swim in Lake Mead. He looked at a tear forming in Sheila's eye and she wrapped her arms around his neck while Duke wiggled, stick in his mouth, at their feet.

"I love you, too."

Sheila leashed Duke, who happily trotted next to her heel. They held hands, and walked next to houses built inches apart. Throngs of people jogged near the surf. A Frisbee floated within easy grasp. Jim snagged it one handed and threw it back in a perfect toss without releasing Sheila's hand. They window-shopped art galleries, occasionally leaving Duke tied outside to go into places for a closer look.

On their way back to Jim's sister's home, an unfamiliar number rang on Jim's cell. He pushed accept and held the phone to his ear. "Hello?"

"Is this Jim Cooper?" a woman's voice asked on the other end of the line. Whoever it was sounded business-like.

"It might depend on who's asking."

"Mr. Cooper, I have needed to speak to you since July."

Awful thoughts of who might be on the other end of the phone rushed into his mind. Was this a mother, sister, or daughter of one of the men he had killed? What would he say? Jim almost hung up, but curiosity demanded otherwise.

"Who is this?" he insisted.

"I apologize, I should have introduced myself. My name is Elaine Packer. I believe you met my son Vincent and our neighbor Brother Allen Coleman last summer."

Jim's tension eased. *I spend too much time worrying over shit that doesn't happen.* "I met several young men, which one was yours?"

"Vincent is the young man who wouldn't eat your candy or drink your root beer."

Jim remembered his conversation with the scoutmaster about the Packer family's position on processed sugar. Her voice sounded stern. Maybe she phoned in anger about him giving the other kids root beer and candy, and he didn't care. Anything would be easier than talking to a widow of his own creation.

"I remember. Your boy did you proud that day. Allen called me last week about a guided fishing trip for the troop next summer."

"You mean, Brother Coleman?" she said in a curt tone.

Jim didn't like her insistent manner, but didn't want to pursue a disagreement over Mormon formalities.

"I think we're talking about the same guy," he said as diplomatically as he could.

"Yes, we are. Brother Coleman has been arranging a guided trip and I'm fully supportive."

"Good," Jim responded. "What can I do for you?"

"I'm calling because on Thanksgiving Day, I call people and tell them something I'm grateful for each year. Something they did that I appreciated, that they might not even remember doing."

"Okay." *When does this lady breathe?*

"Last summer, you gave Vincent a knife he keeps by his bedside and looks at each day. I need to thank you because my son came home different from when he left. He was worried about going, and his father and I almost didn't send him. But when he came back, he talked for days about the man who rode a horse into camp and gave him a gift. Brother Coleman told me why you gave it to him, and I appreciate it. I know sometimes it's hard for him to be the only one not eating sugar. I'm rambling, but I wanted you to know, that it gave Vincent a huge ego boost when you did that for him."

Jim was silent.

"Hello? Are you still there?"

Memories of stopping to help Larry, the young girl with the flat tire, and dozens of other people came into Jim's mind in a single blink. Then he thought about the playground in second grade, and bringing his new best friend back to play at the Cooper Ranch, about enlisting together and returning to Wyoming as part of the security detail that guarded the casket. Jim dropped the phone to his side, let go of Sheila's hand, and wept. He blinked rapidly, but the tears came too fast to stop. Instead, he took a deep breath and pressed the phone back to his ear.

"Did we get cut off? Did you hear what I told you?"

"I did. You have a fine son. Tell him I look forward to riding horses and going fishing with him next summer."

"I will, and thank you again."

Jim said goodbye, and returned the phone to his pocket. He knuckled his eyes dry, exhaled, and smiled.

"I've never seen you like this." Sheila said. "What was that about?"

Jim kissed her on the forehead and scooped her close. "It was about Bradley."

60

Michael gripped the cane, made of the finest eucalyptus, with a solid gold gargoyle embedded in the pommel. He placed the rubber stopper on the ground to lift himself from the car. The fire inside his right foot eased with each step as he moved toward the hospital entrance. "Nerves and soft tissue," the doctor had told him. "The bullet took away some of what you needed to bear weight." Each step reminded him of how life used to be. A bright future, obscene money, working shoulder-to-shoulder with his son and brothers all came to mind as he approached the hospital's revolving door.

The elderly lady at the information desk smiled. *Can't she see how I'm dressed? Do I look like someone who would acknowledge her?* Happy people bothered him, and he gloated over how ignorant most were to their own poverty.

Arriving at the elevators, he pushed the up arrow with his cane and limped through the sliding doors, pushed six in the console and the close button. At the last instant, a hand shot through the slot and the doors slid open again. A young father with his son, both handsome and well dressed in matching slacks and sweaters, got on, as did a nurse.

"Push number five, son," the man said in an encouraging voice.

The boy moved to the console and depressed the button. As it lit, he looked up at his father, the gleam of discovery on his face. The man picked him up, and the boy rested his head on his father's shoulder.

The youngster's brown eyes appraised Michael. "Happy Thanksgiving."

Michael looked directly ahead and ignored the greeting, but the boy reached out and tugged at his silk blazer. "Happy Thanksgiving."

"Happy Thanksgiving," Michael responded.

The child smiled at him and the father turned to make a congenial apology. "I'm sorry. He's been saying it to everyone."

The indicator chimed and the man, child in his arms, was about to follow the nurse onto floor five, but Michael barricaded the doorway with the cane. The man was about to object to the sudden turnstile. Michael dropped the cane and the two adults locked eyes.

"Never apologize for your boy."

The man nodded.

"Never."

The parent holding the child walked through the threshold. The boy waved over his father's shoulder. Michael lifted the cane in recognition as the boy kissed his father's cheek and disappeared behind the closing doors.

Michael exited the elevator on the sixth floor. As he walked to his father's room, he thought of the last four months. If there was an upside to the Wyoming tragedy, it was the opportunity to work with his dad. At first, Michael had worried that Spencer's meddling would make everything worse, but having the old man around had been invaluable. At the funeral he listened from his wheelchair as Spencer put a positive spin on Michael's injured foot.

"We're lucky Mike's alive," his father told the men. "Fighting a decorated soldier and proven killer. Any one of us would be fucking dead. Fucking dead! Where would we be without Mike? A hell of a lot poorer, that's where. I left a decade ago, and look what he's done. My boy's done shit I never dreamed of. And he's just getting started."

Michael smiled as he walked into his father's room. "Happy Thanksgiving, Pops."

"Get me the fuck out of here and it might be," Spencer responded from his bed.

"The doc said day after tomorrow."

"And he knows this how?" Spencer grumbled. "A little chest pain and they cut me open."

"It's a good thing, too. If they hadn't caught it, you'da been gone."

Spencer shifted his weight. "Where's your wife and my granddaughter?"

"At home yelling at the caterer. We'll come by tonight."

Spencer pointed to a fancy alligator-skin attaché against the wall. "Grab my briefcase."

Michael handed the case to his father, who opened it and handed him an envelope. Someone using what looked like a carpenter's pencil had printed WYOMING in the upper left corner. In the same sloppy penmanship the envelope was addressed to: THE BOSS OF RALF FALETTO with Ralf's address beneath.

"What the fuck is this?"

"Look inside."

The envelope had already been torn open, so Michael slipped his fingers through the ragged edges, and pulled out a folded piece of heavy brown paper, probably from a grocery bag. Inside were three identical clothing tags.

XXL

Bulletproof Kevlar Vest
For Law Enforcement or Military Use Only

The penmanship on the paper matched the words on the outside of the envelope. *THE ROAD BEETWEEN HERE AND VEGAS RUNS BOTH WAYS.*

Instead of rage, fear washed over Michael for a moment; his

hands went cold as the blood drained from them. Jim Cooper's warning in the desert four months ago wasn't a threat; it was a statement of fact. *The rancher is coming to kill me.*

"How did Ralf get this?" he asked.

Before speaking Spencer blinked twice. "Michael, you need to listen to me."

"Okay."

"Someone must have killed the bouncers you sent, but it wasn't Cooper."

Wasn't Cooper? "Why?"

"You told me the day he shot your foot, he and the black man took your wallet."

"That's right." Michael paused and then expressed his understanding. "The rancher would've mailed it to me, or not at all. But who would send something to Ralf?"

Spencer looked directly into Michael's eyes. "Ralf was afraid to tell you. After the teenagers followed him in Wyoming, an old cowboy took his driver's license."

"An old cowboy? This doesn't make sense."

"Yes, it does. Cooper has friends, but they're not operating together."

In the last four months he had gained a new appreciation for his dad's clear-headed reasoning.

Spencer shrugged. "Remember the Fillizetti story?"

"Sure, Pops. What about it?"

"Your grandfather waited fifteen years to avenge the situation."

"What are you telling me?"

Spencer adjusted the hospital bed so he was sitting straight up. "The rancher isn't going anywhere. That sheriff who protects him, and all the townsfolk at the bar, it'd be easy to turn them."

Michael considered his father's words, but the searing ache for Jonathan needed more immediate attention. "I'm not waiting fifteen years."

"We can't even get close, not with the townsfolk and the sheriff—not to mention the restraining orders." Spencer scratched at his unshaved face. "All this could change next summer if some fly-fishing guests plant a hundred pounds of uncut blow on the ranch."

"We suspect our money is hidden there as well," Michael offered. "If the law found drugs, they'd give the whole ranch a colonoscopy. Thirty mill would look like serious drug money."

"Now you're with me," Spencer responded. "In the old days, we called it a gang play."

"Gang play?"

"Use the biggest gang to clean up the mess."

It took Michael a second but he caught his dad's meaning. "The biggest gang being the cops."

"Feds, locals—anyone with a badge."

Michael liked the idea. There was no hurry, and if he didn't do it right Jim Cooper would come killing.

"Seeing my grandson's killer rot in prison for a few years before I die would make this old man sleep better. But we need to do it smart."

"Get rested, and we'll figure it out."

Spencer smiled and Michael kissed the old man's cheek. The idea of planning a setup with his father appealed to his sense of rightness. Marcus and Simon—sons and brothers. Johnny had been both a son and grandson, and while he would always miss his child, the blossoming relationship with Spencer had motivated him to curb the drinking, even with the miserably handicapped foot.

Get well, old man.

Alone inside the elevator, the chime sounded a stop at floor five. The same man and little boy got on with the boy riding on his father's shoulders.

"Hello, I'm four." The father looked uncomfortable as the boy persisted. "I'm four."

Good hell! This kid can't shut up. "I wish I was, too," Michael responded.

"Why are you here?"

Michael delayed speaking. In a few seconds he would be out of the elevator.

"Why are you here?"

The father set the boy on the floor beside him. The door chimed, opening on the ground floor.

"Let's go, Jonathan," the father said. The boy's extended hand disappeared inside his father's. "Your mother's waiting for us."

The boy smiled up at his dad as they exited.

Jonathan? Michael stood, not moving, the capillary-deep anger growing as the doors slid closed. In a sudden burst of rage, he splintered the cane over his knee. He hammer-punched the door, leaving dents in the stainless steel.

The door opened and several people got on as Michael limped into the lobby. At the carousel exit, he tossed both pieces of the cane, including the golden gargoyle in the trash.

If it takes fifteen years to do this right, so be it, Michael thought. With no cane to help bear the weight, the screaming pain in his foot matched the agony in his soul. Perhaps he could arrange to have Jim Cooper's foot shot before the penitentiary's sodomite population convened a welcoming party. He liked the idea, but only momentarily because the next thought came to him like it always did. *How do I make him suffer as I have?*

The truth was he couldn't, and Michael knew it. Pure revenge could never happen because Johnny's killer lacked the one thing to make it possible.

If only Jim Cooper had a son.

ACKNOWLEDGMENTS

I'll never have the words for my wife, Janilee, but I'll work each day to have the actions. To my fine offspring, Hailey, Cassity, Abigail, and Mackenzie, your support never wavers.

I heard no, no, maybe, and no. Then I met Christopher Loke and the folks at Jolly Fish Press who said, "Hell, yes! We love it!" Thank you for publishing my unorthodox story.

To everyone I've met within the League of Utah Writers. Your advice over eight rewrites made this possible. Tim Keller, your leadership in our local chapter and statewide creates an environment where good writing happens like the sunrise.

My brothers from life and family, Daniel Coleman, Stephen Watson, Roger Christensen, Muck and Matt, each of you deserve an acknowledgement chapter.

To Michael Zimmer and Rod Miller, your patience and kindness is as big as the west.

Gordon Smith, you have a place on the Bishop family pistol range anytime.

Finally, Dean Koontz, Stephen King, Andrew Smith, and Cormac McCarthy, your words make me a better writer whenever I pick up one of your books.

ABOUT THE AUTHOR

Eric Bishop is known to his friends and family as an "author version of Clint Eastwood." As the owner of a successful marketing firm, Eric spends most of his time on his Utah ranch writing with the music of his adolescence bouncing off the walls. When he's not writing, Eric enjoys spending time with his wife and four lovely daughters at his home in Nibley, Utah. Unlike Jim, Eric hasn't had any run-ins with the Mafia. Yet.

Visit Eric's website at www.eric-bishop.com